THE SUN ON FIRE

William emerged at the top of the steps. Tokugawa was immediately behind him, Philip immediately behind Tokugawa. The crowd was divided into two halves, leaving a clear path down the centre, towards the road and the waiting automobiles. William glanced from left to right, then looked straight ahead and commenced walking.

'Traitor!' someone shouted.

The cry was taken up.

'Traitor!'

'American lap-dog!'

'Disgrace!'

Someone threw a tomato. It burst on the shoulder of William Freeman's uniform jacket, splattering pink pips and juice across his face.

Philip ran forward to protect his uncle. Officers shouted orders. The police thrust into the crowd, seeking the assailant.

'He will be punished,' the other admiral promised.

William's smile was sad. 'Why should he be punished, honourable sir, if he expresses the feelings of the nation?'

THE SUN ON FIRE

Christopher Nicole

THE SHERIDAN
BOOK COMPANY

This edition published in 1995 by
The Sheridan Book Company

First published in 1986 by Arrow Books Limited
Random House, 20 Vauxhall Bridge Road, London SW1V 2SA

© 1986 by F. Beermann BV

Printed and bound in Great Britain by
Cox & Wyman Ltd, Reading, Berkshire

ISBN 1-85501-720-2

CONTENTS

PART ONE

The Patriot

CHAPTER 1

The Pact

'There!' Admiral William Freeman handed his binoculars to his nephew, standing at his elbow. 'That is America!'

Philip Shimadzu levelled the glasses, made out the Chesapeake Lightship and to the left the broad stretch of Virginia Beach, ending in Cape Henry, guarding the entrance to Chesapeake Bay. The country appeared low and swampy, even unhealthy in the October mist, a strong contrast to the mountains and the rocky, sunbathed coast of Japan. Yet it was one of the most evocative sights Philip had ever seen.

'At last, sir,' he remarked, and returned the binoculars.

Like his famous uncle, Philip was tall for a Japanese officer; he betrayed his American blood in his blue eyes and the aquiline cast of his features; if his hair was black and crisp, his complexion was more white than yellow. But, again, like his uncle, he wore the severe dark blue uniform and cap of a Japanese naval officer, unrelieved by any gold braid. Although he had to be content with the insignia of a captain, he still glowed with pride as the huge, thirty-thousand-ton battleship altered course to port, slowly reducing her speed from twenty knots cruising. Standing high on the bridge deck as he was, Philip had no part in conning the ship; that was left to Captain Iyesada and his officers. He was here strictly as aide-de-camp to the admiral. It was a role he would willingly have exchanged for an executive one, yet he knew he was fortunate to be a captain at the very early age of thirty-one, and he owed it all to his illustrious relative, now again peering through the glasses at the slowly developing shoreline. Besides, whether in command or not, this was a sufficiently unique and famous occasion, to be on board the first Japanese warship ever to enter an American Atlantic port; indeed, the *Fuso*, one of Japan's finest capital ships, was the first war vessel flying the Rising Sun ensign ever to cruise upon the Atlantic at all.

This had been a voyage entirely of firsts. First through the Panama Canal, with every inch of space, whether abeam or beneath the keel, having to be carefully measured and utilised, first in the Caribbean Sea, and now, first into Norfolk Navy Yard.

The Americans were aware that history was being made. Despite the lateness of the year, a flotilla of small craft was emerging from the recesses of Chesapeake Bay, led by two destroyers and a coastguard cutter, sirens blaring and flags waving. Philip almost felt tears springing to his eyes. If he was proud of his Satsuma ancestry and of the uniform he wore, he was no less proud of his famous American grandfather, who had fought for both Japan and the United States, and thus no less proud of the deeds of his Caucasian forebears, on whose land he was soon to step for the first time. But already the glories of American naval history were crowding about him. The *Fuso* was sailing over the exact spot where the Royal Navy had been defeated by the French under de Grasse in 1781, thus forcing the surrender of the British stronghold of Yorktown, and in effect, establishing the independence of the United States; Yorktown itself was only a few miles within the bay. And here too, as the great ship nosed her way into Hampton Roads, now entirely surrounded by boats, was the site of the first battle ever fought between ironclad vessels, the *Merrimack* and the *Monitor*, in 1862.

Philip sighed. The Japanese Navy also had glorious deeds to recall, and most of them had happened since his

10

own birth; but he had taken part in none of them. His elder brother, Peter, and he had both joined the navy as cadets at the earliest possible moment, encouraged to do so not only by their uncle and his friend Heihachiro Togo, but equally by their widowed mother Shikibu, William Freeman's sister – but they had still been too young to fight in the immortal battle of Tsushima, the most decisive naval victory ever gained by any navy anywhere in the world. That victory, gained over the Russian fleet in 1905, had established William Freeman's fame, and established, too, the Imperial Japanese Navy as equal to any in the world. It had also been the last fought by a Japanese fleet. Philip and Peter had both served right through the Great War, and yet had seen almost no action save an occasional ship arrest and search, and the bombardment of the German seaport of Kiaochow; there had been no German warships in the Pacific after the very first months.

Now, in October 1921, only three years after the end of that greatest and most bloody of conflicts, war had become a thing of the past, an impossible concept for the future. The reason for the presence of the *Fuso* in Norfolk was so that Mr Tokugawa and Admiral Freeman and the other members of the Japanese delegation, and their aides, could sit down with the British and the French and the Italians, and their American hosts, and discuss ways and means of limiting the possibility of any future naval battles ever taking place. For the Japanese to be here at all, in a conclave dominated by the Western sea powers, was a measure of the importance of this new Japanese Navy . . . even if it also meant that this navy would never have anyone to fight, except perhaps Chinese pirates, and one would hardly use a battleship for that purpose.

The pilot had come on board, and the tugs were standing by to shepherd and ease the warship to its allotted berth. The deck crews stood to attention with their yards of bunting ready to dress overall the moment the ship

11

came to rest. In front of them the naval port was already decked out in its best; the many ships were lying at anchor, and vessels representing all the delegations were already flying flags from bow to stern, while masses of launches and small boats jockeyed for position. When the *Fuso* let go her bow anchor, the nearest American battleship became wreathed in smoke as she commenced firing a salute.

Now, too, Mr Tokugawa had come up to the bridge. He was an elderly statesman, out of place in his silk hat and black frock-coat amidst the smartly dressed officers. He had indeed been out of place throughout the voyage, because he had been dreadfully seasick. But he looked cheerful enough as he observed the land now entirely surrounding the ship, and he gave his little smile of welcome to Captain Shimadzu; the young man was due to become a member of his family in the not too distant future, and if it was undoubtedly a step in the wrong direction for a Tokugawa woman – a direct descendant of the last of the Shoguns, who had ruled Japan for two hundred and fifty years – to give herself in marriage to a Shimadzu man – and one who was not pure Japanese and not even a Buddhist – true nobility was becoming increasingly difficult to find in Japan nowadays, and Philip was at least both handsome and personable.

Mr Tokugawa moved across the bridge, his footsteps hesitant even with the ship at rest, and stood beside Admiral Freeman, dwarfed by the big Japanese-American.

'At last, Freeman San,' he said. 'I wonder what the future holds for us, now we are here.'

'Nothing dishonourable to Japan, honourable sir,' William Freeman said. 'We must always remember that.'

'Oh, indeed,' Tokugawa agreed. 'Nothing dishonourable to Japan.'

America! Philip gazed from the window of the compartment in rapt wonder as the train took the Japanese delegation first of all through Richmond, once capital of the Confederate States, then north to cross the Rappahannock River at Fredericksburg, and thence to ride beside the broad reaches of the lower Potomac before entering Washington itself. How he wished Haruko could be seated at his side, because she too would enjoy this. Haruko of the laughing eyes, the silken figure, so apparently unaware that as a Tokugawa woman she was one of the most privileged and respected in Japan – Haruko always enjoyed everything. Even being betrothed to Captain Philip Shimadzu. He still could hardly believe his good fortune.

She loved history and great occasions more than most. And here were all the great deeds of the past coming to life before his eyes. But he was astonished to discover, when commenting on the famous places they were passing, that he actually knew more about the Civil War campaigns and sites than the American naval lieutenant who was one of the host party accompanying them as guides and, should it become necessary, interpreters.

'You'd almost think you were a Yank yourself,' remarked Lieutenant Parker, a trifle disparagingly; from his drawl it was clear he came from south of the Mason-Dixon line.

'Well,' Philip confessed, 'my grandfather was Ralph Freeman.'

But apparently Parker had not heard of Ralph Freeman. 'Sounds American,' he agreed. 'Lived in Japan, did he?'

Philip gazed at him for several seconds. 'My grandfather was a general,' he said politely. 'He fought for the Mikado and, indeed, aided the Emperor in regaining supreme power from the Shogunate. My grandmother was a Satsuma.'

Parker frowned; this name he had heard before. 'Her folk grew those little oranges, right?'

13

Philip reminded himself that he was a stranger in a foreign land, and that politeness was all that mattered. 'The Satsuma were, are, a great clan,' he said. 'The greatest in all Kyushu. They fought against the Mikado, under their great general, Saigo Takamori, one of my ancestors. But they were beaten, and when our city was burned, my grandmother perished. My uncle . . . ' He nodded at the admiral, who was seated further forward in the compartment with Mr Tokugawa and an American admiral. 'He was there. Only as a boy, of course.'

'Exciting,' Parker commented, not apparently convinced.

'Have you no famous ancestors?' Philip asked, with a touch of malice.

'Well, I guess I have. But ancestors, history . . . ever heard of Henry Ford?'

'He builds automobiles,' Philip ventured. He had studied the American scene most carefully before beginning the voyage, and also during it. 'He is your ancestor?'

'Nope. He once said that history was bunk. And you know what? I reckon he was right.'

Philip was dumbfounded. This man was a serving officer in the navy. A navy with traditions older than the Japanese. 'In Japan,' he said, 'History, the events of the past, the great men of the past, are considered as very important parts of the present. Because those events, those men, made us what we are. From them we have received our understanding of honour, and courage, and right behaviour, which must guide us in our own lives. The past is therefore the guide of the future.'

'Say, I've heard about your notions of honour,' Parker agreed. 'Is it true that if you lose a battle you must commit suicide?'

Philip smiled. 'Only the commanding general is required to commit seppuku in the event of a defeat. Or the commanding admiral, of course. But seppuku is in

14

any event no longer considered obligatory. Some say that bushido is out of keeping with modern thought. Although others claim that without it, a man is nothing.'

'Bushido?'

'The code of the warrior,' Philip explained. 'The law which for centuries dictated everything that is honourable for a man to do, and everything that is dishonourable, too.'

'And it's this law that commands . . . what did you call it?'

'Seppuku. Yes, it is the law of bushido that demands seppuku of a vanquished soldier. It was really very simple, and in fact very civilised, you see, in the olden days. If a dishonoured general, or at a lesser level, a dishonoured private man — bushido only applies to gentlemen, of course, those who were once called samurai — willingly atoned for his disgrace by taking his own life, then the general's followers, or the man's wife and children and belongings, were inviolate; if the dishonoured man refused to commit seppuku, then was he forever disgraced, and his wife and family were at the mercy of his conqueror, as were the soldiers of the conquered but disgraced general.'

'Or the sailors, right?'

'Indeed,' Philip agreed.

'So who'd be an admiral? Not me,' Parker said, another strange remark, as he was an officer. 'And you hold with that idea?'

'I do not know,' Philip said, without thinking. 'I do not know.'

Because he did not know, in his own mind, what he believed. His uncle had always said that bushido was wrong, a relic from a warring, feudal past; yet there was no more honourable man than William Freeman. And there could be no doubt that the great Emperor Mutsuhito, the man who, with Ralph Freeman's help, had abolished the Shogunate, had decreed that bushido should be abolished, at least in its extreme forms. But equally there was no doubt that many Japanese, and especially in the armed services, still believed in it. Not that it mattered, he supposed – as there were no wars left to fight there would hardly be any future occasions on which one could be defeated and disgraced.

Besides, he did not wish to think about ethical questions at this moment. The train was pulling into Washington. Once again, sights and memories of scenes read about and related. He supposed he must be the most fortunate of men. He knew that his people tended to think in rigid lines, overly concerned with honour – and with such intangibles as 'face', which was just another aspect of honour – and with doing what was dictated as right by a thousand years of antiquity, again another aspect of honour. But his rigidity was tempered by his American blood, and his partially American upbringing. His mother, Shikibu, for all her Japanese name and ancestry and indeed husband, had been educated like an American girl, in an American city, San Francisco. And the man she had eventually married was equally unrepresentative of his people, a poet rather than a man of war, a man, by all accounts, of sensibility and feeling, who had also partly been educated in America.

Philip could not even remember his father's face. Although a poet, Taiko Shimadzu had answered the call to arms in 1894 against China, and had perished in that war; Philip had been four years old. But since then, having so largely been brought up by his uncle William, who was also half-American, he had been taught even more to revere and admire this land of the free – even if he could not help but feel that men like Lieutenant Parker were evidence of weaknesses in that system of free thinking, rather than strengths.

To him, to any Japanese, Washington would have been a holy city, the centre not only of government for this enormous land, but also a place where the heroes of the

16

past, such as Washington and Grant, had walked and talked and planned their mighty deeds. The Americans did not seem to regard their capital, however, with any great reverence, any more than they seemed to regard their generals and admirals, or even their president himself, with any special respect.

But the Japanese delegation soon discovered that the Americans were hard-headed negotiators, and they had willing support from the British – which came as a surprise, for Great Britian and Japan were allies, and had been for nineteen years, long before the British and the Americans had got together to fight the Germans; indeed, as British allies, the Japanese had been involved in that war from the very beginning. But now, whereas the Japanese had come to Washington armed with plans for creating a huge modern navy, with ships larger than any ever seen before – ships in which Philip looked forward to serving, and which he even dreamed of commanding, one day – the Anglo-Saxons wanted limitations, not only to the numbers of units in any fleet, but to the size of each vessel. Neither Mr Tokugawa nor Uncle William was happy with the series of proposals which faced them.

'The British, of course, are bankrupt,' William commented in the privacy of their hotel room.

His stepmother – who had replaced Suiko Satsuma when she died in the holocaust which had followed the storming of the Satsuma stronghold of Kagoshima by the imperial troops in 1877 – was English, and William had certainly always admired and respected Alison Freeman. As a serving officer in the Imperial Japanese Navy, and a protégé of the immortal Heihachiro Togo – Japan's greatest sailor, who had learned his craft serving with the Royal Navy – William had always respected the British people as well, and not only as allies, but also as the first Western Power to recognise that Japan might be a worthwhile friend. And he honoured them for the part they had played in the recent war.

Yet he was a man who called a spade a spade, and there could be no doubt that the British wished to scrap half of their enormous fleet and limit new building for some time to come. The reason was simply that, having spent all their wealth in combating the Germans, and being apparently – and so strangely to Japanese thinking – more concerned with social programmes than with maintaining their strength as a Great Power, they could not afford any longer to maintain the Royal Navy as the finest fighting force in the world . . . But obviously they could not disarm themselves until all the other maritime countries had agreed to follow their example.

'Whereas the Americans are merely dishonest,' Tokugawa commented. 'With respect, Freeman San.'

'Oh, you are right,' William said disgustedly. He was also half-American, and had married an American woman, but he was prepared to recognise that even the people who were so nearly his own were concerned purely with their national interests. The Americans wished to agree to the British suggestions, which would stipulate that no battleship should ever be larger than thirty-five thousand tons. But of course the Americans were not bankrupt. They merely wanted, although they would not say so openly, to limit the size of their battleships to those which could pass through the Panama Canal – but they also wanted the rest of the world not to build anything larger. 'The whole thing sickens me,' William grumbled. 'I am a sailor, not a politician or a diplomat. I am glad to be taking a break.'

The conference, having exchanged views and ideas was adjourning for Christmas, a Western festival which meant a great deal to the Americans. Well, it meant a great deal to Philip and his uncle as well, as they were Christians. Of course there was no prospect of returning to Japan for the holiday, if they were to be back at the conference table in early January. But, fortunately, they did not have to travel that far to be with some family. 'We shall go to Connecticut,' William told Philip, 'and spend Christmas with my brother Jerry and his family. They are expecting us. And on the way, we shall stop in New York for a few days.'

New York! Once again Philip was overcome with excitement and emotion, quite out of keeping for a Japanese officer. Yet even Uncle William was excited. He had spent his boyhood in America, and fallen in love there, but it had been on the west coast; this was his first visit to the East as well.

They wandered down Broadway, gazing up at the skyscrapers, attracting attention even though they had prudently replaced their uniforms with civilian clothes: soft hats and long, fur-lined coats, Western-style suits, spats and boots, gold-headed canes and white gloves. But they were too obviously not American.

'Can you imagine, Uncle, what an earthquake would do to this city?' Philip wondered. There was at least one earthquake every day of the year, in Japan.

'All Manhattan would disappear,' William agreed. 'But they do not have earthquakes here. On the west coast, now . . .'

It was fascinating, and exciting, and vaguely disturbing. There was so much to be observed and remembered. Philip still instinctively reached down to remove his shoes whenever he entered the hotel lobby. He instinctively bowed when meeting someone for the first time. He instinctively held his fork the wrong way, and did not know what to do with the knife at all – there were no sharp edges on the foodsticks he had used throughout his life. And he remained amazed at the total lack of courtesy and respect shown by one American to another, the way in which they would argue in public, instead of the junior member of the discussion politely accepting the views of the older or senior.

When Uncle William took him to a Broadway show he hardly knew what to make of it, of the actors who revealed their faces to the audience instead of wearing masks, and of the audience who clapped or booed or shouted comments, not all of them complimentary, instead of sitting in rapt attention and silence as in a Noh theatre in Tokyo. For the first time he was glad that Haruko was not, after all, at his side; Haruko was an enthusiastic theatre-goer, and she would have been deeply offended on behalf of the performers.

'A strange people,' he commented. 'I do not know that I should be happy living here.'

'New York is a city,' his uncle reminded him. 'And probably the most city-like city in the world. It is different in the country. You will like Connecticut better. And there we will be amongst friends.'

Philip could hardly wait.

They caught a train from Penn Station, and rumbled through the greenest country Philip had ever seen. Once again there was a total absence of mountains or even hills, but it looked immensely fertile, and, for fertile land, incredibly unused, when he thought of the way a village of Japanese farmers tilled every square inch of arable land, because there was so little of it. Here there were whole woods standing on level ground, left untouched apparently just for the beauty of them, and little inlets of sea, covered with ice, leading up to delightful sheltered coves; he could imagine what a delight it must be in the summer.

But he remained nervous. He could, in fact, remember his uncle Jerry. Jerry Freeman was the son of Ralph and his English wife Alison, but such had been the vicissitudes of Ralph Freeman's early life that he had actually fathered Jerry before marrying Suiko Satsuma. That had made the relationship between his two sons a strange one, and there had been other factors involved as well, factors which Philip could only surmise, but which would bring shadows across his mother's face when she thought

20

of them. Yet the brothers were the best of friends.

Jerry, standing on the platform to greet the train as it chugged to a halt at the tiny station, was immediately recognisable. He was tall, even for an American – and had the bold, handsome Freeman features, and a mass of fair hair, now equally streaked with grey. He was fifty-seven years old, yet his back was as straight as was to be expected from a career soldier who had only recently retired, and his handshake firm.

'Bill,' he said. 'Welcome home. Oh, welcome home.'

'It is my great joy to be here, Jerry,' William said. 'You remember Philip?'

'I remember a lad,' Jerry said. 'A lad. But Philip . . . and a captain?'

'Gazetted last spring,' William said happily. 'He too will one day be an admiral, Jerry. It runs in my half of the family. As you were a general like Father.'

'As if any sane man would wish to be either,' Elizabeth Freeman remarked, coming forward to take Philip's hands. 'I don't suppose you remember me.'

'But I do, Aunt Elizabeth,' he protested, flushing. He had vague memories, and vague disturbances of memory, too. Elizabeth Freeman was English, tall and spare, and with rather severe features, although they could be relieved by her smile, as now. For a while she had lived apart from her husband, and Philip was sure it was recalling that early and turbulent relationship which still occasionally distressed his mother. But they had been reunited since the end of the Russo-Japanese War in 1905, and had apparently found the differences in their temperaments and outlooks possible to overcome. Because . . . sixteen years, Philip thought, as he looked at the girl.

She was tall for her age, which could not be more than fifteen. And blonde; her yellow curls peeped out from beneath her fur hat. Both of those facts indicated that she was Jerry Freeman's daughter, even if her features were

21

rather softer than her soldier father's. Or her mother's, for that matter. She was undeniably pretty, in a plump, teenage fashion, and smiling as she came forward to present her frozen pink cheek for a kiss. It was impossible to decide what might lie beneath the fur coat, boots and gloves in which she was bundled. As if it should interest a man betrothed to the most beautiful girl in Japan, Philip reminded himself. But it was odd to have reached the age of thirty-one, and now for the first time be meeting such an attractive cousin, even if she was no more than half a cousin. Family ties were the most important aspect of life to any Japanese; here was a whole new family presenting itself for his love and admiration.

'The roads are grim,' Jerry warned. 'So sit tight.'

He drove a Duesenberg, an enormous car with a suggestion of tremendous subdued power. He and William Freeman sat in the front, and Philip sat in the back, between the two women, who each held an arm. 'I've heard so much about you, Philip,' Anne confided. 'And about Japan. I so wish to visit with you.'

'And you shall,' Elizabeth promised her. 'We all shall. Just as soon as you've finished high school.'

Philip leaned back and sighed contentedly. He had come to America anxious only to admire and like, even to love. The hard-nosed admirals and politicians of Washington, the disinterested lieutenants, the brash and cocky New Yorkers, had made him feel a stranger, rejected, even. But here were his own people.

He could even admire the grip of winter, unlike anything he had ever known around Tokyo, where winters were inclined to be wet more than savagely cold. Now they drove between high banks of snow, on a road which was clearly coated with ice; every so often the automobile slid gently sideways, instantly to be corrected by Jerry, who was an expert driver. Snow lay heavy on the tree branches to either side, too, occasionally falling with a *whoosh*. And it was so still; not a breath of air to disturb the almost sinister beauty of the scene.

'Oh, we have wind sometimes,' Elizabeth told him. 'Then we get a blizzard, and real drifts, and the roads are impassable. You're just being lucky today.'

They turned off the main road and on to a lane, where there was even more snow and ice. And when they finally turned off the lane on to a driveway which sloped steeply upwards, the automobile could do no more; no matter how Jerry changed gears, even the chains which covered the wheels failed to grip.

'Well,' he said. 'That's about it. I never thought we'd make this hill.' He turned round to grin at them. 'I reckon we're lucky to have got this far.'

'What happens now?' William asked.

'We walk, old buddy,' Jerry explained. 'It's only a hundred yards. Our house is at the top of this rise.'

Fortunately the two Japanese had only brought week-end valises with them. They set off, up the sloping drive to the Freeman house. Now the ice was even thicker and more slippery. Elizabeth and Jerry, who were apparently used to this sort of thing, each took an arm of William's, to help him up and stop him sliding. Philip and Anne clung to each other behind them.

'What will happen to the automobile?' Philip asked, breath clouding from his mouth.

'This storm will pass over in a day or two,' she told him. 'It'll be all right.'

His boots slipped and he landed on his knees, dragging her down beside him, and then found himself sliding back down the slope. For several seconds they skidded and rolled, Philip panting and embarrassed, Anne shrieking with laughter. Their seniors paused to look over their shoulders.

'Please don't hurt Cousin Philip, Anne,' Elizabeth said severely.

They dined on roast beef, huge, thick slabs of red meat

such as Philip had never seen before; he was at last coming to understand why the Americans needed knives with each meal – apparently the minimum of preparation of each dish was done in the kitchen, where the food was merely warmed and served, with only sauce and pepper for spice. And with the meat they drank head-spinning but belly-warming red wine. After the exertions of the day, and the replacement of the cold outside with the warmth of the house, Philip found himself becoming sleepy, but after dinner they sat in the drawing-room and drank brandy. At least the men did; the ladies drank only tiny little cups of black coffee. Whether the alcohol, stronger than anything he had ever tasted, was meant to counter the coffee, equally as strong as anything he had previously experienced, or vice versa, he couldn't be sure.

He was fascinated by the house. It was built of timber, which was more Japanese in principle than any other American houses he had seen. But these were not thin screens meant to be easily replaced if brought down by an earth tremor; these were massive logs, intended to stand for as long as any stone wall. It was also, after the American fashion, two-storeyed and rambling. The drawing-room was almost a separate wing, a vast and yet strangely cosy room set at right angles to the rest of the house, and oddly reassuring, because it was absolutely filled with Japanese paintings, vases and bric-à-brac – almost it suggested a museum – and there was even a pair of samurai swords mounted above the mantelpiece. Upstairs there were beds covered with thick comforters. He had become used to these, even to the wasteful concept of having chambers set aside entirely for sleeping, and thus empty and unused for the better part of each day. But he still found it difficult to accustom himself to the American way of sitting, or rather, he thought, sprawling would be a better word. Instead of squatting or kneeling on the floor, back straight, shoulders square, Jerry Freeman lounged in an easy chair by the fire, one knee carelessly draped over the other, shoulders almost lower than his knees as he sipped his brandy. Even more incredibly, his aunt, whose fur-trimmed skirt only came half way down her calves, sat with *her* knees crossed, revealing a great deal of leg in a most unladylike fashion as she took an equally unladylike, forceful part in the discussion.

Most incredible of all, but incredibly attractive as well, Anne had kicked off her shoes and curled her feet up on the settee in which she sat. The same settee as he was sitting on, and as her skirt was even shorter than her mother's and barely covered her knees when standing up, every sideways glance revealed him not only a glimpse of stocking-clad feet but of a great deal more besides. He realised he was allowing himself to be rigid again. Anne would be horrified at the thought of ever appearing naked before him, as she might well do in a Japanese bath-house — just as no Japanese woman would ever dream of revealing her legs, or any part of her body save her hands, when fully dressed. Of course, Anne was only a girl — and yet the thought of her in a bath-house was most disconcertingly evocative. But so was the thought of Haruko Tokugawa dressed like that, and sitting like that. The conflicting concepts, added to the red wine and the brandy, made him feel quite dizzy.

Anne, of course, had not had anything to drink, save for a single glass of red wine with her meal. Philip gathered that Jerry Freeman did not approve of the way his people had abandoned all public consumption of alcohol, and certainly indulged in it in his own home — having purchased the French wine at exorbitant prices. But Uncle Jerry, he supposed, was the most relaxed and contented man, at least to external appearances, that he had ever known — which no doubt accounted for the relaxed attitudes of his womenfolk.

Yet Jerry could be serious enough. 'You know they are meaning to limit severely Japanese immigration to the west coast,' he was saying to Uncle William.

William Freeman nodded. 'I know there is a bill before Congress to that effect,' he said.

'Oh, there's no doubt it will be passed,' Jerry said.

William frowned. 'But why? You will have to explain it to me, Jerry. Do you know, all of my life, certainly when I was a boy in San Francisco, I remember the Japanese and the Americans as being the best of friends. Your people could not do too much for us. And indeed, I have built my entire concept of life around that friendship. Now, suddenly I get the impression that we are almost your enemies. In Washington I felt that we were not there to negotiate and discuss the future, but to be put in our proper place, as regards the British and the Americans.'

Jerry sighed, and leaned forward to knock out his pipe. 'I wouldn't say that is too wide of the mark,' he agreed. 'You see, when Japan was an emergent nation, in Western terms, which had to do what it was told, why, then we were eager to be your guide and mentor. Even when you started flexing your muscles, when you licked Russia, we were on your side; no American could ever dislike anyone who took on the Tsar. But now, the fact is, Bill, you've just become *too* big. For our boots, anyway. You work too hard, and you don't seem to play hard enough. In fact, you don't seem to play at all. Your immigrants have just about taken over Hawaii and the west coast, at least around the cities. They're keeping Americans out of jobs. And you're becoming just too powerful in the Far East. You know, we don't want any empire like the British, but we sure do like to feel we're the boss in our own backyard. And we do regard the Pacific, both sides of it, as our own backyard.'

'And you expect us to accept that?' William asked. 'It may be your backyard, Jerry, but it's our front yard. And we have to live in it, and survive, in a harsh economic world.'

'I'm on your side,' Jerry said. 'You asked me to explain it.'

'Surely we can talk about something else apart from politics,' Elizabeth protested. 'You haven't told us how Hilary is, Bill. Or Shiki and Maureen. Or Peter.'

'They're all well, and wish they could be with us here,' William said. 'And hope you'll all be coming out to see us, before too long, now that travel is getting back to normal.'

'Well, of course we are,' Elizabeth said. 'We're certainly coming over for Philip's wedding, the year after next. You are going to invite us, Phil?' She looked at the young man.

Who flushed; he had been looking at Anne.

'Today we went tobogganing and walking,' Anne Freeman wrote in her diary. 'Philip fell down three times, and fell off his toboggan twice. He has never tobogganed before, and I don't think he has walked in the snow very often, either.'

She paused, chewing the end of her pen, gazing at the wall on the far side of her desk. He was in the next room, just a wooden wall away. And she didn't really want to write about him at all; she wanted to go to bed and dream of him. But she had made a rule to record every thought in her diary, so that she could never forget what she had once thought, or felt, or even imagined.

'He is such a strange man,' she wrote. 'He is so tall, and strong, and *old*, and yet so deferential to his uncle and to Daddy. There are so many things he does not ever seem to have done. But then, I suppose, when I go to Japan, I will discover there are so many things I have never done either. How I want to go to Japan.'

Another chew. But it had been her dream since she could remember. Which made sense, she supposed. Her father had been stationed in Japan as a military attaché to the American Embassy in Tokyo for several years, before she was born. This had been natural, not only because he spoke the language fluently, and had in fact been born there, but because he was Ralph Freeman's son and William Freeman's half-brother. He was entirely Japanese in his sympathies and in many ways in his outlook; his house was filled with Japanese *objects d'art*. Anne herself spoke the language quite well, taught by her father; she had anticipated having to speak it with her cousin, forgetting that he spoke English like an American.

It was natural for her almost to feel Japanese. But if she wore a kimono every night to write in her diary before going to bed, it was more of a dressing-gown over her nightdress than a usable garment; she would never dream of wearing such a thing on the street. And as she had observed so quickly with Philip, there were many areas in which she and any girl he might know in his home town would be utterly different. But she so wanted to be like them, and to live with them, too. It was her ambition, shared by her parents, to qualify as a doctor. It was also her ambition to go to Japan to work, in the huge Anglo-American hospital outside Yokohama, just south of Tokyo. This ambition was so far private, because although she knew her father would certainly encourage it, she equally knew that her mother would oppose it. Her mother agreed that there were many fine things about both Japan and the Japanese, and she was happy to welcome her Japanese relatives by marriage, but Anne suspected that certain things she had seen and perhaps even experienced during her stay there, before the separation which had all but ended their marriage, had caused her to distrust them as a people.

As if anyone could really distrust a people represented by someone like Philip Shimadzu.

Anne wondered if she had a crush on her cousin. She thought about such things, about various aspects of herself, very seriously. She had had a crush on a football player the previous year, and had quite felt bereft when he went to college, although he had only ever carried her books three times. But how childish he seemed compared to Philip. On the other hand, Philip was so old . . . But that also meant he was experienced, and kind; and he certainly liked her, she knew.

She had been overwhelmed on Christmas morning when he gave her a present, brought all the way from Japan, and for a cousin he had never even seen before, had not known whether he would dislike on sight. It was a pin box, made of lacquered wood, and with a lid of utterly exquisite *cloisonné* work which the Japanese craftsmen had raised to the level of a fine art. It sat on her desk now, its marvellous blues and greens and pinks seeming to wink at her as she wrote. She had been so delighted she had thrown both her arms round his neck and kissed him. He had been taken by surprise, she knew; kissing was not a very usual custom in Japan. But then his arms had gone round her and he had held her close for a moment before releasing her, both of them covering their embarrassment in laughter.

'He is so handsome,' she wrote. 'So tall, and strong. He is everything I knew he was even before I saw him, when I first heard he was coming to visit. And I know he must be very good at his profession. How could he not be, and be a captain at his age? But I wish he were not so old. I wish he were not betrothed. I wish . . . '

But there were some things one did not confide even to a diary, which might one day be read by some alien mind. Especially as she had no idea of what the thoughts really were. They were composed of a mishmash of romantic snippets, remembered from all the books she had ever read or the movies she had ever seen. Philip was every bit as attractive as Douglas Fairbanks, and much quieter and less demonstrative. He would be a treasure to adventure with. But such things could only happen in dreams. He was, after all, just about exactly twice her age. That seemed incredible.

'I wish him every happiness in his marriage,' she wrote. 'I'm sure that Miss Tokugawa must be the most beautiful woman in Japan, as he says she is. How strange she is only one year older than I.'

Again she paused to chew. Because that meant he was just about twice her age as well, and yet he was going to marry *her*.

'How I envy her,' she wrote. 'And tomorrow he and Uncle William leave, to return to Washington, and the Conference. But he has promised to return here for a visit before he goes back to Japan. Oh, I hope he does. And he will. I know he will. He is a man who will always keep his word.'

She closed the diary.

'Well, honourable sir?' William Freeman demanded.

Tokugawa sighed, and laid down the paper he had been studying. 'It is the final draft of the agreement.'

'How can it be an agreement, if we do not agree?' William inquired. Philip had never seen his uncle so angry, and the admiral had not yet actually read the offending paper.

Tokugawa sighed again. 'This is not perhaps as bad as we had feared, honourable Admiral,' he said. 'It has been decided to operate on the ratio of five tons each of American and British ships, to three tons of Japanese, to one and three quarter tons each of French and Italian. The French and Italian delegations are prepared to agree to this.'

'And that should concern us?' William remarked. 'France and Italy are not islands. They need armies, not fleets. Five to three. That means, in effect, honourable sir, that for every five American warships, and every five

British warships, there will be but three Japanese warships. That is more than three to one against us.'

Tokugawa raised his head. 'Are you envisaging a war between Japan and America and Great Britain, Admiral?'

'God forbid, sir. Nor is there any possibility of such a war ever breaking out. The British are our allies . . . '

'Ahem,' remarked Tokugawa.

William paused, and gazed at him.

'It is proposed, and accepted by the British, that as part of the general agreement, the alliance between Great Britain and Japan shall be terminated.'

'It has been proposed by whom?'

Tokugawa shrugged. 'One presumes, by the British and the Americans. In any event, as I have said, the British have agreed to this.'

'And so we must also,' William said bitterly.

'It is difficult to have an alliance unless both sides wish it,' Tokugawa pointed out mildly.

'The British,' William growled, loading the word with contempt. 'Have we ever failed them as allies?'

'Indeed not. But times change,' Tokugawa observed. 'And it is pointed out that fears of any Japanese inferiority in the Pacific are groundless. The British are committed to maintaining the bulk of their fleet in the North Atlantic, and they have a vast colonial empire to patrol. The Americans are committed to a two-ocean navy, half in the Atlantic, half in the Pacific. In point of fact, it is stated, we shall remain the most powerful fleet in the Pacific.'

'Thus we are confined *to* the Pacific,' William said savagely. 'And thus consigned to inferiority for the foreseeable future. Suppose *we* feel the need for a two-ocean navy? Suppose *we* wish to create a vast colonial empire?'

'Such contingencies are remote,' Tokugawa said, continuing to speak in a mild tone. 'I think these terms are the best that we can hope to obtain.

'Terms?' William shouted. 'Are we then a defeated

nation, crawling to a conference table in the hopes of avoiding the consequences of our humiliation?'

'It is our business to do the best we can, without antagonising the other powers,' Tokugawa reminded him. 'Now, it is also proposed to limit full fleet strengths to the same ratios I have already mentioned. This is the distasteful part. Our hosts have prepared a schedule of possible reductions in every navy, the concept being that the United States and Royal Navies should each be limited to a total of five hundred and twenty-five thousand tons, which means that the Japanese Navy will be limited to a total of three hundred and fifteen thousand tons. This involves, I am afraid, the decommissioning of . . . ah . . .' He gave the admiral an anxious glance. 'Our fourteen oldest battleships.'

'What did you say?' William asked, his voice low.

'Well, no modern ships are involved, of course. Really only the *Settsu* was launched after 1910.'

'And that renders the others too old for service? A stroke of the pen is to destroy two-thirds of our battle fleet? That will surely be the greatest naval defeat in history.'

Tokugawa gave another of his sighs. 'The British and Americans will be reducing their fleets in equal proportion, honourable Admiral. And we will still have six battleships left. Six modern vessels.'

'Eight, honourable sir,' William corrected him. 'The *Kaga* and the *Tosa* will soon be completed.'

'Six,' Tokugawa repeated.

William stared at him with his mouth open.

'Work is to cease on the *Kaga* and the *Tosa*,' Tokugawa said. 'They are designed to displace more than thirty-eight thousand tons. That is three tons over the limit. Of course, it may be possible to convert them to other uses. But they cannot become battleships, under the terms of this agreement.'

'I see,' William said, ears glowing in rage. 'Well, then,

the sooner we get redesigning and rebuilding the better. We must keep within thirty-five thousand tons, you say. Well, we can build more ships of the *Nagato* class, and improve them too. Yes, indeed. We will . . . '

'We will build nothing for fifteen years, honourable Admiral.'

Once again William's mouth sagged open – and then snapped shut. 'Fifteen years?'

'There is to be what the British and the Americans call a naval holiday for that time. There will be certain exceptions, of course. The Americans are to be allowed to complete their recently launched Maryland class ships, to bring them up to the required ratio, and the British are to be allowed to build two entirely new battleships . . . '

'To bring *them* up to the required ratio?' William asked savagely.

'No. They already have the required ratio. But they have no ships armed with sixteen-inch guns. Both the Americans and ourselves already have such weapons. It is felt that the British would thus be placed in a position of intolerable inferiority, were they not allowed to build two comparable vessels.'

'Comparable,' William snorted. 'If they are starting now, with all the advantages of our research to draw upon, they will build the two most powerful battleships in the world, believe me. Even at thirty-five thousand tons. So tell me what exceptions are to be made in our favour, honourable sir.'

'I am afraid, none. We already have a full quota of capital ships, and they are amongst the strongest afloat. It is a matter, as I have said, of getting rid of our older vessels, and of not building again until 1936.'

'And the four battle-cruisers we already have laid down?'

'Those orders will have to be cancelled, and the hulls broken up.'

William gazed at him, then glanced at Philip, standing

in horrified silence beside his chair. 'You do realise the consequences of this agreement, honourable sir?' the admiral asked.

'Only too well.

'You understand that it will throw more than half of our shipyards out of business, with their attendant work forces?'

Tokugawa nodded glumly.

'That it will mean abandoning the recently started recruiting drive for the navy?'

'Yes,' Tokugawa said.

'That it will display to the world that we are a second-class Power? That indeed there are only two first-class Powers in the world, Great Britain and the United States?'

'I think that is an established fact, honourable Admiral.'

'But you propose to accept this agreement?'

'I do not think we have any alternative. I believe that to make enemies of the British and the Americans at this juncture would be far more disastrous to Japan than accepting a position as the third strongest naval power in the world, or accepting a certain amount of domestic inconvenience. I propose to accept this agreement, yes, honourable Admiral. And I would be very pleased if you would lend such acceptance your full support. It is essential that we present a united front when we return home.'

William Freeman gazed at him.

At last Tokugawa allowed himself the vestige of a smile. 'The alternative is to admit that we have suffered a defeat, as you have suggested, and then perhaps to commit seppuku. I am of course prepared to do that, but I do not believe that such a course will in any way help our country. It is our duty to return to Japan and convince our countrymen that the way we have chosen is the best. After all, honourable Admiral, we are dealing with honourable men, are we not? What, are you not half-American yourself? Do you not know and trust the British? Their concept is that between the three of us, our great ships will patrol the waters of the earth, and ensure perpetual peace. Can there be any end more desirable than that?'

It was William's turn to sigh. 'I do trust the Americans, and the British, honourable sir. And in that spirit, I will give you all the support you wish. I can only hope and pray that the people of Japan are also capable of understanding the situation, and of understanding too our trust in an Anglo-Saxon future.'

'He's not coming back.' Anne Freeman put down the letter and gazed at her mother and father in dismay. 'Philip and Uncle William aren't coming back.' She looked at the date on the letterhead again. 'They've already left for Japan.'

'Yes,' Jerry said. He also had received a letter from his brother, which he was now folding back into its envelope. 'I'm afraid they've received a rough deal, and aren't very happy about it.'

'Oh, really, Jerry,' Elizabeth said. 'I've been reading about the agreement in the newspapers. Everyone seems to think the Japs have done very well out of it.'

'Everyone, meaning the British and American newspaper commentators.'

'Well, really, how could a nation like Japan, a tiny nation like that, expect to be put on the same footing as England?'

'Has it ever occurred to you, my dear, that there are damned near twice as many people in Japan as there are in England?' her husband inquired.

'Oh, well, possibly. But half of them are hardly civilised. And then there's our empire to be protected, and . . .'

'Yeah. Well, I've never been one hundred per cent sure

35

empires are a good thing, except of course for those who happen to have conquered them,' Jerry remarked. 'No, my love, no matter how we may choose to look at it, the Japanese have been ganged up on in every way. When you think how they had virtually to beg to obtain any mandates over the German colonies in the Pacific, where Britain and France were collecting mandated territory wherever they happened to point. And now, this so called agreement . . . The decisions they have had to accept were taken long before they ever got to Washington. They were virtually given an ultimatum: take it, and we'll pat you on the head, or leave it, and we'll treat you as an outsider. We'll put you back into your isolation of a hundred years ago. Only this time we'll be isolating you, not you isolating yourselves. That's virtually gunboat diplomacy. Add to that the new restrictive immigration law, aimed solely at the Japanese . . . They've had a *very* raw deal.'

'And you are, as ever, utterly pro-Japanese,' Elizabeth snapped.

'Sure. I admire them. I don't think there is a nation in history that has accomplished what they have in the past fifty years. Or possibly, could have accomplished that much.'

'When I think of some of the things they've done during those fifty years,' Elizabeth said. 'The way they massacred the Chinese in Port Arthur . . . '

'Now wait a moment. That happened because the Chinese massacred their Japanese prisoners first. Including young Philip's father, remember'

'They didn't!' Anne cried.

'I'm afraid they did,' Jerry said.

'Oh . . . That doesn't excuse what the Japanese did in return,' Elizabeth insisted. 'And when you think of things like bushido, and hara-kiri . . . '

'What's hara-kiri?' Anne asked.

'Something quite horrible,' her mother told her.

36

'It's what the British call seppuku,' her father explained. 'You know, ceremonial suicide. But no one does it any more. Sure the Japanese had some tough customs, once upon a time. So did we. Now they're trying desperately to be one of the modern, civilised nations, and we say to them, okay, you can play in our game, but strictly under our rules, and strictly as the junior member of the gang. We had better hope they never get tired of that and decide to make some rules of their own.'

Anne gazed at him with her mouth open. 'There won't be a war between America and Japan, Daddy? Say there won't.'

'Oh, of course there won't, sweetie. Japan could never fight us. That's what makes the blood boil, to see them pushed about like that. It's sheer bullying. Never mind. Philip doesn't bear a grudge against you, obviously, or he wouldn't have written you a letter.'

'Yes,' Elizabeth said, thoughtfully. 'Anne, darling, would you mind terribly if I read that letter?'

'Of course not, Mummy.' Anne handed her the envelope.

Jerry winked at her. 'Your mother thinks you have developed quite a crush on that young man. She wants to make sure he doesn't have one back. After all . . . '

'He's engaged to be married to the most beautiful woman in Japan,' Anne said, suddenly angry, and getting up.

Jerry raised his eyebrows. 'Why, so he is. I was going to say that he was twice your age, and related, as well.'

'Only just.'

'True.' He pointed at her, laughing. 'You *do* have a crush on him.'

'Jerry!' Elizabeth admonished. 'Stop teasing poor Anne. Philip's letter is entirely correct.' She handed back the envelope. 'And he does apologise most humbly for not being able to keep his word. How strange these people are. He seems to think not being able to come up here for a last visit is positively dishonourable.'

'Well, he would think so,' Anne said. 'He gave his word.'

It was Elizabeth's turn to raise her eyebrows. 'Did he? To whom?'

'To me.'

'Did he?' she asked again, and looked at her husband.

'So maybe he had a crush too,' Jerry said good-naturedly. 'Far away from home, and fiancée, and all that. And he's a sailor.'

'Jerry!' But Elizabeth was looking at Anne, and perhaps remembering Christmas Day. 'Anne . . .nothing, well . . . '

'Oh, Mummy. He didn't even kiss me goodbye, just shook my hand.'

'Well, thank heavens for that,' Elizabeth said. 'I mean to say . . . '

'He's twice my age, and he's related. And he's going to be married. And he's *Japanese*.' Anne ran from the room, and locked her bedroom door behind her. Then she reread the letter, before stowing it carefully in the top drawer of her bureau, next to his Christmas present. Then she sat and gazed at her diary for several minutes. But there was nothing to write tonight. She would not see him again until he was about to be married.

She cried herself to sleep.

CHAPTER 2

The Doubt

With a roar the anchor chain of the battleship *Fuso* ran through its hawse-pipe to plunge into the mud of Tokyo Bay, and the huge ship came to a halt. For a few seconds the noise of the plunging anchor echoed across the bay, and the sea-birds uttered raucous cries as they wheeled and turned above the new arrival. Then there was silence; there was no sound from the sailors lining the foredeck, or those aft, also standing rigidly to attention. Equally was there no sound from the officers on the bridge; once the last command had been signalled to the engine-room by telegraph, and the last hum had ceased from within the steel hull, the silence was utter.

There was no sound from any of the warships anchored around them, either. When the *Fuso* sailed, several months before, the riggings of the warships had been lined with cheering sailors, the air harsh with the whistle of sirens, the boom of signal guns. Now there were again men standing to attention on the decks of the waiting fleet, as custom and discipline demanded, but no cheers, no sirens, no salutes. News of the Washington Naval Agreement had been radioed ahead.

'Well, honourable sir,' William Freeman said. 'We had best go ashore.'

Mr Tokugawa nodded. His face was even more grim than usual.

The admiral's barge was swung out and lowered into the water, her crew already on board. The gangway and embarkation ladder were in place. William descended to the main deck, accompanied by Philip and Tokugawa. There they turned to salute the bridge and Captain Iyesada, Tokugawa removing his silk hat and holding it against his breast. Then they went down to the launch, which immediately cast off.

'We shall report directly to His Majesty and Count Saito,' Tokugawa decided.

'Of course,' William agreed. 'There is no need for you to accompany us, Philip. You will return home, directly. Your mother will be anxious to see you again after so long. Tell her, tell Hilary, I also will soon be home.' He smiled at the young man's expression. 'You did not really expect to be welcomed, did you?'

Philip did not know what he had expected. Certainly not this. They might have become pariahs, or emissaries of some hostile country. Those men out there were his own comrades. He had served with many of them, knew most of the officers on those ships by name. Did the fools not realise his uncle had brought back the best terms he could possibly have obtained? Well, they would just have to learn that.

The launch nosed into the dock and was made fast. There was a party waiting to greet them, three other admirals, two other black-clad officials from the Admiralty. 'Welcome home, honourable Admiral,' the first officer said, his face grim.

'Indeed, it is good to be here,' William said, also bowing. 'You have automobiles ready?'

'Of course,' the other admiral said. 'His Majesty, the entire Cabinet, are waiting to hear the truth of the situation from you.' He looked up as they climbed the steps to the dock itself; there was a large crowd of men, restrained by policemen, staring at the new arrivals in silence. 'At times like these, honourable Admiral, it is good to recall that one is a naval hero.'

William said nothing as he emerged at the top of the

steps. Tokugawa was immediately behind him, Philip immediately behind Tokugawa. The crowd was divided into two halves, leaving a clear path down the centre, towards the road and the waiting automobiles. William glanced from left to right, then looked straight ahead and commenced walking.

'Traitor!' someone shouted.

The cry was taken up.

'Traitor!'

'American lap-dog!'

'Disgrace!'

Someone threw a tomato. It burst on the shoulder of William Freeman's uniform jacket, splattering pink pips and juice across his face.

Philip ran forward to protect his uncle. Officers shouted orders. The police thrust into the crowd, seeking the assailant.

'He will be punished,' the other admiral promised.

William's smile was sad. 'Why should he be punished, honourable sir, if he expresses the feelings of the nation?'

The taxi-cab drew to a halt in front of the gate leading up to the little house. Set in one of the outer suburbs of Tokyo, Shikibu Shimadzu's home was one of a series of delightful small villas facing the road. The front garden was of course small; the real beauty of the garden was at the rear, where half an acre of shrubbery and cherry trees filled with birds composed the main part of the property. There was a goldfish pond, alive at once with fish and floating lilies and surmounted by a curved bridge, and damp sloping areas of brilliant green grass, the whole representing the best of Japanese decorative horticulture. It was a garden where all things were at peace. But then, it was also a house where all things had been at peace, ever since Philip could remember.

He paid the taxi-driver, and offered a tip. The man gazed at the extra coin, then shook his head and drove away. It had, in fact, been a long and uncomfortable drive from the naval docks. Not a word had been spoken after Philip gave the address, but the taxi-driver's thoughts had been easy to interpret. He felt as one with the crowds on the quayside.

Philip had never been so angry in his life. He only wished there could be one individual on whom he could centre his sense of outrage. To see his uncle, the greatest man in Japan, in his opinion, reviled by a mob . . . The same mob had cheered his departure and recalled how he had taken his crippled cruiser virtually alongside the Russian flagship – a battleship carrying twice the weight of guns as his own vessel – in order to sink it at Tsushima. Now it was all gone for nothing.

He squared his shoulders and walked up the path to the open front door, and his mother. Shikibu was the youngest of the three children Ralph Freeman had fathered by Suiko Satsuma; she was only just past fifty. She was also the most Japanese, small and delicate, intensely pretty and quiet of demeanour. There were only occasional streaks of grey in the black hair which was so carefully gathered into a huge bun on the back of her head. Although she had been a widow for some twenty-five years, she still wore the plain white mourning kimono, with no trace of design or pattern, and no jewellery. But she was smiling happily as she watched her son coming towards her.

'Philip!' she said. 'Oh, Philip!'

Reassurance swelled Philip's heart. Knowing his mother's enormous, almost fanatical patriotism, he had been so afraid of this meeting. But now he bowed, and then took her hands. 'It is so good to be home, honourable mother,' he said. 'So good.'

Shikibu held him close; she had to stand on tiptoe to kiss his cheeks. 'Everyone is here to greet you,' she said. 'Everyone.'

She held his hand to lead him into the house, where a

serving-girl was waiting to assist him out of his boots and encase his feet in soft slippers. He entered the main room, moving silently on the tatami mats which entirely covered the floor, and bowed to the people standing there. Then it was a time of embraces and kisses, first of all from his Aunt Maureen Freeman, Shikibu's elder sister, a big, more Caucasian than Japanese-looking woman, who had never married, and then from Hilary Freeman, the handsome, grey-eyed American woman William Freeman had married after many adventures, and then an embrace and a handshake from his brother Peter, who was also wearing naval uniform. Peter was as tall as Philip, and slightly more heavily built; he was two years the older. He sported a little black moustache, but that apart, the two brothers were remarkably alike.

'Welcome home, Phil,' he said. 'Oh, welcome home.'

Sake was waiting, as were cushions for them to sit on, and more serving-girls to take Philip's sword and dirk and cap.

'You must tell us all about it,' Shikibu said, sitting next to him and holding his hand.

'Is William well?' Hilary asked. 'I had expected him to come with you.'

'He felt it to be his duty to report immediately to His Majesty and the Cabinet,' Philip explained.

'I want to hear all about the voyage,' Maureen said. 'And about what America is like nowadays. And I want you to tell me about Liz. Oh, how I want to hear about Liz.' She and Elizabeth Freeman had been great friends as girls, and had indeed wandered the world together before Elizabeth had settled down.

'But first,' Peter requested, 'tell us what really happened in Washington. What was actually agreed? There have been so many rumours.'

'None of which we have believed, of course,' Shikibu said. 'Tell us the truth, Philip, and set our minds at rest.'

*

43

Philip took a long breath. 'I do not know what these rumours are saying,' he said cautiously.

'The most terrible things,' Peter told him. 'That our navy is to be cut in half. That we are to be subservient to the British and the Americans.'

'That no more Japanese are to be allowed to emigrate to the United States,' Shikibu said.

'That the Anglo-Japanese treaty of alliance is to be ended,' Hilary added anxiously; her two children by her first marriage were both British, and lived in England.

Philip looked from face to face; how he wished he had gone to the palace with his uncle and Mr Tokugawa. 'Well,' he said. 'I think that in substance the rumours would appear to be true.'

They gazed at him incredulously.

'Except,' he went on, feeling exactly as he imagined he would were he about to plunge his short sword into his belly, 'that the navy is actually to be reduced by two-thirds, at least as regards battleships.'

'I do not find your jokes amusing,' Peter said stiffly.

'I am not joking. Fourteen of our twenty capital ships are to be removed from service. The oldest ones, of course.'

'Fourteen . . . ' Peter was speechless. He also held the rank of captain: he had spent the past two years on the staff, but was looking forward to a seagoing appointment in the near future.

'And all new building is to cease,' Philip went on.

'But . . . William agreed to this?' Shikibu asked.

'Uncle William and Mr Tokugawa, and the other members of the delegation, felt they would do no better,' Philip explained.

'And I am sure they were right,' Hilary said loyally.

'You . . . ' Shikibu stared at her sister-in-law. 'You do not understand,' she said. 'If this is true, we might as well have been defeated in a war.'

'Now, Shiki, that is not so,' Maureen protested. 'The

Americans and the British are also reducing their fleets. Aren't they?' She looked at her nephew for confirmation.

'Oh, indeed,' Philip said. 'After the British have built two new sixteen-inch gun ships. But they will be within the thirty-five-thousand-ton limit, like our *Nagato* class.'

'I cannot believe Uncle William agreed to that,' Peter declared.

'I am sorry,' Philip said. 'But there it is.'

'What will His Majesty say?' Shikibu wondered. 'What will the nation say?'

'They will understand, when it is explained to them,' Philip said.

'Understand? How can they understand?' Peter shouted, getting up. 'How can anyone understand such a betrayal?'

Philip also got to his feet. 'You cannot use such a word about our uncle. He did what he felt was right.'

'And destroyed our navy with a stroke of his pen,' Peter sneered. 'Understand? I am ashamed. Ashamed!' He stamped from the room.

Philip would have followed him, but Shikibu stopped him. 'It is better to let him go,' she said. 'He is angry. We are all angry. Are you not angry, Philip?'

'I was angry, Mother, when I first heard of the agreement. But I now believe it may well be for the good of the world. We have all talked about stopping the arms race, so that another world war can never happen. Well, is this not a first step in that direction? It may not please everybody, but it is a definite step. Now, if the armies will follow the example set by the navies . . . ' he checked at his mother's expression, and gave a sigh of relief as he heard his uncle's voice outside.

'William!' Hilary ran forward, then hesitated at the sight of his stained tunic. 'My God, you're hurt!'

'Only a tomato,' William said, and drew her to him for a close embrace. Then he reached past her to hold Maureen close as well. Only Shikibu hung back.

'I saw Peter on the way out,' William said. 'But he chose not to see me.' He looked at Philip. 'You've been breaking the news?'

'Yes, sir,' Philip said.

'You have come from the palace?' Shikibu asked her brother.

William went towards her, his arm still round Hilary's waist. 'Yes.'

'What did His Majesty say? Viscount Saito?'

'They understand that we did what was necessary,' William said. 'Although I will not pretend it was a pleasant interview, it was, at least, a short one.'

'What was necessary?' Shikibu demanded, still refusing an embrace. 'What was necessary about it? Has the Japanese fleet been defeated in battle? Has the Japanese fleet *ever* been defeated in battle?'

'Of course it has not,' William said. 'But we are not talking about battles in the past. We are talking about avoiding future battles.'

'And you will do that by making ourselves so weak we cannot fight anybody? By crawling to the British and the Americans?'

'Now, Shiki,' William said, placatingly.

'Our father fought to make Japan strong,' Shikibu said, her voice low and filled with venom. 'My husband *died* to make Japan strong. And you – you give it all away.' Like her elder son, she turned and left the room.

The Tokugawas lived in a palace. Compared with the ten tatami mats which was all Shikibu Shimadzu's cottage measured, Philip supposed this house would contain some fifty mats, each six feet by two. It was single-storeyed, but set on high ground which looked down on Tokyo, and was entirely surrounded by deep verandahs. There were grounds, rather than a garden, with lawns, and lakes, and rushing waterfalls, tended by a dozen gardeners. There were three automobiles in the garages, and a driving-range behind the house so that the new craze for golf which was afflicting the upper-class Japanese could be indulged. And there was a butler, solemnly bowing as he removed the young naval officer's shoes; a footman stood by to take Philip's hat and gloves, sword and dirk.

A maidservant waited to escort him through the house. How his heart pounded as he followed her through an antechamber, and thence down a corridor, which he knew led to the gardens at the back. He had deliberately postponed his visit for a day, to give Mr Tokugawa time to make his explanations to his various relatives, and to give them time to digest what he had done. Even so, Philip had absolutely no idea of the reception awaiting him. His mind remained filled with the anger of his mother and his brother — anger which had not abated in twenty-four hours.

The maidservant opened the door for him, bowing very low, and he went through, on to one of the side verandahs, from which steps led down to the rose garden. And Haruko. As it was already March, the weather was dry, and not even truly cold any longer. Haruko wore a crimson kimono and carried a crimson parasol, almost matching the blooms as she appeared to study them most carefully, but half inclining her head as she heard the door.

'Shimadzu San!' she said, her voice quiet, and yet . . . filled with pleasure?

He ran down the steps. 'Haruko . . . '

'Shimadzu,' she said again, turning to face him, while the prettiest of blushes caressed her cheeks. She was the most beautiful woman in Japan; for a few weeks, on the return voyage from Washington, his mind a turmoil of concern at the reception which would be awaiting him — justifiable concern, as it had turned out — and kaleidoscopic memories of that happiest of Christmases he had just celebrated, he had almost doubted. His thoughts had been too clouded with Anne Freeman, so full of life and vitality, so bubblingly self-confident, so outgoing in her attitude towards the male sex – so different from a well-born Japanese girl.

He had, in fact, almost been unfaithful, in his mind. How carelessly, how stupidly, and how criminally. And most of all, how wrongly. Now he gazed at the magnificent raven hair, parted exactly in the centre to reveal the whiteness of the scalp, before drifting down her back to her thighs: at a perfect heart of a face, in which high forehead, small nose, wide-set black eyes, wide mouth, and pointed chin were all perfectly delineated. He knew nothing of the rest of her; Haruko Tokugawa had never attended a public bath in her life. But her feet, safely encased in white stockings but occasionally peeping from beneath the skirt of her kimono, were so exquisite it was safe to assume her body was not less so.

Her mind was no less a stranger to him than her body. She was his betrothed – but the business had been decided several years before, when she was only twelve, by his uncle and the Tokugawas. He vaguely remembered meeting her before that time, but as a naval officer in his mid-twenties he had not been terribly interested in a ten-year-old girl, however pretty and well-born. Since their betrothal he had seen her more often, but never alone. It had of course not crossed his mind to question Uncle William's decision; a man married where his father, or, lacking a father, his guardian, directed. And it was certainly going to be an advantageous marriage, into all the wealth and power exuded by the Tokugawas. But he simply had no idea whether or not she even liked him. Her manner had always been composed and quiet, acquiescent and compliant. It was impossible to decide what went on behind her eyes. Her expression in repose was thoughtful, even serious. On the other hand, when she smiled, her face lit up as if there were a thousand musical candles behind the mask.

And she was smiling now.

Equally, he had not seen her for several months. 'Haruko,' he said again, and reached for her.

She gazed at him, moving slightly backwards, and allowing her eyes to drift sideways.

'Ahem,' said her aunt, who was seated by the steps.

Philip sighed, and hastily allowed his arms to fall back to his sides. His meetings with Haruko had always been overseen by a female member of her family. He had never kissed her or held her close. Strange to think he had done that with Anne Freeman, and never with his future wife. Of course, he had had sex with geisha girls in his time; that went with being a Japanese officer and a gentleman. But it had never been sex with love. And how he wanted that, now. And needed it, now.

'You have seen your uncle?' he asked.

'He dined here last night.' Her voice, too, was like music.

'And?'

'It is a sad day for Japan,' Haruko said. 'My family knows this.'

'And you?'

'I know it too.'

'I wish to know your feelings about what has happened,' Philip pressed.

'Sadness, and sorrow.' She looked at him in that direct way she used so devastatingly. 'But for you, more than for Japan. I understand how you must feel. And your uncle. My uncle is a politician. He describes politics as the art of the possible, and he has always been successful. But the navy is there to achieve the impossible, should it ever become necessary, and your uncle has been a successful naval officer. I understand your thoughts, my Shimadzu.'

'Can you forgive me?'

'Forgive you? Who am I, to forgive my future husband?'

'Haruko,' he said, relief flooding through his system

49

almost like a glass of brandy.

'I have heard that your brother is angry and has left your home,' she said.

How rumour did travel. 'He will come back,' Philip asserted confidently. Suddenly he was confident about everything.

'I am sure he will,' she agreed. 'I have heard, too, that you are to be appointed to the staff.'

Philip frowned at her. 'Am I?'

She smiled. 'I would not have you go to sea, my Shimadzu, when we are so soon to marry.'

'But . . . ' Not even Uncle William had mentioned this. Possibly because he had not known of it; the Tokugawa still exercised an enormous influence in Japanese affairs. 'I am overwhelmed, of course. I but wish our marriage did not have to wait for more than a year.'

'You would perhaps prefer it to be celebrated this year?' Haruko asked, her eyes dancing.

'This year? Oh, if it were possible.'

'It is to be arranged.'

He was speechless for a moment. 'But . . . you will not be . . . '

'Eighteen? I shall be seventeen in June,' she said. 'My parents have discussed this matter, in the light of recent events, and it is my father's intention to approach your uncle and your mother with a view to bringing the wedding forward by a year. He may already have done so.'

'Haruko,' he said, 'that is the most splendid news I have ever heard.'

'It is felt,' she said, smiling at him, 'that at this critical juncture in Japanese affairs, it is essential to show the solidarity of our two families.'

'Oh, indeed it is,' he said. 'But you, Haruko . . . ?'

She allowed her fan to open and flick across her face. 'I, too, am delighted, my Shimadzu.'

Philip stared at his brother in consternation. He had

come home bubbling with so much news, and now . . .
'You have resigned from the navy?' he asked, and looked
at his mother.

Who said nothing.

'I can no longer serve a force which has betrayed the
interests of my country,' Peter said.

'But . . . have you told Uncle William?'

'He will no doubt learn of it soon enough,' Peter said.
'It is not my business to tell my uncle everything that I
decide to do.'

'But . . .' Again Philip looked at Shikibu. 'Can you not
stop him?'

'He is a grown man,' Shikibu reminded him. 'Nor am I
convinced that he is making a mistake. I share many of his
sentiments.'

'But what are you going to do?'

'I have been offered a commission in the army,' Peter
said.

'The army? You will go from the navy to the army?'

'With equivalent seniority,' Peter said. 'I shall be given
the rank of colonel. The army has not allowed itself to be
bullied and humiliated by any foreign powers. The army
has never lost a battle. Until last January it was equally
possible to say that of the navy. Now that is no longer
true. It is to the army that Japan must look for any future
greatness, that is plain. I wish to take my part in that
onward march.' His voice softened somewhat from its
rhetoric. 'The army welcomes any naval officer who
seeks true glory. They would welcome you as well,
brother.'

'I shall never leave the navy,' Philip said. 'And you are
wrong in your estimation.'

Peter shrugged. 'I have taken my decision.'

'And I am sorry for it,' Philip said. 'But I would not
have us be enemies. I had hoped you would stand with me
at my wedding.'

Philip bowed. 'You are not my enemy. I do not hold

51

you personally responsible for the errors of my uncle and others. However, I feel it would be best for you to find your groomsman from amongst your brother officers. I shall attend your wedding in a private capacity. And I wish to congratulate you on your good news.'

'You have heard?' Philip glanced at Shikibu.

'Yes,' she said, and at last smiled. 'I am very pleased, Philip. It will be good. Good for you, and good for us. You will be happy with Haruko Tokugawa, and she will make you a good wife.'

'Have you also heard I am appointed to the staff?'

She nodded. 'I congratulate you on that also.'

He looked at his brother.

'And I also, Philip. You will take my place, and make plans for future wars.' He smiled. 'Be sure you have the ships to fight them with.'

'Come in, Captain Shimadzu, come in.' Isoroku Yamamoto stood up behind his desk, and came round to shake hands. Big for a Japanese, with a barrel chest and powerful shoulders, he still had to look up at the tall young man. Seven years the elder, he was himself still a captain, but senior in the rank, and Philip knew his reputation as one of the finest officers and sharpest brains in the service, clearly earmarked for promotion. He wondered if *he* would ever be earmarked for promotion again?

'Welcome aboard,' Yamamoto said, squeezing his fingers. 'Let me see, it must be nearly a year since last we met.'

'Almost exactly a year, honourable Captain,' Philip agreed. 'It was at the party to celebrate my promotion. You were kind enough to congratulate me.'

'And since then you have travelled half way round the world and back,' Yamamoto said. 'I congratulate you again.' He stared into Philip's eyes. 'I was sorry to hear of your brother's decision.'

'So was I,' Philip said, and waited. He had entered the

52

Admiralty building with some trepidation, and was still uncertain what sort of a reception he would receive.

'Still, every man must do as he thinks best,' Yamamoto said. 'As only he can answer for his actions when he confronts his ancestors. Sit down, Shimadzu San.' He himself returned behind his desk. 'But I am very pleased to have you in his place. You may not be aware of it, but I have asked for you as my permanent assistant.'

Philip raised his eyebrows. 'I am flattered, honourable Captain. And surprised.'

Yamamoto smiled. 'Because you are not the most popular officer in the service at this moment? I am told that when they burned the American flag yesterday in Osaka, they burned an effigy of your uncle as well. That is sad. I fought at the Battle of Tsushima myself. I saw a great sailor in action. But people forget, too easily. Perhaps they will forget this incident easily as well.' His finger pointed suddenly. 'However, I did not request your assistance out of sympathy, Captain Shimadzu. I believe you can be of great value to the future plans of the Japanese Navy.'

'I?'

'Indeed. Because of your American blood, your ability perhaps to think with an American mind. This is our task, yours and mine. America is our subject, and our objective. And it is the most important subject in the world, to any Japanese officer.'

Philip frowned. 'With respect, honourable Captain, but are we contemplating a conflict with America?'

Yamamoto leaned back in his chair. 'Ultimately, there can be no other course open to us.'

Philip stared at him in consternation.

'The army, of course, does not appreciate this,' Yamamoto said. 'To them, six thousand miles of water is an insurmountable obstacle. And they do not think of things like gasoline supplies, and oil supplies, and even food supplies. They have no concept of how vulnerable these islands, and their people, are to overseas blockade, how our ability to wage a modern war could be ended like that . . . ' He snapped his fingers. 'Simply by the refusal of other nations to trade with us. They suppose that they can march wherever they wish to go on their own two feet, and find whatever they need along the way. Thus while they share our common sense of destiny, they think only of China as our enemy. Every private soldier is taught from his first day that he will one day kill Chinese soldiers for the glory of Japan. One day soon, perhaps. Their plans are well advanced, I believe. But to suppose that the army can conquer China, or even sufficient of it for our needs, without interference from the United States, and perhaps from other Western Powers as well, is a ridiculous dream. It is our purpose to consider the possible consequences of that dream, and take steps to make sure it does not become a nightmare.'

'Forgive me, honourable Captain,' Philip said. 'But my brain is spinning. I had no idea that Japan was planning war against anyone. I had thought wars were a thing of the past.'

'How can that be, where one man has more than he needs, and another less, Shimadzu San? And how may man live, and be a man, without war? War is a part of his nature. So is eating, and drinking, and hopefully, improving his lot. That is what war is all about. I wish you to begin by considering certain facts about our country. We barely produce sufficient rice to feed our population. And our population grows every day. For the past twenty years the consequences of this have not been as apparent as they should have been, partly because we have managed to expand, in a modest fashion, and partly because so many Japanese have emigrated to the Hawaiian Islands and America. Now we are told that must cease. That is going to cause a very severe economic problem here at home. We are also told that expansion is no longer civilised – by countries who have already expanded over half the globe, mind you. But *our* adventures in Korea and Formosa were uncivilised. Even so, we must have Manchuria. We would have had it by now, had not the Western Powers prevented us from taking it. Yet must we take it, before long. And before not very long, either. It is a simple economic necessity, if the Japanese people are going to be fed. Would you argue with that?'

Philip had never considered the matter in that light. He had never gone short of food in his life. 'Obviously, our people must be fed . . . '

'Exactly. And yet, can you argue against the fact that should we decide to ignore world opinion – which of course merely means the opinions of Great Britain, the United States and France – and go into Manchuria anyway, we will be risking conflict with those three powers?'

'We most certainly would,' Philip agreed, happy at last to perceive an element of sanity entering the conversation.

'Good,' Yamamoto said, rather like a schoolmaster who has succeeded in teaching his pupil to spell a first word. 'Now I would like you to consider another point. Would you seriously argue that the Japanese are the most intelligent, the most forward looking, the *best* race in Asia? Think of our history of progress over the past half century.'

'Well . . . ' Philip immediately thought of the two and a half centuries of stagnation before 1850. But certainly a miracle had been wrought since then. 'I would agree with that estimation, yes.'

'So are we not the natural leaders of Eastern Asia? Is it not absurd that the peoples of China, and Burma, and Siam, and Vietnam, which the French so arrogantly call Indo-China, and of the Philippines and Malaya and the Dutch East Indies, all basically of one racial origin, should be held in thrall by Anglo-Saxons and Dutchmen and Frenchmen? That is a negation of the natural order of things. And I have not even mentioned India, a country of

55

four hundred million souls ruled by a few white-skinned Englishmen.'

'Well,' Philip said cautiously. 'I suppose . . . '

'It is our duty, to lift Eastern Asia, at the least, from the level of a colonial province to an awareness of its place in the world,' Yamamoto told him. 'So, would you not agree that if Japan is to accomplish this, it must first become a great industrial power?'

'That is certainly desirable,' Philip said, glad to be enthusiastic at last.

'Now tell me how, in your opinion, this is to be done, when we lack so many of the natural resources on which industrial power rests? We have no oil. We have no tin. We have no rubber, here in our islands. We must obtain these from outside.'

'But we are already doing so,' Philip argued.

'We trade our meagre goods for these things,' Yamamoto pointed out, 'with the Western Powers who control them: the Americans in the Philippines, the British in Malaya, and the Dutch in Celebes. Thus we are at the mercy of these nations. Can you doubt that, should we proceed with our very necessary expansion into Manchuria, the Western Powers would seek to bend us to their will by refusing to supply us with such commodities at all? And yet, you have just agreed with me that unless Japan expands, merely in order to feed its people, it is doomed virtually to extinction.'

Philip pulled his nose. He did not think he had actually agreed to that.

'Therefore,' Yamamoto went on, 'it is a situation which needs to be redressed – if necessary by force of arms – if Japan is going to survive, much less prosper.'

'With respect, honourable Captain,' Philip said. 'But you are speaking of conquest.' What had Uncle William said in Washington? Suppose *we* wish to create a vast colonial empire? And they had agreed that was impossible.

56

'Does the word conquest frighten you?' Yamamoto asked. 'Did not your American ancestors conquer an area virtually the size of China in their search for greatness? In their pursuit of "manifest destiny"?' He smiled. 'But actually, I am speaking less of conquest than of an inevitable chain of logical events, Shimadzu San. I see our immediate task as this: supposing that expansion into China *must* lead to the threat of conflict with the Western Powers, we may make the logical assumption that the first essential to any plan of expansion by the Japanese people must be to secure the oilfields of the Dutch East Indies, the rubber and tin of Malaya, and the rice of the Philippines. Would you agree?'

Again Philip could only stare at him.

'Having established that,' Yamamoto said, 'we can move forward to another phase. Our very first step must be to prepare, in great secrecy, a fleet and an army, and strike south before anyone is aware of what we are about, and invade the Philippines, Malaya and the Dutch East Indies, and secure them. Our task, yours and mine, is therefore to create the plans for such a pre-emptive strike.'

'Plans . . .' Philip was aghast. 'You are talking of going to war with the entire world.'

'Would it entail that? This is the task to which I wish you, in particular, to address yourself, Shimadzu San. I wish you to tell me what would be likely to happen, if the events I have outlined to you took place. Tell me, firstly, how soon you think such a rapid expansion could be carried out. After, of course, the necessary fleet and army has been assembled, and assuming this could be done in the utmost secrecy.'

Philip's brain seemed to be tumbling. This man was absolutely serious. And presumably he had been given his directive by someone in the Government. Or in the Naval High Command. 'I think it would be a very lengthy operation, honourable Captain,' he said. 'And for that reason, virtually impossible.'

'Tell me why.'

'Because, to begin with, it would mean conquering the garrisons of the Western Powers . . . '

'There are perhaps a thousand British soldiers in all Malaya,' Yamamoto reminded him. 'I doubt there are that many Americans in the Philippines. There are, I agree, considerable numbers of Dutch soldiers in Celebes and New Guinea, but they are spread over a vast area.'

'Would they not be supported by the local populations? And as you have said, it is a vast area.'

'I doubt the local populations will prove a problem. I would expect them to be on our side.'

Philip frowned.

'That is, of course, not our province,' Yamamoto said. 'Yet it seems likely, according to reports I have read. In any event, we would have to make that a prerequisite of any plans we may draw up. And I do not think it would prove difficult, over, say, a ten-year period. We already know that there are great numbers of local leaders, especially in the Dutch territories, who are eager to overthrow white colonial rule and would accept any help to do so. Do not forget that India is on the verge of another mutiny. The British have taken up shooting them down in great numbers. This can hardly make them love the British. However, I note that local support is prerequisite number one. Let us assume it is obtained. What next?'

'Well . . . Great Britain, Holland and the United States would immediately declare war upon us.'

'Would they, Shimadzu San? The Dutch, perhaps. Their East Indies are ninety per cent of their colonial empire, and the only part of any great value to them. But the Americans are busily pretending to everyone that the Philippines are being prepared for full independence. Oh, they will retain certain rights, and military bases. But they have had a bellyful of war, and there are large sections of the American population who are against *any* colonial adventures, however disguised as preparing nations for independence. Would they be prepared to go to war, across six thousand miles of water, for a group of islands which really mean very little to them? *They* are not dependent upon the Philippines for anything. The Americans do not even eat a great deal of rice. But this is a subject which is peculiarly your own. I will bow to your opinion.'

Philip gazed at him, because he suspected Yamamoto was right. Would the Americans wish to go to war for the Philippines? Would Lieutenant Parker seriously wish to leave his comfortable desk in Washington to fight for some emergent nation nine thousand miles away?

Yamamoto smiled. 'That leaves Great Britain. The British might very well wish to defend Malaya, principally because of its proximity to India. But supposing the British do decide to go to war against us, what then? There is scarce a brigade of regular troops in Malaya itself, as I have said. There are only a few cruisers and destroyers in the British Pacific Fleet. There is nothing we could not brush aside with contempt. Would they then assemble the forces of the Empire against us? Could they? Did Australia and New Zealand and Canada and South Africa back them against legitimate Turkish aspirations in the Middle East? They did not.'

'The Australians would back Britain if we were to move into, for instance, New Guinea,' Philip ventured.

'And that should frighten us? Do the Australians have an army? Do they have a navy? I believe they have a couple of cruisers. Anyway, it will be part of our government's task to assure the Australians that we intend no invasion of their continent. And we do not. They have nothing there that *anybody* wants. No, no, only Britain is capable of sending forth an army or a navy against us. But would the British *people* back a British government hell-bent upon a major war in the Far East? I doubt that. And if they did, by the time they could assemble their armies and their fleets, and find the money, we would have Malaya. Possession is nine-tenths of the law, is it not? And do not forget, any British force operating in and around the Indian Ocean would always be looking over its shoulder at the Indians themselves.'

It occurred to Philip that Yamamoto was perhaps placing too much store by an Indian revolt; he did not suppose the Indians truly wished to acknowledge the Japanese as their masters any more than they enjoyed acknowledging the British. But he chose a different argument. 'The British have allies apart from their dominions,' he murmured.

'Of whom are you speaking? France? Hardly to be counted on at this moment, or for the foreseeable future. France is exhausted. The United States? Because she and Great Britain presented a united front against us at Washington? That was because they had mutual objectives. They have no mutual objectives when it comes to colonial empires. Besides, I do not think the United States will ever wish to go to war on behalf of a European power again. They have even refused to join the League of Nations.'

Philip had forgotten about the League of Nations. But it was a straw. 'Yet are we members of the league, honourable Captain,' he said. 'We would be breaking every objective of that organisation. We would become pariahs in the international community.'

'There are a great number of Japanese, Shimadzu San, who do not regard the League of Nations as necessarily vital to the future of our country. I am one of those. The league is concerned with maintaining the status quo, for the benefit of Great Britain and France. I do not see the League of Nations ever providing the Japanese people with rice. Thus I do not think that Japan can afford to regard criticism by the league of any future action as a deterrent to such action. We are more concerned with the reactions of individual countries, and especially the

United States. But this, I repeat, is your province. I do not wish categorical answers here and now. I wish you to study the project, and give me carefully considered opinions, supported, wherever possible, by facts. However, let us conclude this discussion by considering the ultimate, that all three colonial Powers, Britain, Holland and America, decide to act against us. What do you envisage then?'

'An impossible situation,' Philip suggested. But he knew he was about to be corrected yet again.

Yamamoto smiled. 'For the Western Powers, indeed. You will agree that there is no possibility of preventing us from obtaining our objectives, providing we act with sufficient speed and secrecy. Now, once that is done, there will equally be no possibility of them imposing trade sanctions upon us, cutting us off from our vital supplies, especially oil, because we shall then have all the oil we need, from the Dutch East Indies. So, they will be left only with the option of direct assault. With what? Their fleets?'

'Our fleet has just been reduced to a third of the combined British and American strengths, honourable Captain.'

'Not here in the Pacific. And we have the two *Nagato* class battleships. The two most powerful vessels in the entire world, thirty-four thousand tons and armed with sixteen-inch guns. They are worth any three existing ships.'

'The British are also about to build sixteen-inch gun ships,' Philip reminded him.

'About to build. We shall have to wait and see how they get on. They will not, in any event, be able to build any ship more powerful than either the *Nagato* or the *Mutsu*, for the simple reason that they are forbidden to do so by the terms of the Washington Agreement, which they themselves drew up. But supposing they do build these ships, they will then have to send them, with

61

adequate support, twelve thousand miles. That will not only denude Great Britain of any defensive, or offensive, capability in the North Atlantic, it will also remove that fleet many miles from its home port or any adequate port facilities at all – providing we hold Singapore by the time the British fleet reaches the Indian Ocean. They will have to operate out of Colombo. Do you not see that we are envisaging a scenario where the conditions of Tsushima could be re-enacted? Then the Russians sent a fleet from the Atlantic, half way round the world, to fight us, and we were waiting for it, and utterly destroyed it. I was there, remember. So was your uncle.'

'The Americans . . . '

'*If* they come in, which is doubtful in the extreme, as we have already agreed, they would still be operating several thousand miles from their nearest base. Once we hold Manila and Subic Bay, Pearl Harbour is *their* nearest adequate port installation. And they too would be denuding themselves of any Atlantic capability, if they are to have any chance of defeating our battle fleet.

'It is possible, you see, Shimadzu San, to turn any situation to one's own advantage, however unpromising it may look at first sight, if one approaches it in the proper frame of mind. I am not proposing that we strike south tomorrow morning. There are also certain political situations which have to be resolved to our advantage; the complete destruction of China as a possible enemy, for one, and the penetration of Malayan and Philippine and Dutch anti-colonial opposition; these things will take time. But often such things take *less* time than is at first supposed. And the world situation is ever changing. It is possible that long before the scenario as I have outlined it is absolutely right for us, other circumstances may have arisen which are entirely favourable to us. Who can tell? Our duty is to prepare the necessary plans, down to the last detail, which will enable us to act at a moment's notice, when that moment arises. This involves absolutely accurate calculation of ship speeds and requirements, of when our various invasion forces can be made ready following the issuing of the necessary orders, and so on. I intend to create a large team to implement these ideas. Your task will be to head a special body which will monitor all American thought as regards the East Asia situation, and even more important, to monitor all American naval developments. Doing this, you will be performing a great duty for your country.' He held out his hand. 'As I have already said, welcome aboard, Captain Shimadzu. We are the architects of the future of Japan.'

'Is he mad?' Philip asked William, as they sat in the garden of Shikibu's house.

'Hardly. He is regarded as a brilliant man. Certainly a future admiral.'

'And he is charismatic, I must admit. But really, what he is proposing . . .'

'Something you should hardly be telling me,' William reminded him. 'I am a serving officer, not a planner. I have always been a serving officer. A carrier-out of orders rather than a creator of orders. How I ever allowed myself to be talked into a diplomatic mission . . .'

'Because you are half-American, Uncle,' Philip said. 'That is apparently my great value as well.'

'Well, I am taking a sea command next month,' William said. 'Not that I shall be going to sea all that often. There is nowhere to go. And not that many ships to take.' He gave a grim smile. 'My last command. Of a destroyed navy.'

'Yamamoto does not think so. But how I wish I were coming with you. I am not a staff officer. And how can I even pretend to be a staff officer when I do not believe in the task I have been assigned? When I am horrified by it?'

William rested his hand on the younger man's. 'You are appointed to the staff, partly because Yamamoto asked for you, as one of the most promising officers in the service, and partly because the Tokugawa wished it, as a future son-in-law. You know, Philip, even at sea a man is sometimes commanded to do things he abhors, and a serving officer must always carry out his orders. At sea, this is without any chance of redress. You are really in a most fortunate position. You have been given a task which you can use for what you consider the good of Japan. It is your task to convince Yamamoto that his plans are impossible. And you must support your opinions with facts. Doing that, you will be of far more value to Japan than standing on the bridge deck of a warship.'

'Supposing I *can* convince him,' Philip said gloomily.

'Nothing lasts forever. No man holds the same appointment forever. Yamamoto has been appointed to direct naval planning, so that his superiors can assess his capabilities. He is an enthusiastic, ambitious officer. He believes that by producing plans such as those he outlined to you he will be bringing himself to the notice of the admirals, and promoted. No doubt he will be. But as he *is* ambitious, and desires to reach the top, he will not long remain in charge of strategic planning. Bear with him, and correct his tendency to excess. This is often the lot of the supporting officer. And do not feel that you are being disloyal to your American heritage, or that you can harm the United States in any way; you may be sure that the Americans are also making plans in case a war with Japan should ever be forced upon them.' He smiled. 'It is interesting work; you should enjoy it. You are young; you should also be happy. You are about to make a famous marriage. You have a tremendous career ahead of you. You have but to do your duty under all circumstances, to love Haruko under all circumstances, and you will wind up as Commander-in-Chief of the Japanese Navy. I make this a prophecy.'

'And if my first duty as Commander-in-Chief is to lead

our fleet into battle against the Americans?'

William shook his head. 'That will never happen, Philip. I make this prophecy too. Yamamoto may one day command the navy, but he will never command Japan. Neither will any of these hot-headed generals. Japan is governed by sensible and honest men. No sensible and honest man could ever wish war with anyone, much less with the United States.'

CHAPTER 3

The Occasion

If Uncle William had a fault, Philip knew, it was a tendency to urbanity, to believing that everything would always come out right in this most perfect of worlds. Because for him, everything *had* turned out right. He had himself clashed with authority in his youth, when commanded to carry out duties of which he had not approved – but he had basked in the support and friendship not only of Heihachiro Togo, Japan's greatest sailor, but even of the Emperor Mutsuhito, who had been such a firm friend of his father's. Thus, whatever the ups and downs of his career, the disaster of his first marriage to a Russian countess, he had triumphed over all. Not with entire joy, of course. His son by that Russian marriage, Boris, was lost to him somewhere in Soviet Russia – Philip wasn't even sure if his cousin had survived the Revolution, or the Civil War which was still raging: Uncle William never spoke of him. And there were also the children of Hilary's first marriage, to the Englishman Henry Dawson. They lived in England, and were both married – his aunt regularly went home to visit with them. But she was seldom accompanied by her husband on these lengthy journeys. William preferred to devote his life to his two nephews, the sons of his favourite sister and his closest friend.

Now even that had turned partly sour. William had never discussed the matter with him, but Philip could tell that he had been deeply hurt by Peter's decision to abandon the navy for the army. The two services had always been far apart in their thinking, their beliefs, their ethics. For a very good reason. The army had been created by Prussian officers, on the Prussian model, and with Prussian moral values – it was no coincidence that the army remained the last stronghold of bushido, or that it believed it could defeat the world if need be. The navy, on the other hand, had been trained by British officers, on the model of the Royal Navy – and not even the Royal Navy of Nelson, but that of Victorian England. While it, too, undoubtedly believed it could beat the world if it had to, it had been taught to keep such thoughts to itself. Not even Captain Isoroku Yamamoto would ever voice his ambitions in public.

But there were other factors dividing the services, as well. The army had only ever fought in Korea and Manchuria, against Russians and Chinese. If the navy had never fought anyone else either, the sailors necessarily came into contact with more of the outside world, understood more of Japan's place in that world. Perhaps still not enough. It was a thousand pities, Philip thought, that Yamamoto had not made the journey to Norfolk Navy Yard, and gained just the smallest glimpse of the immense power that was the United States.

The army, of course, regarded the Washington Agreement with total scorn. No outside nation, or group of nations, was ever going to tell them how many divisions they could have, how many men would compose a division, or with what weapons they would be armed. The army had read about the immense forces unleashed in Flanders between 1914 and 1918, but without great interest. Conditions in Western Europe were far different to any envisaged in East Asia. Besides, they preserved a certainty that a Japanese army would have overcome the obstacles of entrenchments and barbed wire and machine-guns, as indeed they had done against the Russians in 1904. They had not stopped to consider that

67

the Germans had also found it easy to defeat the Russians – and that the British and the French and the Americans had found it, if not easy, certainly practical to beat the Germans, simply by the application of overwhelming force. That was not a train of logical thought that appealed to the army. They dreamed of conquest, of a Greater Japan dominating all Asia. And Peter was now one of them.

And because of those dreams, the navy must also dream. But, Philip knew, William retained his innate trust in the honour and sense of mankind, and especially Japanese mankind – at least that small portion of it ever likely to control the country's destiny. Let the generals, let Peter, dream of world conquest. Let the navy, let Yamamoto, make plans to aid them on their way. No admiral, and no general, either, would ever fashion the future of Japan – surely.

Thus life was there to be lived and enjoyed, in confidence of the future. If possible.

In fact, Philip found that he enjoyed his new job enormously. He had always been interested in the planning of naval warfare, the envisaging of various circumstances, and equally, of the limitations and the possibilities of ship design and performance, at least as much as in commanding at sea. And he was relieved to discover, when he got down to it and correlated all the facts which were obtainable, that he had no need to misrepresent anything to Yamamoto in order to press his point of view.

He could not deny his superior's claim that there was no opposing force available in the Pacific which could possibly offer battle to the Japanese fleet for a period of several weeks after war commenced. But, he pointed out in his reports, such a war could not take place until after the British had completed their two new vessels, which were to be named after the two most famous of British admirals, Horatio Nelson and George Rodney. Equally, the Americans would have their sixteen-inch gun ships –

albeit these were each some two thousand tons smaller than the *Nagato* and the *Mutsu* – either at their naval base of Pearl Harbor in Honolulu, or able rapidly to gain the Pacific by means of the Panama Canal.

It was therefore necessary, he stressed, to envisage a situation whereby within six weeks of the commencement of any war, America and Britain, should they work together, could unite in the Pacific a fleet of as many as six – four American and two British – of the newest and best battleships afloat. In addition, there was the British battle-cruiser *Hood*, which at over forty thousand tons was already the most powerful warship afloat – even if battle-cruiser armour remained suspect after the Battle of Jutland, in which three British battle-cruisers had been sunk in a few minutes.

'I feel that such a concentration would pose the Japanese Navy a near impossible task,' he wrote, 'and therefore feel that this foreseeable situation must be resolved in a manner satisfactory to us before it can be possible to proceed further with the Strike South concept.'

Yamamoto was impressed, not with the possibility of an American-British alliance, which he derided, but with the thoroughness of the report, which included projected mobilisation periods for the British and Americans, passage through the Panama Canal, and carefully considered elapsed times from home-port departure to arrival at a given point within striking distance of Japan.

'I do not believe such a scenario can ever arise, Shimadzu San,' he said. 'But you are right to say that it must be our duty to make sure it never *can* arise, before we can be expected to proceed further.' He gave one of his grim smiles. 'I shall have to form a study group to consider the possibility of blowing up sufficient of the Panama Canal to prevent its use for some months.'

But that was clearly something out of Hollywood,

Philip reflected. And presumably Yamamoto forwarded his report to their joint superiors. He could at least feel that he had delayed serious study of the 'strike south' concept for some time to come.

There was, however, little else in his professional or social life to be satisfied about, except his approaching wedding. In fact, nothing else mattered; he was almost counting the hours, much less the days, to the great occasion. But until then, life was strangely empty, and unhappy. He called on Haruko every week, and they walked in the garden together and discussed serious matters, such as the building of their new home, which Haruko naturally regarded as the most important subject in the world. And rightly so, he knew. She was moving out of a palace into a small house, and that was sufficiently a miracle in itself; he was entirely in agreement with her that everything about her new home should be just so.

She was, as always, unfailingly respectful and loving, as her birth, her sex and her upbringing required. No man could possibly ask more in a future wife – but he could never hold her close, never share with her his innermost thoughts and desires. He had never done that. Simply because they were never alone. He could never attend the theatre with her, except as part of a large family group, and he could never take her walking or riding in the country. He remembered how he and Anne Freeman had gone off by themselves, tobogganing, rolling down slopes together, bouncing against each other – while he and Haruko could not even visit their new house without an elderly relative in tow.

He could not help thinking about Anne, because to his surprise, he received a letter from her, two months after his return to Tokyo. It was a very typical letter. She thanked him for his apology for having been forced to break his promise by his uncle's decision to return immediately to Japan, and reiterated, several times, how she

70

was looking forward to visiting his country – she had apparently heard that she might well be doing so this very summer – and then went on to tell him all the things she had been doing, the picnics and the beach parties as the weather had commenced to warm up, and the visits to New York. She bubbled, as he remembered her doing, while he found himself quite out of sorts at the thought that she was probably rolling down some other slope with some other man at this very moment. Some young man, perhaps, unengaged and unrestrained by manners, who might wish to take advantage of her ebullient nature.

He could not even be with Haruko in the company of male friends. That was simply not done. It was rare even for a wife, except at intimate family gatherings, to attend a male party. For a fiancée it was unheard of.

He had now been engaged to Haruko for four years, and he had never found it any hardship before. Of course, the glimpse of the freedom enjoyed by American women, of the intimacy they could share even before marriage, had unsettled him. But equally his own changed circumstances were to blame. He had no male friends any more. He had never had a great circle of friends. As a younger brother, he had been content to follow the lead of Peter. Peter's friends had been his, and he had tagged along at their games and pastimes as very much a junior partner. Now, suddenly, Peter was no longer his friend. Peter studiously avoided revealing his own feelings since his angry outburst on the day of William's and Philip's return, and was always politeness itself to both of them, but he never wished to be with them, never invited his younger brother to any social gathering in which he might be involved. He had new friends, in the army.

While Philip did not even have a groomsman. The Tokugawa had not raised the matter – presumably they assumed Peter would be filling that role. But with the wedding now only two months away the situation was becoming acute. He even thought of asking Yamamoto himself, but was too afraid of being turned down.

The officers of the navy continued to look at Philip Shimadzu with caution. He had only been an aide-de-camp at Washington. He had played no part in any of the decisions taken there, and it was easy to see that he did not approve of them, however loyally he supported his uncle and his uncle-to-be-by-marriage. Yet he had been *there*. Only Yamamoto treated him with confidence, but it was more an association of two officers who were, as far as Yamamoto was aware, working towards a similar goal – he did not suppose they could ever be true friends, because of the considerable differences in their temperaments.

He had never felt so alone, because even at home his mother treated him with reserve: he had been at Washington! He began spending a good deal of time with his aunt Hilary, who was entirely on her husband's side, and with Aunt Maureen, who took no sides at all, and was a brusque, jolly, no-nonsense type of woman. He attended the officers' club as was his duty, but more often than not found himself drinking alone, or standing on the fringes of a happy crowd. Even the geisha houses were barred to him. This was a personal choice. With his wedding now so close he felt it would be wrong of him to seek passion with another woman, however bought, and however loveless.

But if only the day would come. How slowly it crept closer. He gazed at the card presented by his secretary, raising his eyebrows in a question.

'An English naval attaché,' the young man said.

'Wishing to see me?'

'Indeed, sir.'

'Well, show him in.' Philip got up and walked round his desk to greet the incoming officer.

'John Graham, Lieutenant-Commander, Royal Navy,

Captain Shimadzu. This is a great pleasure.'

Philip had his fingers squeezed by a powerful hand. John Graham was, he estimated, a few years younger than himself, and, as it was June, wore the somewhat ridiculous dress indulged in by the British in what they considered the tropics: white shirt and shorts, white knee-length stockings and white leather shoes; his epaulettes were his only sign of rank, apart from, presumably, his already discarded cap. But he was an interesting-looking man, not big by English standards, certainly, with sandy hair and a sharp nose, but a flat, strong mouth and quickly moving blue eyes — and possessing a powerful grip.

'Welcome, Commander Graham,' Philip said. 'Please be seated. Would you prefer to speak English?'

'I say, could we?' Graham asked. 'May as well face it, you know; I find your language dashedly difficult.'

'It is, dashedly difficult,' Philip agreed, making a mental note; like so many British officers, Graham was putting on a silly-ass act — but he did not doubt there was a very shrewd brain behind those eyes.

'Thought I'd make my number, what?' Graham remarked. 'I've only been here a few weeks.'

'What brought you to me?' Philip asked.

'Well, old man, I have to say . . . you're half-American, aren't you?'

'One-quarter American,' Philip said.

'Enough. My business, well, it's to find out what you chaps are up to. I thought it'd be easier to start with someone who understands English, don't you know.'

Philip gazed at him. The Englishman might just be overdoing it, he thought. But such a simplistic approach to naval intelligence could be more devious than he suspected. He thought it might be amusing to counter it in a similar style. 'I'm afraid I have very little to offer you,' he said. 'I am concerned with planning. For war against Great Britain, one day.'

73

'Oh, quite,' Graham said, apparently unsurprised. 'Our Far Eastern johnnies are working out how to beat you too, don't you know? But it's hardly likely to happen, now is it? Japan and Britain have been friends for too long.'

'We were even allies, down to last year,' Philip murmured.

'Indeed we were. I think that ending that alliance was one of the great mistakes of English foreign policy,' Graham asserted.

Once again Philip gazed at him.

'One of my dreams, as a young officer,' Graham went on, 'was of steaming into battle, the Royal Navy and the Imperial Japanese Navy, in line abreast . . . '

'Who would we have been steaming against?' Philip inquired.

'Well . . . ' Graham smiled. 'When I dreamed, of course, it would have been Germany. Now there's nobody *to* fight, is there? Except maybe the Americans.'

The two men looked at each other.

'But that is a nonsensical idea,' Graham continued. 'I mean, you may not actually like the Yanks, what? But one wouldn't really want to fight them. No, no. I really don't see what I am doing here at all. Still, duty is duty, what? Just thought I'd make my number.'

Philip was intrigued. Less about what the Englishman, or rather Scotsman, he supposed from both name and accent, was after – although he was certainly after something – than the quite remarkable way he was going about it. He reminded himself that the British hadn't succeeded in conquering the greatest empire in history merely by sending silly asses to the far corners of the earth.

'I'm glad you did.' He got up. 'My grandmother was English, don't you know? Or rather, Scottish. Name of Gray.'

'How splendid,' Graham acknowledged. 'You've a

look of the highlands about you, Captain.'

'So have you, Commander. Shall we lunch together?'

'You'll have to teach me how to use these dashedly odd sticks of yours,' Graham said. And then proceeded to master the art of eating with foodsticks so quickly that he proved he had practised often before. Either he was playing a gigantic game, Philip thought, or he was trying to establish some very profound point, which for the moment quite escaped him. Either way, he thought it would be intensely easy to dislike his new acquaintance.

But that feeling disappeared when Graham began to talk. 'Shame you never got to grips with the Germans out here,' he remarked. 'Dashedly fine seamen, you know. And they made fine ships, too. And manned them well. I served on *Lion*, you know.'

Philip was immediately impressed. The battle-cruiser *Lion* had been the flagship of Sir David Beatty, easily Britain's most successful admiral of the Great War, and had probably seen more action than any other ship, as well.

'You were at Jutland?' he asked.

'Only a middy. My word, we took some stick that day. You should have seen them go up. *Indefatigable*, *Queen Mary*, and then, a little later, *Invincible*. Just a whoosh, a bang, and nothing. More than three thousand men lost. Everyone said the battle-cruisers were poorly armoured. Point taken. We hit the Germans a few times and none of them blew up. But you have to give it to Jerry for his shooting. It was twice as accurate as ours.'

Gone was the silly-ass image; his eyes were burning.

'*Lion* was hit as well,' Philip ventured.

'Oh, quite. We should have gone up as well. Jerry landed one right on a turret, with the ammunition hoist right beneath. But for one of our officers flooding the magazine, he was dying at the time, from splinter wounds, you know, we'd have been playing harps as

75

well.' He grinned. 'Or stoking fires. I sometimes wish I was a Muslim; they have no doubt that if they die in battle it's going to be the heavenly houris for ever and ever.'

'What did it feel like?' Philip asked. 'To watch those three great ships just, well, disintegrate?'

Graham frowned. 'Do you know, old boy, I don't think one felt anything. You know the famous saying, that old David turned to his flag captain and remarked, "Something seems damned wrong with our battle-cruisers today." Battle is like that. You never believe it can happen to you. But you must remember what it's like, from Tsushima.'

Philip sighed, and drank some sake. 'I was not at Tsushima.' He gave a shamefaced grin. 'I was too young. I have never seen a fleet action. Even a ship-to-ship action.'

'Well, old boy, I wouldn't lose any sleep over that,' Graham remarked.

'Wouldn't you? I hold a captain's rank, and I have been in the service for fifteen years, and I still do not know whether or not I am a hero or a coward.'

'Being under fire doesn't always prove that either,' Graham said.

'Where were you when *Lion* was hit?'

'Well, ah, in the turret, don't you know.'

'*In* the turret?'

'I was blown out. Wasn't even hurt. And talk about scared. I was pissing like a fire-hose.'

'But you saved your ship.'

'No, no. It was the marine officer did that. And died. Now there is heroism. But you know . . . ' he gazed at Philip. 'I think I would have done it, if he hadn't done it first. Given the order to flood the magazine, don't you know. No matter how scared I was.' He pointed, suddenly, very like Yamamoto. 'And you would have done the same, Captain Shimadzu. Because we're trained to do

76

that, you see. To take command. It's training that counts, not raw courage. That's what makes all naval officers brothers, regardless of their nationality, the politics of their superiors. When the time comes, Philip, as come it must, you'll find you're as much of a hero as the next man.'

The next day they played tennis, and the evening after that Philip invited Graham to have a drink with him at the club. Graham had won at tennis, and Philip, who ranked himself as a good player, was impressed. He had led by two sets to love, and four games to two, but Graham had never surrendered, had worked away, slowly taking the initiative, saving two set-and-match points in the third set, and two more in the fourth, before clinching it in the fifth. The Scot was as fit as a professional athlete, and Philip rather suspected his brain was cast in the same mould.

While in the club he was totally relaxed and easy-going, soon entrancing his audience – all serving officers, but all without a fraction of his experience – with tales, this time of the engagement off the Dogger Bank, making the battle come alive with his descriptions and his sense of urgency. Of course, one or two eyebrows were raised at this friendship between a staff officer and an official spy, and next morning Philip felt it necessary to explain what he was doing to Yamamoto.

Yamamoto listened as thoughtfully and courteously as ever. And then nodded. 'Of course, openness is always the best defence. I will have Commander Graham's background investigated, but there is not much we can do about a British Embassy official, unless he actually tries to bribe you into giving him information. However, I will mention his name to the Kempai.'

'The Kempai?' Philip frowned. He had heard the name before, without understanding its meaning.

'Our intelligence services,' Yamamoto explained.

'They like to know about these things. They probably already have a file on your Commander Graham.' He smiled reassuringly. 'Do not worry. I shall see that you are not involved. I would involve no man with the Kempai intentionally, unless he is the most utter villain – or a foreign naval attaché, of course.'

Philip wondered whatever he could mean, but did not press the point. He was at once relieved to have got the matter off his chest, and a little concerned that he was perhaps not being quite honest with Graham.

The more he saw of the Scot the more he liked him. Graham's rather inconsequential conversation, on all matters unrelated to ships and the sea, was indeed a cover for very sharp observations, and for an encyclopaedic knowledge of world affairs. But when he could be persuaded to talk about the sea, he was entrancing. He knew every detail of every Japanese ship, and of every British ship, too, and discussed them with an easy fluency.

'*Rodney* and *Nelson*,' he asserted, 'are to be of a totally revolutionary design. There is no doubt they will be the most powerful ships the world has ever seen. Oh, I know your *Nagato* and *Mutsu* are so rated at the moment, but consider this: your ships displace about thirty-four thousand tons, perhaps a shade more deep-loaded. So will ours, officially, but I can tell you that deep-loaded they will be something over forty thousand. Your ships have eleven-inch armour plating. Ours will have fourteen. And while your ships have eight sixteen-inch guns, ours will have nine. Using triple turrets, of course.'

'It has not yet been proved that triple turrets will actually work,' Philip argued.

'Oh, they will. But the principal difference between *Nelson* and *Rodney* and all other ships is that in them, *all* turrets will be forward of the superstructure.'

Philip frowned. 'You intend to superimpose *two* triple turrets?'

'Ah, no. That would be going it a bit, don't you think?

78

We will superimpose one triple turret, B, above A, as you do. C turret will be immediately behind B, on deck level. Of course that means only six guns will fire straight ahead. But all nine in broadside.'

'And none astern,' Philip commented.

Graham grinned. 'I understand it is the principle that the Royal Navy never steams away from an enemy, don't you know. But even the siting of the guns is not the truly revolutionary concept. It is the island. Don't you see, old boy, all the ship's vitals will be clustered aft, in one area, which means that they can be protected far more adequately than any ship now afloat, but at the cost of far less weight.'

'Yes,' Philip said thoughtfully.

He duly reported what had been said to Yamamoto, who was delighted, although he pointed out that he was already in possession of all the information yielded by Graham – and that Graham undoubtedly knew that. Philip was relieved about this. He really hated having to betray his new friend. And if he remained worried about the day when the Scotsman would seek some classified information from him, that day never came.

As a naval attaché, Graham was the oddest Philip had ever encountered. So odd, in fact, that he simply had to be genuine, in his often-professed admiration for the Japanese people and all they had accomplished, and in his liking for *his* new acquaintance. Certainly he was the type of friend Philip had sought throughout his life, and never found until now. Graham's knowledge of history, and Japanese as well as world history, was on a par with his knowledge of ships. His respect for the events and the great people of the past equalled Philip's own. His humour was infectious and he could laugh at himself, the greatest of human gifts.

Graham also very rapidly became universally popular in Tokyo. He had only been in Japan a few months but he had already accumulated a wide circle of other friends, for, despite his remarks at his first meeting with Philip, he spoke Japanese with total fluency.

Yamamoto himself could not help liking him, and as he said to Philip, 'Not even the Kempai can find a bad word to say of him. He actually did fight in battle-cruisers throughout the war, was present at Dogger Bank, Heligoland and Jutland, as he claims, has the Distinguished Service Cross, even if he never wears the ribbon. The man is a genuine war hero, who, it seems, opted for Japanese studies after the war ended, and so winds up here as naval attaché. Truly, the British must have talent to spare if they can send one of their best to a dead-end job like this.' He smiled. 'Unless he has come as a goodwill ambassador to make up for the abrogation of our treaty.'

Philip was delighted. Soon he invited Graham home, and discovered that his mother and Aunt Maureen, and even Uncle William and Aunt Hilary, were also prepared to be delighted with him. So, a fortnight before the wedding, Philip took his friend along to meet Haruko. She was surprised, but very quickly warmed to the stranger, and soon they were chatting away like the oldest of friends. He left early, and Haruko remarked, 'What a very pleasant man, my Shimadzu. I did not know the British could be so pleasant.'

'I like him too,' Philip agreed. 'In fact, my Haruko, with your permission, I have asked him to stand with me at my wedding, as my brother will not.'

'Why, Shimadzu,' she cried, 'I am delighted. I can think of no one I would prefer.'

Japan! Anne Freeman could hardly contain her excitement as the ship rounded Nojima Point and entered the waters of Tokyo Bay. The bay stretched some twenty miles into the distance, and Tokyo itself was lost in the summer haze, but already she could make out the bustling seaport of Yokohama, and by looking west, beyond the quays and warehouses and dwellings, she could still see in the distance the mighty peak of Mount Fuji, rising twelve thousand feet into the sky from its position dominating the Hakone range. They had, in fact, sighted Mount Fuji the previous evening before retiring, when Japan itself was still hidden beneath the horizon. She had hardly slept.

Now she clung to the rail and her father's arm as the ship reduced speed. In front of them were several ships of the Japanese Navy, lying at anchor. It was possible Philip might be on board one of those vessels. She wondered if he would identify the *SS William Tell*? With binoculars he might even be able to make her out, as she and Jerry and Elizabeth, with most of the other first-class passengers, were on the boat deck.

If he did, she knew he would probably smile and say to himself, silly little girl. She had not told either her mother or her father about writing to him. She had contemplated writing almost from the day she had learned that he would not, after all, be returning to Connecticut for a last visit. At first she had resisted the temptation, because she was not at all sure what she would say, and because there had seemed time to think, and consider. The news that his marriage had been brought forward by a whole year had changed all that. No one had been able adequately to explain the reason.

'I guess he must have found he missed Miss Tokugawa more than he knew,' her father had suggested, smiling in that easy way of his.

Anne formed the opinion that he had not actually missed Miss Tokugawa at all, while in America. Certainly he had hardly ever spoken of her, except to repeat that she was the most beautiful woman in Japan, as if trying to reassure himself, and that she was a member of the oldest and most famous family in the country as well, excepting only the Royal House itself. But he had also confided to her that the marriage was arranged four years earlier, when Miss Tokugawa was only a child. It seemed ridiculous that he could possibly love her in such circumstances; it seemed even more ridiculous that such an old-fashioned system could still obtain anywhere in the world. But her opinion clearly did not matter; he was still going to marry his selected fiancée – in a week's time.

She had written to congratulate him, and then had added a lot else besides, about the things she had done since he left, about how she hoped he would be able to pay the States another visit before his marriage, about how she looked forward to her visit to Japan. She very much feared that she had gushed. But she had still received a reply, courteous and serious, reciprocating in kind as regards news. He had written that he looked forward to their next meeting as well. But perhaps he had just been being polite.

She knew now that she did have a crush on him, after all. He seemed to epitomise every romantic notion she had ever had about Japan and the Japanese. How she hoped he would be on the quayside to greet them, and would notice how she had grown, really, from a girl into a young woman, all in six months. She had not only gained in height, but in figure as well, as she had shed almost all of her puppy fat; but where her hips had slimmed her breasts had grown – her mother was becoming quite disparaging about them, remarking that large busts simply were not fashionable any more. But Anne could remember Philip looking at her breasts six months ago, when they had been much smaller, and blushing furiously when she had caught him at it.

And he was on the quay. With William Freeman, and a tall, slender American woman who turned out to be her aunt Hilary, and a stout, jolly woman, her aunt Maureen, and a small, slender woman with the most splendid black eyes, her aunt Shikibu, Philip's mother. Philip stood beside her.

He was twice as handsome as she remembered him, and when he held her close to kiss her cheek she nearly fainted. She was such a mass of blushes and stammers she hardly knew where to look, and had no doubt at all that her secret was immediately revealed to all the world – but no one commented, although they all laughed when he observed, 'My goodness, Anne, but how you have *grown.*' Which had her blushing all over again.

She remained quite unable to concentrate on the drive from Yokohama up to Tokyo, unable to grasp that she was actually standing on Japanese soil, something she had dreamed of for so long. When they passed one of the huge vermilion-painted temple gates, called tori, she could only blink in wonder; when her father pointed out the huge bulk of the Anglo-American hospital, standing on its cliffs above the bay, she hardly noticed it, although she still intended to come and work here. Even the streets of Tokyo, which they reached in half an hour, failed to register sufficiently, although she did notice there were as many taxi-cabs as man-drawn rickshaws, which was a disappointment.

She could not stop staring at Philip. He drove himself, with his mother seated beside him. She and her father and Hilary were in the back. William was driving the other car, with her mother and Maureen, who had greeted each other with more warmth than Anne had ever before observed in her mother, and had immediately started a chat which would undoubtedly last the journey. But all she wanted to do was gaze at the back of Philip's neck, and at least she could do that without being noticed.

'And how is Peter?' her father asked.

'Well,' Philip answered. 'He asks to be remembered to you. You've heard he's in the army now?'

'Indeed,' Jerry Freeman said.

'He is working very hard,' Shikibu commented. 'And leave is difficult to obtain.' She and her son exchanged glances.

'What she means is,' Hilary remarked, 'that he belongs to the anti-American school. He'll get over it. But it's very popular right now.'

'So I understand,' Jerry agreed. 'I half-expected to be stoned in the street.' He grinned.

'It's not quite as bad as that,' Philip said.

'And how do you like being on the staff?' Jerry asked.

'I'd sooner be at sea.'

'But it is the ideal position for a young man about to be married,' Shikibu pointed out. 'And building a house. There are so many things to be seen to, all the time.'

'I can imagine. Say, you won't forget that we're dying to meet the young lady?'

'Ah, I'm afraid that won't be possible now,' Shikibu said. 'Until the wedding. It is not proper.'

Anne felt a sense of relief. She had no desire to meet the famous Haruko Tokugawa, the most beautiful woman in Japan, and certainly not before the wedding. She thought there could be no woman in the world to whom she had taken so complete and instant a dislike, without ever having laid eyes on her.

To her disappointment, she and her parents were not to stay with Shikibu and Philip and Maureen, but rather in the somewhat larger house, some distance away, owned by William and Hilary. She did not know what she had hoped from spending the last few days of his bachelorhood in the same house as Philip, but she certainly had hoped to see a great deal of him. Now it appeared she was hardly going to see him at all, until the wedding. She suspected her parents had had something to do with the decision as to where they would stay; they were not entirely unaware of her feelings. And considered them exceedingly unhealthy, if not so very unusual in a young girl. Anne supposed they were right, even as she sighed when, after several cups of green tea, they drove away from Shikibu Shimadzu's house, leaving Shikibu and Philip waving to them from the front garden.

The house itself had been like a painting coming to life;

she had not before understood how Japanese houses could be so starkly empty, and yet so perfectly attractive. She had thrilled to removing her shoes on entering, and then to walking on the tatami mats of which she had read so much. She gazed at the – living-room, she supposed it was, really quite small, but made to seem larger than it was by the absence of furniture, and yet the epitome of flawless simplicity, with the half-dozen cushions arranged on the mats for them to sit on, and the vases of flowers on low pedestals in each corner, while exquisite Japanese silk paintings hung on the walls – but again, only one to each wall, unlike so many cluttered American houses.

This same room would become a bedroom that night, by the simple expedient of removing the cushions and spreading the necessary mattresses. She could actually be sitting in Philip's bedroom. But it was Shikibu's bedroom, as she discovered when she was taken on a tour of inspection, through sliding and therefore utterly noiseless doors, so unlike the banging and handle-turning American variety. She was shown the spare room and the kitchen, where two smiling serving-girls bowed low, and then indeed Philip's room, different to any other in the house because of its bookcase, crammed with naval textbooks and manuals, in both Japanese and English, but also with a good selection of American novels. She could only gape in wonder when he illustrated that, should either he or his mother wish to entertain on any scale, the partition separating the two rooms could be removed with the greatest of ease to make one large room, and then replaced again just as easily when the guests had gone. Such simplicity, which at the same time was so elegant, was almost sublime.

Then Philip himself took her on an inspection of the garden, and showed her the bath-house – again totally different to any American bathroom, and yet enormously evocative – with its slatted floor, where the real business of bathing took place. And then the enormous, deep, quadruple tub with its sitting-ledge, in which, she knew, men and women would sit together and soak – without, of course, the slightest suggestion of impropriety. And yet the thought that, were she actually living here, she might share the tub with Philip left her again almost faint.

But it would probably never have happened, anyway. When they reached William's house, there was no suggestion of communal bathing. She did not know if William and Hilary ever indulged; she suspected they did, because they seemed to be awfully in love with each other for two people of over fifty who had been married for seventeen years, and had, by all accounts, been lovers for some twenty years before then. But they were determined to do nothing to contravene American manners and morals – again, she suspected, principally not to offend her mother, who certainly could not be imagined ever sharing a bathtub with *anyone*. Least of all, her father.

So no doubt Philip and her aunt Shikibu would have behaved in the same way. Yet she was astonished to find, when she visited the bath-house the next morning, having deliberately waited until all her seniors had either done so or were obviously not going to, that a maidservant was waiting to assist her. She didn't know what to do. She had never bathed in front of anyone in her life before. She had been naked in the presence of another person only once in her life, the day she and Nancy Coleman had gone swimming together in the river below her home. It had been more of a dare than a pleasure, and they had only looked at each other once, with mutual embarrassment, before turning their backs on each other.

But to her consternation, the Japanese girl had already removed her kimono, and was ready to assist her. Feeling gloriously wicked, she submitted, while reflecting on how thin the child was. Was Haruko Tokugawa that thin? Then how on earth could Philip really love her? But perhaps Japanese men also liked thin women. The girl was certainly astounded by the roundness of the body she had to assist. But she seemed delighted, and wished to soap her victim. Anne refused that, and then wondered if she should have – the girl looked so upset. But she emptied buckets of cold water over her, to create an even more alarming impression of size, and then ushered her into the hot tub at the end of the room. Anne was afraid she would wish to get in beside her, but apparently her duties did not include that; she merely retired to the far end of the room and waited with a voluminous towel. But she insisted on wrapping Anne in it and making sure every inch of her body was dried.

It was quite the most remarkable experience she had ever had, and her imagination simply could not cope with the thought of her mother being so ministered to, and then came to a full stop at the thought of her father . . . but there were no male servants in the house.

She found it difficult to concentrate for the rest of the day. She had come to Japan not only to see, but to bury forever her girlish dreams and fantasies. She might have a crush on Philip Shimadzu, but he was about to be married, and next year was to be her last at school, before college, and womanhood, and medical school. Even if her father, who was far more observant than he liked to appear, had recently suggested that a girl who day-dreamed as much as she did was more suited to be a novelist than a doctor. She knew she day-dreamed too much of the time. And all of her life she had day-dreamed about Japan. Over the last year Philip had appeared as the living embodiment of all that Japan stood for in her imagination. Now she was here. Japan was reality, no longer a dream. And Philip would soon cease to be available for dreams. But after the bath, and she began bathing every morning, she felt that surely she could indulge a last week of dreams, before closing that book forever.

It was a busy week. William naturally wanted to show them all of Tokyo and the surrounding countryside, to drive them out to Hakone and show them the lakes and the mountains, to take them on tours of old castles and museums and new cloisonné works, and to show them some of the great ships of the Japanese Navy as well. He even took them to the Admiralty to see Philip at work, and to meet his immediate superior, Captain Yamamoto, a stern-faced man who was yet polite and left an impression of enormous strength of will and determination.

Philip also had friends for them to meet, especially his best man, who, very oddly, she thought, turned out to be a British naval attaché named John Graham. He seemed a great favourite of the family. It did not take her long to understand why; he was charm itself, a brilliant conversationalist and an absolute mine of knowledge. She was delighted that he seemed very smitten with her, sat next to her at dinner, and asked her about her schooling and what she intended to do afterwards, Philip had never shown that much interest in her.

'A doctor,' Graham said. 'Now there's ambition for a pretty young woman. Even in this day and age.'

'Are you against women usurping men's traditional fields, Mr Graham?' she asked. 'Or only when they are pretty?'

'Heaven forbid, dear lady,' he said. 'I look forward to the day when a woman stands upon the bridge of one of His Majesty's ships. Not that I suppose it will happen in my lifetime. But of course, when they are pretty, or at least as pretty as you, Miss Freeman, being a man myself, it seems to me that your only proper function is to make men, or one special man, happy.'

She suspected he was poking fun at her, and had had just sufficient sake to be bold. 'Would you not say that is backwards, Mr Graham?' she asked. 'If a woman is truly that pretty, should it not be the proper function for all men to make *her* happy?'

He gazed at her thoughtfully for several seconds before replying. Then he smiled. 'Touché. And I shall have to reconsider my estimate. If there are a lot of girls like you in the United States, I may indeed live to see a woman in command of an American battleship, at the least.'

After dinner Philip found the occasion to stand beside her and say, 'I am so pleased you like John, Anne. He is quite the most splendid fellow, don't you think?' As if her opinion really mattered to him. She realised this had been the most splendid evening of her life.

Then it was the day of the wedding. Both Anne and her mother had special new dresses for the occasion – and both were terribly aware that theirs would be the *only* two dresses amidst a sea of kimonos. Even Hilary was going to wear the kimono, and she offered to lend one to each of her guests, but Elizabeth decided against it, although it was simpler to sit properly on a cushion on the floor in a kimono than a dress. Elizabeth was determined not to fade into the Japanese scene.

Anne was tempted, but she knew it would displease her mother, and besides, she did wish to wear her new dress, which was quite the finest thing she had ever owned, and her first utterly adult outfit as well. The dress was made of pale blue voile, a colour which suited the silky pale yellow of her hair to perfection. There were small flower designs in pink and yellow, but these were well scattered and only enhanced the purity of the blue. Her waistline was fashionably low, and helped to disguise her bust, which her mother felt to be very necessary. Her petticoat, most important when one would be squatting on the floor, was white muslin, matched by her white stockings and white suede gloves. Her shoes were brown suede, with buckles, and her handbag was heavily embroidered. And her hat was simply beautiful, an enormous blue silk, several inches wider than her shoulders, low crowned, with pink velvet ribbons and ruching. She had no doubt that she was going to stand out like a sore thumb amongst the Japanese ladies – but equally she had no doubt it was going to be a sore thumb well worth a second look.

She had never been so excited in her life. She had been to several weddings in Connecticut, and last year she had even been a bridesmaid at the marriage of the elder sister of a close friend of hers whose father, a retired general, had inherited a considerable fortune, and none of her parents' friends were less than reasonably wealthy – but she knew she had never attended quite so classy a function as this wedding was going to be.

It was going to take place at night in the Tokugawa Mansion, instead of a church, because the Japanese did not use churches for such functions. Anne had wondered if there was actually such a thing as a mansion in all Tokyo, barring the Royal Palace itself, but she soon discovered how wrong she was. She and her father and mother, together with Hilary – William had gone to Shikibu's house, as he was acting as guardian of the groom – found themselves that evening in the midst of a huge crowd of people, slowly walking in line across wide verandahs into a room some thirty yards square, she estimated. Once again, simplicity, except in the flower arrangements, was the keynote. For the occasion, a low dais had been erected at the far end, and there, she saw to her delight as well as her concern, sat Philip and John Graham, on cushions on the tatami mats. They were watching the arriving guests but not greeting them in any way, occasionally exchanging a word with each other, and taking sips of sake from tiny cups proffered by serving girls. Both men wore naval uniforms, Philip's blue and Graham's white duck, and both looked extremely hot and somewhat nervous, as well they might be, she supposed.

The guests were being presented to Mr and Mrs Tokugawa, another reversal of an American ceremony, as the wedding had not yet taken place. It was a slow business, and after each introduction the new arrivals were escorted by serving-girls to the space on the floor allotted to them.

Anne, aware that she was indeed attracting a number of surreptitious glances, found herself giving a good number back. The women were all dressed very similarly, at first glance, all wearing the kimono, all with their glossy black hair – or, in Hilary's case, reddish-brown hair – gathered in a loose pompadour and secured with enormous highly-carved and decorated ivory pins. Anne and her mother were the only two in hats. And yet, all the women were carefully and subtly different. There might apparently only be so many colours available for the kimono, and each shade of red and blue and green was repeated several times, but each kimono had its own special design, sometimes hardly discernible from a distance, leaving each woman completely distinct from any rival.

The men also mostly wore the kimono, except for a sprinkling of uniforms, but their garments were far more utilitarian and less interesting.

Anne had arrived in front of Mr and Mrs Tokugawa, immediately behind her aunt Hilary, when to her consternation she discovered that the other couple greeting the guests – whom she had assumed were also family – were none other than the Crown Prince Hirohito and his wife. She simply did not know what to do. The Japanese all bowed almost to the floor when presented. She knew that if she did that her hat would fall off, so she curtseyed instead, right down to the floor, and found that she was stuck there. Without her father's hand under her elbow to return her to her feet she would have overbalanced.

'Quite a to do,' her father whispered, as they took their places beside Maureen and Hilary, right in the front of the guests as they were family of the groom. 'Philip really is leaving us all behind, don't you think?'

Elizabeth, who was very hot, merely snorted.

'You have not met Peter yet,' Hilary said, indicating the young man seated on her right. Anne had already noticed him because, apart from the little black moustache adorning his upper lip, he was remarkably like his younger brother. But he wore the kimono, and she would have expected him to be in uniform.

Peter Shimadzu rose to his knees, and in that position gave a stiffly formal bow to his American relatives. 'It is an honour, Uncle Jeremy,' he said, 'and Aunt Elizabeth, to welcome you to Japan.'

'Well, it's a pleasure to be here, Peter,' Jerry said. 'This is our daughter, Anne.'

Peter bowed to her in turn. But she saw that his eyes were cold and disinterested. Presumably he still belonged to what her aunt had called the anti-American school. Suddenly she shivered; she wondered how many other people in the room hated her father, and therefore probably her mother and herself, just for being Americans?

Serving-girls brought them tea and plates of exotic titbits, and the conversation became general while they waited. Anne didn't know if the Tokugawa girl was exercising a bride's privilege of arriving late or if this was normal. But she seemed to have been sitting for well over an hour, and her legs were quite cramped, when suddenly Philip and Graham, having obviously received some kind of a signal, got up. Graham remained standing on the dais, looking distinctly nervous, while Philip left the room. At the same time she heard a slow and rhythmic clapping from outside.

'Those are the servants,' Jerry whispered. 'Mixing rice grains together, to symbolise the coming union.'

She found she was holding her breath, and glanced carefully from side to side to see if anyone was looking over their shoulder. Most were, so she turned her own head to watch the bridal procession enter the room, amazed at the total absence of music – but that seemed to enhance the solemnity of the occasion.

The bride and groom came first. They did not hold hands or even look at each other, which would have been difficult anyway, because Haruko Tokugawa was entirely shrouded in her deep pink veil, which matched her deep pink gown. Another surprise, then Anne remembered that in Japan white was the colour of mourning. Certainly the girl was invisible, save for her tiny slipper-clad feet, which appeared from beneath the skirt of the kimono. Philip looked so proud.

Behind them came the three parents, and William, who in his capacity as Philip's guardian walked beside Mrs Tokugawa. They took their places on cushions at the foot of the dais, while Philip and his bride mounted the three steps and sat there, Haruko remaining veiled so that no one could see her face. Graham now came down the steps and took his place with the congregation, so presumably the ceremony had commenced. But it was the strangest ceremony Anne had ever attended: no priest and no prayers, indeed, no suggestion of religion at all. Instead two ladies, apparently members of the Tokugawa clan, knelt on the dais beside Philip and Haruko, and fed them titbits from lacquered trays waiting on the floor, together with sips of tea. Each morsel of food was accompanied by a speech from one or other of the ladies, in which they praised the beauty, industry and virtue of Haruko, and the manhood, valour and fame of Philip. They spoke in Japanese of course, and Anne found it a little difficult to follow, although everyone else in the room seemed to be hanging on their every word.

While the speech-making continued, serving-maids were arranging little lacquered tables before all the guests; apparently they were now to eat properly. Anne watched the toast-mistresses, who were ceremonially, and rather indecently, she thought, laying the large paper model of a female butterfly on its back before the couple, and then placing the paper model of a male butterfly on top of it, while themselves drinking a toast to the future happiness of the couple. And now at last Haruko removed her veil — but to Anne's consternation she was still invisible, as every inch of her face, save for her eyes and her red-coated lips, was painted white, to form a sort of doll-like mask. Still she did not look at her future husband, but gazed straight ahead; Anne did not suppose she was seeing any of the guests, either.

Now the real ceremony began, and it was conducted by the two principals themselves. Anne watched Philip pour a full cup of sake from the kettle which had been placed beside him, drink half of it, and hand it to a waiting maidservant; she took the cup to Haruko, who drank the remainder. Then Haruko refilled the cup from a kettle placed at *her* elbow, and repeated the ceremony. This was done three times, and then Haruko rose and left the room, followed by her ladies. Philip and Graham immediately exited by a different door.

'Time for refreshment,' Jerry said, as conversation became general and several people got up to stretch their legs, rather like the intermission between acts at a theatre, while the serving-girls produced pickles and sweetmeats and cups of tea and sake.

'Is it all over?' Anne asked.

'Good heavens, no,' her father told her. 'The principals have merely gone to change their clothing.' He winked at her. 'It's going to be a long night.'

Indeed it was. When Philip and Haruko returned, after perhaps fifteen minutes, there was another wine ceremony, which was followed by an enormous banquet of carp soup, various kinds of meats, pickles, course after course after course, which Anne could hardly digest. She gazed at the bride and groom, who were, presumably, now married, although she was not at all sure of the exact moment when this had happened. They were eating as heartily as everyone else, but still never looked at each other, as was apparently required by etiquette, much less exchanged a word. But they were both power-fully affected by what was happening, plainly enough; they were each removed by the attendants twice more in order to change their sweat-soaked clothing.

But at last the meal was over, and it was time to withdraw into a smaller room, where a priest waited before a makeshift altar to perform the Christian cere-mony. Only the immediate families and those members of the audience who were Christians attended this, perhaps twenty people in all; the remainder stayed in the larger room, and no doubt continued to eat and drink.

Although this ceremony was also conducted in Japanese, it was far more intelligible to Anne; when she saw Philip place a ring on Haruko's finger she felt that he was, at last, truly married. But still he did not kiss her. She found this very strange, and then had to brace herself, as now Haruko was introduced to all those members of the family she had not previously met, bowing low before Anne's father and mother, as befitted youth, of whatever rank, meeting an older person. Then she stood before Anne. Once again Anne simply did not know what to do, as she gazed into the midnight eyes. She began to curtsey, even as Haruko began to bow. And they both laughed together.

Had she ever heard such a heavenly sound as that tinkle of laughter?

Philip was beside his bride. 'This is my cousin, Anne Freeman,' he explained.

'Why, my Shimadzu,' Haruko said, 'why have you not told me of her before? She is quite lovely.' She spoke in Japanese, but Anne could understand her well enough, and felt herself beginning to blush.

'I am not so beautiful as you, Miss Tokugawa,' she said, also in Japanese.

Haruko's painted eyebrows moved upwards. 'Miss Tokugawa?' Once again the tinkle of laughter.

'Oh . . . Mrs Shimadzu,' Anne stammered.

'Of course. And you cannot tell that I am beautiful, beneath this paint,' Haruko said. 'But you must come to see me, as soon as we return from Hokkaido, and we will talk together. Would you not like that?'

'Would I?' Anne cried. 'Oh . . . but I won't be here. We are leaving next week.'

'That is a great pity. Then you must come to Japan again, and stay with me. I wish to be your friend.' Haruko's hands closed on Anne's, in a grip delightfully light, and yet strong and compelling as well. 'Will you promise me that?'

'Oh, I will,' Anne said. 'I will.'

Haruko smiled and went on her way, Philip proudly at her side. How could he not love a woman so utterly elegant, confident, charming . . . and beautiful. Having heard her voice, Anne knew she had to be beautiful.

She felt tears spring to her eyes. But were they tears of sadness, or joy? She had no idea.

CHAPTER 4

The Husband

There was, of course, a great deal still to be done after the ceremony, although unlike a Christian wedding this did not consist of speech-making or toasting; in Japan that had taken plce at the start of the proceedings. Now it was necessary for the formal goodbyes and salutations. William and Shikibu left as soon as the Christian marriage was completed, while Haruko retired with her own parents to bid them farewell; fifteen minutes later she also left the Tokugawa mansion, with her maid, to be driven to Shikibu's house and greet her new mother, for she was transferring herself entirely from the Tokugawa to the Satsuma clan, and specifically to the Shimadzu family.

Philip remained behind, to bid farewell to his father-and mother-in-law, and the rest of the guests. It was a ceremony and a proceeding he had studied very carefully for some time, yet it was still odd to be so suddenly separated from his new wife, just as it was even odder to be married to a woman he had not yet kissed. However, there was one Western custom to which they were most definitely adhering; he had not only established this, but had made the arrangements himself – they were going to honeymoon, all by themselves, up in the northern island of Hokkaido, to which they would be travelling by train first thing next morning. Until then he could afford to be patient.

He moved amongst the guests, saying goodbye to each

of them, bowing low before the prince . . . and found himself face to face with Anne. She was quite the most spectacular woman in the room, and certainly the most beautiful – so long as Haruko's face remained covered in paint, he reminded himself. It was truly remarkable how the girl had blossomed in the six months since he had last seen her. She seemed to have grown at least an inch, principally, he estimated, in the leg, and she reminded him of a young colt in her movements. While above, she had a quite spectacular bust measurement; it was impossible to imagine any Japanese woman with a figure quite as hour-glass as that, even had the kimono been a garment intended to illustrate curves. Or legs. Her hair, worn disappointingly short as was apparently the new American fashion, was still suggestive of the most perfect silken strands. She was going to make some man very happy, one day soon; and no doubt she would be a marvellous wife. And yet he had the strangest feeling that she would fall into *his* arms were he to hold them open.

It was not a thought for any man to think on his wedding night, and it was not a thought possible for any well-born Japanese girl, who would, like Haruko, have been totally obsessed with parental blessing, and correct behaviour, and polite manners. American girls rated those qualities below the upsurge of passion, which they approximated with love itself, which they regarded as the most important event in their lives, however often repeated. He could only hope that Anne would find lasting love and passion, and never have to seek a second chance.

Now she was smiling at him, although he was sure he could see tears in her eyes. 'That was just wonderful, Philip,' she said. 'So different, and yet . . . so special as well. I am so happy for you.'

'I'm feeling pretty happy myself,' he said. 'But Anne . . . I'm so happy too that you could be here. Do you know, you've never looked lovelier?'

She gave a little curtsey. 'Why, thank you, sir,' she said. 'Do I get a kiss?'

He brushed her cheek with his own, and whispered in her ear. 'Haruko meant her invitation, you know. She would love to have you visit with us, when you have finished school.'

Her head turned quickly, and her lips as well, to touch his for a moment. 'Oh Philip,' she said. 'I do love you so. Mind you're happy. Real happy.'

She pulled away from him and hurried into the crowd.

John Graham accompanied him in the taxi. 'Quite an occasion,' he remarked. 'I can't say I've ever been to anything quite like that before. What does it feel like to be married to Haruko Tokugawa?'

'I don't know yet,' Philip confessed. 'Maybe it hasn't sunk in.'

'I can believe that. By the way, I must tell you that I found your young cousin absolutely delightful. And a real beauty, too.'

'She's not actually my cousin, you know,' Philip pointed out, wondering why he was doing so. 'Her father is only my father's half-brother.'

'Complicated,' Graham agreed. 'Doesn't alter the fact that she's a real looker. Shall I come in?'

'Well, of course,' Philip said. 'We must at least have a nightcap.'

It was past midnight, but Shikibu and Maureen were waiting for him with cups of warm sake. 'Haruko has retired,' Shikibu said. 'But she is expecting you to go to her. She has dismissed her maid.'

'I'll be away then,' Graham said, finishing his drink and reaching for his shoes. 'Have a good holiday. My word, what an inane thing to say. All the very best, Phil old boy.'

'But John . . . I haven't thanked you.'

'When you come back,' Graham suggested, and closed

the front door behind him.

'I would not delay,' Shikibu advised. 'A new wife does not like to be kept waiting.'

'But . . . now?' Philip looked at his watch. 'There is the train . . .'

'Not for seven hours. Philip, you are the strangest boy.'

He bit his lip, and drank some sake. Somehow it had not occurred to him that he would be expected to consummate the marriage here in his own house, and so immediately. Did he not wish to? Certainly he felt more sexually anxious than ever before in his life – but he could not be sure that was not at least partly caused by the taste of Anne Freeman's lips on his own. He knew that were it Anne waiting beyond that thin partition he would be in there already, because they would love without restraint, without manners, without etiquette. He knew so much about Anne – and so little about Haruko. And suddenly he was afraid to find out.

'Now go to her,' Shikibu commanded, taking the empty cup from his hand. 'And make her the happiest woman in the world, as she is eager to be.'

Was she, he wondered? Or was she performing a duty, just as she had accepted him for her betrothed when he must have seemed old enough to be her father? He allowed his knuckles to brush his bedroom door before sliding it open and stepping inside. There was but a single light in the room, a glow emanating from a candle placed on a low stand in one of the corners. Before it knelt Haruko Tokugawa. But she was no longer Haruko Tokugawa. She was Haruko Shimadzu, his wife, and by Japanese custom, his entirely. As she would know.

He stood by the door, waiting until she had finished her prayer and raised her head. 'I did not mean to keep you waiting, my Shimadzu,' she said, her voice soft. She wore a loose blue kimono, and had washed her face clean of paint. Her hair was loose down her back, and as she stood up he realised that her feet were bare. So she was

100

naked beneath the single garment.

'I have kept *you* waiting, my Haruko,' he said.

She smiled, and bowed. 'That is your privilege, my husband.'

He stood before her, and raised her so that he could look at her. She was more than a foot shorter than he, and he suspected less than half his weight. He licked his lips. 'Haruko, if you would prefer to wait until we reach Hokkaido . . .'

The tiniest frown lines appeared between her eyes. 'You would prefer to wait, my husband?'

'Oh, no . . . I mean, I wish only to please you.'

'No, no, Philip,' she said, the first time she had ever used his given name. 'I am here to please *you*.' She slid the kimono from her shoulders.

Presumably she had been told by the ladies of her family this was an act she must perform. But it was not something to which she herself was accustomed; as the garment slipped past her thighs to the floor she closed her eyes, while her entire body seemed to glow. But what an entrancing body it was. Hardly more than that of a child, by Western standards, but perfectly fashioned: square shoulders, if narrow; slender rib-cage; slender thighs; slender legs. And then . . . small, bud-like breasts, but with surprisingly large, and surprisingly erect, nipples; flat belly; pubes suggesting strands of black silk.

'Haruko,' he said.

Her eyes opened. 'Do I not please you, my Philip?' Her voice was as low as ever.

'Oh Haruko,' he said, and took her in his arms. For a moment her body was stiff, but then it relaxed as he lifted her from the floor and found her mouth, and when their tongues touched, to his enormous pleasure her legs went round his waist, so that she sat on his thighs while she clung to him, a movement of almost abandoned love. And confidence.

'I will please you, Philip,' she said. 'I will please you.'

101

'And I you,' he promised, and gently set her on the mattress while he started to undress. But she came to him again, to help him. He had to presume that this too had been taught her by her women relatives, as part of a bride's duties; certainly she was unsure of herself, or of his clothes. But she was eager. Because she loved. Perhaps, he thought with a spasm of guilt, she had always loved, where he had been afraid to let himself.

'Do *I* please *you*?'

She knelt, to brush his penis with her lips. Again, uncertainty, but certainty of what must be done. 'I had not expected such beauty,' she said, and raised her head. 'But Philip . . . '

He knelt beside her. 'He is afraid of you. With reason. Because he had not expected such beauty either. He will soon be ready. Haruko . . . ' He took her on his lap, caressed her breasts, taking each nipple between his fingers and very gently elongating it. She shivered, and sought his mouth again, while her own hands, small and darting, wandered over his body anxiously. Oh, indeed she loved. But she had also been well taught, as a Tokugawa woman should have been. She brought his legs together and turned to straddle them, kneeling, so that she could reach his mouth and feel his entry at the same time. For now he was hard. He held her close, and tightened his hands on her buttocks, and felt another of those delightful shivers as he slipped into her, and she moved her body, seeming to suck him further and further into her, suppressing the pain she must be feeling, for she was small, and tight, and yet liquid in her desire.

'We were too quick,' he said, at last lying down, while she remained on his chest, closing her own legs upon his fast dwindling penis. 'I was too quick.'

She smiled, and kissed him. 'Then next time we will be slower, my Philip. I but wished to know if it was as wonderful as my mother promised me.'

'And was it?'

'No,' Haruko said. 'It was twice as wonderful as anything she described.'

They walked hand in hand over Hokkaido's rock-strewn beaches, each knowing the other was naked beneath their kimono, each only counting the minutes until they could reasonably return to the hotel, and the erotic privacy of their room. They loved in a fashion Philip had never thought possible. She wanted so much, wanted to experience so much, even to the basically uncomfortable Western position. She smiled, and loved. He was a wonder-world to her, of muscles and arteries and tendons she might have dreamed of touching all her life. As she was a wonder-world to him, of secret valleys and entrancing curves, and sighs and scents and unexpected responses, even if he remained haunted by the supposition that were he to hold her just a shade too closely, he might crack her into two. She was a blanket which he could spread across his thoughts and his fears, and use to shut away the outside world, because the outside world had no meaning when she was in his arms. No man, he thought, could ever have been so blessed.

Yet the outside world was there, good and bad, and as she was not afraid of it, had no disturbing thoughts and not a single apprehension, she was not so disposed to reject it. 'Your American cousin is so very lovely,' she remarked, as they walked, the great Pacific rollers tumbling sand and spray only a few yards to their right. 'I had no idea she was so old.'

'She is just a child. A year younger than you,' he said.

'And I am just a child?' she asked, with a tinkle of laughter. 'I do hope she can come to visit with us. I should like to know her better. I think perhaps from her I could learn much of America, and American ways.'

'I am sure she will come,' Philip said. 'If you ask her again.'

She glanced at him. 'You do not like Miss Freeman?'

103

He shrugged. 'I have never thought about it one way or the other, I suppose.' His first lie to his wife, on the fourth day of their marrige. But it would be a lie no longer. Because he had never thought about it, one way or another, since he had first taken Haruko into his arms. And he never would again.

'Why are you unhappy in your work?' she asked, two days later.

'Me? Unhappy in my work?' Lie number two.

'Yes,' she said. So perhaps she knew he had lied about Anne Freeman too. 'But I understand the reason,' she went on. 'I have spoken to Papa about this, and it will be changed.'

'Eh?'

'I understand that I made a mistake in asking you to go on to the staff,' Haruko said. 'I understand that you would prefer command of a ship. After all, you are a captain. You should have command of a ship.'

'But Haruko . . . ' He had been going to say, one cannot have anything one chooses merely by wishing it, and mentioning it to one's father. But he realised that Haruko Tokugawa could do that, and would. 'I thought you wanted me in a shore job?'

'I want you to be happy, my Philip,' she said. 'Only that.'

A wife who could make dreams come true, while still enveloping him in her love. Could *any* man ever have been so blessed?

A barge took him out into the sparkling waters of Tokyo Bay, moving between the anchored warships, the mighty *Nagato* and *Mutsu*, the *Fuso* on which he had made that so fateful voyage to America, and then the smaller cruisers, before finally pulling in to the side of the *Yahagi*. Philip, seated in the stern, pretended little interest in the grey-painted hull rising above him.

The accommodation ladder was in place, and a guard

of honour waited at the top of the steps. A boatswain's whistle played a salute, and Philip stood to attention and in turn saluted the bridge. Only then did he allow himself really to take in the four hundred feet of steel, the five thousand tons of displacement, which was now his to command. He gazed up at the three funnels and the fighting top from which the Rising Sun of Japan proudly fluttered, forward and then aft at the six five-point-five-inch guns which were the cruiser's main armament, then looked over the assembled ship's company, standing to attention, but carefully watching their new captain. Did not every man present amongst these five hundred sailors know that he had been a part of the Washington delegation?

Lieutenant Mashada stepped forward, saluted again, and then bowed; the two men already knew each other, of course. 'Welcome aboard *Yahagi*, Captain Shimadzu,' he said. 'Welcome honourable Captain. It is our privilege to serve you.'

'It is my privilege to be here, Lieutenant,' Philip said, and went to the bridge.

'There is a signal, honourable Captain,' Mashada said, at his elbow. 'From the Fleet Commander.'

Philip read the printed letters.

CONGRATULATIONS ON FIRST COMMAND STOP YOU WILL BRING NOTHING BUT HONOUR TO THE JAPANESE NAVY STOP PERMISSION IS GRANTED FOR YOU TO TAKE *YAHAGI* TO SEA FOR ONE WEEK'S INDEPENDENT SHAKE DOWN CRUISE STOP GOOD LUCK STOP FREEMAN

Philip looked across the water to the flagship. 'Make to Fleet Commander,' he said. "Message received and understood. Will avail myself of your permission immediately." And then, Mr Mashada, prepare the ship for sea.'

*

'It is so small,' Haruko complained. She stood in the captain's sleeping-cabin in the stern of the cruiser, and looked from the bunk-bed to the shower-bath and toilet and hanging locker, then through the door into the day cabin, hardly larger, containing a settee bolted to the bulkhead, a desk, a chair and a filing cabinet.

Philip grinned at her. 'It is only intended for one person, my love,' he said. And she was in his arms. She had been on the quayside to welcome him back, perhaps, he suspected, already regretting her generosity in allowing him to go to sea at all.

'I wish I could sail with you,' she said, 'next time you go away for a week.'

'That would be difficult. We would have to install a double bunk, for a start.' She raised her head to discover whether or not he was poking fun at her, and he kissed her again. 'But who knows, it may one day be possible. John Graham believes women may one day be able to join navies.'

'Not in Japan,' Haruko said. 'He has been to call. Graham San, I mean. Often.' She smiled. 'I think he considers he has been substituting for you.'

Philip raised his eyebrows, and her smile widened. 'With perfect propriety, my Philip. There can be no greater gentleman than John Graham.'

'That I can believe. Now, my love . . . '

'Although he does ask so many questions.'

Philip frowned. 'Questions? About what?'

'Well . . . you.'

'Me? He knows everything there is to know about me.'

'He does not appear to think so. He wants to know all about your family background in the States. He knows about how your grandfather fought for the Mikado, of course. But he wanted to know about the shipping company he founded in San Francisco, and about your uncle's career in the American Army . . . ' She gave one of her little tinkles of laughter. 'I am afraid I could not tell him much.'

'Hm,' Philip said thoughtfully. 'He is an odd fellow. But as you say, a most likeable one. Now, my love . . . '

Haruko frowned. 'You are not coming ashore with me now?'

'There is a great deal to be done. One cannot simply drop the anchor and walk away from a ship. Especially if one happens to be in command. But I shall be with you for dinner.'

'And then?'

'Every dinner. For at least a week.'

'Then I must make the most of my time, my Philip,' she said. 'Until dinner.' She turned her head as there came a knock on the door.

'Yes?' Philip said.

His personal servant, Hagi, bowed. 'With respect, honourable Captain, but Captain Yamamoto seeks permission to come on board.'

'Yamamoto! But of course. Invite him up, Hagi. You remember Isoroku Yamamoto, my love?' He escorted Haruko into the narrow corridor, and towards the companion ladder leading to the quarterdeck.

'Of course,' she said. 'He was the man you did not enjoy working with.'

He checked, and glanced at her. 'As he will undoubtedly be an admiral long before I,' he said, 'I would be grateful if you would keep that opinion to yourself.'

'Of course I will,' she said again. 'But who knows when *you* may become an admiral, my Philip? It could happen tomorrow.'

'I doubt that even you could bring that about, my sweet.' He took her to the gangway, where Yamamoto was at that moment emerging. 'Honourable Captain.' Philip saluted, then bowed.

Yamamoto bowed in turn, and then to Haruko. 'I have

107

timed my visit unfortunately.'

'By no means, Captain Yamamoto,' Haruko said. 'I was just going ashore. But be sure you bring my husband when *you* come ashore. We have a date for dinner.' She went down the steeply sloping steps of the accommodation ladder with the same certainty she did everything, one hand resting lightly on the rail, the other daintily holding the skirt of her kimono just clear of her ankles, not a hair of her carefully pompadoured head moving, even in the fresh breeze.

'I congratulate you, honourable Captain,' Yamamoto said. 'On everything, but especially on your wife.'

They looked at each other. They had spoken only briefly when Philip turned over the contents of his desk and his files; the command had been waiting for him when he returned from his honeymoon. Yamamoto had revealed no emotion on learning that he was about to lose the services of one of the principal members of his planning team. Yet Philip could not doubt that the senior captain knew who had been responsible for his so-abrupt transfer.

Now Yamamoto smiled. 'Will you not show me your new kingdom?'

Hagi had brewed sake, and the two captains sat together in the day cabin to drink and talk.

'She is a fine ship,' Yamamoto said. 'In every way worthy of her commander. I understand there is a report on her boilers before the Admiralty?'

Philip nodded. 'They are actually only ten years old. That is the age of the ship, in fact. But they are no longer efficient. And I understand that it will be possible to replace the existing sixteen boilers with only six, far more powerful.'

'That is true,' Yamamoto agreed. 'When are you due for refitting?'

'Well, I have been informed by Admiral Freeman that

it will probably not be for at least two years. There are other ships with more serious problems than mine.'

'There is not a ship in this navy without serious problems,' Yamamoto said. 'Have you ever heard of a General Douhet?'

Philip frowned. 'He sounds French.'

'He is Italian, as a matter of fact. One may not rate the Italians as great seamen, Shimadzu San, but they are most profound thinkers. This man Douhet is one of their best, and his thoughts are actually so disturbing that I believe he was imprisoned for a while during the Great War, because of the chance that his opinions might have a subversive effect on the Italian soldiers. I would recommend that you obtain a copy of a book he has written, called simply *War in the Air*, and read it most carefully.'

'*War in the Air*?'

'Write it down,' Yamamoto suggested. 'Then tell me, have you heard of an American General called Mitchell?'

'Billy Mitchell. Yes, I have heard my uncle Jerry speak of him. He is some kind of a crank.'

'You think so? He, too, has written a book, called *Our Air Force*. It is about the United States Army Air Force, but his conclusions are valid for any air force, and for any service that may have to oppose an air force. Especially a navy. I recommend that you study both of those books.'

'Of course I shall, honourable Captain. But am I allowed to ask why they are so important?'

'Simply this. Do you realise that a single bomb, dropped from an airplane, could destroy your vessel?'

Philip frowned. 'So could a single shell fired from an enemy ship.'

'Not so easily,' Yamamoto corrected him. 'You are *expecting* to be hit by another ship, and your own vessel has been designed accordingly. Thus your armour is

109

arranged so that its greatest strength is on the vertical as opposed to the horizontal plane, in order to repel shot travelling in a roughly horizontal direction. There will, of course, be a parabola, but not a pronounced one. And this applies even more to battleships than to cruisers. Have you ever studied the Battle of Jutland? Three British battle-cruisers were sunk at Jutland, by plunging shot which landed on their decks rather than on their sides and penetrated the armour there, because of course that was much less thick.'

'I have been told of this,' Philip said thoughtfully, remembering Graham's reminiscences.

'There were other factors involved, of course,' Yamamoto said. 'The Germans had better armour-piercing shells and their fire was remarkably accurate. But that does not invalidate the point, that any warship is much more vulnerable to plunging shot than to parabolic shot. And there is another point to be considered, Shimadzu San. No matter how hard he tries, providing your engines are working, your shipborne enemy will not be able to fire at you at less than a distance of several thousand yards, and your ship will presumably be constantly changing position to present a most difficult target. An aircraft will be able to fly immediately above your decks before dropping its bombs. You may well be able to avoid one bomb. But suppose there were four, six, perhaps a dozen aircraft, all flying immediately above you? There would be no action you could take to avoid being hit.'

'Is that what this Douhet claims? And General Mitchell?'

'Amongst other things. What they do say is that future naval combat will be controlled from the air, rather than the big gun at deck level.'

'I cannot believe that,' Philip said, thinking of the might of the *Nagato*, and the might that, according to

Graham, would be the *Nelson* – floating fortresses with over a thousand men aboard, independent townships at sea, and armed with the heaviest weapons ever invented. To be sunk by one small airplane?

'It is difficult to believe, certainly,' Yamamoto acknowledged. 'Nevertheless, it is a possibility that must be considered. I cannot impress upon you too strongly, Shimadzu San, that it is a possibility against which we must prepare the most active defence.'

'What defence is there?'

'In the first place, the obvious defence is to shoot down the enemy aircraft before it can drop its bomb. Before it can even get overhead. I strongly recommend that, when you receive notice of your refit, in 1924 or whenever, you put in for a battery of anti-aircraft guns. They do not have to be large-calibre. Big machine-guns will do. But they will protect you against the plane coming too close.'

'Then I shall do so, honourable Captain. And many thanks for bringing this matter to my attention.'

'But machine-gun fire is of course purely defensive in concept,' Yamamoto went on. 'The next thing we must do is prepare a bigger and better air force than any other nation.'

'Oh, indeed . . .'

'And that,' Yamamoto said triumphantly, 'will not be limited by any international agreement.'

'Yes,' Philip said. 'But, honourable Captain, one thing puzzles me. I do accept that a ship may be vulnerable to air attack, but surely only if it lies within range of enemy aircraft. When the fleet is several hundred miles offshore . . .'

'We must expect that our future enemy, whoever he may be, will carry aircraft with their fleet. I am not talking of catapult-launched planes from battleships or cruisers, but of whole ships converted entirely for the

111

carriage of planes. You know that the Western Powers were experimenting with such ships towards the end of the war?'

Philip nodded. 'But I do not believe they were very successful.'

'They will be successful in the future. And therefore so must we, in the same field. I have already recommended that the hulls of at least one of the battle-cruisers we have been forced to abandon because of the Washington Treaty be used for the building of an aircraft-carrier. This will be a revolutionary step. But we are in a revolutionary situation.' He smiled. 'I am even considering entirely altering the essentials for our Strike South Project. But that no longer is your province.'

Clearly he was not going to elaborate. But obviously, sending a fleet south to the Philippines and Malaya and the Dutch East Indies would be an enormously hazardous operation if what he had just said was ever remotely likely to be true; the ships would have to carry out the whole operation within reach of shore-based aircraft.

Philip could not help being secretly pleased, and relieved, if these new developments meant that the whole project would be thrown still further back in possible time.

He discussed the possibility of aircraft having an influence on the future of sea warfare with Graham, who was as usual completely knowledgeable about the subject.

'Yamamoto is, of course, quite right,' Graham said, walking with his friend on the quarterdeck of the *Yahagi*. 'Aircraft will make a difference to the future of sea warfare. As to whether or not it will be quite so revolutionary as he fears, at least in regard to large ships, I have my doubts. But ships like this, essentially unarmoured, will be very vulnerable, even to near misses from large enough bombs. You must have adequate anti-aircraft batteries. And not machine-guns, Phil. Yamamoto is wrong there. You want two- and three-pounder pompoms. The Swedes are developing a very good weapon – people called Bofors – which I suggest you study. A Bofors gun will give you increased range and accuracy, and more hitting power, and it really is important to shoot the enemy down long before he can even come close enough for a near miss.'

Philip took out his notebook and wrote down the name. 'I shall certainly look into it. We are due for a refit, some time in the next two years. I will accumulate all of these recommendations in my report.'

'Two years?' Graham raised his eyebrows. 'Then there will be no war for two years?'

They gazed at each other. 'One sincerely hopes not,' Philip said. 'Are you expecting one?'

'The Royal Navy is operating on the premise that there will be no major war for the next *ten* years,' Graham said. 'They are instructed to take this attitude by the Government, and it applies to design and building as well as to strategy. And the ten-year period is being carried forward from year to year.'

'An admirable concept,' Philip said, wondering if he should report this to Yamamoto. But Graham was not a fool. He never revealed any information which could not be obtained from any observer either studying British newspapers or military literature, or the reports of the debates in the British Parliament. Yamamoto undoubtedly already knew just what the British strategic thinking consisted of . . . and he had no desire to betray his friend.

'And a sensible one?' Graham asked. 'Obviously it does not make sense unless all other nations capable of fighting a major war are equally reluctant to do so.'

It was the first time he had ever probed. Except, so strangely, to Haruko. Philip had almost forgotten about that. But surely that had been mere curiosity; Philip was well aware that he *was* an object of curiosity to many people, because he was so American both in appearance and background, and yet a serving officer in the Imperial Japanese Navy.

But he *was* a serving officer in the Imperial Japanese Navy, a fact Graham well understood. So what was he seeking? Reassurance, as it appeared? Or actual information? Philip had no means of knowing what other contacts he had, what other information he might have obtained from a separate source. But it was unbelievable that he could have found out about the Strike South Project. Equally, it was out of the question for him ever *to* find out about the Strike South Project; the project, if ever carried out, or even suggested, could set the world in flames – but hopefully it would never happen, simply because Japan would never be able to achieve all the preliminary requirements established as essential to success by Yamamoto. It was, perhaps, a reassuring thought that Yamamoto knew that, too.

'I am sure it is a sensible one,' he said.

'I am glad to hear it,' Graham said. 'One hears so many rumours, of Japanese demands on China, of Japanese plans . . . One hears that you have more than ten thousand soldiers on guard duty in the International Concession outside Shanghai.'

'The British also have concession guards. So do the Americans and the French.'

'Of course. I believe we maintain a company of marines. The Americans have even less. But ten thousand men! That is an entire army division, just about. To protect a few diplomats and merchants and their families? That is an unheard of situation, in a foreign country, in time of peace.'

'The Chinese have raised no objections,' Philip reminded him.

'What would your government do if they did?'

114

Philip smiled. 'Ignore the protest, I imagine. China is our traditional enemy, something no Japanese can ever afford to forget. But I agree with you, that in some directions we overdo our present strength *vis-à-vis* Chinese weakness. Believe me, John San, I do not approve of everything my government does. But as I serve it, I am not prepared to be over-critical, either.'

Graham gazed at him. 'In no circumstances that you could possibly envisage?'

Philip frowned. He had never known his friend so serious. Therefore he *must* have discovered something . . .

Graham's face broke up into his usual smile. 'I am being hyper-philosophical, would you not say, old friend? Believe me, there are many things the British Government does of which I do not approve, either. I serve it; and therefore, like you, I cannot criticise. And yet . . . I wonder, sometimes, if a situation ever could arise where I would *know* my country's course was so wrong that I would find myself turning against it. Even actively. Or is that unthinkable to a Japanese?'

'I would say it would be unthinkable to any serving officer, whatever his nationality,' Philip said. 'All of us must hope and pray that we are never faced with even the consideration of such a choice.'

Yet Graham's words kept lingering in his brain during the long, lonely winter months when the *Yahagi* was on patrol duty off the Ryuku Islands, looking out for Chinese pirates and smugglers, who found the scattered chain of rocks and islets to the south of Japan a haven for their illegal activities.

He had hoped to be home for Christmas, but his replacement was delayed by mechanical troubles, and he soon realised he would not return to Tokyo before the end of January. Haruko would be upset. Their first Christmas as man and wife . . . although she was not a

115

Christian she had been looking forward to experiencing this festival of which he had told her so much. Now she would be alone, with the other members of his family, of course.

Meanwhile he was left to pace his storm-swept bridge, or sit in his day cabin and write up his log, between coping with the various administrative requirements of captaining a ship at sea, or lie in his bunk and gaze into the darkness . . . and brood. Because he could not get away from the fact that his government, his nation, was already embarked upon a course of action he not only believed to be wholly wrong, but even to be virtually suicidal. Had Graham been trying to warn him? Or had the discussion contained a far more sinister element? Far more likely, it had just been a discussion, from Graham's point of view.

Of course it was absurd for Japan to maintain a division of troops in a Chinese city; of course it would not be tolerated by any other nation in the world, in time of peace. But then was it not equally absurd, and unacceptable, for Japan to maintain a whole army corps on the borders of Manchuria, constantly encroaching into Chinese territory, as if daring the Chinese to attempt to expel them so that they could seize on an acceptable *casus belli* to put before the world – that the Chinese had fired first. He could not understand why the Government did not insist that the army pull out.

That was bad, and was gaining the Japanese a bad image throughout the world. But far worse was the knowledge, which Graham did not possess, surely, that in the course of time, if the circumstances proved suitable, the Japanese intended to do the firing first, as part of the army's plan to create an East Asian Empire which would leave them independent of the entire rest of the world in raw materials, and thus in power. And thus, equally, in opinion. It was an ugly, vicious, insensate dream. One which his uncle William claimed would

116

never happen, because the Japanese were not an ugly, vicious, insensate people. Quite the contrary.

But what of those Japanese who composed the army leadership, with their increasing appeals to the laws of bushido, their strident claims that only arms and battle were of consequence in the life of a man?

And would not the British, the French and the Americans claim to be sensitive and honourable people? Yet they had all sought empire during their emergent years. Not in one fell swoop, perhaps, but none the less effectively. The British claimed to have created their empire by accident, merely following with their ships and their soldiers the penetration already made by their merchants and their missionaries – but had not that penetration been caused by the British need to establish unchallengeable food supplies and supplies of essential raw materials for their burgeoning economy, as much as by any great desire to spread the word of God? The French claimed to have only been trying to check British expansion, but the end result had been the same. The Americans had been slightly more honest. They had conquered half a continent in the name of their 'manifest destiny'. Many Americans now looked back askance at the rampant imperialism which had swept aside Indians and Mexicans alike with irresistible ease – but America was not about to give New Mexico or Arizona or Texas back to their original owner.

During all those centuries of expansion by the Western Powers, there was no record of any English, American or French officer standing up and saying, This is wrong. Presumably one or two had resigned the service when asked to carry out an utterly immoral order. And had never been heard of again.

Was this the ultimate recourse? It would be a pretty futile one. And a soul-destroying one. He loved the sea and the navy, and he desired only to bring honour to his family, and even more important, to his uncle William.

117

Standing on the bridge of his ship he was happier than anywhere except in the arms of Haruko.

And there was another unbreakable link in the chain of duty and responsibility – and loyalty – tying him to his profession. He was married, to a beautiful and loving, and entirely patriotic woman, who was also a member of one of the great houses in the land. He owed her and her family a duty not less than he owed his country or his own family. His feet were set on a path, and could never leave that path, no matter how muddy or even obscene the puddles through which he might have to wade.

A conviction which became irrevocable when he returned to Tokyo at the end of January and found Haruko to be pregnant.

CHAPTER 5

The Catastrophe

'Congratulations!' Jerry Freeman said.

'Oh, you are a good girl,' Elizabeth Freeman said. 'And we have a little present for you.'

Anne took the small box slowly, carefully flipped open the lid and gazed at the ring. 'Oh Mummy,' she said. 'It's beautiful.'

'Try it on,' her father suggested.

She slipped the ring on to the third finger of her right hand. 'It's just perfect. But . . . is it a real sapphire?'

'Of course,' Jerry said. 'A present for a young lady who has finished top of her class. Now, what would you like to do with your summer vacation? Name it, and it's yours. Europe? London, Paris, Rome, Vienna, Berlin . . . or Antarctica?'

'Will you be able to come?' Anne asked.

'Ah, not for the whole three months. I should be able to join you for the last few weeks, though.'

'Operas,' Elizabeth said in a dreamy voice. 'Concerts. Ballets. The Champs Elysées. The Via Veneto . . . We could do Venice as well. And, of course, England. London. Oxford Street. We've missed Ascot.' She sighed, and then brightened. 'But we'd be in time to catch Henley Regatta.'

Her mother would be coming for the whole summer. But while Europe with both parents might be fun, Europe with her mother alone would be impossible; the two of them just did not see eye to eye on almost anything. Their

119

tastes were entirely different.

And anyway, she had absolutely no desire to go to Europe.

'Doesn't exactly fill you with joy,' Jerry observed. 'Does it?'

'Well,' Anne said. 'Of course it's a magnificent idea, and I'm so grateful to you both for suggesting it. I should just love to see Europe . . . But don't you think I'd enjoy it even more when I'm a little older?'

Her parents exchanged glances; this was the first time they had ever heard their daughter suggest she wasn't old enough for anything.

'I see,' Jerry remarked. And she realised that he did see, and that anything further she might say would be redundant. 'You'd rather go somewhere else.'

Elizabeth also understood. 'Oh, really,' she protested. 'Not back to Japan?'

'Well, why not?' Anne asked. 'It's nearly a year since I was last there. It'll be a year by the time I can get there again. And our last visit was so rushed. It was all wedding, and Tokyo . . . I'd like to explore, and get to know the people, and – '

'Why?' Elizabeth asked bluntly.

'Because . . . ' Anne had to bite her lip to stop herself from falling into the trap of confessing that she intended to live there once she had qualified. That might just be sufficient encouragement for her mother to refuse to let her attempt medical school at all – she was still doubtful about the entire project, in any case. 'Because I'm related to them, I suppose.'

'You are not related to any Japanese in any way,' Elizabeth declared. 'Your grandfather happened to father some children by a Japanese mother. That is all. I do not call that a relationship. And if you think I am going to spend an entire summer in that . . . well . . . ' She glanced at her husband, and flushed. 'So many of their habits are positively indecent.'

120

'I'm sure they consider a great many of our habits indecent,' Anne argued. 'It's all a point of view.' She looked at her father in turn. 'And you said I could go anywhere I liked. Even Antarctica.'

Jerry gave one of his easygoing grins. 'Well, I guess we did.'

'And Haruko Shimadzu did invite me to visit with them,' Anne pressed.

'She's hardly likely to want you around at this minute,' her mother pointed out. 'Isn't she several months pregnant?'

'I might be able to help,' Anne insisted.

'Oh, really . . .'

'She could stay with Shiki,' Jerry said.

'Jerry!' Elizabeth snapped. 'Anyway, she cannot possibly travel by herself.'

'I've been before,' Anne said, her mind starting to jump for joy; her only fear had been that her mother might change her mind and come after all.

'My dear girl, your father and I were with you.'

'We did promise,' Jerry said again. 'I tell you what: I'll put her in the charge of old Whateley. He'll take care of her as if she were his own daughter.'

Captain Whateley was the senior commodore of the Freeman-Pacific Line, the shipping company founded by Ralph Freeman after his triumphant return from Japan forty-five years before. Jerry was the President of the company, from which the Freeman fortune came – although, partly due to his military career and partly because Elizabeth did not like the West Coast, he was a very inactive president. But he was still the majority shareholder, and what he wanted usually happened.

'Oh, that would be just great,' Anne said. 'I do so like Mr Whateley.' She didn't, actually. Captain Whateley was probably the most boring man she had ever met. But she would sail with the devil to get back to Japan.

*

121

Why, she wondered? For the excitement of the journey, for a start. The excitement of the Pullman trip across America with her father, who was coming to see her off. The excitement of San Francisco, and looking at the old family house on Nob Hill. The excitement of steaming out beneath the Golden Gate Bridge towards the setting sun. The excitement of actually travelling alone, for the first time in her life, even if, clinging to her father on the bridge deck before he went ashore, she had suddenly wanted to change her mind and go back to Connecticut — and even if Captain Whateley virtually insisted on tucking her into bed.

At the end of it all, there would be the excitement of Japan. There was the true crux of the matter, because bound up with Japan were thoughts, feelings, she dared not even put into coherent thought, much less talk about with anyone. Much less even write about; since returning from Philip's wedding, she had stopped keeping a diary.

Yet she knew now that it was no longer anything to do with Philip himself. She had not seen him for a year, not, in fact, since the moment she had kissed him goodbye at the wedding. She still remembered that kiss, but she could hardly remember his face. And he had now been married a year, and was about to become a father. He would be utterly content with his beautiful wife, and she would not have had it any other way. He had been a girlhood crush. And now she was a woman.

So the crush, on a single person embodying a dream, had suddenly centred on the entire people. The ambience of their lives, their history and their aspirations. And this was the inadmissable part, because it was an erotic ambience. It had not seemed so when she was there, although she had been aware of feeling more continually alive than ever before in her life. She had, on that visit, experienced so very little that was truly Japanese, because of the presence of her mother and father, and the desire of everyone to make their stay as American as possible.

Even eating with food-sticks had been less because Aunt Hilary and Uncle William had felt they should – there had been Western cutlery available – than to prepare them for the wedding. And yet, that little she had experienced had been so very much. How much, she had only understood since her return to America when she had endeavoured to remember things and found herself thinking only of the erotic. Not only the bath, but the very clothes, the way of life, the total subservience to the male partner – certainly not in line with current American thinking, but appealing to her. Providing, of course, one found the proper male partner.

That was the ambience she sought, an ambience as far beyond understanding and acceptance by her mother as the stars were beyond the sun. And she felt, she knew, that staying with Haruko she would experience so much more, uncover the real heart of Japan, discover if the people and their civilisation really was as beautiful as it seemed at the surface. It could even happen, as was to be her fate, while staying with Shikibu. For all her apparently resigned widowhood, her aunt, like all Japanese women, exuded a subtle eroticism in her every movement, almost like perfume.

So what was she looking for? She had no idea. She had no real desire to think about it too deeply. Certainly she did not want a flirtation with any Japanese man, not even Philip, were he unmarried. She wanted to experience the country. That was it, she supposed. She was in the midst of a love affair with a country, a culture, so completely alien to any she had ever known. So why not enjoy it to the full?

'I am so glad you have come back to us,' Shikibu said, meeting the ship. By herself. She smiled at the question on Anne's face. 'Philip is away at sea, as is William. But Hilary would like you to spend some time with her. I told her you would do so, after you have spent some time with me. Peter is in Manchuria, you know, with his regiment.

And Maureen is away on one of her summer hiking expeditions. She'll be back in a week or so; she intends to be here for the birth of Haruko's child. But I am all alone at home now.'

Anne's heart went out to her. She was so glad she had come. 'Haruko is well?' she asked, as the taxi took them through Tokyo's crowded streets.

'She is expecting you to call,' Shikibu said. 'She does not go out, you see, because of her condition.'

Anne nodded. She understood this was another un-American aspect of Japanese life.

'But she too hopes you will be able to visit with her,' Shikibu said. 'After the babe is born.'

'I should like that,' Anne said, and gazed out of the window at the people. 'Are Americans still very unpopular in Japan?'

'Oh . . . ' Shikibu gestured with her shoulders rather than shrugged. 'There is much unemployment, still. And many people blame America for it. But things will improve, and it is better for our people to learn to fend for themselves, than to run away to another country. You will encounter no anti-Americanism, my dear. You are here to enjoy yourself. To relax, and do whatever you like.' She paid the taxi-driver, and called one of her maids to take Anne's suitcase up to the house. 'So tell me, what would you like to do first?'

She was here to do whatever she liked. To get back the ambience as quickly as possible. To fall in love all over again, as quickly as possible. 'I should just adore to have a bath,' she said.

'Of course,' Shikibu said. 'We will have one together.'

'Anne,' Haruko Shimadzu said. 'Anne Freeman.' She spoke in English, surprisingly, and uncertainly; she was clearly still in the process of learning the language. And she *was* beautiful, Anne realised, seeing her face for the first time. There was superb artistry in every feature.

Shikibu as she might have looked as a girl, perhaps. For the moment all Anne's thoughts centred on Shikibu. Shikibu had sent away the maid and soaped her niece herself, and then requested her to do the same in return. And Anne had not refused this time. It had been the most unforgettable experience of her life.

She had not known what to expect, what to expect it to lead to, actually touching another woman's body, and being touched in return. Her memory once more went back to one day with Nancy Coleman, when they had both been discovering that they were indeed women – a day which had again ended in mutual embarrassment. But instinctively she had known there would be no embarrassment with Shikibu, even had there been a sexual connotation at the end of it. Would she have refused? She simply did not know. And the question had simply not arisen. If Shikibu's fingertips had been like little darts of feeling all over her body, and Shikibu's eyes had closed with sensuous relaxation – she had kept *her* eyes open in excitement – her aunt had never crossed, or suggested that she might wish to cross, that invisible line between sensuality and sexuality. And when Anne had soaped her, she had laughed at the girl's obvious embarrassment. Then they had rinsed each other, and sat in the tub together and talked, while the hot water slowly seemed to penetrate every recess of Anne's body, inducing the most delicious sensations. Sitting in a tub with a woman three times her age, and her father's half-sister into the bargain, feeling utterly erotic and yet utterly unguilty about it, with a suggestion of a total mental intimacy – which emanated from the physical intimacy of the bath and the soaping, and yet contained not an iota of suggestion that what they were doing was in any way indecent or obscene; and even more, that if they chose to progress a step further, that would not be indecent or obscene either, simply because it would be a mutual decision, an extension of the mental rapport which had already

125

enveloped them – there was the essence, and the beauty, of Japan.

It now enveloped her like an outer coat, as it did all Japanese woman. Haruko was grotesquely large for so small a person, and yet retained the beauty of her face, the smallness of her hands and the calmness of spirit.

'It is a tiresome period,' she explained. 'And I wish Philip were here. But he has promised to be home for the birth, and I must be patient until then.'

She seemed to have no doubt that she would.

Anne was just as happy that all the men should be away. Shikibu was in the habit of visiting her daughter-in-law every day, and Anne always accompanied her. But there were other things to be done as well. Shikibu was not merely a widow sitting at home and remembering her youth. She took a regular class in physical education at a kindergarten school near her house, more as a hobby than as a means of earning a living – as Jerry Freeman's half-sister she was also a shareholder in Freeman-Pacific and was really a wealthy woman, however quiet her mode of life.

Shikibu invited Anne to accompany her to the school, and Anne was delighted to do so. The Japanese children were utter charmers, even if they were awestruck when the American girl also shared in their calesthenics, and chatted with them, and played games with them; more than ever she was resolved to return to Japan as a pediatrician.

Shikibu was pleased. 'You are Jerry's child,' she remarked. And then smiled. 'Forgive me.'

'I know what you mean,' Anne said. 'But I must have *something* of Mother hidden away inside me, as well, you know.'

'Keep it hidden,' Shikibu advised, and they both laughed.

Philip did not return in time for the birth of his son, in the last week of July. Again, Anne was happy about that;

however, she could tell that Haruko was far more disappointed than she allowed herself to reveal. But childbirth was surely a strictly female occasion, with Maureen pitching in to help as she hurried home from her expedition, and Hilary as well, while of course the Tokugawa women were also anxious to be involved, even if they had to bow to the superior family status of the bride's mother-in-law. Anne allowed herself a delicious imaginary glimpse of her mother in Japanese society, accepting her daughter's mother-in-law as her superior, however she might suppose the woman to be of a lower social class than herself.

But Haruko had not entirely forgotten the glories of her Tokugawa forebears. 'We will call him Iyeyasu,' she announced, when the tiny scrap of humanity was placed in her arms after a strictly no-nonsense birth.

'Iyeyasu?' Anne asked.

'He was the founder of our family's greatness,' Haruko told her. 'The first Tokugawa Shogun. They called him The Lord of the Golden Fan, because the Golden Fan was the Tokugawa emblem, in those days of armoured knights and ferocious battles. Iyeyasu will surely also be a great warrior.'

The oddest sentiments to come from the mouth of a new mother, Anne would have thought. But she was not disposed to criticise. It was so exciting to be actually a part of a happening like this, to be in the room at the birth, to watch Shikibu and Maureen and Hilary and the Tokugawa ladies carrying out their duties so expertly and confidently, and to see Haruko smile as she looked at her son.

'I am going to be a pediatrician,' she announced. 'And I am going to come to work in Japan, no matter what happens and who says what. Will you let me be Iyeyasu's doctor, Haruko? Or at least, the doctor of your other children?'

'You will be the doctor of all my children,' Haruko

127

promised. 'And next week you will come and stay with us. Philip will be home by then.'

'Oh, but . . . ' Anne didn't know what to say. She did so want to stay with Haruko for a while, but she no longer wanted to be in the same house as Philip. And she did not actually want to leave Shikibu, even less so now that Maureen had returned home.

The three of them made such a jolly trio, sharing everything, talking and laughing together late into the evenings, discussing sexual matters with a freedom Anne had never known in Connecticut, had in fact never dreamed to be possible anywhere. She was even given an illustration by her aunts of how a woman should use the two magic balls; and a woman *should* use the magic balls, apparently in their opinions, whenever she felt the need or the urge – men were all very well, but at the end of the day a woman was her own best friend, and lover. What should have shocked her, and perhaps even appalled her, suddenly became the most natural thing in the world, even if she found their philosophy difficult to accept. The feelings of guilt which had troubled her ever since puberty simply disappeared, even if when, greatly daring, she tried the ivory playthings herself, she was far too tense to gain full value from the experience.

But this freedom of mind was what she had come seeking, because, entirely without proof, she had been sure it was there. The other delights of Japanese life were eating the most exquisite food, drinking sake and green tea, and divorcing the mind entirely from male pre-occupations such as politics and economics – subjects which had always seemed uppermost in her mother's mind – in favour of cooking and caring for one's hair and body, and flower-arranging. Shikibu was a mistress of the art of *nageire*, literally, 'throw in', that of creating an entire vase of flowers around a single central stem or branch all apparently thrown together with total carelessness as opposed to the ancient, formal flower-arranging known as *rikka*. Wearing the most comfortable and exciting of clothes was another delight. Soon she entirely discarded Western dresses, and took to wearing the kimono, which she loved for its freedom from clinging undergarments.

'I do love this place,' she told her aunts. 'I do so want to live here for the rest of my life.'

'Then you shall,' Maureen declared. 'If I have to wring Lizzie's neck.' She looked quite capable of doing that. But then she laughed, in that hearty manner of hers. 'But I think I can probably persuade her without violence.'

Yet she did also want to see Philip again, if only to illustrate to him how well she fitted into the life of his country. Why? She simply had no idea. And she began to suspect the rapidly approaching meeting was preying on her nerves, and thus on her health. Certainly she awoke, on the day he was due to bring his ship into Tokyo Bay, with a streaming cold and a sore throat, and she had not had a cold for over a year.

'You must have caught something from one of the children,' Shikibu said. 'I think it would be best if you did not go out today.' She smiled. 'Do not worry, Philip will come to see you. As soon as he has seen Iyeyasu.'

Did Shikibu know, or suspect, anything of the un-spoken bond between them? How could she, when Anne was not sure even Philip knew of it. It existed in her imagination. It *had* existed; it could do so no longer. Even if now she felt she was capable of thinking like a Japanese woman. And thus, acting like one? That she did not know. She was not sure she truly wanted to find out.

And she was, in fact, grateful for the extra time to prepare herself. She waved Shikibu and Maureen good-bye as they left for the docks, and returned inside the house, frowning and blowing her nose. She really felt absolutely rotten, as if the base of her skull was gripped in

129

a steel vice, making it difficult to concentrate upon anything. Of all the bad luck. But surely it was only a cold.

Yet it was a fever as well. She knew she had a temperature. She wondered if it was something to do with the kimono, after so many years in constricting Western dresses. She wondered . . .

'Missee is not well?' asked one of the maids.

Anne stared up at her, only slowly realising that she was lying on the floor. She had no recollection of having got down there, could think of no reason for having done so. She watched the maid's face, seeming to drift out of focus although the girl did not appear to have moved, and with an immense effort, made herself sit up. But then she was lying down again, and moving, legs and arms thrown thither and hither without any intention on her part, while in the distance she could hear someone screaming.

Only slowly did she realise the screams were her own voice.

Philip was on the quayside to greet his aunt and uncle.

'Is she . . .?' Jerry stared at the young man.

'She's all right,' Philip assured him. 'She's going to be all right. They're pretty sure about that.'

'Pretty sure?' Elizabeth demanded.

'Well, as sure as they can be, Aunt Liz. You know what these things are like.' He had obtained special permission for them to avoid customs, and he himself carried their bags straight out to the automobile, where Haruko and Shikibu waited.

'Jerry' Shikibu said, embracing her brother. 'Oh, Jerry. I am so terribly sorry.'

'It wasn't your fault, Shiki,' Jerry said. 'Can we . . . ?'

'Of course,' Philip said. 'We shall drive down to Yokohama immediately. You remember Haruko?'

'How could we forget,' Jerry said, and kissed her on the cheek. 'I feel so bad about the baby . . . '

'He was in no danger,' Haruko insisted. Although he had been, of course. Probably in more danger than Anne herself, Philip knew. But Haruko had acted throughout with the supreme calmness and confidence which was her greatest beauty and most attractive strength.

He started the engine and turned on to the street, meaning to reach the highway south as rapidly as possible.

'Tell me what happened?' Elizabeth begged. 'Everything.'

'It was the day Philip came back, three weeks ago,' Shikibu explained, holding her sister-in-law's hand. 'Anne had caught what seemed to be a cold, so she stayed at home, and when we got back from the docks, we found her lying on the floor. The maids were terrified. She had had a convulsive fit, and had screamed at them, and twisted her body. They had just not known what to do. I called the doctor immediately, and we put her to bed, but the high temperature and the sudden loss of feeling in her legs made him suspect right away that it could be infantile paralysis. So he insisted she go into an isolation ward immediately, and arranged admission to the Anglo-American hospital. It was the best thing we could do.'

'I cabled you that same day,' Philip reminded his uncle.

'All of you did everything you could,' Jerry agreed. 'And we are so very grateful. But you say she's going to be all right?'

'They think so,' Haruko said. 'She was very ill for a week, right after we wired you. It was truly touch-and-go, for a while. But then she started to pull round . . . We sent another message to the ship. Didn't you get it?'

'Yes,' Jerry said. 'And thank God for it. I reckon we were both just about going nuts, standing there on deck, watching the minutes tick away, not knowing . . . '

'It must have been terrible for you,' Shikibu said.

'But she *is* going to be all right?' Elizabeth asked again. 'No – no paralysis?'

131

'The doctors are hoping for a complete recovery,' Philip said, increasing speed as they reached the comparatively open road leading to Yokohama, only ten miles away.

'But you said there was no feeling in her legs.'

'For that first week or so. Then a reaction was found in the toes of her right leg and then her left. They've been giving her the works, you know – massages, exercises, and she's been coming along very well. She'll have to remain in hospital for at least another month, they say, for final checks, but she seems able to move all her limbs quite freely now.'

'Has there been an epidemic?' Jerry asked.

'No, remarkably. Just a few cases, mostly isolated from each other.'

'Then I don't see how Anne contracted the disease.'

'The doctors say that it's possible for someone to carry the poliomyelitis organisms without themselves suffering from it,' Philip explained. 'So Anne could really have picked it up anywhere.'

'She was fond of exploring the Tokyo bazaars by herself,' Shikibu said. 'I didn't see any harm in it. It just never crossed my mind . . . '

'Of course it wouldn't, Shiki,' Jerry assured her. 'Of course it wouldn't.'

'If only we'd made her go to Europe,' Elizabeth muttered, staring out of the window as the houses sped by. They were already in the suburbs of Yokohama.

'Oh, come now, sweetie,' her husband protested. 'There's just as much risk of getting polio in Europe as there is in Japan.'

Elizabeth shivered, and hugged herself.

Philip pointed at the Anglo-American hospital rising above them, perched on the edge of low cliffs overlooking Tokyo Bay. 'She has a good view,' he said, attempting to lighten the atmosphere. 'Right out over the ships. Her favourite.'

132

Elizabeth said nothing, and a few minutes later he pulled into the car park. 'They don't really like their isolation wards too crowded,' he said. 'You'd better go up with Uncle Jerry and Aunt Liz, Mother. Haruko and I will wait here.'

Jerry nodded, and escorted the two women through the glass-fronted doors to the reception desk.

'Will we get back to Tokyo by noon?' Haruko asked, looking at her watch; it was just eleven. And noon was when Iyeyasu was due for his next feed.

'Oh, sure,' Philip said. 'They won't allow them more than fifteen minutes with her, and it's only a half-hour drive back.' He stared through the windshield, drumming his fingers on the wheel.

'I know how you feel,' Haruko said.

He turned his head.

'Well . . .' She shrugged. 'You have only been to see her once. It is so tragic, a beautiful, healthy, vigorous, energetic girl like that, being reduced to a wreck . . .'

'Don't you believe the doctors that she will make a full recovery?'

'I don't know. Oh, I hope they are right, my Philip. But it makes you think. Do you know, when I heard what her illness was, I hated her. I could only think, that wretched girl has held Iyeyasu in her arms, and breathed on him . . . Oh, I hated her, my Philip, when I should only have felt sorry for her.'

'We were lucky,' he said, and squeezed her hand.

'And she was unlucky,' Haruko said. 'So unlucky.'

She was right, of course, Philip knew. It was odd how some people were totally lucky, and others were equally unlucky. It was tragic for a girl like Anne, so young and full of life, as Haruko had said, to be struck down by so terrible a disease – even if she was able to make a full recovery. But then, was she not equally unfortunate to have fallen in love for the first time with a man who was not only related to her, and virtually twice her age, but was also betrothed to someone else? Shikibu, having observed her both a year ago, just before the wedding, and now for several weeks on end this last summer, was sure Anne *had* fallen for him, and when he remembered their games together in Connecticut, and her last words to him on his wedding night, he knew that his mother was right.

The thought haunted him, and not only because of the wasted sadness of it: he would not have been a man had he not been affected by the realisation that so magnificent a woman was there for the taking, and probably on whatever terms he might propose. Of course he had never for a moment actually contemplated taking such a villainous step . . . But now she was a magnificent woman no longer.

How did one reconcile ill fortune of that magnitude, with the fortune which seemed to pursue himself and his wife and family? Anne must have been carrying the disease for several days before her collapse, days during which, as Haruko said, she had been holding Iyeyasu in her arms, breathing on him. Days, too, when she had been sharing a house with his mother and Maureen. Polio was supposed to strike more at the young than the old, however; perhaps his mother and aunt were past the age when they would easily contract the disease. But what of Haruko herself? She was only a year older than Anne. Why had one caught the germ and not the other?

What would he have done had Haruko also gone down with polio? He thought he would probably have gone mad. Certainly he too would have hated Anne with every fibre in his body.

He leaned back in his chair and gazed at his wife's photograph in its silver frame. It stayed on his desk in his day cabin every moment the *Yahagi* was in port, even if he had to stow it safely at sea. Haruko, smiling at him, leading him confidently through life.

She was quite marvellous to Anne, as well, despite all. She went down to Yokohama every morning, with Jerry and Elizabeth, to visit the Anglo-American hospital. Almost as if she felt guilty for that spasm of hatred. He had only been back once in the week since the Freemans' arrival. He had in any event viewed Anne's return to Japan with mixed feelings. The girl's earlier adoration had embarrassed him, and he could still remember that kiss. Because the temptation still remained, lurking at the dark edges of his subconscious? He did not know. He knew he had feared what a seventeen-year-old Anne Freeman might be like, remembering as he did what a sixteen-year-old Anne Freeman had been like. And in the event, he had found only a crumpled wreck lying on a floor.

He really did not want to see that wreck again too often. Perhaps there was guilt involved, a Christian, and totally un-Japanese, concept that had he never allowed himself to think of her carnally she might not have been struck down. An absurdity, really, in this world of harsh realities. But not the less disturbing. There would be time to see her again, regularly, when she was fully recovered. Which by all accounts would not now be long. Today was 1 September, and the doctors all seemed to agree that she might leave the hospital the following week, unless there was a relapse. So . . .

He was aware of noise. A very loud noise, but one he could not identify. It was totally chaotic, like a huge giant belching after a satisfying meal. Then he realised that he was lying on his back on the cabin floor, his chair on top of him. For a moment, remembering the maids' description of what had happened to Anne, he had a spasm of fear that he might have caught polio himself. But he certainly did not have a cold in the head, or any loss of sensation in his limbs. He sat up, and rubbed his head, watching the photograph of Haruko go sliding across his desk and then fall to the deck, the glass shattering.

He was aware of anger. Some fool was shaking his ship, in harbour. And still making a lot of noise; his ears were ringing. And Haruko's portrait had smashed.

He scrambled to his feet, and the door burst open, to admit Hagi. A Hagi who had forgotten to knock, and who was now forgetting to bow. 'Captain, he gasped. 'Captain.'

Philip found himself sitting on the settee, Hagi on his lap. The fellow seemed to have gone mad. But the entire day seemed to have gone mad, because he was gazing at the port, which was fortunately closed, and there was water splashing against it.

'Captain,' Hagi screamed again, sliding to the floor. 'Captain!'

Philip reached his feet once more, ran into the corridor. The ship lurched yet again, and he was thrown against the bulkhead; he supposed he might have sprained his wrist. He ran for the companionway, met two sailors coming down. Falling down. The entire world had gone mad.

He threw them aside and started climbing, bursting past the wardroom, where people were shouting, and reached the lower bridge. There he checked, gazing in horror at the sea. Half an hour before, when he had gone below, Tokyo Bay had been its usual calm self, with little breeze and scarce a ripple on the water. There was still no wind, and yet now the surface seethed as if boiling, rolling all the ships to and fro, while the worst was still to come. Even as he watched he saw a solid wall of water, a wave some thirty feet high and of unimaginable depths, riding up the bay. He listened to sirens blaring as other ships saw the coming catastrophe, but could not turn his head. Riding at anchor, *Yahagi* was at least facing the coming avalanche, but she had no power, and but a single anchor down – no more had ever been considered necessary. She was also one of the furthest ships out, and therefore first in line.

'By all the gods,' Mashada gasped beside him.

One of the sailors moaned.

'Hold something,' Philip said, and himself grasped the bridge rail as the tidal wave burst on the bows of the ship, completely obliterating them, forcing them down as it careered aft. Visibility disappeared in green water as the wave broke against the bridge screens, which fortunately held. But even above the immense roaring of the water Philip heard the *crack* of the snapping anchor-chain.

He shook his head, stared forward as the water cascaded to port and starboard, and watched the severed chain snaking in the air before coming down with a crash on the forward gun turret, denting the steel which was supposed to resist a six-inch shell. He was dimly aware of the men to either side of him scrambling back to their feet, gasping and shouting. But only the thought that his ship was adrift and out of control occupied his mind. He whipped open the speaking-tube to the engine-room. 'Give me steam,' he snapped. 'Give me steam.'

Fortunately, as *Yahagi* had been the duty ship that week, or first in line should any naval presence be required outside Tokyo Bay, her boilers were at least partly stoked. Philip reckoned it would be possible to raise full steam in an hour. An hour! When every second meant possible disaster.

Mashada was grasping his shoulder and pointing. The tidal wave had crashed amongst the other ships, and several of them, too, had snapped their chains and were drifting, colliding, while sirens blared and voices shouted. Not all had survived; he saw a fishing-boat turned upside down, its crew disappeared. But he had problems of his own, for behind the wave had come a wind, hot and vicious, and strong, seeking victims from amongst the shattered fleet. It marked *Yahagi* as its own, driving her across the still-turbulent sea towards the rocks on the eastern side of the bay. An hour would be too long.

'Mashada,' he said, 'break out two more anchors. We must bring her up.' Once again he picked up the speaking-tube. 'It is very necessary to have steam at the earliest possible moment,' he said. 'The ship is in danger.'

Mashada was already on the foredeck, where water still ran through the scuppers. Men were emerging from hiding to assist him. Their faces were blanched with horror and fear. If they knew what had happened, they also knew that the earthquake had been on a scale none of them had ever seen before.

But having been given the lead by their captain and officers, they were prepared to work to save the ship. The auxiliary anchors were shackled to the spare chains with what seemed agonising slowness, while the tumbled rocks came ever closer; then the anchors plunged into the water, and the ship slowly came to a halt – Philip estimated the nearest rocks were only fifty yards astern. But the seas were already subsiding, and for the moment his command was safe. It was time to think, to take stock, to try to understand what was happening. And what had happened elsewhere.

The noise was tremendous. Philip went outside on to the bridge wing, where there was still water dripping everywhere. He felt the September sunshine incongruously hot, and realised for the first time that he was on duty without his cap, thus contravening every navy regulation. He gazed at the now distant Tokyo shoreline and saw that the wave, having continued up the bay with ponderous and deadly slowness, was now breaking over the docks. Even at a distance he could see the entire waterfront being submerged, small craft being tossed into the air, great warehouses being smashed down. He could not see beyond the wave, but he knew that he was watching Tokyo being destroyed. Tokyo! His entire family was there.

No, he remembered. Not his *entire* family. He turned, to stare down the bay towards Yokohama. On a clear day, it was possible to see the Anglo-American hospital for miles, and this was an exceptionally clear day. But yet he could see nothing. He heard someone behind him, and Hagi pressed his binoculars into his hand. He took the glasses, levelled them, swept them up and down the coast. Of course the tidal wave had swept the Yokohama coast as well. It would have been stronger there, further out. But even with the glasses he could make out very little of what might have happened down there. Yet he could no longer refuse to accept what his first glance had shown: the Anglo-American hospital was no longer there.

Duty! As John Graham had said, duty made heroes of them all. Just as duty protected their sanity. Only duty mattered. Above wife and child, family and friends? Above everything.

By one-thirty, sufficient steam had been raised for *Yahagi* to weigh her spare anchors and cautiously return to her berth. Most of the other ships were now under control, and it was nearly impossible to tell that anything had ever happened, so calm was the sea. And as long as one did not make the mistake of looking shorewards; because now there was smoke rising above Tokyo. Smoke and dust, the final agents of destruction.

Carefully concentrating, Philip lined up the necessary bearings which told him he was exactly where he should be, and ordered Mashada once again to let the reserve anchors go; *Yahagi* was once again safe and sound. 'Make to the Fleet Commander,' he said to his signal lieutenant. ' "Permission requested to release maximum number of men." '

He waited, hands tight on the bridge rail, looking now at Tokyo. The dust which had earlier clouded the interior of the city had settled, and the waters seemed to have subsided. Now there was only a huge pall of smoke, rising briskly, not dissipated by the gentle breeze.

'Signal from the Fleet Commander, honourable

Captain.'

Philip took the sheet of paper.

PERMISSION GRANTED FOR TWELVE HOURS PROVIDING SUFFICIENT CREW RETAINED TO WORK SHIP IF NEED BE STOP CONGRATULATIONS ON SUPERB SEAMANSHIP AND COURAGE STOP PERSONAL TO SHIMADZU ACT FOR ME STOP FREEMAN

Philip could only imagine the feelings that must be going through his uncle's mind. But the Fleet Commander had to remain with the fleet until further orders were received, until the magnitude of the disaster became known. He looked at Mashada.

'I have already taken a consensus of the crew, honourable Captain,' the first lieutenant said. 'I will remain in command while you go ashore.' Mashada's family, lucky people, lived down in Honshu. 'Only those men whose families are in the Tokyo or Yokohama areas need shore leave at this time.'

Philip nodded. He could not speak. Now that the immediate crisis was over, his mind was too full of unthinkable thoughts.

They used all their liberty boats to take some two hundred men ashore. Sailors were landing from other ships as well, gazing in horror at the scene before them. On the waterfront itself, the earthquake had done less damage than the tidal wave. They looked at whole docks torn from their pilings and scattered to and fro like matchsticks; at great warehouses with doors smashed down and roofs torn off, with their contents, heavy bags of rice and sugar, bales of cloth, huge hunks of frozen meat, new cars awaiting delivery – all flung haphazardly, in and out of the water, or perched at absurd angles on equally absurd remnants of once-strong structures. It was as if Tokyo had been looted by an invading army of giants.

At least there was no fire here; that lay beyond, and could now be smelt as well as seen, not merely the lung-destroying odour of smoke, but the nostril-filling stench of burning wood – and burning flesh. And with it, an awful moan, emanating from the throats of several millions of people slowly realising what had happened, slowly understanding that the worst was yet to come.

To Philip's amazement, John Graham waited on the dock. The Scot's white uniform was black with soot and dust, and he had cut his knee; he too had lost his cap. 'My God,' he said, as the steam pinnace nosed between broken piles and floating timbers to find a semblance of dry land. 'What was it like out there?'

'Nothing as severe as here,' Philip said. He stepped ashore to squeeze his friend's hand, because here was the true measure of friendship, that Graham's first thoughts should apparently have been of him. 'And you?'

'I'm all right. The embassy's a bit knocked about. Nothing that can't be repaired, providing they manage to block this fire before it reaches there. The palace seems undamaged. But the main part of the city . . . whew. Are you going to try to make it home?'

'Yes,' Philip said. 'Is there transport?'

Graham shook his head. 'You couldn't move it, anyway.'

Philip dismissed his men. 'Twelve hours,' he reminded them. 'You will reassemble here at midnight.' He also dismissed the boats to return to the cruiser; all except his own steam pinnace – his instincts were telling him he was going to need it long before the twelve hours were up.

'I'll come with you,' Graham said.

They walked away from the docks and into a scene out of Dante's *Inferno*. The tidal wave had penetrated the first few streets of the city and wreaked as much insensate destruction there as in the docks area, but now it had been replaced by the hissing, darting, consuming flames, above which rolled the growing clouds of brown smoke.

141

Yet it was the damage done by the earthquake itself which first caught the startled eye. There were great fissures in the streets, out of which bent and buckled tramlines emerged like iron snakes. Masses of overhead wires lay in clusters, like unearthly spiders' webs dislodged by a strong wind. They were now harmless enough as all electricity supplies had been cut off, but they had clearly been deadly for a few seconds at the beginning of the catastrophe, as they could tell by the blackened body of a man on whom one cluster had fallen. Burst water-mains still seeped spreading liquid, the fresh mixing with the salt puddles left by the inundation of the sea. Shattered houses, many of them reduced to piles of wood, others left with but a single wall standing or even a single wooden upright, had their intimacies, their beds and their stoves and their clothes, torn about by the invading giants. Many burned fiercely, and it was easy to see that the earthquake had caused tens of thousands of small fires, which had come together in the general conflagration, because the people of Tokyo would all have been preparing their midday meal when the tremor occurred.

And of course there were people. People standing, staring at what had been their houses, expressions of utter horror on their faces; people shouting at the heavens which had permitted this holocaust, and tearing their hair in anguish and despair; people sitting, weeping; children, in groups, traumatised into silence by the power of the cataclysm; and people lying, some moaning in pain from broken limbs, others absolutely still, men and women and children, their white limbs pathetically thin and frail, while terrified dogs crept amongst the living and the dead, unable to comprehend.

But there were other people as well, screaming their fear and their agony from inside collapsed buildings, begging for help before the flames reached them and they burned to death. Philip and Graham immediately went to the assistance of one old woman trapped by a falling timber. They pulled her free easily enough, but there could be no doubt that her leg was broken.

'Is there no help?' Philip asked, and looked around to see if he could recall some of his sailors, as if even his two hundred men could bring any succour to so many.

'The army has been called out,' Graham said. 'They are taking over the city.'

And indeed a moment later, while they stood uncertainly by the woman, who was moaning and weeping, they were surrounded by a company of soldiers, armed and ready to deal with any looting or rioting. They were also equipped with spades and axes to dig out the living – and accompanied by a medical unit.

Philip showed them the woman, and they nodded and got to work. Then he and Graham went on their way, drawn by the horrific vision of those they knew and loved having become anything like those they now passed. They hurried. It had never occurred to Philip that he would ever walk across the breadth of Tokyo. But it was surprising how quickly it could be done, even if they were forced left and right by fresh outbreaks of flames and had to make several lengthy detours to avoid great palls of smoke which sought to choke them. But they could also travel nearly in a straight line, where there was no fire. They picked their way through the rubble of people's houses to shorten their journey; they paused from time to time either to reassure the distraught or, on more than one occasion, to help free the trapped; they saw sights they would never forget, and they heard prayers and imprecations and expressions of despair they would never forget either. They came across a tramcar filled with people, all of whom had been electrocuted by the short-circuiting of the overhead cables; miraculously, the earthquake had not touched the passengers, and they sat, stiff and lifelike, like wax dummies in a museum, one woman's hand still outstretched as if she had been about

143

to pay the fare. They waded a canal filled with people, where the fire had swept only minutes earlier; the people had leapt into the shallow water to escape the flames, and there they had died, their heads scorched beyond recognition, their bodies still seated in the shallow water. But despite all, they kept their own lurking suggestions of despair under control. It was clear that Graham was as anxious as Philip; the Freeman family, and its offshoots, were his closest friends in all Japan.

Finally they reached a street which was only partly damaged. Philip wanted to scream with joy, and now he ran. There was hardly any fire, and the breeze was blowing the flames the other way. There was one wall thrown in. Nothing more. Some shattered vases, some scattered flowers, some dislodged tatami mats. Even the garden gate remained on its hinges.

And there was Shikibu, clinging to his arm and holding Iyeyasu, and Maureen, weeping with joy, and Hilary, asking after her husband.

'Thank God!' Philip said. 'Oh, thank God!' He held his baby son close. 'Uncle William is all right. All of us are all right.' He looked from face to face, knowing what a grotesque lie that was. 'What time were they returning?' he asked.

'By noon,' Hilary said. 'Jerry, and Liz, and Haruko. By noon. Haruko had to feed Iyeyasu, at noon.'

Three hours ago. And the earthquake had struck at ten minutes to noon.

'They would have left the hospital,' Graham said.

'I must get down there,' Philip said.

'We,' Graham reminded him.

'How will you get through?' Shikibu asked. 'If the roads are torn up all the way down the bay . . .'

'They are,' Hilary said. 'We asked those soldiers, remember?'

'We'll go down by boat,' Philip decided; his instincts had been too accurate. 'The odds are that they would have left. When the tremors started they would have returned to the hospital.'

Only the hospital isn't there, he thought, despair again smashing at his mind. The hospital isn't there.

But the women didn't know that, and he wasn't going to tell them now. He kept clinging to the desperate hope that being unable to see it might have been an optical illusion caused by the dust, or by the movement – by anything.

He and Graham made their way back through the stricken city, the clouds of smoke. It was nearly four in the afternoon, and they had not eaten since breakfast. Or drunk: their throats were parched. But neither had anyone else eaten or drunk since morning, and the work of rescue was progressing so very slowly. The cries and moans, the smells and the sounds, were even more harrowing than they had been an hour before.

They hurried, wanting only to get on, to breathe the clean air of the bay. Philip's pinnace waited at the broken dock, manned by three seamen whose families lived in the security of Hokkaido, and who had had the sense to keep the boiler stoked.

'Yokohama,' Philip said, and himself took the helm.

They kept as close to the shore as they could, but had also to keep a sharp look-out. The bay was filled not only with flotsam from the shore and from those vessels which had been overwhelmed by the tidal wave, but also with floating bodies, dogs and pigs, cats and chickens . . . and humans, sucked away from the shore by the power of the receding tidal wave. It was inhuman to drive through them without attempting to reclaim at least the human carcasses – but this was an inhuman day.

They studied the coast as they steamed past. The highway up and down which Philip had driven so often at speed was virtually non-existent. Great gaps had been torn in the embankments, into which the road appeared to have collapsed, and those houses built on the seaward side had also been swept away into jumble; the tidal wave must have broken right over this low-lying area. They saw people, in the distance, conforming to the same pattern as in Tokyo, standing and staring, or poking hopelessly amidst the ruin of their homes, for loved ones or loved possessions. Some noticed the naval pinnace and waved and shouted. These they could bring themselves to ignore, but they also saw shattered carts and upturned cars, people driving to Tokyo and caught by the sinking road, the surging water. The temptation to put into the shore and examine every one was almost irresistible. But they could afford no such futility. They had to believe that Haruko and Uncle Jerry and Aunt Liz had not begun their return journey before the tremors started. And they could do nothing to help anyone else. That was the army's task, and already they could see soldiers moving down the road. Now it was a case of thank God for the army.

At last they could make out the tall buildings of Yokohama, those which had survived the shock. The Anglo-American hospital had been north of the sea-port, perched on its cliff, a landmark peering out over Tokyo Bay. Anne Freeman's favourite view. Now Philip could no longer delude himself, or even hope. He gazed at the rubbled earth, which had slid down from the cliff edge, taking the hospital with it. They looked in awestruck silence at shattered timbers, strewn to and fro on the shore; at beds, upside-down, twisted, half-covered in earth, half in and half out of the water, some even with their neatly folded white sheets still in place; at surgical instruments and broken bottles; at seeping drugs and medicines; and at white-clad bodies, floating in the shallows, scattered up and down the slope.

And they smelt the stench of death.

Philip reduced speed to dead slow, and they eased through the floating debris towards the shore, Graham in the bows to look out for unsuspected obstacles. The

146

Anglo-American hospital had once had its own dock –
but that too was gone. It was a matter of gaining the shore
itself, if they could.

'Port a point,' Graham called. 'Steady. Steady. Hard
starboard. Steady. Port a point . . .'

Philip obeyed the instructions without thinking,
watched the various baulks of timber and dislodged
rocks, passing by to either side. He could not think about
anything. He dared not think about anything. He could
only wait.

'Slow astern,' Graham commanded. The pinnace
glided to a stop, within a few feet of an outcrop of rock
which had either survived the earthquake or been thrown
up by it. Graham had guided them right to the shore with
consummate skill. One of the sailors jumped ashore with
a line, and a moment later they were secure.

Philip left the helm, stood at the foot of the slope and
gazed up. He saw a white body draped round a crag
about twenty feet above his head. A small body. A child.

'Christ!' Graham exclaimed. 'It just doesn't look as if
there were any survivors.'

But immediately they heard a shout. 'Hallo!' someone
was calling. 'Hallo!'

They looked to their right, and saw a man waving at
them. He also wore white. 'Hallo!' he shouted again.

They scrambled towards him. 'Dr Azuma,' he said, as
they came closer. 'Thank God you have arrived.'

'Captain Philip Shimadzu,' Philip told him. 'This is
Lieutenant-Commander John Graham, RN.'

Azuma shook hands. 'You had relatives in the hospital?' he asked.

Philip nodded. 'Did anyone survive?'

'Oh, indeed, quite a few. Thanks to prompt action by
my staff.' Azuma had a cut on his forehead from which
blood had seeped; his hair was untidy and thick with
dust; his white jacket was split up the back and only
stayed on his shoulders by virtue of its arms and collar;

the rest of his clothing was equally in tatters. No one could doubt that those who had survived had done so by this man's efforts. But he remained totally, and remarkably, calm. 'We have some forty people up there. The hospital disintegrated, you see. It just slid down the slope into the sea. Many of those people need urgent medical attention. Can you take forty in your boat?'

'No,' Philip said. There was so much he wanted to ask this man, but he just could not. Again, he could only take refuge in duty, and facts. 'I cannot take more than twenty.'

'There was a young lady here,' Graham said. 'In the isolation ward.'

'Ah. Miss Freeman, the American. Of course,' Azuma said. 'Captain Shimadzu. I am sorry, I should have recognised you. We talked, when your cousin was first brought in.'

Philip stared at him.

'Is she . . . ?' Graham bit his lip.

Azuma smiled. 'She is not dead, Mr Graham. She is perfectly all right.'

'Oh, thank God,' Philip said. 'Thank God!'

'He has sent you to us,' Azuma said. 'Now, sir, if you can take twenty people, as you say, the badly hurt, and Miss Freeman, of course, I should be eternally grateful.'

'Yes,' Philip said. He still could not ask the question.

Neither, it seemed, could Graham, this time. 'But, what about the rest of you?' he asked. 'I mean, food, water . . . '

'We will manage,' Azuma said. 'Until the army gets here. Now, do you think . . . ?'

'Of course,' Graham said, and signalled the Japanese sailors to come up and join them.

'That will be a blessing,' Azuma said, and led them to the cluster of people on what had once been the car park.

Philip surveyed the battered group. Some were lying only semi-conscious on the tarmacadam. Others rose to their feet as the men approached. They were mostly women, patients and nurses.

'Philip!' Anne pushed herself up, unsteady after so many weeks in bed and the events of the day, swaying as she staggered towards him. 'Oh, Philip!'

'Anne!' He had not seen her for ten days. Then she had been a thin wisp of a girl, in bed. She hardly looked different now, thinner and paler than before, covered as she was in dust. Her brain would also be covered, he knew, as he looked into her eyes. Covered with horror. 'Is – is there no one else?'

The doctor frowned. 'You had another relative with us?'

'Not with you. Visiting Miss Freeman. My wife. My aunt and uncle.'

'They left me,' Anne said. 'They left fifteen minutes before the earthquake.' She stared at him, her eyes even more tragic than before. 'Oh, my God! Philip . . .'

'Fifteen minutes?' Philip looked at Azuma, and then they both turned to look at the road, which could be seen below the car park, winding towards Tokyo. But today, as they had seen from the pinnace, winding was the operative word. The road was a twisted pathway, a jumble of stricken houses and cars and telegraph poles, and people.

'Fifteen minutes,' Azuma said. And shook his head.

PART TWO

The Lonely Man

CHAPTER 6

The Despair

Philip Shimadzu ran from the shattered remains of the hospital, across the car park, and down the road. He leapt great holes and sudden ravines, scrambled over rocks which had become uncovered, paused to look at a dead body. He heard voices behind him, shouting, and ignored them. The last fibres of his self-control had suddenly and finally snapped.

He tore his uniform when he fell, regained his feet, looked at more dead bodies and shattered houses. He had seen so many of these already today that they hardly registered. But there were living here, too. They stared at him, incomprehensibly. He wore naval uniform, but he was capless, and his jacket was unbuttoned.

'Have you seen an American automobile?' he panted. 'This morning? Before the earthquake? Have you seen an American automobile?'

They stared at him, and he ran onwards, and paused for breath, heart constricting. He stood above where the road dipped down to the sea. Where the road *had* dipped down to the sea. Now it was entirely gone, for a stretch of perhaps a mile; on the landward side there was nothing but swamp, where the tidal wave had been, and not entirely receded. There were several cars down there, sticking out of the mud at grotesque angles, one or two upside down and sunk into the mud itself. There was no sign of life.

Graham panted behind him. 'You cannot run all the

way to Tokyo, Phil,' he said. 'And we must get those injured people to help.'

Philip pointed. 'They would have been down there when it happened,' he said.

'You don't know that.'

'Fifteen minutes from the hospital? From leaving the isolation ward? Five minutes on the stairs and getting the car started; five minutes driving out through the suburbs; five minutes on the open road. They would have been down there.' He began to climb down into the valley, and after a moment's hesitation, Graham followed. They waded through mud and sludge to the nearest of the automobiles, then moved on to the next.

'We could search forever,' Graham said.

'I must find her,' Philip said. 'You take the pinnace and go back to Tokyo with the injured. I will stay here and search, forever.'

Graham sighed, and hesitated . . . then gave a little groan and pointed. Just emerging from the mud, about forty yards away, was the rear bumper and number plate of another automobile. Philip ran forward, because he too had recognised the number of William's car. He dashed into what must have been a field, and sank to his waist, having almost to swim to make his way forward. Graham came behind him, as they reached for the doors of the car Jerry had been driving.

'You must drink something,' Shikibu said.

Anne Freeman shivered. She had shivered all evening, lying, wrapped in blankets, on a mattress on the floor of her old room in Shikibu's house. But the cold was not outside. It was in her stomach and her heart . . . and in her mind.

It was nothing that could be analysed. She dared not analyse, comprehend what had happened. Lack of comprehension stretched too far back.

Her mind was a maelstrom of emotions and conflicting

154

memories, ever since she had found herself lying on the floor. She had seen people clustering round, some faces familiar, others unfamiliar. She had tried to speak to them, to tell them that she was really all right and would be getting up in a moment, but they had not seemed to understand.

Then memory became incredibly fuzzy. She remembered a car ride, of some sort, but a strange car because she seemed to be in a bed. Then there was another bed, and a contraption into which she had been fitted, and which had forced her to breathe even when she had really been too tired to breathe. And now all the faces were strange.

Awareness, and understanding, had returned slowly. And fear. She had polio. An utterly dread word, with all the connotations of lifelong paralysis. Not so, Dr Azuma had said. The nurses had inserted her into a bathing costume, and the doctor had himself entered the bathing pool with her and held her up while she slowly moved her arms and legs. She would recover. No one had any doubt about that.

But she had been struck down, first. Now guilt had taken the place of fear and uncertainty. She had plunged wildly, irresponsibly, into a lifestyle of which she really knew nothing, and understood nothing. Shikibu had no doubt bathed with other women all of her life, perhaps even with other men. Nudity, physical intimacy, did not carry the obscene connotations in Japanese society that they did in the Judeo-Christian world. She had wanted to take advantage of that point of view, to indulge her desire for total freedom . . . but she was not Japanese, and all the time she had been waiting for *something* to happen. And for that crime, almost that sacrilege, she had been struck down.

Seeing her mother and father had been almost unbearable. Seeing them with Haruko even more so. Yet no one else seemed to suspect her guilt. Everyone was so kind, so

155

anxious to reassure her, so eager to make plans for when she was well again; and with every day she *had* felt more and more well again. Guilt had slowly faded into the background. She was being childish again. There could be no guilt in desiring freedom, to do whatever one wished whenever one wished with whoever one wished. Surely . . . then she had watched the light-fitting above her bed begin to move, watched her dressing-table begin to move, watched her bowl of fruit smash on to the ground, listened to an enormous, terrifying and truly obscene groaning, which had been accompanied by screams of terror from the other wards. She had tried to get out of bed, and fallen, and been plucked from the floor by Dr Azuma. She had been carried down shuddering corridors, surrounded always by the groan and the screams, watching whole walls falling outwards, great cracks tearing the floors apart. The whole world, it seemed, was being torn apart . . . but she was escaping. To remember? And know that she was guilty?

Because the whole world *had* been torn apart. Her world. The bodies had been brought down to the pinnace wrapped in blankets, and she had not seen their faces. Philip had. He had looked at the death frozen expressions of horror piled upon horror, as first of all the car must have spun wildly out of control as the earth had buckled beneath its wheels, and then the three people inside had watched that solid wall of water rearing up over the bay like a cobra head, and rushing at them, striking, implacably destructive, insatiably seeking the end of their lives. They would be buried with those expressions still on their faces.

The three people. She could not think of them more clearly than that, or she would have screamed until her heartstrings snapped. But, not thinking of them, of Mother and Father and Haruko, hurled so abruptly into eternity, she could not think of any other member of the family, either. Shikibu, kneeling beside her, her own face a mask of tragedy. Maureen, standing, all her infectious good humour dissipated in streaming tears, because she had loved Elizabeth as much as her brother – as young women they had adventured together, during the breakdown of Elizabeth's marriage, had travelled the world together, sharing experiences given to few women, and perhaps sharing even more than that: no other member of the family had ever discovered the truth of their relationship; Hilary, solemn and pensive; Uncle William, massively calm, although his cheeks also showed the signs of tears. He and his brother had lived separate lives, for the most part, following their different destinies, east and west. But they had also fought side by side in their time, and once, she knew, they had even loved the same woman – a love which had ended in tragedy. They had, despite the thousands of miles of physical distance and the no less yawning chasm of national cultures which had divided them, shared a great deal.

William was already aware of his responsibilities. 'You will come home with us, Anne,' he said. 'We . . .' He sighed, and left the sentence unfinished. But she knew what he had been going to say. He and Shikibu and Maureen were all the family she now possessed. Her Japanese family. The family her mother had refused to recognise ever existed.

Her dream come true, so suddenly changed into a horrible nightmare.

She nodded, and tried to get up. Once again Shikibu pressed the cup of sake into her hand, and this time she drank, and listened to the baby crying. He had still been at Haruko's breast, which was why her visits to the hospital had been confined to the mornings between ten-thirty and eleven-thirty, and despite Shikibu's efforts with a bottle, was now hungry. Certainly he did not yet miss his mother. Haruko had visited the hospital every day, leaving the babe with her mother-in-law. Oh, if only she had not come every day. Because there was the

157

greatest horror of all. A horror which, she knew, would stretch on and on and on, throughout the rest of her life. And Philip's, too. She had reached the door, slowly and hesitantly, the only way she could move anywhere nowadays, William at her elbow ready to catch her if she should begin to fall. Philip was in the next room. Only a few hours ago he had held her close and said, 'Thank God,' because she was alive. But that had been before he realised that his wife was dead. Dead because of her. Had she not been in hospital, Haruko would have been in Tokyo, in her own house . . . and that house had not even suffered more than a few broken vases. Now Anne gazed at him, and he gazed back, and then turned away. She knew that she must be the most hateful sight in the world to him, at this moment.

And forever?

'William and Hilary have decided to take Anne back to America,' Shikibu said. 'William has to go there, anyway, to see to Jerry's estate. But they feel it would be best to continue the girl's education exactly as Jerry had planned it. We are fortunate that she has always expressed the wish to make Japan her home, when she finishes college. Do you not think so?'

She looked at her younger son anxiously, but Philip did not reply. He sat, and stared at *his* son, wriggling on the floor. Did Iyeyasu still remember his mother? Probably not. He would never remember his mother.

Shikibu sighed, and looked at Peter in turn. She was grateful for his presence, and she knew Philip appreciated the way his brother had obtained leave of absence to be with him in this tragic hour . . . But they had drifted too far apart, she feared, for Peter ever to be able to exert any more influence on his sibling.

'It is unfair,' she said, 'and unreasonable of you to blame Anne for what happened, Philip. She is sufficiently distraught as it is.'

'I do not blame her,' Philip said.

'But you will not speak to her, or comfort her in any way.'

'No,' Philip said. 'No, I cannot do that, Mother.' It was his turn to sigh. 'I do not expect you to understand.'

'Which does not mean that I do *not* understand,' Shikibu told him. 'But the fault is yours. She is quite innocent of being anything but an impressionable young girl.'

He turned his head, frowning at her. If they had discussed the ill fortune of Anne's having developed a crush on him, he had never expected her to raise the matter before anyone else — even if the third party was his own brother.

'Because you have *shared* her feelings,' Shikibu said. 'I have seen you looking at her, in the past. I know that you have thought how easily you could love her, just as easily as she would love you. I know too that as you are an honourable man, you have always rejected such thoughts, because of your love for Haruko. So that now you feel doubly guilty. But do you not suppose she too feels doubly guilty?'

'You do *not* understand, Mother,' Philip said angrily, and got up. 'You will excuse me.' Because she understood too well.

He walked into the garden; even at dusk he could still hear the growl of engines, the sound of hammers. Tokyo was rebuilding, with all the tremendous energy and dedication of purpose that was the Japanese national characteristic. And with the help of its friends. One hundred and fifty thousand people had died in that shock on Saturday, 1 September, 1923, at ten minutes to noon, either in the tremor itself, or as a result of the tidal wave and fires which had followed. Another hundred thousand had been seriously injured. Seven hundred thousand homes, one hundred and fifty-one Shinto shrines, six hundred and thirty-three Buddhist temples, and seventeen libraries, including that of the Imperial Palace, which had been caught in the fire. Even the cabinet building where Count Yamamoto, uncle of Isoroku, had been attempting to form a government, had been destroyed, with twenty potential members killed when the floor had collapsed. Yet the city was being rebuilt. If for some thirty-six hours most people had been too shocked even to realise what had happened, after that the entire nation, the entire world, it seemed, had been galvanised into action. Help, money, supplies, had poured in, especially from the United States. If any good could come out of such a catastrophe it surely had to be that the Japanese could no longer hate the Americans, because the American people had proved their generous friendship.

Now it merely seemed that Tokyo and Yokohama might have decided upon a gigantic rebuilding exercise – there was no longer any evidence that either city had been driven to that decision by the hand of God.

The hand of God, he thought bitterly. As if he could ever believe in God again. How arrogantly had he sat at his desk that Saturday morning, and compared Anne Freeman's ill fortune in contracting polio with his own increasing good fortune, which had followed him throughout his life. And then left him, in the twinkling of an eye. That too was not something his mother could ever understand, because although brought up as a Christian she had imbibed too many of the Shintoist beliefs of her husband. Life was a business of survival, amidst the myriad snares laid for one by the malignant forces of the universe. An earthquake was only to be compared with a typhoon or an illness or a war. When these things happened, people died, and people lived. Only the manner of the dying, or the manner of the living, the determination that no dishonour should be brought upon the name bequeathed to one by illustrious ancestors, was truly important. Certainly, to wish oneself also dead would be regarded by Shikibu, by any sensible Japanese, as absurd.

There was no way he could tell her that his only wish at this moment was that he could have been inside that automobile, with Haruko's hand in his, together at the very end. Lacking the ability to make that be, he had no desire at all. Not even to touch his son, the fruit of her womb. So how could he make himself smile upon the girl who had shared his thoughts equally with his wife, and whose very presence had brought such catastrophe upon him? And upon herself, of course. But it was now necessary for them each to find their own salvation. She was seventeen years old, and had suffered a grievous illness which might well leave her debilitated for the rest of her life. She had now in addition suffered a tragic loss, which had turned her into an orphan in a single moment. But she *was* only seventeen, with her life in front of her, and with relatives to care for her and guide her towards an eventual happiness.

He was thirty-three, and had climbed to the very top of the happiness tree – and been shaken from it and hurled to the ground. If he chose to indulge the cloying appeal of self-pity, at least for a while, that was surely his privilege, at this moment in his life. Whatever he did, wherever he turned, he saw Haruko at his elbow. *She* had only been eighteen. She had been happy. Happy with the utter confidence of birth and privilege and health and motherhood, and love. Happy as perhaps no human being had any right to be. That could have been her only possible crime in the eyes of the gods.

And as she had made him so happy, thus now he could only be unhappy. Slender limbs, slender body, beautiful black hair, flawless features and pulsing heart, all his, his to love, his to worship, his to cherish, his to caress, his to *know*. His to carry, lifeless, through the mud and the sludge, back up to the wrecked hospital. Even in death, she had been as light as a feather. And when the mud and mucus had been cleaned from her mouth and eyes and nostrils, she had still been beautiful. His, for eternity. But

161

eternity had lasted for just over a year.

'What will you do?' Peter asked.

Philip turned his head. He had not heard his brother follow him into the garden. He had not really expected that much sympathy, from Peter. Yet they were brothers, as Jerry and William had been brothers. They were required to share their grief, as once they had shared their joys.

'Your leave of absence expired two days ago,' Peter reminded him. 'And you have not rejoined your ship. Mother is worried.'

'I have resigned from the navy,' Philip told him. 'I mailed the letter the day before yesterday. They will have it by now.'

'Well, I cannot criticise your decision, of course,' Peter said. 'Will you join me, in the army? We should be happy to have you.'

Philip shook his head.

Peter frowned. 'What *will* you do, then?'

'I do not know . . .'

'Philip . . .'

'I do not know,' Philip said. 'I do not *know*.'

'You may enter, honourable Captain,' said the flag-lieutenant.

Philip raised his eyebrows. Why did the fellow persist in addressing him as 'Captain' when he must know he was no longer a serving officer? He was not even wearing uniform. He had only come to the Admiralty at all because he had been commanded to do so by his uncle, and he knew that William was leaving for the United States within the week.

The lieutenant was holding the door open, and bowing as he did so. Philip stepped into the office, then checked. Apart from William Freeman, now rising from behind the desk, Isoroku Yamamoto was also present, and a third officer, also wearing naval uniform, and also dis-

162

playing the insignia of a captain's rank, a small, wizened man who looked older than he should – for the rank. His face was vaguely familiar, but Philip could not remember his name.

He bowed. 'Honourable Admiral.'

'Come in, Captain Shimadzu,' William said. 'You know Captain Yamamoto?'

William bowed again.

'And Captain Kitabake?'

Another bow. But the name stirred his memory. Ikita Kitabake was something of a mystery figure in the Japanese Navy. He had served longer than any other captain – and yet remained a captain. He had served longer than any other captain – and yet had never commanded a ship. Because he had spent his entire career on the staff, certainly. But he had spent his entire career on the staff – and yet had never been associated with strategic planning, or design planning, or tactical planning . . .

'Sit down, Captain Shimadzu,' William said.

Philip obeyed.

'This letter of resignation . . .' William flicked the sheet of paper on his desk. 'It will not, of course, be accepted.'

'With respect, honourable Admiral . . .'

'It is recognised,' William said, 'that you have suffered an enormous personal loss, an emotional catastrophe. Some others of us –' he paused, and gazed at his nephew – 'have some small idea of your feelings. But a man's worth is to be found in the way he rises above the disasters of life, not in the way he sinks beneath their load.' He glanced at Yamamoto. 'You are an officer of too much talent, too much experience, and too great value to the Imperial Japanese Navy for us to allow you to wander away from us.'

'But it is also recognised,' Yamamoto said, picking up his cue, 'that command of a ship may at this moment be

163

too great an ordeal for you. Believe me, believe us all, Captain Shimadzu, when we say that the entire navy is filled with admiration for the manner in which you saved your vessel from destruction on 1 September. Your behaviour on that day was in accord with the highest traditions of the Imperial Japanese Navy. And I may add that your crew would happily serve beneath you, now and always. However, as I say, it is felt that perhaps, for a year or two, it would be in your best interests to assume entirely new responsibilities, carry out entirely new duties, which will further your reputation and your fitness for high command in the near future, and which will be of inestimable service to your country.'

Philip waited, frowning.

'Captain Kitabake?' William Freeman invited.

The little figure stirred. 'I would welcome you in my organisation, honourable Captain,' he said.

Philip looked at his uncle, mystified.

'Captain Kitabake is the commander of Naval Intelligence,' William Freeman explained.

Of course, Philip thought. That would explain everything. But naval intelligence? 'I know nothing of intelligence work,' he said.

Kitabake smiled. 'It is not difficult. There would have to be a small period of training, to acquaint you with such things as codes and other procedures, but you would find these simple. Intelligence is more a matter of –' his smile widened – 'intelligence. That is, common sense. It is a matter of watching, and listening, and considering what one has seen and heard, and drawing conclusions. It is intensely interesting, I do assure you.'

'And who would I be watching?' Philip inquired. 'And listening to? And considering?' He could not possibly accept such a task and remain close friends with John Graham, for instance. And that was a friendship he valued too highly to consider giving up.

'We feel, in the beginning, that it would be best for you

164

to leave Tokyo, to leave Japan, indeed, for a while,' Kitabake said, gazing at him.

Philip looked at his uncle, but it was Yamamoto who spoke. 'This makes sound sense, Shimadzu San. Tokyo, Yokohama, they can have nothing but sad memories for you. A complete change of scene, of culture, even of climate, is perhaps what is needed to return you to your best.'

'I would appoint you naval attaché at Shanghai,' Kitabake said.

'Shanghai?'

'It is a very responsible post,' Kitabake assured him. 'Perhaps the most important I can offer you. You know something of our relations with China?'

Philip looked at Yamamoto. 'I know something of the army's relations with China, and their intentions.'

Kitabake gave another little smile. 'That is well put, honourable Captain.'

'However,' Philip went on, 'I do not speak any of the Chinese dialects, or Mandarin.'

'I am sure you will learn, at least Mandarin, quite easily, honourable Captain. But in fact, a knowledge of Chinese is not a prerequisite of a naval attaché in China, for reasons I will explain in a moment. And of course most Chinese connected with the coast or the sea speak at least some English, a language with which I understand you are completely conversant. However, let us consider the task before you.

'I take your point regarding the army's ambitions, and agree with you. But while all of us may not agree with the army's priorities, they are none the less valid, and of vital importance to the nation. Certainly it behoves us in the navy to endeavour to keep the army under control, to restrain them from rash adventures. Good intelligence is essential for this. And nowhere is it more essential than with regard to China.

'For the past seven years, ever since the death of Yuan

Shih-kai, China has been in a condition of utter chaos. It is no longer a nation, but a haphazard accumulation of several nations, each ruled by its own warlord, save for the Nationalist enclave in the south-east. However, it appears as if the Nationalists, this fellow Dr Sun Yat-sen, may at last be putting his house in order, and it is his avowed intention to reunite the country beneath his rule. This is nothing less than a declaration of war upon all other would-be rulers of China. Now, once upon a time it might have been possible to smile at such aspirations on the part of the amiable Dr Sun, whose efforts at unifying China beneath his rule in the past have not proved very successful. But circumstances have changed and may now be moving in Dr Sun's favour. The principal change has been the overthrow of the Tsar and the emergence of a Communist regime in Russia.

'If China and Japan have ever shared a bond, and it is the only bond our two countries have ever shared, it is a common awareness of the threat that is Russia. And I believe that most Chinese still hate and fear that colossal bear. For a while we even supposed that the threat from the north had dwindled, because of the chaos into which Russia itself seemed to be sinking, following the revolution of 1917. But now that revolution has triumphed. The Civil War is ended, and Lenin and his crew appear to be firmly in control. This too would not concern us greatly for the foreseeable future; they have more than enough internal problems. But it has now come to our notice that the Soviets, as the Russians now call themselves, are supplying Sun Yat-sen with money and arms as well as military experts, and you may be quite sure they are supplying political advisers, as well.'

'I did not know the Kuomintang was a Communist organisation,' Philip said.

'It is not, officially. And we know that there are many Nationalist leaders, especially Dr Sun's chief general, Chiang Kai-shek he calls himself, who are violently

opposed to Communism as a political system for China
. . . But that does not mean they will not ally themselves
with the Communist menace in order to achieve their
objectives. This would obviously be a worrying situation
for us, should China be united under a regime which has
even the slightest ties to Moscow. In fact, it would be an
intolerable situation, and events in China need to be
monitored very carefully. I may also repeat that the more
information we obtain on Chinese plans, the more certain we can be of preventing an accidental clash between
Nationalist troops, as they move north, and our own
soldiers in Manchuria. Such a clash, as I am sure you
appreciate, honourable Captain, could have disastrous
repercussions, and even lead to war.'

Philip stroked his chin. Of course he did not wish to
leave the navy. It was the only career he had ever considered, from his earliest memories. But equally, as these
men all clearly recognised, he was not at this moment in a
fit mental state to command a ship at sea. It was that
knowledge which had led to his resignation. But if it were
possible to remain in his chosen profession . . . and what
harm could it do? Even to his friendship with Graham, if
he was to be posted outside Japan. It might indeed help
towards a further postponement of the Strike South project, and thus give more time for a complete rapproche-
ment to be reached between Japan and the United States,
which was his greatest ambition; as Kitabake had
pointed out, the more information they could obtain on
Chinese aspirations the less likely it was that war between
the two countries could come about by accident – a war
in which the United States might well be forced to become
involved, on the Chinese side.

'I am interested in your offer, of course, honourable
Captain,' he said. 'But I am afraid I do not quite understand how I, as naval attaché in Shanghai, may obtain
any useful information at all.'

'Ah,' Kitabake said. 'Shanghai, honourable Captain,

may be regarded as the most important city in China, at this moment. It is already the greatest seaport in China; some sixty per cent of all Chinese trade leaves and enters through Shanghai. As such, it is the most valuable prize the Nationalists can gain. At present, Shanghai is virtually an independent city-state, but it has little in the way of defences; its defences rest in the warlords who control the Upper Yangtze, and whose armies are situated south of the river. But there can be no doubt that the city will be the first objective of the coming Nationalist offensive. It is also, however, a hotbed of Communist agitators and subversives. Naturally this is of enormous importance to us.

'But there is an even more important aspect of the situation, from the point of view of intelligence: Shanghai, from its importance as a trading port, is also the very centre of American, and British, and French influence in China. We also maintain a considerable presence there, as you no doubt know. Now, there can be no doubt that these Western Powers, who are just as opposed to Communism as ourselves, are also watching the situation very closely, and preparing to take certain steps in the event of certain eventualities, such as a Communist-controlled, or even a Communist-allied, Nationalist government ever taking power, or even appearing to be ready to take power.

'Obviously, for our own security it is essential for us to understand just what the Western attitudes are, how they change from week to week, and what is likely to be their eventual stance, not only *vis-à-vis* China, but *vis-à-vis* Japan as well. Especially in regard to the naval units they would deploy in these waters should it ever become necessary. You will have observed that there has been a movement, since the end of the Great War, to treat Japan as being of inferior status to the Western powers. This is a mistaken impression, one we would hope to correct in the course of time, but at *this* time we must accept the possi-

bility that the Western Powers may decide to act uni-
laterally in China, as they have more than once in the
recent past, without referring to us at all. Certainly without inviting our participation. This would of course be
intolerable. They are interested only in maintaining their
trade rights. But the sort of government which eventually
rules China is important to our very existence. All of
these things have to be discovered and considered, and
fitted into the overall strategy of our nation.'

Philip looked at his uncle.

'I would say you are being offered a very responsible
post,' William said.

'And it is not an end in itself,' Yamamoto pointed out.
'After a year or so, if you choose to request an active
command, you will of course be given priority consideration.'

'It is also possible, and indeed desirable, for you to
make yourself a home in Shanghai,' Kitabake said. 'We
would expect you to take your son, and . . . ' He raised
his eyebrows inquiringly, and glanced at the admiral.

'I am sure your mother will be able to find you a
suitable nurse for the boy,' William said, 'however sad
she may be to see you depart from Japan. But again, it is
only a temporary posting.'

Shanghai, Philip thought. Naval intelligence. A place,
and a subject, he had never supposed would touch his life
in the slightest. But also a chance to think, and perhaps
take stock of himself and his future, and give the terrible
pain in his heart the opportunity to subside.

'I accept the post,' he said. 'And am most grateful for
your understanding, honourable sirs.'

'That is very satisfactory.' William stood up, and the
other officers rose with him. 'Now, if you gentlemen
would be good enough to leave me alone with my
nephew . . . '

Yamamoto and Kitabake bowed, and left the room.
William clasped Philip's hand. 'I know you have made

the right decision, and I am proud of you for doing so. Now, there is one more thing I would ask of you. As you know, your aunt and I are leaving in three days' time for the United States. Anne is, of course, accompanying us. I would be most grateful if you would come to supper with us tonight, to say goodbye, as it were. Your mother is coming, and also your aunt and your brother.'

'I would beg to be excused from attending, honourable Uncle,' Philip said.

William Freeman's eyes narrowed. 'It is permissible to ask why?'

'I am in mourning for my wife, sir. I can attend no convivial occasions.'

'I have never heard mourning extended to a family group,' William said. 'There will only be family present tonight.'

'Nevertheless, with respect . . . '

'You do not wish to sit down with Anne Freeman.'

Philip gazed at him. 'I do not think I would contribute anything save gloom to the evening, honourable Uncle.'

William Freeman considered him for a moment, then nodded, sighing as he did so. 'A man must make his own decisions in this world, Philip. But he must also hold his own opinions. It is my opinion that you are wrong in your attitude, and that you do much wrong to an unfortunate woman. However, the decision is yours. I shall not press you further. Go to Shanghai, and come home with a smile on your face.'

'Shanghai,' John Graham said thoughtfully. 'Naval attaché. Well, Philip old son, I don't know that I can honestly congratulate you. Spying is a filthy business, at any level.'

'Do you feel filthy?' Philip asked.

'Of course,' Graham said, with his usual devastating candour. 'However, I accept that your friends, and your uncle, are only trying to help you, and if the posting keeps you in the navy, it has to be a good thing. But I shall miss you.'

'As I shall miss you, old friend,' Philip agreed. 'But I am only going for a year or two. That has been established. Will you not be here when I get back?'

'Oh, God, I suppose so. The number of reasonably junior officers in the Royal Navy who are fluent in Japanese can just about be counted on one finger. So I'm afraid I'm stuck here for some time yet.'

'Then maybe you can come down and visit with me, some time,' Philip suggested.

'Maybe,' Graham agreed. But strangely, Philip felt instinctively that his friend had no intention of ever doing that. Even more strangely, and instinctively, he felt that, without warning or reason, a sort of mental shutter had suddenly fallen between them. Because he too was now in intelligence? There could be no other reason. And yet he and Graham were friends. The very best of friends. It seemed incredible that their friendship could be affected by a purely professional requirement. But there could be no doubt that Graham regarded this farewell as final. Philip returned to his home in a deeply saddened state of mind.

'Shanghai,' Shikibu said. 'Well, no doubt it is for the best.' But she too looked utterly saddened. 'I will find you a suitable nurse for the boy.'

'Why don't you come with me?' Philip asked, holding her hands. 'You can nurse Iyeyasu yourself.'

Shikibu smiled at him. 'I do not like the Chinese,' she said. 'They murdered my husband. I can never forget that, and I would not have you forget that either. They are our natural enemies.' For a moment the smile had died, but now it returned. 'Anyway, I have things to do here. What do you wish done with your house?'

'I shall never live in it again,' Philip said. 'I do not even wish to see it again. Sell it.'

'I will rent it, for a year at least,' Shikibu said. 'Feelings change. And then,' she hurried on, as he would have protested, 'there is Maureen. I could never go away and leave her, especially now that Hilary and William have gone to the States. They are both deeply concerned about you, you know, Philip.'

'I know,' Philip said.

'Yes,' Shikibu said. 'Well, as I said, perhaps a year in Shanghai will be good for you.' She squeezed his fingers. 'I shall miss you. And the babe. Be sure you come back to me my own Philip again.'

He kissed her on the cheek. 'I shall do that, Mother. You have my word.'

Shanghai! The more he thought about it, Philip realised that the translation into this entirely different world was indeed good for him. It was not only the sights and sounds of Tokyo and Yokohama, the sights and sounds of the *Yahagi* herself, which constantly brought back the memory of that dreadful day, of everything that had happened, and was still happening, in his mind. It was the people he saw every day, too. Even his own mother. He desperately needed to be away from everyone, for a while, to think, and reflect, and to compose himself to face the rest of his life without Haruko.

But with Iyeyasu. For a month after the earthquake he had hardly been able to look at the babe. He wondered what Iyeyasu thought of it all, what he was truly aware of, in his childish subconscious. Instead of his mother, his grandmother, no less loving, and tender, and kind . . . but would not even a babe have observed a difference, in scent, in the pressure of the arms holding him? Instead of a father cooing at him and dandling him on his knee, surely his earliest memory, he now knew only a stern figure who merely kissed him good night. And instead of a mother's breast, the teat of a bottle.

But at least there was a loving hand holding the bottle.

172

He glanced down at the girl who stood beside him at the rail, the babe in her arms, also gazing at the approaching shoreline. Her name was Idzuma, and she was twenty-two years of age. She came from what would once have been known as the honin class, the serfs in Japan before the upheaval of 1867. His grandfather, Ralph Freeman, he recalled, had helped to free those serfs. But Idzuma, separated from those grim old days by three generations, fully aware of her freedom and her rights as a citizen, still understood that, compared with a Shimadzu or a Satsuma, much less a Tokugawa, she was lower than the dust beneath their feet. Yet perhaps that did not stop her aspiring; certainly she appeared to wish only to please, and in that endeavour bestowed upon her infant charge more love than even a mother could have done.

In those olden days of the last century, of course, there would have been no decision involved. A samurai slept with his honin women as a matter of course, whenever his own wife was not available, or even if she were, and he felt like variety. The honins had accepted their masters' advances because they had to, but so aware had they been of that simple fact that anger or humiliation had probably never entered into it at all; any honin woman would have been equally aware that her lord and master could chop off her head, if he wished, even if such behaviour was not generally approved save where she had actually committed a crime. But certainly he could beat her like a dog, if he chose, and be sure of approval. In many ways life had been a remarkably simple affair sixty years ago; one was what one was born, and for that reason, either lucky or unlucky.

This girl would, he knew, willingly come to his bed at the slightest invitation, and for similar reasons to those her grandmother would have felt. He might not own her, in 1924, but he was her employer, and he was a captain in the navy, and he came from a great and wealthy family. All of these factors had undoubtedly been weighed by her

173

parents when they had accepted Shikibu's offer of employment, and that they had accepted the offer indicated that they also accepted that their daughter was about to become a concubine, and would therefore never make a satisfactory ordinary marriage. They had, in effect, sold Idzuma in the hopes that she might thereby better herself, and them – and the only route to that betterment lay in the arms of her widower employer. She was a pretty little thing, too. But she was not a *thing*. There was the difference between 1924 and 1864. She could not even be taken as one might take a geisha, enjoyed and forgotten, in the knowledge that, unless one actively wished it, one would never see her face again.

Idzuma, as the nurse of his son, was a part of his life. As the nurse of his son, she could be dismissed and forgotten, should she prove dishonest or incompetent. But once she took off her kimono for him, she would be a part of his life forever. His fault. He had no doubt that should she ever take off her kimono for Hagi, standing on her other side – and he was her most likely fate, certainly once she had abandoned hopes of him – she would certainly not become a vital part of Hagi's life. But then, Hagi was of honin stock himself.

Philip's brain was too confounded by memory and ideals and fears and uncertainties. He desperately wanted a woman, physically, because he had refused himself the slightest physical relief since Haruko's death. He desperately wanted a woman, emotionally, and he desperately wanted to find a true mother for his son. But he could have none of those things, because he could never find another Haruko. And the only possible substitute for Haruko was now six thousand miles away and, in any event, so totally rejected that she must by now loathe the very thought, much less the name of Philip Shimadzu.

And there was no one else, and could be no one else, even if he knew that by prolonging this celibacy he was but perpetuating his own misery. So he merely returned

Idzuma's smile, and ruffled the thin hair on Iyeyasu's head, and gazed at the approaching shore.

The coastline was certainly interesting enough, and different enough, in every way. As he had not taken up his new appointment until after Christmas, because of the three months' training in intelligence procedures and grounding in the Chinese language that had been thought necessary, he had sailed away from Tokyo in ice and snow. But here the climate was almost sub-tropical. Japan had no great rivers; here for some miles offshore the sea was discoloured by the amount of silt brought down by the immense flow of the Yangtze Kiang. Now the ship made its way through buoyed channels between several islands, while the bottom visibly shoaled, before the huge sweep of this greatest of Asian rivers opened before them, winding its way past innumerable cities all the way from the mountains of Tibet.

The steamer proceeded, dead slow and with a pilot aboard, past a shore built up with embankments to keep out the flood waters, and for the rest low and swampy, so unlike Japan, so reminiscent in many ways of Chesapeake Bay. A subsidiary river only a few miles inside the bar led away to the south. This was the Whang Poo; and already in the distance they could see the rooftops of the biggest city in China.

Anchors plunged into the soft mud, and the steamer came to rest in the midst of several other large vessels, which were flying the flags of almost every maritime nation on earth. Launches were on hand to ferry the passengers ashore, to a dock area where Customs and Immigration waited beside the railway line which would carry the European and Japanese passengers the short distance to the International Concession. The sprawling colonial town where the non-Chinese lived, behind walls of barbed wire, was protected from any upsurge of well-remembered hatred for the 'foreign devils' by an international force which could almost be called an army, the dominant factor in which, Philip recalled, was a 'brigade' of ten thousand Japanese soldiers.

For a member of the diplomatic corps and his entourage formalities were virtually non-existent, and then they were welcomed by a secretary from the embassy who gravely introduced himself as Mr Nikuma, and added, 'Welcome to Shanghai, Captain Shimadzu. We are most pleased to receive you. We have heard much about you.'

That appeared to be the tag line which would follow him for the rest of his life, Philip supposed. But he preferred not to inquire exactly what aspect of him Nikuma was referring to – his American ancestry, his dubious credits as a sea captain, or his recent tragic past; he suspected that the last was most likely, and it was the most unwelcome to discuss, with anyone.

'It is my great pleasure to be here,' he said, and took his place in the carriage, beside Idzuma and Iyeyasu, with Hagi, unused to travelling in the same compartment as his employer, sitting opposite in silent embarrassment. Nikuma looked as if he might have been about to make some comment on the new naval attaché's domestic arrangements, but changed his mind.

'You will like the concession,' he stated. 'Do you play polo?'

'Badly,' Philip confessed.

'Ah. Auction?'

'If you mean bridge, passably.'

'Ah.' Mr Nikuma looked faintly concerned. Obviously the new naval attaché was going to require a crash course in the social graces.

Philip was more interested in the countryside through which the train was passing, low-lying and swampy and featureless, devoid of any interest save for the odd pagoda. And for the people. They passed groups of soldiers, in somewhat shapeless khaki uniforms; and groups of peasants, peering at the train as if still unused to such iron monsters careering about their countryside. They wore broad-brimmed and crownless hats, and shapeless clothes consisting of blouses and trousers, in bright colours, certainly, with reds and blues predominating, but all clearly filthy, and making it utterly impossible to tell at a distance the difference between the sexes.

But the difference, he thought, between the two dominant peoples of East Asia, was quite remarkably distinct. Physically, in that the Chinese were on the whole larger and somewhat paler of complexion than the average Japanese, but even more in their lifestyles. Japan stood for neatness and intensity; China, apparently, sprawled with careless indifference to either. From the window of a Japanese train one would see only cultivated fields or mountains or lakes; here there were only rice paddies or open pasturage or swamps. One would never see a Japanese woman in trousers, or other than recently bathed, freshly perfumed and coiffured, and neatly dressed; it was difficult to suppose some of the women he was now looking at had ever encountered soap and water, much less brush and make-up. Japanese men hurried, pursuing their daily tasks and their ambitions with equal fervour; Chinese men lounged, and moved without enthusiasm, when they moved at all.

'They are savages,' Idzuma commented, briefly and disparagingly.

'That is unfortunately true of most of them,' Mr Nikuma agreed. 'But we make them work in the concession.'

There was only one railway station between the docks and the city itself. Here they left the train, without regret, and entered a comfortable American-made automobile, which whisked them through wide, clean streets and between neat little houses; this was still not a Japanese town, but it was an English or American colonial one rather than Chinese.

'Your house is in here,' Nikuma explained, as the automobile turned in to what seemed a large compound.

The whole concession vaguely reminded Philip of a compound, isolated from the rest of the countryside as it was, and surrounded by its barbed-wire fencing and strongly guarded gateways. But now it appeared that the interior of the concession, apart from the shopping centre, was a series of smaller compounds. Above this one there flew the Rising Sun of Japan, and there were armed Japanese soldiers on the gates; the houses within, some twenty of them, were also entirely surrounded by individual wire fencing.

'Are we being placed in a prison?' Philip wondered.

Mr Nikuma smiled, deprecatingly. 'Arrangements such as this make it easier for security. You must remember that all foreigners are hated by the average Chinese, and that we Japanese are hated more than most. It was we who brought the Manchu pack of cards tumbling down to defeat, and however much the Chinese may be glad to have seen the back of the Manchu as rulers, they still remember us as their natural enemies. Thus we restrict entry to the concession to those who are needed to work here, or who have business here. Of course, the guards on the gates make it difficult for any unauthorised person to get in, but still, some do get through even the check.'

'For what purpose?' Philip asked.

'Well, at the very least, to burgle. They are a very poor people, and anyone who lives in the concession is by their standards necessarily a millionaire.' Nikuma's tone did not betray any sympathy for those very poor people who sought to redress the inequality of society. 'But some also come to murder,' he went on. 'They are quite fanatical in their hatred.'

Philip looked at Idzuma, who was clutching Iyeyasu somewhat nervously; she clearly hadn't contemplated finding herself in some kind of front line when she accepted this post.

Mr Nikuma observed her reaction, and gave another

of his smiles. 'However, no one has ever got inside the Japanese diplomatic compound,' he told them, 'and lived to tell about it. This is your house.'

The house was equally unlike anything either Idzuma or Hagi had ever seen before, being simply a European-style colonial bungalow, as were all the other houses in the enclosure. A wide front verandah gave access to a living-cum-dining room, behind which to one side was the kitchen, while to the other a corridor led to three bedrooms and two bathrooms. The whole was surrounded by green lawns and occasional flower-beds.

'The gardener is supplied by the embassy,' Mr Nikuma hastened to explain.

Philip allotted the back bedroom to Hagi, and the smaller of the two front ones to Idzuma; Nikuma had made the necessary arrangements and there was a cot already waiting for Iyeyasu, who would share the room with his nurse.

'This is a palace, honourable Captain,' Idzuma said, gazing in wonder at the size of the place, while Philip wondered what she would make of the Freemans' house outside Stanford. Then he wondered what would become of that house now, and hastily changed the direction of his thoughts.

'You are pleased?' Nikuma asked.

'Oh, very,' Philip said. 'I am sure we will be very comfortable here.'

'That is satisfactory,' Nikuma said. 'Now, here is Major Mori to greet you.'

Philip turned in surprise, faced the man who had just entered the front door. In place of uniform he wore a white duck suit and carried a soft straw hat. He was rather small, even for a Japanese, and about Philip's own age. He wore a little moustache, like Peter, and carried himself with the trained stiffness of an army officer. Now he gave a stiff, brief bow.

'Captain Shimadzu?'

179

Philip bowed in turn. 'Major Mori?'

'That is correct. You have heard of me?'

'Only from Mr Nikuma,' Philip said. 'But I am pleased to make your acquaintance.'

Mori glanced at Nikuma, who hastily bowed, having clearly performed his allotted task. 'I shall leave you now,' he said and almost scuttled for the door.

'Your servants?' Mori asked.

'Are unpacking my things.'

Mori nodded, and carefully closed the door to the corridor. 'I have some things to say to you in private, honourable Captain.'

Philip raised his eyebrows. As a captain in the navy he outranked a major in the army, but Mori hardly seemed aware of that fact, except in his respectful address. 'Are you the military attaché?' he asked. 'And should you not be in uniform?'

Mori returned from the door. 'The answer to both of those questions is no, honourable Captain. Is it permitted to sit?'

'Of course.' Philip also sat down. Now he was intrigued.

'Kitabake San did not mention me to you?' Mori asked, placing his hat carefully beside himself on the settee.

'No,' Philip replied.

'Ah. But he has written to me to expect you. Our families share a considerable bond.'

'Indeed?'

'Oh, indeed. Your uncle, Admiral Freeman, killed my father, Colonel Mori, in a duel.'

Philip gazed at him. Good for Uncle William, he thought.

'I was just a boy then, of course,' Mori explained.

'So was I, I imagine,' Philip said. The old devil; what a lot of magnificent secrets Uncle William had tucked away up his sleeves.

180

'Still, that is in the past, and has no bearing upon the present,' Mori went on, 'except to convince me, as it has obviously convinced Kitabake San, that you are a man of much courage and ability, coming as you do from such a redoubtable family. That is good. We shall work closely together, you and I.'

'Doing what?' Philip asked.

'Protecting the interests of our country,' Mori said severely. 'All information obtained by you will be passed immediately to me, and correlated to such information as I myself have been able to glean, before my people forward it to Tokyo.'

'Your people? You are a marine officer?'

'No, honourable Captain. I hold a military rank.'

'Then I do not understand,' Philip said.

'Have you never heard of the Kempai?'

Philip frowned. 'I have heard of the Kempai.'

'And were you not aware that all naval and military attachés, all embassy staff, indeed, on foreign stations, and especially where those foreign stations are situated in countries which may be regarded as hostile to Japanese interests, come directly under the jurisdiction of the Kempai?'

'No,' Philip said. 'I did not know that.' Or I would not have accepted this posting, he thought. And then wondered if Graham had known that – which would account for the Scot's sudden coolness towards him.

'Well, it is so,' Mori went on. 'As Captain Kitabake is well aware. He is a member of the Kempai himself.'

'Kitabake?' Philip wondered if his uncle knew *that*. But William was in America on extended leave of absence.

'It is surprising he did not mention it,' Mori went on. 'However, you are welcome to use the embassy telegraph to contact Captain Kitabake and confirm the truth of what I am saying.'

'I do not doubt the truth of what you are saying for an instant,' Philip protested. Nor did he. However instantly

181

dislikeable, Mori was a Japanese officer, and for a Japanese officer ever to lie was unthinkable. 'I am merely surprised, as Captain Kitabake did not appraise me of the situation. However, I am perfectly willing to cooperate with the Kempai in every way.' Until, he thought, I can obtain a transfer, as rapidly as possible. 'Perhaps you will inform me of the name of the commanding officer here in Shanghai, and how soon I may meet him.'

Mori smiled. 'You have already done so, Captain Shimadzu. I am the officer commanding the Kempai in Shanghai, and indeed, all Eastern China. As of this moment, you will take your orders from me.'

CHAPTER 7

The Anger

Philip's consternation was complete, and obvious. Mori smiled contentedly. 'It is considered best that I should hold the rank of major,' he explained. 'And be considered assistant military attaché. I do not wish to attract any more publicity than is necessary. But we are faced with an immense task here, Captain Shimadzu. Has Nikuma San told you anything of the situation?'

'He considers all Chinese to be thugs, I gather,' Philip said.

'He is unfortunately quite correct in that assumption,' Mori said. 'And they are thugs who hate us. They hate all foreigners, but the Japanese more than most. While those of them who are Communist are the worst of all. You will remember that unpleasantness we had in Korea five years ago?'

Philip frowned. He remembered that there had been a revolt against Japanese rule in Korea towards the end of the Great War, and that it had been put down with great severity by the Japanese army.

'I see that you do,' Mori went on. 'Well, that was Communist-inspired. I regard them, emanating as they do with their pernicious doctrines from Russia, another of our hereditary enemies, as the most severe threat our nation has to face. I understand that you have been told your chief duties will be to consider the possible unification of China under a Nationalist regime from a naval point of view, and more importantly, to learn all you can about Western naval strengths in Chinese waters, and their projected strengths as well. I would not have you neglect your duties in these directions; it is important work. But above all you must fight the Communist spectre. *We* must fight it, shoulder to shoulder, and we must extirpate it wherever we can. To this end, it is sometimes necessary to, shall I say, bend the rules of international diplomacy, international usage, from time to time. But as it is necessary, it must be done. I wish you to understand this.'

Philip listened; he had no idea what the man meant.

'That is why I make my headquarters *here*,' Mori continued, 'and not in Canton, or Peking. Shanghai is the very centre of the Communist movement in China. The city is riddled with Communist cells. The students and young people are controlled by them. It would, for example, be highly dangerous for you ever to enter the Chinese city, even with a strong escort; you would be mobbed and perhaps even lynched, and the authorities would just stand there and look on. Every movement against Japanese interests emanates from Shanghai, and is Communist-inspired. They are our enemies. And they must be defeated. I do not wish you to have any doubts about this, honourable Captain.'

'How could I?' Philip murmured, wondering if he had ever met a Communist in his life, and if he would recognise one if he did.

'Good,' Mori said, and his face relaxed into a singularly charming smile. 'So come with me, and I will show you the hub of my organisation: my house. My automobile is outside.'

Mori's house was not, surprisingly, in the Japanese diplomatic compound, but in fact some distance away, standing in its own grounds, and considerably larger than the average bungalow, although it was single-storeyed. But it, too, was surrounded by a wire fence, and there were even more guards here than at the compound.

The front of the house was conventional enough, but from the kitchen a door led into several small, inter-connecting rooms, used as offices and containing a great deal of radio and coding equipment, and occupied by several male secretaries, all apparently hard at work.

'The centre of the intelligence system for all of China,' Mori told him proudly. 'Here we are in constant contact with Tokyo, as well as with army headquarters in Manchuria.'

'But, do not the Chinese know of the existence of this place?' Philip asked.

'Indeed they do. There can be no doubt of it. But there is nothing they can do about it. They would need an army to get in here. And it would be an act of war, for any Chinese military force to enter the International Con-cession. War, honourable Captain, upon all the world. Indeed, it would suit our strategy admirably were they to attempt to do so.'

Philip took his point. But how galling must it be, he thought, for the Chinese to have to admit 'international concessions' at all. Was it possible to imagine Japan permitting a foreign enclave within its own territory, quite beyond the reach of Japanese laws? Or the United States? Or Great Britain?

'Now, here,' Mori was continuing, but stopped as a man entered the farthest door and gave a stiff bow. 'Yoshine,' Mori said, obviously pleased to see the new arrival. 'I had not expected you back so soon. Captain Shimadzu, I would have you meet my aide, Captain Yoshine. Captain Shimadzu is our new naval attaché.'

Yoshine bowed again, before shaking hands. 'It is a great honour, honourable Captain.'

'You have information for me?' Mori asked.

Yoshine smiled. 'I have more than information, honourable Major. It is possible to say that the venture was a success.' Like his superior, he wore civilian clothes, somewhat crushed and soiled. But he looked very pleased with himself. 'I have one.'

Mori raised his eyebrows. 'But that is success indeed. We will come immediately. This will interest you, Shimadzu San. It will show you what we are up against.'

Mystified, Philip followed Mori and Yoshine through the final door and down a short flight of steps into a sunken garage. The doors of the garage were closed, entirely shutting out all light and sound from the outside world, and presumably preventing any from escaping the interior as well; electric bulbs gleamed on two cars, one of which had clearly just arrived, and on four men, Japanese, also in plain clothes, standing about it.

'In the boot,' Yoshine said.

'Have you spoken?' Mori asked, very quietly.

'English.'

'Then we will continue that. Open it.'

Yoshine nodded to one of his henchmen, who unlocked the boot and raised it. Mori moved forward, and Philip followed him, still totally mystified. Yoshine helpfully shone a flashlight into the interior, to reveal the huddled body of a young Chinese man, bound wrist and ankle, and also blindfolded. But he was no coolie; he wore Western-style clothes. And even through the blindfold he could see the glare of the lights. 'Where am I?' he asked, in English. 'I will have the law on you. I . . . '

'Take him out,' Mori commanded, also speaking English.

Two of the waiting men seized the young man by the shoulders and jerked him out of the car; he hit his head and fell to the oil-stained concrete floor of the garage, gasping in pain.

'Do you mean you have powers of arrest?' Philip asked, aghast at seeing another human being so ill-treated.

'Unfortunately, no,' Mori said. 'It is necessary to use persuasion to get these vermin to come and visit us.'

'You mean you have kidnapped this man? But on what grounds? Is he guilty of some crime against . . .'

Mori held up his finger warningly. 'Against mankind, my friend. He is certainly guilty of murder. Amongst other things. Of that we can be quite sure.'

The young man's head jerked; he had been listening. Now he twisted from side to side. 'Who are you?' he gasped. 'What do you want with me? You have kidnapped me. You are criminals. You . . .'

Mori nodded, and Yoshine stepped forward, seized the young man's lank black hair to lift his head and slapped him hard across the face. The young man gasped again, and blood dribbled from his burst lips. 'We are pleased that you are anxious to speak with us,' Mori told him. 'But you must simply answer our questions.'

Two of the guards pulled the young man to his knees. He still panted, and tears rolled out from beneath the eye-bandage. He was starting to shiver as well.

'What is your name?' Mori asked.

'My name is Tang. Henry Tang,' the young man said.

Mori looked at Yoshine, who stepped forward again, tore open the young man's jacket, turned out the pockets of his jacket and trousers, and thumbed through a wallet. 'That is his name,' Yoshine said.

'You have no right,' the young man gasped. 'You . . .'

'What is your occupation?' Mori asked.

'I am a schoolmaster in Shanghai. I am . . .'

'You are also a Communist courier and agitator,' Mori's voice hardened.

The young man's mouth closed.

'That is why you are here,' Mori told him. 'We know who you are, and what you do. You plot the murder of foreign officials and businessmen. You belong to a society which is determined to drive all foreigners from China. Is that not so?'

'You are Japanese?' the young man asked.

Yoshine kicked him in the belly. Henry Tang retched

187

and then vomited, his body writhing, but still he was held on his knees by the men grasping his shoulders.

'I will ask the questions,' Mori reminded him. 'Now, Henry Tang, we know that *your* principal occupation is carrying messages from Shanghai to a certain Wu Chi in Nanking, and then orders from this Wu Chi back to your people in Shanghai. We know that this Wu Chi is your superior, and an important member of the Communist conspiracy. What we do not know is who this Wu Chi is. That is what we wish you to tell us. Our agents in Nanking have been quite unable to discover the identity of this mysterious fellow with the woman's pseudonym. Satisfy our curiosity.'

The young man's head turned right and left again; now vomit had joined the blood staining his chin.

'If you do not tell us,' Mori said, 'we shall cause you much pain. Much pain,' he said thoughtfully. 'And much sadness.'

The young man inhaled, trying to get his nerves under control as the pain of the kick began to fade. 'You have kidnapped me,' he said again. 'On Chinese soil. You have . . .'

'Take him to the table,' Mori commanded.

The guards dragged Henry Tang across the floor, feet trailing, to the inner recesses of the garage, where there was a large work-bench, stained with a variety of liquids . . . To Philip's horror, he was sure that at least one of them was blood. On this table they dumped Henry Tang, on his back, their companions moving forward to assist them. The boy gasped and tried to resist them, but was helpless, bound hand and foot as he was.

Mori stood above him, while Philip watched, feeling faintly sick. *I would involve no man with the Kempai intentionally*, Yamamoto had said: *unless he is the most utter villain.* Had Yamamoto known? Known what? But he was about to find out.

'I wish you to identify Wu Chi,' Mori said quietly.

'Otherwise you will never enjoy a woman again.'

Henry Tang gasped and heaved his hips and belly, the only parts of him that could move.

Mori nodded to Yoshine, who unbuckled the prisoner's belt, dragged trousers and underpants down to his knees, leaving him exposed and helpless, and alert, as if his penis knew what might be going to happen to it. Philip found he was holding his breath, aware of a most peculiar mixture of feelings pervading both mind and body: revulsion and horror, certainly – but also excitement and expectation, which he knew would leave him ashamed in retrospect.

Yoshine went to the wall, where a variety of tools were hanging, and returned with a large adjustable wrench, which he handed to his superior. He then stood by Tang and grasped his thighs, pressing them into the table, as his men did with the boy's shoulders and ankles. Obscenely, the penis was now hard, as terrified blood pumped into it.

'For the last time,' Mori said. 'Will you identify Wu Chi?'

'No,' the boy gasped. 'Never . . .'

Mori took the penis in his left hand, as a butcher might have held a piece of meat he was about to carve for a customer's satisfaction. But more tenderly, Philip realised. Mori even stroked the blood-filled flesh before tightening his grip, as if seeking sexual satisfaction for them both. With his right hand, he slid the jaws of the wrench over one of the testicles, and thumbed the wheel to close the jaws until the sac was held firmly. Another turn of the wheel, and the young man gasped and moaned and made a convulsive, but futile, effort to move.

'Mori,' Philip said, his voice thick. This could not really be happening.

Mori ignored him, and turned the wheel once more. The jaws sank into the flesh and the young man screamed, and now Yoshine needed all his strength to keep him flat on the table.

Mori thumbed the wheel again, and Philip struck his shoulder. Mori turned in surprise, and the wrench slipped to the table. The boy gasped.

'This is medieval,' Philip snapped.

'But efficient,' Mori told him. 'Our ancestors knew a great deal about forcing confessions. And they did not have such tools readily to hand.'

'You will kill him.'

'No, no,' Mori said. 'Not until he has told me what I wish to know, anyway. But I will crush his balls to powder.'

'I will report this to the ambassador,' Philip said. 'If you do not stop, this instant.'

Mori smiled. 'You are being childish, Shimadzu San. Do you not suppose the ambassador knows the methods we are forced to employ?'

'Nevertheless, you cannot so ill-treat this man. Any man.'

'I can, and I will, do anything that furthers the cause of Japan,' Mori told him, and turned back to his panting victim; at least the pain had caused the erection to collapse. He fitted the spanner to the testicle again, and the boy screamed.

'Wu Chi,' he shrieked.

'Yes?' Mori asked, bending his head.

'She *is* a woman,' Henry Tang gasped. 'But you will never touch her.'

'Tell me why,' Mori said, and thumbed the wheel.

The young man cried out again, and resumed his writhing. 'She is the daughter of the mayor himself. The daughter of the mayor.'

Mori straightened. 'How foolish we are. Of course. Mr Wu. Do you know, Shimadzu San, it just never crossed my mind that Wu could be her real name?' He smiled. 'And you say my methods are not efficient?'

Philip left the garage.

*

190

Ambassador Shirikawa gave a sad and somewhat tired smile. 'Sit down, honourable Captain, please. I repeat, it is a great pleasure to have you in Shanghai, and to meet the nephew of so famous a hero as Admiral Freeman. But even men like you must take the world as they find it.'

'Honourable sir, I came here under a mistaken impression.'

'You were, perhaps, improperly briefed. If it is any comfort to you, your predecessor suffered from the same drawback, but he remained here for his term of duty. I think it is possibly a failing amongst naval officers, that they are too able to divorce themselves from reality. Consider, honourable Captain, you spend your life in a private world, a world of men dedicated to the same cause, the same profession, the same arts, as yourself. No one else may, or can, impinge upon that sense of unity and purpose, once a ship is at sea. And then, when you engage an enemy, it is at a distance of several miles. You never see the face of the man you kill, never feel his hot breath on you, never see the blood-lust in his eye.'

Philip began to wonder if the ambassador was not a frustrated actor.

'It is different with the army, where one shares perhaps a greater intimacy with the object of one's hate,' Shirikawa said. 'I would put it to you, Captain Shimadzu, that Major Mori is doing a most valuable and important job. A thoroughly distasteful one, I do assure you . . .'

'Not to him, honourable sir,' Philip interrupted.

'Possibly not, now. But then, if he did find it as distasteful as you have done, would he be able to perform his duties at all adequately? And we need the information he obtains. All nations use intelligence services, and counter-intelligence services, and the task is never pleasant. And you must not forget that this man – Tang, did you say his name was? – is certainly an avowed enemy of ours. It may have sickened you to see him tortured, but do not be under any illusion that were he to see you

191

walking alone down a deserted street he would not immediately stick a knife in your back, and laugh as he did so.'

'Nevertheless, honourable sir . . . '

'As his ancestors killed your illustrious father,' Shirikawa said gently. 'In a most brutal and horrible fashion, I have heard.'

Philip gazed at him. There was no argument to put against that. 'It is still my intention to seek an immediate transfer, honourable sir.'

'And I would recommend that you do not.' Shirikawa held up a finger as Philip would have spoken. 'There are aspects of this situation you have perhaps not fully considered, Captain Shimadzu. Firstly, that by returning to Tokyo you will harm no one but yourself; certainly you will not change anything that may happen to any Chinese Communist who falls into Mori's hands. Secondly, that you were sent here because it was felt that, in your recent tragic bereavement, you could not be asked to command a ship at sea; to flee within a week might arouse doubts as to whether you can usefully be employed anywhere. Thirdly, Mori has no cause to love you. He has no cause to love anyone related to Admiral Freeman. It is somewhat, not to say very, unusual for him to display his methods to a new attaché within hours of his arrival. Do you not suppose he was throwing down a challenge, hoping that you would, indeed, turn tail and run?'

'You make it seem like a matter of honour,' Philip grumbled.

'It is, in many ways,' Shirikawa agreed. 'And you are an intensely honourable man. I should be sorry to see you go. I need honourable men about me.'

'So I stay, and accept that what happens must happen?'

'That is the wisest course, for the time being.'

'I will never work closely with a man like Mori, honourable sir.'

Shirikawa shrugged. 'You do not truly have to. I will explain your feelings to him, and you may remit your information directly to Tokyo. Now come, I am pleased with your decision. It is a victory for common sense. I would have you meet Colonal Asawa, who is the real military attaché. And then we must make preparations for a dinner party to welcome you to Shanghai . . . and introduce you to the society here.'

Asawa turned out to be as charming as Mori was unpleasant. But Philip none the less returned home in a thoroughly unhappy frame of mind. He had acted as a Japanese officer should, according to both Shirikawa and Asawa, but he had certainly not acted as an honourable man, he was sure. And now he must just accept the situation, knowing, whenever he met Mori, that that smiling face might just have come from tormenting some other poor creature, whose only crime was that he resented the way the foreign devils lorded it over his beleaguered country.

Because he had no alternative. He knew Shirikawa was right. Everyone was bending over backwards to help him through his misery. But there was a limit to how much help even his uncle could give, if he continually shied away from every unpleasant task he was given to perform, or was forced to associate with.

'Master will kiss Baby goodnight?' Idzuma asked from the doorway.

'Yes.' Philip went into the nursery and gave Iyeyasu a perfunctory peck on the cheek.

'Master is unhappy,' Idzuma suggested, softly.

He turned to look at her; her fingers were playing with the sash of her kimono. 'Yes,' he said.

'Then why does Master not be happy,' she said, and the kimono fell open.

*

She seemed to be as hungry as he. After so many weeks he thrust again and again, and she responded with almost triumphant spasms of her pelvis. His ultimate fate, a honin woman. But was that not in perfect harmony with what he had now become: a Japanese officer who obeyed orders and believed utterly in the integrity of the state, regardless of any evidence he might obtain to the contrary. How foolish he was ever to have supposed he could be anything different.

In that mood, he could throw himself whole-heartedly into his new duties which, as the ambassador had suggested, first of all necessitated social acceptance by the other residents of the concession. This did not present any difficulty whatsoever for a handsome young widower with a tragic background and a delightful baby son. Invitations flooded his office, to attend tea parties and luncheon parties and dinner parties, to join such and such a consul or vice-consul and his family in their box to watch horse-racing – which was a very popular pastime, the concession having its own racecourse within the perimeter – or polo matches.

It seemed a remarkable occupation for a naval officer, and he could not see that he was actually learning anything of any value to Japan. He played tennis with the British naval attaché and his wife and the wife of the British consul, and discovered that *HMS Nelson*, on completion, might well make a combined shakedown and show-the-flag cruise to the Pacific, but she certainly would never be stationed there.

He discussed the importance of this with Asawa, but the colonel merely snorted. 'The British, Shimadzu San,' he said, 'are a has-been nation. They are like a snake with its head cut off, which continues to wriggle for several minutes. But those are the muscular convulsions of a dying creature.'

Thinking both of John Graham and the fact that in *Nelson* and *Rodney* Great Britain now possessed the two

194

most powerful battleships in the world, Philip could not really agree with that point of view. But he kept his opinions to himself and duly relayed the information to Tokyo. In any event, the Shanghai naval attaché was not the least like Graham: he *was* a silly ass.

He played cards with the French consul and his beautiful wife and the Swedish chargé d'affaires, and learned that the French had not yet made up their minds what kind of battleships to build. 'They are such costly toys,' M. Defarge pointed out. 'And it has not yet been proved which designs are the best.' Philip did not bother to relay that information at all, nor did he discuss the situation with Asawa; he had no doubt the military attaché considered the French even more passé than the British.

He had dinner with the American consul and his wife. Mr and Mrs Carruthers had known Jerry and Elizabeth Freeman, and were deeply sympathetic about their tragic fates. 'You just never can tell what's going to happen,' Carruthers opined. 'Life can be one hell of a messy business.'

He divulged over the port that the Americans were thinking more in terms of aircraft-carriers than battleships at this moment, but that naval opinions in Washington were hopelessly divided. He also revealed that Billy Mitchell, the apostle of air as opposed to sea warfare, was to be courtmartialled for criticising his superiors – which seemed a little hard if the United States Navy was actually in the process of taking his advice. 'Crazy, mixed-up world, isn't it,' Carruthers agreed.

Asawa was more interested in that, because, he said, 'Clearly America is the only foe we have to fear in the near future, Shimadzu San. And it may interest you to know that they feel the same about us. Indeed they do,' he went on, as he observed the sceptical look on Philip's face. 'Their war department classifies us as Code Word Orange, as opposed to Black or Grey for a possible war against a European adversary. And our information is that they are concentrating more and more on Orange, as opposed to any of the others. And that, honourable Captain, means they are concentrating on your navy, not my army, for the simple reason that a war between Japan and the United States can only ever be a naval war.'

Philip refused to take him seriously; it was just too far-fetched to be believed. In fact, life for a naval attaché in a place like Shanghai was a make-believe existence at every level. It had never before occurred to him that he could actually be working by attending dinner and cock-tail parties or playing tennis, or boating on the Yangtze in the company of half a dozen laughing men and pretty girls of every nation under the sun. As for the Chinese, he hardly ever saw them. Mori had apparently been right in his opinion that for a Japanese officer to venture into the Chinese city would be to provoke an instant riot; he was expressly forbidden to undertake such an adventure by the ambassador.

Equally, it had never occurred to him that he would ever have a mistress, much less maintain her in his own home. Presumably everyone supposed he slept with his son's nurse, but Idzuma was a very level-headed girl and never treated him with less than uttermost respect, even when they were alone together. She was not Haruko, in any possible way. But she helped to dull the sharp edge of memory, and in many ways she preserved his sanity, he was sure; because almost every day it was necessary to encounter Mori, and bow politely.

He did not know if the Kempai commander was aware of his conversation with the ambassador. But he did know that Mori regarded him with contempt, just as he knew that the Kempai was going on its way, making up its own rules of ethics and conduct, as Shirikawa had said it would. And that therefore he had played the part of the most arrant coward, no matter how he tried to convince himself that he was, in fact, following the necessary paths of duty and patriotism.

Thus not even in the eager arms of Idzuma was it possible to be happy. After his first month in Shanghai he felt so depressed and bedevilled, so much the charlatan at having to laugh and smile and flirt with all the unattached young English and American and French and even Russian women in the concession who considered him fair game, regardless of his existing domestic arrangements, that he sat down and wrote Anne. It was less a letter than an outpouring of spirit, in the one direction where he felt sure he would not be criticised or reminded of his position and his responsibilities . . . But he was wrong, because she never replied.

It was only a few weeks after he had realised that she was not going to reply that an incident occurred which entirely changed his attitude to life. He was in any event feeling resentful at the way she had let him down, even as his own better self was reminding him that it was he who had refused to say goodbye to her, when he was awakened one morning by a tremendous burst of noise – rifle shots, screams and shouts – from the direction of the concession railway station. Mori had said that it would be an act of war for the Chinese ever to attempt to gain control of the concession, and this certainly sounded like a war.

He dressed in great haste, warned Hagi and Idzuma not to leave the house under any circumstances until his return, and hurried out, to encounter both Asawa and Mori, although the Japanese soldiery were conspicuous by their absence.

Mori was in a state of high glee. 'The British were on guard at the station,' he explained, 'when some Communist youths came up and began stoning them. They opened fire. I am told a good number of the students have been killed. Good riddance; they were all Communists, of course. But it is good that the British have been drawn closer to our problems. They spend too much of their time in criticising us. Now, perhaps, they will understand that we must face this menace shoulder to shoulder.' He gazed at Philip. 'It would be for the good of Japan were everyone to realise that.'

He was a dedicated man, Philip thought. Even if also a scoundrel.

That the British could shoot down stone-armed students was almost as unthinkable as that a Japanese officer could squeeze the testicle of a Chinese suspect with a wrench. It seemed to make nonsense of everything Philip had always believed, and certainly to make nonsense of Graham's disapproval of his new posting. It almost convinced him that people like his uncle and Isoroku Yamamoto and Ambassador Shirikawa were right, and that one should take an absolutely pragmatic view of the world – and that one's honour should also be viewed in that light. The ideal concept was obviously to do his duty and fear no consequences.

This new resolution was helped by the arrival in the summer of Shikibu, to his great delight; he had been able to convince her that she need not meet a single Chinese if she did not wish to. His mother, with her virulently nationalistic principles, was the ideal person to reassure him that his new attitude was entirely correct.

He had warned Idzuma that she must be utterly circumspect during Shiki's visit, but Shiki herself immediately understood the situation. 'She is a good girl,' she said. 'And for you, as well. It is well said, no man need ever marry more than once, presuming he has a son by that marriage, and a willing servant.'

A totally Japanese point of view. But one which it seemed he needed to adopt. Yet the doubts remained. The following year, 1925, he returned to Tokyo for a long leave. The family were all well, and it seemed that the very last scar left by the earthquake had been removed. Even Anne, by all accounts, was doing well in medical school, although of course there was a long way to go before she could dream of qualifying.

Perhaps it was the memory of her which still haunted him – just as her refusal to answer his letter angered him whenever he thought of it – that led him back into self-doubt. 'I am marking time,' he told his uncle as they strolled in the garden. 'Stagnating.'

'Everyone marks time, occasionally,' William remarked in his usual philosophical manner. 'Do you wish to return to active service?'

Philip hesitated. He did not know. His last memory of active service was of standing on the bridge of the *Yahagi* watching that tidal wave coming towards him. And from that memory stemmed so many others. He did not know what his reaction would be, should he ever find himself standing on a bridge at a moment of crisis again.

'I think you should give it another year or two,' William suggested, watching him closely. 'You are doing good work, and more important, it is work that has to be done. And you are gaining in seniority. Another two years, perhaps. You could be ready for a battleship.'

Philip stroked his chin. 'You know that I am really working for the Kempai?'

'I know that the Kempai are everywhere,' William answered.

'More than that,' Philip said, and told him of Mori, in the most general terms.

'A small world,' William commented, more interested in the man himself than in Philip's suggestion of sadism in his treatment of prisoners. 'Still, you know, his father was a fine officer. We fought in 1905 over a difference of opinion as to his treatment of Russian prisoners of war, much indeed as you have found cause to quarrel with this Mori. But I have often regretted my duel with his father. I am glad the son does not appear to bear a grudge.'

Which was very typical of Uncle William's attitude to life, Philip thought. But not everyone regarded the Kempai in so relaxed a light, apparently, whatever their own national weaknesses. When he telephoned the British Embassy to invite John Graham for a set of tennis, the Scot politely refused.

It was a polarisation which Philip deeply regretted. But the British were now in deep water in the Far East, as the Chinese as a whole launched a boycott of British goods in retaliation for the shooting of the students in 1924. Graham himself therefore had to carry a burden of guilt.

For Philip, life after his Tokyo holiday settled into a very easy rhythm. It was even possible, now, to look on the bungalow in Shanghai as home; more so, indeed, than his house in Tokyo, which was being let by Shikibu. But the fact was that he had only lived for one year in the Tokyo house – and then had been away at sea for nearly half of that time – and he had already spent two years in Shanghai. Besides, there were no unpleasant memories connected with the Shanghai house; he no longer saw Haruko coming towards him whenever a door opened. In fact, her memory was at last beginning to fade at every level, even if he still kept a photograph of her on his bedside table. As his mother kept saying in her letters, it was time, and it was surely possible, to start thinking of re-creating his domestic life. If only, as Shikibu put it, for the sake of the boy. In July 1926 Iyeyasu was three years old, and he had lived nearly all of his life in China. This alone was a disturbing thought. Shikibu made no reference to Idzuma. She regarded the girl as good for Philip, but in a limited fashion. A Shimadzu could never form a permanent attachment to a honin woman. Well, for that matter, Philip knew that he did not look at Idzuma with any permanency in mind; but for the moment he was not prepared to look anywhere else.

He realised that taking a second wife, from his own class, was as imponderable a future as ever again standing on the bridge of a warship. He did not even know if he would be able to consummate a sexual relationship with a new wife; there were difficulties enough, whenever he allowed memory to intervene, with Idzuma. He had, in a most un-Japanese but entirely American fashion, managed to allow the tragedy of his life to get on top of him, like a cold, wet blanket, and now he did not know how to kick the blanket off. Or even if he wanted to. Idzuma supplied his physical requirements, without intrusion or argument, and above all, without emotional involvement. He could well remember his feelings as they had first steamed into the Yangtze. Idzuma had indeed become a vital part of his life. To throw her out for a more permanent mate did not appeal to him in the least.

As for the young ladies of the concession, who in the beginning, be they English or American or French, or even Russian, had found him so attractive, they were at last concluding that he did indeed have a mistress tucked away at home, because he had never availed himself of the many opportunities carefully placed in his way by both ambitious females and their equally ambitious mothers.

So where did his future lie? He had been sent to Shanghai to think, he reminded himself, as much as for the obtaining of any useful information, which was fairly widely known anyway. And it was occurring to him that thinking was never a pastime he had indulged in to any great extent. He had imbibed a great deal of knowledge, not only in seamanship and naval warfare, but in classical literature and maths and the various important Japanese arts such as swordsmanship and wrestling, and had come to regard himself as an erudite and even a talented man — as others certainly considered him. But he had spent his entire life beneath the aegis of his uncle, and beneath the aegis of his family name. That had taken him, ever since he could remember, in the direction of the navy, and since becoming a cadet he had never done anything more than

201

obey orders; even in his marriage he had done nothing more than carry out the edict of his family. Happily, in the case of Haruko.

But he had never thought for himself, and wherever such thoughts had even started to intrude, he had hastily rejected them. That had been the case with Anne, and it had been the case with his instinctive rejection of the Strike South Plan.

But then, he *had* no other task in life but to obey orders, carefully, and rigidly, looking to neither left nor right, until he himself assumed command. But even then he would obey orders. The orders of his superiors, the orders of his caste – and, he very much feared, the orders of bushido. Only the tactical carrying-out of such orders would ever be left to his discretion.

So where did the orders originate? With some unsuspected ambition, lost in the interior of the Imperial Palace? He did not believe that. The orders were lost in the mists of the past, an unfolding of the destiny of the Japanese people, which must drive them on either to victory or disaster. And these preordained attitudes, which became translated into physical orders, were interpreted by various staff officers who were not afraid to think, and plan, and do. Yamamoto, for instance. And Mori? No, he was sure Mori was carrying out orders simply because he enjoyed his job. Mori was the thug to end all thugs. But he was apparently considered a necessary thug, to the future of Japan. Philip could not help wondering how many of his kind were about.

202

CHAPTER 8

The Rebel

'It is the honourable Major, honourable Captain,' Hagi said, bowing low.

Philip, sitting on the floor of his living-room and playing at lead soldiers with Iyeyasu, who was already revealing himself to be passionately fond of uniforms and guns, looked up in surprise. He had not paid much attention to the knock on the outer door, supposing, as it was not yet dusk, that it could only be another of the interminable invitations to which he was subjected.

'Forgive the intrusion, Shimadzu San,' Mori said. And gave one of his charming smiles. 'What a pleasant domestic scene. It has always been my great sorrow that I have never found the right woman to marry, and bear me a son.'

'She might have found some of your habits difficult to accept,' Philip remarked.

Mori shrugged. 'Is that not the case with every marriage? Is it possible for us to be alone?'

'Of course,' Philip got up and nodded to Idzuma, who had appeared from the kitchen. Now she hurried forward to scoop the little boy from the floor. 'Will you take tea, honourable Major?'

'Ah, no, with great respect, honourable Captain. I am in some haste, and I think you will be too, when you hear what I have to say.'

Philip frowned, gestured Idzuma and Iyeyasu from the room, closed the door behind them and sat down. 'Yes?'

203

Mori sat down as well, drawing his chair closer. 'Do you remember, three years ago, when my people managed to lay hands on that scoundrel Henry Tang?'

Philip gazed at him. Lay their hands on him, he thought. A very apt description. 'Yes,' he said. 'I reported the incident to the ambassador.' If Mori had just found that out and wished to fight a duel in this generation as well, he was more than welcome.

'Of course,' Mori said, smiling. 'His Excellency told me of it that same day. I was pleased to discover that you are a man of your word, Shimadzu San. But also a man of good sense.'

'You think so?' Philip snapped, thoroughly disgruntled by the other's urbanity.

'I do indeed. Which is why I have come to you now. Do you recall the name that Tang let slip, under interrogation?'

'Interrogation,' Philip said. 'Is that your name for it? Don't tell me Tang has allowed himself to fall into your hands again?'

'No,' Mori said. 'I am sure Tang has more sense. Or indeed, ability.'

Philip frowned. 'Don't tell me you murdered him, on top of everything else?'

'Good heavens, no. We turned him loose. With good reason. Why do you suppose those students attacked the British outpost, three years ago? Tang told them he had been kidnapped and tortured by the British.'

'Mori,' Philip said. 'You are the most unutterable scoundrel who has ever lived.'

'What nonsense,' Mori said. 'I do my duty. But Tang is neither here nor there, except in relation to the information he gave us. Do you remember what that was? A name, and an identity?'

'No,' Philip said.'

'Ah. Well, you are not trained in these matters. We wrote it down, of course, and filed it, for future reference.

204

Wu Chi. The daughter, one of the daughters, of the mayor of Nanking. Giving orders to a Communist cell in Shanghai. Even you must agree that is a most sinister development.'

'I agree it suggests that the mayor of Nanking, or one of his daughters, at any rate, may have Communist sympathies,' Philip said.

'That is undoubtedly so. But do you know what these orders concerned?'

Philip waited; he did not doubt that he was about to be enlightened.

'Nothing less than a Communist *coup d'état*,' Mori said triumphantly. 'Aimed at taking over Shanghai as a Communist state, from which would be founded an entire East China Communist state.'

'Oh, come now,' Philip said. 'That is hardly a practical proposition.'

'You think not? You are aware that the Nationalists, under Chiang Kai-shek, have launched an attack upon the warlords controlling the upper Yangtze?'

Philip nodded.

'That means, does it not, that the entire Nationalist army is committed to what will probably be a long and bitter struggle. No one can even be sure it is a struggle they can win. Thus China is once again totally without any central authority. Can there be a better moment for the Communists to seize control of the country's largest and most prosperous city?'

'I take your point,' Philip agreed. 'But they will hardly dare attack the International Concession.'

'Perhaps not. Indeed, it would be good for us were they to do so, as then we could openly fight them and defeat them. But they are too smart for that, I fear. However, the prospects of a Communist-controlled Shanghai, and of Communists controlling most of Kiangsu Province, is certainly unattractive. We must stop them, if we can. And it so happens that I believe the means is to hand.'

205

'Indeed?'

'Yes.' Mori was looking more triumphant than ever. 'I have received information from my spies in Nanking that this arch-Communist agitator, this Wu Chi, is actually on her way to Shanghai at this moment. Would you believe it? Undoubtedly her arrival will be the signal for the *coup*.'

'Oh, come now,' Philip said again. 'Some young girl?'

'Hardly a young girl. She is thirty-six years of age.'

Good heavens, Philip thought; my own age.

'And she has never married, which is most un-Chinese and distinctly suspicious. As for being a woman, they are the most dangerous of all agitators, believe me. Was not Rosa Luxemburg a woman?'

'Who was Rosa Luxemburg?'

'She was a Communist agitator in Germany, in 1919,' Mori explained. 'She tried to pull off a *coup d'état* against the government. They shot her. We may have to be more circumspect with this Miss Wu, but I certainly intend to stop her ever reaching Shanghai.'

'Mori,' Philip said, as usual deliberately using the rudest form of address he could think of. 'One day you may go too far. You are talking of kidnapping. As you kidnapped Henry Tang. Well, you may have been able to get away with kidnapping some unimportant school-teacher, and making him believe the British were responsible, but you are hardly likely to get away with the kidnapping of the daughter of the mayor of Nanking, whatever the colour of her politics.'

'I am prepared to risk anything for the good of Japan,' Mori declared. 'In any event, there will be no risk. My people, Captain Yoshine in particular, are experts, and we have a technique which has never failed. I but wondered, as you were in at the beginning, Shimadzu San, if you would also like to be in at the end, so to speak.' He looked at his watch. 'The Nanking ferry is due to dock at six o'clock. I must be there to meet it.'

206

'You intend to try to kidnap this woman in broad daylight?'

'Six o'clock is dusk at this time of the year. It will be very simple. She will not be travelling from the dock by train, you see, but by private automobile. I have been informed of all this. It really will be very easy. And I am sure you would find it most interesting.'

Philip gazed at him, realising that he was absolutely serious. And that there was nothing *he* could do about it. Running to the ambassador would not help: Shirikawa would merely give him another lecture on where his loyalties should lie. But, he determined, at least he could make sure that this Wu Chi underwent nothing like what had happened to Henry Tang, even supposing Mori seriously intended to ill-treat a woman who was also a member of China's ruling class. Besides, he was curious to watch Mori's thugs at work; it occurred to him that might be useful one day, if it was ever going to be possible to bring the Kempai to account for its crimes.

'Yes,' he said. 'I imagine it will be . . . interesting. I will come with you.'

It was indeed fascinating to watch Mori, and his men, at work. Mori himself ostentatiously wore uniform, which he did very rarely, and insisted Philip also be fully and properly dressed. They drove in an embassy car flying the Rising Sun of Japan ensign on its bonnet, leaving the concession through a gate guarded by American marines, who stood to attention as the *corps diplomatique* number-plates and flag were identified. The car stopped, and Mori carefully signed the book with the time of exit.

'I shall be back in one hour,' he told the Marine sergeant. 'We are but meeting a colleague on the Nanking ferry.'

Then they drove slowly along the rutted road which led to the docks area, several miles away down-river; it was impossible to drive any faster without constant danger to springs and shock-absorbers. The road roughly followed the railway track, at a distance of some two hundred yards, and they were actually passed by the train, chugging on its way to meet the incoming ferry steamer. However, the road was not in sight of the railway all the time, and at one place dipped away behind a stone quarry. The quarry was no longer being worked, and in it there waited a black van. Philip felt his adrenalin begin to flow, even as he was increasingly disturbed by the totally arrogant ruthlessness of Mori and his henchmen.

They pulled into the docks area, and were greeted by the captain in command of the duty detachment of Japanese soldiers. As usual, there was a large crowd of Chinese onlookers and relatives waiting to welcome people, staring out at the ancient paddle-steamer, which belched black smoke from its funnel as it slowly came into the wooden pilings, brown water swirling away from the huge sidewheels. It might have been a scene out of a film set on the Mississippi, Philip thought – but for the Chinese and Japanese, and but for what was about to happen. What *was* about to happen? He had no idea.

The gangplank was run ashore, and sailors made it fast, then stood by to assist the passengers. Philip stared in both amazement and consternation, because the first passenger off the ferry, while definitely Chinese, and definitely, he estimated, in her middle thirties, was dressed in the very height of Western fashion. The hem of her pink-printed chiffon dress might have hung a couple of inches below her knee, and thus somewhat lower than they were currently wearing them in New York, but the waist was fashionably low, in fact right down over her thighs, and consisted of a red velvet sash, secured with an enormous bow; her shoes were black patent leather, her stockings flesh-coloured, and her hat an enormous brimmed black silk, decorated with a red ribbon. She would have been striking in any circumstances, but she was also an extremely attractive woman, her black hair cut short to expose boldly handsome features, while if her bust was somewhat unaccentuated, again in keeping with modern fashion, the stocking-clad legs, by far the most protected and concealed part of the average female Chinese body – or Japanese body, for that matter – were perfectly shaped.

'You see how she reveals herself,' Mori growled. 'She is an absolute wanton. All Communists are wantons.' He was in a fine fettle of excitement, and Philip began to doubt that his inclinations were quite as homosexual as he had at first supposed. He was more than ever glad he had decided to come along.

Wu Chi was greeted in Chinese by two young men, who had driven up in an automobile, with much affable chat and counter-chat. Philip was by now fluent in Mandarin, but so far as he could make out at a distance their conversation was entirely commonplace. Meanwhile, Mori was hurrying forward to greet one of the other passengers, an unmistakeably Japanese gentlemen, who was also wearing Western dress. 'Mr Yamaguchi,' Mori gushed, bowing as low as if the new arrival had been the Emperor himself. 'Welcome to Shanghai.'

Yamaguchi bowed in return. As he clearly checked himself from bowing even lower than Mori, and as his presence on board the same ferry as Miss Wu was so fortuitous, Philip could not doubt that he was actually a Kempai agent assigned to shadow the Chinese woman, and was merely acting the role of prominent business-man. 'It is my great pleasure to be here, honourable Major,' he said.

'I would have you meet my superior, Captain Shimadzu of the Imperial Japanese Navy,' Mori said, telling the lie without the slightest suggestion of a smile. 'He has been looking forward to making your acquaintance.'

Philip obediently moved forward, and found himself gazing into Wu Chi's eyes as she turned her head at

209

hearing Japanese being spoken. Then she looked away, almost appearing to toss her head in disgust.

'I am most honoured, honourable Captain,' Yama-guchi said, bowing again.

'Japanese dogs,' someone shouted from the crowd of onlookers outside the station, but peering at the arrivals through the iron bars.

The cry was taken up. 'Japanese dogs!' The crowd surged forward, waving sticks.

'Good heavens!' remarked Mr Yamaguchi. 'Are we safe, honourable sirs?'

'Tell your soldiers not to shoot,' Wu Chi snapped, in English, turning to look at the guards, who were lining up, rifles at the ready.

'So, sorry, no speekee English,' Mori said. But he winked at Philip. 'We do not wish to copy the British, eh?' he asked in Japanse, and then hurried off to speak to the captain in command.

The mob continued to shout threats and imprecations, surging against the railing. Once again Philip found him-self returning Wu Chi's gaze. She was not disturbed by the incident, as of course she could be sure that no one out there wished to harm *her* – but she was also mystified; the last thing she would have expected or wanted was a demonstration against the Japanese at this moment, to trumpet her arrival in Shanghai to the world.

Her two friends also seemed totally taken by surprise, and Philip suddenly understood, especially as Mori now came hurrying back, smiling. His network of spies and *agents provocateurs*, and what they could command, was really frightening.

Mori paused beside Miss Wu and her escorts, and gave a deep bow. 'So sorry,' he said. 'We do what we can. But who can say what mob will next do? My people no shoot unless forced. But missee, I would leave here, chop chop.' He rejoined Philip and Yamaguchi. 'Let's leave while we may,' he said in Japanese.

They got into the embassy car. The chauffeur already had the engine running, and drove away at great speed, heedless of the uneven surface, for all the world as if they were terrified. Philip looked over his shoulder, but the Chinese car was not following.

'Oh, they will,' Mori promised him. 'And we do not want them to come too soon. It must be clearly established in everyone's mind that we left the docks well before Miss Wu and her friends.'

'You engineered that demonstration,' Philip accused.

'But of course. Here we are.' The automobile had reached the quarry and swung off the road, causing its passengers even more bone-shaking discomfort as it hurtled across the ruts and came to rest behind the black van, which utterly concealed it. Mori rolled down his window. 'Five minutes,' he called.

Yoshine nodded, and he and his men, all wearing Wetern-style civilian clothes, donned face-masks, while the van engine was started. With perfect timing the van moved forward just as the Chinese vehicle came round the corner. The Chinese blared their horn and swerved to the right, ploughing out of the ruts and into the ditch. The van followed it, coming to rest bumper to bumper, while Yoshine and his men leapt from the back, armed with automatic pistols.

The car doors also opened, and the two Chinese men got out, but without hesitation Yoshine's men opened fire. There was a flurry of sound, and the two Chinese fell like sacks of rice, leaving bloody marks against the now punctured bonnet of their vehicle. Philip opened his own door to get out, hardly believing that he had just seen two men shot down in cold blood, but Mori grasped his arm. 'Not yet,' he said. 'She must not see our faces.'

Philip gazed in horror as Wu Chi also got out, throwing her door wide, and then checking as Yoshine stood before her. She made to retreat into the car, but Yoshine grasped her shoulder and jerked her forward. She gave a

211

gasp and landed on her hands and knees. As he pulled her to her feet, she struck at his mask with her clawing hands. He easily avoided the blow, and two of his men came forward to grasp her arms.

'Help me!' Wu Chi screamed in English.

'One minute more,' Mori promised, as again Philip made to get out. So he waited, and watched. Yoshine had moved round in front of the woman, who attempted to kick him, but only succeeded in dislodging one of her shoes, while two more Japanese soldiers hurried up to seize her flailing legs. Wriggling, twisting and screaming whenever she could catch her breath, Wu Chi was lifted from the ground and then brought down again, one man to each limb. Yoshine knelt beside her and calmly tore open her left sleeve. Wu Chi raised her head and snapped her teeth at him – her hat had come off and rolled away. Still utterly calm and unhurried Yoshine took a box from his pocket, removed a hypodermic needle and syringe from the box, dabbed Wu Chi's arm with a piece of iodine-coated cotton wool, and injected her, for all the world as if he were a doctor.

Wu Chi screamed and tossed and turned, fighting with even greater desperation as she could feel the drug beginning to take effect. But already her struggles were dwindling, and a moment later her head drooped.

Now at last Mori got out of the automobile. Philip followed him to where the woman lay on the grass. Yoshine's men were binding her wrists behind her back and carrying the cord down to secure her ankles, treating her as if she were nothing more than a meat carcass. Yoshine himself produced a roll of sticking-plaster from another pocket and placed a strip of it across her eyes.

'It is, of course, highly unlikely that she will regain consciousness before we reach my house,' Mori said. 'But it pays to be careful. Now make haste,' he told his men. 'Put her in the boot.'

*

The American marines stood to attention as the embassy car returned, the flag flying, Mori sitting in the front seat beside the chauffeur, Philip and Yamaguchi in the back.

'That was a quick trip, Major Mori,' remarked the sergeant of the guard, presenting the book for him to sign.

'Well, you see, for once the ferry was on time,' Mori explained. 'If they would repair the road now, we could do the journey in ten minutes.'

'You can say that again, sir,' the sergeant agreed, saluting as the car moved on.

Philip's brain was still reeling. He could hardly believe what he had just experienced. His brain could not accept the fact that two men had been shot down in cold blood, and that a well-dressed, civilised woman was lying in the boot of this automobile, drugged and bound hand and foot . . . to awaken in Mori's unthinkable garage.

'That was an act of banditry,' he said. 'An act of war. My God . . .'

'It was an act of necessity,' Mori asserted. 'But I am truly beginning to doubt that you have the stomach for this business, Shimadzu San. I am forming the opinion that it would be best for you to return to more normal duties.'

'You are right,' Philip said. 'I should have done that long ago. I should have done that the moment I reached Shanghai, regardless of the consequences. I allowed myself to be persuaded otherwise.'

Mori shrugged. 'The decision is yours. Ah, here is the International Hotel. You will excuse us for a moment.' He opened his door, and then looked over his shoulder. 'I would advise you to sit absolutely still until I return, Shimadzu San. I would take a grave view of any rash act of chivalry. The woman is quite unconscious, and will remain so for some time yet. You could not set her free even if you wished, and you would also be destroying your own career. I shall only be five minutes.'

The chauffeur had also got out, and was opening the door for Yamaguchi, who passed him the suitcase – which he had of course kept with him inside the body of the automobile. The doorman and two bellboys came hurrying out of the interior of the hotel, and Yamaguchi bowed to Philip. 'It has been a great pleasure, honourable Captain,' he said loudly. 'I look forward to resuming our so interesting conversation in the near future. Please to excuse me now.'

He and Mori entered the hotel foyer together, talking and laughing, followed by the bellboys and the suitcase, while Philip stared after them.

As Mori had predicted, the kidnapping had worked with flawless ease. He and his aide had gone to the docks to meet an important businessman returning from a visit to Nanking, and now they had delivered him to his hotel. Mori had signed them out of the concession and then signed them in again; anyone who wished to check the time they had been absent would be forced to conclude that they had driven at a normal speed there and back – certainly there was no possible evidence that they had stopped along the way, for any purpose whatsoever. The fact that a few minutes after they had left the docks there had been a case of murder and kidnapping on the road behind them would have to be attributed to Chinese bandits. If anyone did have any suspicions, he could never prove it . . . unless the woman were to turn up and give evidence. And if she did that, she would once again be pointing the finger at the British, not the Japanese. After having suffered what unimaginable and obscene tortures?

So, what was he going to do about it? Try to help her here and now? But he knew that was impossible, on every count, because Mori had been quite right. Forcing the locked boot open, even supposing he could do such a thing in time, and tumbling an unconscious woman out on to the street would accomplish nothing towards saving

214

her . . . and it would be the end of him. Driving the car off promised a better solution – but the chauffeur had taken the ignition key into the hotel with him, and Philip simply did not know enough about automobiles to start the engine without a key. Besides, to do that would still enable Mori to classify him as a traitor. If he was going to do anything at all, it had to be in the privacy of the garage.

But was he going to do anything at all? It was a haunting thought. Did he have the courage? Or the training? The ambassador had also been right: he had never been trained for the hurly-burly of physical combat. On the bridge of a ship he was as brave and as capable as the next man – and as ruthless. He would hurl several tons of steel across the ocean without hesitation, seeking to destroy the enemy, and he would not cavil with the whim of Fate, which might bring several tons back to blow him to eternity. But he had never in his life faced a man in anger, at arm's length.

Mori returned and got into the back seat beside him. 'An eminently satisfactory exercise,' he remarked. 'Now, Shimadzu San, as it is possible that our guest may soon wake up, if you will permit me, I will take her to my home first, and then the car will take you to yours the moment she has been unloaded. Will that be satisfactory? And then, may I suggest that you put in your application for a transfer immediately? I will endorse it. And you should not feel disappointed in yourself. Intelligence work requires qualities which are not always present in the average man. The fault is Kitabake's for not recognising that you lack such qualities. But do not worry. No harm has been done.'

'I will remain for the interrogation,' Philip said.

Mori raised his eyebrows.

'With your permission, honourable Major,' Philip said sarcastically.

'My dear fellow, you are more than welcome.' Mori smiled. 'I understand. She is a pretty thing, is she not? She

215

will be great sport. But you will remember to speak only English. And also, please, not to interfere with my methods.'

'I wish merely to watch,' Philip said, feeling the adrenalin begin to flow. But what was he considering? What could he consider, which would not make him a traitor just as much as if he had started something on the street? And for a woman who would probably murder him as soon as look at him, and whose ancestors had murdered his own father? He could only hope to prove his honour, by interfering in private, if he dared. But surely there were Japanese somewhere who would condemn Mori's actions? The problem was, were there any in Shanghai?

The car turned through the gate and then down the short sloping driveway to the sunken garage. The doors of the garage swung open – like jaws, Philip thought – and then closed behind the automobile. There were six men waiting for them, but not Yoshine: he would, of course, still be getting rid of the black van.

Mori got out, blinking in the electric-light glare, and pointed at the boot. One of the men threw it open, and two more reached inside to grasp the woman and tumble her on to the stone floor, where oil immediately soaked her dress.

She was still unconscious. Mori stooped beside her and thrust his fingers into her hair to raise her head. Then he let it fall again, and instead thrust his fingers into the bodice of her dress, tearing it open to expose her chemise. This, too, he ripped down to the waist, showing her breasts.

'Is that necessary?' Philip asked, his voice thick. But he was telling himself that he had to follow a plan, which was to do nothing until he had indisputable evidence that Mori meant to torture his victim. As if tearing her clothes to shreds was not a form of torture . . .

'Of course,' Mori said, 'the most important thing about interrogation, far more important than mere pain,

216

is to make one's antagonist feel at a disadvantage. Tie this woman to a chair, fully dressed and properly groomed, and then pour sulphuric acid into her lap, and she would probably defy us to the end. Make her aware that she has already been defiled, take away her sense of dignity, and she will surrender to threats. You will see.' He snapped his fingers, and one of his aides came forward with a chipped enamel jug filled with water, which he upended on the woman's face. Wu Chi gasped and choked, and one of the men seized her hair to drag her up to a sitting position. For a moment she acquiesced limply, body almost inert, then she suddenly swung her feet, pivoting on her bottom to create a scything movement aimed at anyone who was close to her. But the man avoided her easily enough and let her fall over again. She rolled, deliberately, away from the car, until she came to rest against Mori's shoes. There she checked, almost watchfully even if she could see nothing; her skirt had ridden up to expose her thighs and she was aware of this, because she made one more movement, attempting to pull her body a little further along the floor while pinning the skirt in place with her weight.

Very delicately, Mori placed his shoe on Wu Chi's shoulder and rolled her on to her back. 'We have not properly been introduced, Miss Wu,' he said. 'But it is our great pleasure to see you.' He spoke English.

Wu Chi inhaled slowly, her nostrils dilating, her breasts swelling. Then she sat up – a feat that revealed surprising physical strength and fitness as she could not use her hands. Then she turned on to her knees.

'Where am I?' she asked in a low voice, also speaking English.

'You are paying me a visit,' Mori said.

'You have not told me your name,' she said.

'I do not intend to.'

'But you are English.' She spat the word.

Mori bowed, even though he knew she could not see

217

him. 'We have that privilege. And you are a Communist agitator.' His voice hardened in turn.

Again the quick fluttering breath, while her head moved as if she was trying to see from beneath the plaster; she could tell her clothes were not as they should be, without quite knowing why. But Philip could tell that the true horror of her situation was slowly beginning to penetrate her brain as the effects of the drug wore off. Yet she kept her voice low; it was a singularly attractive voice. 'And that gives you the right to kidnap me?' she asked.

'It gives me the right to do whatever I choose to you,' Mori told her. 'But first, I would like you to answer one or two questions. I wish to know about this *coup d'état* your thugs are planning for Shanghai. I wish to know names, and numbers, and above all, dates.'

'And you shall know *nothing*,' the woman spat at him. Mori regarded her for a few moments, then he went to the tool bench, opened a drawer, and took out a length of silken cord, very fine but also, Philip knew, very strong. He nodded to two of his men, and they stooped, grasped Wu Chi's arms and raised her to her feet. Again her head turned to and fro, but this time she did not attempt to fight. She knew she had to save her strength.

Mori stood before her, one end of the cord wrapped around the fingers of each hand. The cord was pulled tight, and then he stroked it along her chin. Wu Chi's head jerked, and she gasped.

'Do you recognise that?' Mori asked. 'It is a cord. Very thin and strong. Were I to wrap this cord round your neck, you would be dead in seconds. You would like me to do this, would you not, Miss Wu?'

Wu Chi hissed at him, her teeth bared.

Mori smiled. 'But I am not going to oblige you. The cord has other uses. It also cuts. I will show you.' He freed one hand and tore her dress some more. Once again Wu Chi jerked her head, and this time she moved against the

218

restraining hands as well. But the men pushed her forward again, and Mori reached into her dress and pulled out her right breast, rather as he might have taken something from a pocket. The breast was larger than it had seemed beneath the dress, and had an attractive sag. Mori took the cord again, held it tight, and gently passed it beneath the flesh until it reached her chest. Then he raised his arms, and the breast rose with them. Wu Chi gasped, and Mori commenced moving the cord to and fro against the flesh while still pressing upwards. Wu Chi's mouth clamped together and a little moan escaped her lips.

'You see,' Mori said, lowering the cord. 'I could perform a mastectomy with that cord. In seconds.' He gave the breast a reassuring squeeze. 'But I am not going to do that either. The cord, you see, permits me to question you, and, indeed, to cripple you in a way that only a doctor would ever be able to tell . . . should you ever care to ask one, in all the circumstances. Now, will you not tell me when is your coup, and how many men you lead, and who are their commanders?'

'I will tell you *nothing*,' Wu Chi said, and went on speaking in Chinese. She had clearly never learned to curse in English. Now she cursed Mori and his ancestors and his descendants most fluently in her native tongue.

'Put her on the table,' Mori said, and two more men came forward to lift her legs from the floor. Now Wu Chi did fight them, with the fury of utter desperation, but with utter futility.

Philip wiped his forehead. He was pouring sweat. And his mind was the same jumble of confused emotions as when he had watched Henry Tang being similarly manhandled, similarly dehumanised. As Mori was dehumanised. As he would be dehumanised were he to allow this to continue.

So, was he about to destroy himself, after all? Himself, and Iyeyasu, and perhaps even his family? No, only himself. There was a way to prevent any harm, even any

219

blame, ever accruing to Shikibu and Iyeyasu, to William and Peter. It was a way that, as a Christian, he considered repulsive and criminal. But it was also the way of honour, even in Christian societies. Once he had rescued the woman.

He took a step back from the table, looked from left to right to establish his situation. No one in the garage noticed. They were all too interested in the coming sport.

Wu Chi was placed on the table, heavily enough to leave her winded and gasping, and momentarily still. Mori stood beside her, threw up her skirt and dragged down her knickers to her knees. Now the gasp became an exclamation of outrage, but there was nothing she could do; two of the men were holding her bound ankles very tightly, and the other men were holding her shoulders equally firmly, and pressing them into the wood.

Mori inserted his hand between the quivering muscles of Wu Chi's thighs, carrying one end of the string with it. Then he withdrew his hand, but grasped the cord from the other side. Then he moved the cord up until it reached her body, arranging it with great care so that it fitted into the cleft of her buttocks and of her vagina. Then he beckoned two of the other men to take an end each.

'Now you see, Miss Wu,' Mori said. 'With this cord in this place I believe I could cut you in half. Certain it is that after fifteen seconds of sawing, you would entirely cease to be a woman, now and forever. Do you wish that to happen, Miss Wu? Can you not see what a waste that would be? Because once we start to saw, you will tell us. You will tell us because you will be half-mad with pain. And yet, alas, once we start to saw, the damage done may well be irreparable. Consider that, Miss Wu.'

Wu Chi's head twisted from side to side, as Henry Tang's had done, and a tear escaped the blindfold and trickled down her cheek. In a moment it would be too late, but Philip had at last found what he wanted; the guards had discarded their weapons on entering the garage, and stacked them neatly by the stairs leading up to the house. He could only hope and pray that they were loaded. Slowly he began to move in that direction.

'Well, Miss Wu?' Mori asked.

Wu Chi spat at him.

Mori smiled. 'Do you know, Miss Wu, I suspected that would be your attitude. And I am glad of it. To stroke you with this cord is going to be very enjoyable. But why should we hurry? We have all night. I think that before I use the cord, I will give you a treat, as well as provide you with a further opportunity to consider your position, and perhaps change your mind. I am going to let my men have you, for a little while. They will enjoy that, and you will enjoy that, and it will remind you of what you are about to forgo forever.'

Wu Chi cursed him again in Chinese. And now Philip stood by the guns, still ignored by everyone in the room.

Mori nodded to the men holding the cord. One of them released it, and the other pulled it through. Wu Chi gasped.

'Release her ankles,' Mori said.

One of the men produced a knife and cut the rope holding Wu Chi's ankles. Immediately her knees came up, protectively, and then slowly went down again, as she realised that to protect she had also to expose.

'You will find this interesting, Shimadzu San,' Mori said. 'And also useful. It is of course only useful with a woman who is aware of herself, of her position, who has pride. But to strip a woman of that pride is often the first step towards her complete surrender. In fact, why do you not mount her yourself, first? I am sure you will enjoy it.' Still smiling, he at last looked away from Wu Chi to where Philip had been standing, then turned further, inquiringly, and looked down the barrel of an automatic pistol. 'Are you mad?' he asked.

'Tell your men to release Miss Wu's hands,' Philip told him.

The men had already checked in their assault on Wu Chi, and were staring at Philip in consternation, although they still held her.

'Quickly,' Philip snapped, and pointed at the man with the knife.

He slit the rope holding Wu Chi's wrists.

'Now all of you,' Philip said, 'get away from the table and against the wall. Turn round and face it, hands in the air.'

'You *are* mad,' Mori remarked. 'Do you not realise you will be cashiered? You will be shot.'

'You too, Mori,' Philip said. 'Face the wall. And press the release for the door. Remember, if the door does not open immediately, I will shoot you in the genitals.'

Mori retreated to the wall and pressed the switch; the door rose into the roof.

Wu Chi slowly sat up, touching herself, as if unable to believe she was free. Then she reached up hesitantly and pulled the tape from her eyes. She blinked at the light, only slowly focussing, gazing first of all at Philip, and then at the men lining the wall; even with their backs to her there could be no doubting their nationality. 'Japanese,' she whispered.

'You will not escape,' Mori said, his voice almost a hiss.

'Just be quiet, Mori,' Philip recommended. 'And don't move. Killing you would be one of the great pleasures of my life. As killing your father must have pleased my uncle. Now, Miss Wu, will you get into the automobile, please.' He backed away from the table towards the car as he spoke.

Wu Chi hesitated only a second, then pulled up her knickers, jumped down from the table, and ran to the car. Philip opened the driver's door and sat down, passing the pistol through the open window to keep it pointing at Mori, his finger tight on the trigger.

'Now, Mori,' he said, 'I have here a witness as to what

222

you do to people, down in this garage. I would like you to think very carefully. If you consider the matter, you will realise that it would be better to keep this incident within the family, so to speak. I have nothing to lose, now. You have everything, should I take this woman to the concession newspaper, for example. Whereas, if you do nothing, it will be a simple matter of her word against yours. I would think about these things, if I were you, before you act.'

He started the engine, reversed the automobile out of the garage, still holding the pistol trained on the men, then turned quickly and drove up the ramp into the night. Mori had not moved.

'You are not Japanese?' Wu Chi asked.

The streets were empty. Philip instinctively drove towards the diplomatic compound, and then slowed and turned away again. He had, as Mori had said, committed an absurdly maniac act. There probably was nothing left to him now, save seppuku. Yet he felt not the slightest regret, and it would be senseless to consider the future until he had completed his self-appointed task.

'Yes,' he said. 'I am Japanese.'

'But you do not look Japanese,' she said. 'Not entirely.'

'I have American blood.'

'Ah. But yet, you wear a Japanese uniform,' she remarked. 'Is that man right? Will you suffer for this?'

'Perhaps.' He slowed as the gate came in sight; the American marines were still on duty.

'You will escape with me?' she asked.

'Yes,' he said. The marines came to attention as the car stopped. Wu Chi held her torn dress closed across her breast, but in the semi-darkness no one could tell what had happened to her. And if the sergeant somewhat raised his eyebrows at the appearance of a Japanese officer leaving the concession for a drive at night with a woman, he was not about to comment. Philip signed the

223

book, and drove through, turning down the road towards the Chinese city, only a mile distant.

'You were very brave,' Wu Chi said. 'And you have saved my life, I think. You will find that I can be very grateful. You will come and live with me, and I will make you very happy. I will make you very rich. If you will serve with me, I will also make you very powerful.'

The road was empty, and the guards were almost out of sight in the gloom. Philip braked the car. 'I cannot do that,' he said. 'Now, listen to me, Miss Wu. If you get out here, will you be able to walk into Shanghai in safety? I'm sorry about your clothes.' He looked into the back seat, remembering a rug he had noticed there, dragged it out and gave it to her. 'Wrap this around your shoulders.'

She gazed at him.

'Have you no friends, in Shanghai?' he asked.

'I have many friends, in Shanghai,' she said. 'I will be safe there. But . . . ' She frowned. 'You will not come with me?'

'I cannot,' he said again.

'You will go back to face imprisonment? To be shot, as Mori said?'

'I do not think I will be shot,' he said.

Once again she gazed at him for several seconds, then she leaned across and kissed him on the cheek, before getting out of the car and walking down the road, the rug held about her shoulders; she did not look back.

Philip watched her disappear into the darkness, then he turned the automobile and drove back through the gates and into the Japanese Diplomatic Compound. He parked the car before his bungalow and went up the steps. There were men already inside the house, waiting for him.

224

CHAPTER 9

The Lover

William Freeman sat behind his desk and regarded his nephew for several moments; there was no one else in the office. At last he said, 'I am at a loss for words. So is the ambassador. He writes that he simply cannot account for your actions, either in intervening on the woman's behalf – a Chinese woman, a member of the race that murdered your father . . . '

'With respect, honourable Uncle,' Philip interrupted. 'Every man who took part in the murder of my father was executed by the Japanese Army, thirty-three years ago. One cannot hate an entire people forever.'

'You think so? You can be sure the Chinese hate us, and will do so forever. But His Excellency is also unable to explain your other actions . . . '

'Such as why I did not commit seppuku when left alone with my swords?'

'Well, that is a point, certainly.'

'Would you have been pleased, had I done so?'

'Of course not. It would have killed your mother. And hopefully it will not be necessary. But if only I could understand *why* you acted as you did.'

'Because it had to be done.'

'That is your reason?'

'Yes,' Philip said. 'And I demand the right to a court martial.'

'So that you can bray to the world about the iniquities of the Kempai? What will your reaction be when the

225

court commands you to commit seppuku?'

'I shall obey it willingly, providing I can first tell the truth to the Japanese people about what is being done in their name.'

'Do you suppose they wish to know?' William asked. 'Do you suppose the Kempai is unique? Do you not know that every nation on earth has its secret intelligence services, and that no one wants to know how they operate? Least of all, the people. All the people ever want to know is that their interests are being looked after by a group of dedicated men.'

'Dedicated men. Do *you* believe that, honourable Uncle?'

William sighed, and gestured him to a chair. 'What I believe hardly enters into the matter. We do not live in an ideal world, Philip. It is a pragmatic world, alas, where only the result of one's actions matters, not the intention. You are aware that three days after you left Shanghai, the Communists seized control of the Chinese city?'

Philip nodded.

'Mori claims it happened because you released that female into their midst.'

'I cannot believe that, with respect, honourable Uncle. The plans were laid. She was one of their leaders, to be sure, but the coup would have been carried out on schedule whether she was there or not.'

William shrugged. 'It is possible that you are right. Yet there could have been a connection. And in any event, it was a wasted gesture. Are you also aware that she is dead?'

Philip raised his head slowly.

'Oh, indeed. The Communists did not succeed in grasping power without resistance. There was considerable street-fighting. And, as you are aware, we have agents inside Shanghai itself. One of these has reported that Miss Wu was shot dead when attempting to enter the house of a prominent anti-Communist merchant. The

226

man and his family were of course lynched. It is a sad world, indeed. But you could have ruined your career for nothing, without in any way changing the course of events, the course of history. Without even prolonging the woman's life by more than a few days.'

Philip frowned at his uncle. The words 'could have' were the first suggestion he had heard, in the four weeks that he had been under officer arrest, that his career was *not* ruined. But he still did not see how it could be otherwise, in all the circumstances. And did it matter? As his uncle had said, he had actually accomplished nothing, save perhaps to save Wu Chi a few minutes of agony. It was even possible to suppose that, had he let Mori torture her and then contemptuously throw her aside as he had thrown Henry Tang aside, she might still be alive, too battered a hulk ever to take her place in the Communist revolt. But would she not rather be dead, killed in the very moment of her glory, the very pride of her feminine health and beauty, than to live, a hulk? He had to believe that, just as he had to believe that perhaps, at the very moment of death, a memory of him, of a man who had sacrificed so much to save her from mistreatment, might have flashed across her brain.

'So we are left with a serious situation on our hands,' William was saying. 'Undoubtedly Shanghai will have to be retaken from the Communists, presumably by the Nationalist army, whenever Chiang Kai-shek can spare the time. That will mean more fighting. And it will also bring the Nationalist army to the very gates of the concession. That could be a serious matter, perhaps even more serious than having a Communist regime sitting *outside* the gates of the concession, and endeavouring to control all our very considerable trade up the Yangtze Kiang. The army are determined to do something about it. Cooler heads are endeavouring to dissuade them from wild action, to make them wait upon General Chiang Kai-shek, who surely has too much on his plate to want to fight us as well. But the situation is fraught with danger. You were sent to Shanghai to play your part in preventing a war, not in provoking one.'

'I have said, honourable Uncle, that I do not believe my actions influenced the situation in any way,' Philip insisted. 'And I have been taught all my life that one's actions should be guided solely by one's personal honour and the honour of one's country. You taught me that. I could not stand by, as a man, and watch what Mori intended to do to that woman. Even less could I stand by as an officer in the Imperial Japanese Navy. Have you read my report?'

William nodded. 'I did. Before burning it.'

'Before . . . you had no right, sir.'

William pointed. 'I had every right. You speak to me of honour? Have you any right to bring dishonour upon your fellow officers, your country's armed services? You have no proof that any of these things you describe would actually have happened, or actually happened. Your witness is dead, and you yourself are disgraced.'

'And Mori will lie,' Philip said grimly.

'Major Mori has stated that he intended to frighten the woman into a confession. That he had no desire or intention to use that cord. That you panicked and lost your head.'

'As he had no desire or intention of emasculating Henry Tang?' Philip demanded.

William sighed. 'You are accusing a fellow officer of lying. I would not have you do that in public. I wish none of this affair made public, ever. Fortunately, this is possible. The woman Wu Chi, so far as we have been able to ascertain, made no report regarding her kidnapping or the murder of her bodyguards, except perhaps to her immediate associates. No doubt she did not wish the entire world to know of her arrival in Shanghai. Certainly, nothing has appeared in any newspaper that we have been able to discover. As I say, this is very fortunate for you. Your arrest has been kept a closely guarded secret, and this too will never be made public. Mori has agreed not to pursue the matter . . . '

'Which surely indicates his guilt,' Philip said.

'Perhaps. Or his maturity. He quarrelled with a fellow officer over the treatment of a Communist suspect. This is regrettable, but the sooner it is forgotten, the better. We made a mistake in thinking you suitable material for intelligence work. I made a mistake. I recommended you to Kitabake. I will shoulder the blame.'

'You? I do not wish you to shoulder the blame, honourable Uncle.'

'Listen to me, you silly boy. You have a life to live. You have a son and a mother to care for. You have a career. Not every man can be fully successful at everything. You have proved yourself both a brilliant executive officer and a brilliant staff officer. As well as a brave and honourable man. Japan needs men like you to face the future. Let others do the dirty work of calculating what that future may be, in what direction it may lie. You are being returned to the staff. Yamamoto himself recommended it. You know that he now holds a rear admiral's rank, and a command?'

'I know that, honourable Uncle, and congratulate him. I also would prefer a command.'

'You will obtain one, in the course of time. But for the next couple of years we must bury you where you will not come too much before the eyes of your fellow officers, especially those in the army. With the best will in the world, aspects of this affair must eventually become known. You could find yourself fighting a duel.'

'Do you think I am afraid of that, honourable Uncle? I would welcome the opportunity.'

'To kill Mori, perhaps? Those days are in the past, fortunately for us all. You will take overall command of naval design in succession to Captain Hiraka. Captain Hiraka has a brilliant record, so you have much to live up to. However, I know it is work in which you have always been interested.'

'Indeed, honourable Uncle.' Philip could hardly believe either his ears or his good fortune. 'I am proud to have been chosen for such a responsibility.'

'You may find it a frustrating one, I imagine,' William said. 'Restricted as we are by the terms of the Washington Agreement. Now there is talk of yet another naval conference, this time to be held in London, in a year or two. You will have to attend that as an observer, certainly. But I know you will do the best you can.'

'Thank you, honourable Uncle. I would wish you to know how grateful I am for your forebearance in this business, and for your continued trust in my abilities.'

'You are my nephew,' William said. 'My favourite nephew, as I think you understand. It would make me a very happy man were you not again to abuse my trust.'

Philip gathered the interview was at an end. He got up and stood to attention. Yet there was still something he had to know. 'May I ask one more question, honourable Admiral?'

'Yes?'

'What are *your* feelings, about the work of the Kempai, of men like Mori, honourable sir?'

William Freeman regarded him for several seconds. 'I thank God I am not one of them,' he said.

'But you feel their work is necessary.'

'Yes,' William said. 'I have to feel that. And so do you. As I have told you, do not suppose interrogating prisoners in an unpleasant manner is an art limited to the Japanese alone. There are aspects of life which none of us like to investigate too closely. Your business is to do your duty to the best of your ability, which is considerable; and let others, as I have said, worry about where that duty may eventually take you. Understood?'

'Yes, honourable Admiral.' Philip stood to attention.

'Now, I have one more thing to say to you, honourable

230

Captain,' William continued. 'In your new duties, you will, of course, be bound publicly by the Washington Agreement, and in due course by whatever agreements may be reached in London. But it will also be your duty, within the framework of the tonnage permitted by those agreements, to order the design and commission of the best possible ships for the Imperial Japanese Navy. Such ships may have qualities other navies lack, perhaps through the development of your own insight and imagination — qualities which may be absent in other design-planners. Such innovations and improvements on our part must, of course, be kept very secret. The lords of the Admiralty therefore feel that it would be unwise for you to renew your friendship with foreign naval attachés, and especially Commander Graham, RN.'

'Graham? Is he still in Tokyo?'

'Very much so. But I hope you have taken my point?'

Philip hesitated, and then nodded. He could not argue with the principle. 'I shall avoid Commander Graham,' he said regretfully.

But on the other hand, he reflected, as he went down the stairs, John Graham would almost certainly no longer wish to know him.

'Philip,' Shikibu said. 'O Philip.' She held him close, closer than he could ever remember. 'What are we to do with you?'

'Love me and support me always, Mother,' he said. 'I would hope.'

She held him at arm's length. 'Even when you do the craziest things?'

'Do you know of it?'

She nodded. 'William told me. In the strictest confidence.'

'Well, then, I would hardly expect you to condemn me.'

'A Chinese?' She shuddered. 'I do not know how you

231

could even touch one. But it is in the past.' She held his arm again. 'Isn't it?'

'Oh, yes,' Philip said. 'I am Admiral William Freeman's nephew. I am untouchable, even by the Kempai.'

'And that offends you?'

'No, honourable Mother. No. I am being stupidly proud. I have even been promoted. I just do not know whether I am standing on my head or my heels. Is Iyeyasu here?'

'Of course. And Idzuma. And I have given notice to your tenants to leave your house. I would love you to live here, with me, but I know you will wish a place of your own.'

'Mother!' He held her close again. For four weeks he had been confined to a room at the Officers' Club, allowed out for exercise, and to see his son once a week. At least part of his confusion was at attempting to grasp that it was actually over.

'She is such a good girl,' Shikibu confided, as they walked, their arms round each other, towards the lounge. 'Such a good girl. And she worships the ground upon which you walk.'

Philip looked down at her.

Shikibu smiled. 'Oh, do not be absurd, my son. I would never expect you to marry a honin woman. But that does not stop me being pleased that she is there, for the sake of both Iyeyasu and yourself. You will not find a better.'

He suspected she might be right. And what a delight it was to sleep that night in his own bed, Idzuma in his arms, and to know that his mother approved. Or to play with Iyeyasu again – he was as bewildered as his father, at four years old capable of being concerned at the sudden upheaval in his life which had taken him from Shanghai back to Tokyo in such haste, but incapable of understanding why it had happened, or why he had been separated from his father for so long.

But now it was over. Did he have any regrets? How

could he, as it had turned out well . . . save for the death of Wu Chi. But suppose it had turned out badly and he had after all been condemned to seppuku? What would he have felt then? He had acted like some romantic American film hero, not like a well-disciplined, patriotic Japanese officer. The romantic side of his character was clearly one he was going to have to subdue, to bury, in fact, if he was going to reach the top in his career. Supposing that were still possible.

But at least, now he had been given a position where he had always wanted to be. Naval design had always been his greatest interest, and if, as William had warned him, he was virtually hamstrung in developing any large ideas by the terms of the Washington Agreement, there were still a thousand and one possibilities to be considered, and perhaps put into practice, which would raise the Japanese fleet to a higher standard of efficiency and offensive power than any other navy in the world – even if he hoped and prayed such power would never have to be used.

But he had barely been at his new desk a week when Admiral Yamamoto was announced. 'Shimadzu San,' Yamamoto said. 'Welcome back aboard. Oh, welcome back.'

Philip bowed deeply. 'It is my great honour and privilege, honourable Admiral.' He gazed into Yamamoto's eyes. 'You know about Shanghai?'

Yamamoto nodded. 'And I am proud of you.'

'Are you?' Philip cried. 'Oh, honourable Admiral, if you knew how those words go straight to my heart.'

Yamamoto smiled, and sat down. 'Not that I think you were wise, or even correct. But every so often a man must act as his heart dictates, or he is not a man. You and I, Philip, are fighting seamen, not medieval torturers or spies. Oh, do not misunderstand me, we need these things, these people, just as did our ancestors. But it is our privilege to lead from the front, and die in battle,

233

gloriously, when the time comes. Now, what have you got to show me? What do you think of the *Akagi*?'

'A magnificent conversion, honourable Admiral. She must be the largest aircraft-carrier in the world.'

'No,' Yamamoto said. '*Kaga* will displace more, deep-loaded. This is something we are trying to conceal from our rivals. Has *Kaga* completed trials yet?'

'Not yet, honourable Admiral. But she will be completed by the summer. She too is a magnificent vessel. I most heartily congratulate you on the design.'

'I simply told Hiraka San what I needed, Shimadzu San. Because the more I have studied the subject we discussed five years ago, the more I am convinced that these are the true capital ships of the future. Unfortunately, it seems that the Americans also hold this point of view. Have you details on *Lexington* and *Saratoga*?'

'Only that they have commenced trials, honourable Admiral.'

'And how do they compare with *Kaga* and *Akagi*?'

'They will certainly also exceed forty thousand tons, deep-loaded,' Philip told him. 'But I understand their aircraft capacity is to be about sixty machines, whereas both *Akagi* and *Kaga* are designed for ninety.'

'They are designed to *carry* ninety aircraft,' Yamamoto pointed out. 'Which is to say there is hangar space for that number. But how many of those can ever be operational at one time?'

'Well . . . sixty, I would say.'

'So that in plain terms,' Yamamoto said, 'their carriers are every bit as large as ours. And they have others. *Ranger* for example.'

'She is less than twenty thousand tons, honourable Admiral,' Philip pointed out. 'And is therefore easily matched. I have been considering the matter. We still have some thirty thousand tons available to us under the terms of the Washington Agreement. We can use this tonnage for two small carriers, each quite capable of matching *Ranger*. I intend to have the plans drawn up and submitted as soon as possible.'

He expected approbation, but Yamamoto did not look pleased. 'Bah,' he said. 'Small carriers are a waste of time. They will have neither the range nor the speed to keep up with the main fleet.'

'Agreed. But it is the best we can do, in the circumstances.'

'Is it, Captain Shimadzu?'

Philip gazed at him. 'Without contravening the terms of the agreement, honourable Admiral.'

'When does this agreement expire, Philip?'

'1931, honourable Admiral. But . . . '

'And how long would it take to design, gain approval for, lay down and complete — let us say — a fifty-thousand-ton aircraft-carrier?'

'Fifty thousand tons! Honourable Admiral . . . '

'How long, Philip.'

'Well, not less than five years.'

'So we are talking about virtually the end of 1932, supposing you commenced work this instant. That is already two years after the termination of the present restrictive agreement.'

'Indeed it is, honourable Admiral. But perhaps you are unaware that we have already been invited to attend a fresh conference, to be held in London as soon as it can be arranged, and in any event not later than 1930. It is generally accepted that a new naval holiday will be proposed there, and probably accepted.'

'Is it generally accepted that we must adhere to any such proposal?'

'Well . . . no, honourable Admiral. But if we do not, we shall be isolated.'

Yamamoto smiled. 'Is that not all the more reason for possessing a fifty-thousand-ton aircraft-carrier, the greatest ship in the world, by then? She will, of course, need to be adequately supported. At least two battleships

235

of a similar size and speed, and adequate cruisers, destroyers and above all submarines to provide protection above and below the surface of the sea. Such a ship, supported by *Kaga* and *Akagi* and our present battleships, would represent the greatest fleet in the world. The greatest fleet, in terms of hitting-power, that the world will ever have seen.'

'Indeed it would, honourable Admiral. But the cost, and the damage to our international relations . . . '

'Must be taken into account, of course,' Yamamoto agreed. 'None the less, I think this is a matter which requires your most urgent attention. It is not your province to consider cost, unless specifically commanded to do so by your superiors, or to consider our international relations. We have a foreign office to do that. It is your province to be prepared for whatever contingency may arise, and I can tell you, in the strictest confidence, that a national emergency could arise at any moment. Here in East Asia, events are moving away from agreements and towards settlements. This is frankly far sooner than I had anticipated. And I am only too well aware that the navy is not ready to guarantee victory against any other major power, and certainly not against a combination of two such powers. Thus we must be ready, and soon.'

Philip could only stare at him in consternation; the only two powers to which he could be referring were the United States and Great Britain. 'Do you mean the Strike South policy is to be implemented, honourable Admiral?'

'No,' Yamamoto said. 'That is a part of the problem. There is no coherent national policy at this moment. The Government says, quite correctly, that the nation is not able to sustain a war economically, and looks at the navy. The navy points out that the only way any major conflict can be sustained is by implementing the Strike South Plan, but that this is impossible while our forces are hamstrung by the absurd restrictions of the Washington Agreement.' He wagged his finger. 'Your reports, from the old days when you were my planning officer for the USA, have helped their lordships become certain of this. And while this is going on, the army says, we are going to carry out our plans anyway.'

'But is not the army ultimately subject to the decisions of the Government?'

'Theoretically. But it would be a bold prime minister who would take on the generals. The fact is, the army has logic and common sense on its side. The generals are right in claiming that if we do not act now we may soon be in a position where we lack the strength to act at all. I suppose you have not heard that Chiang Kai-shek has won his offensive against the warlords on the Upper Yangtze, and has re-taken Shanghai from the Communists, at a single stroke? He now controls all of Eastern China south of Chihli Province. And he is preparing to advance against Peking at this very minute. Manchuria will be next, and then all China will be unified, as it was under the Manchu. And this will be no feeble, fading regime, dominated by a half-mad Dowager Empress, that we will be confronted by. This will be a young and virile nation, led by a young and virile dictator. Chiang Kai-shek is a dangerous man, Philip. Make no mistake about that. He is far more able, far more determined, than Sun Yat-sen ever was. Even the army have been caught napping by his successes. It is as yet in no position to make a move in Manchuria. But it is none the less determined to act. Within the next few months, we shall seize the Shantung Peninsula.'

'Do *what*?' Philip was aghast. The Shantung Peninsula was a part of China itself, the southern half of the Gulf of Chihli, only seventy miles from the great city of Peking.

'I am to command the covering fleet,' Yamamoto said, with simple pride. 'I do not anticipate any difficulties. There is a good port there, you remember it, Wei-hai-wai? We bombarded it and then took it from the Germans in 1914. And during our occupation of the port we undertook considerable reconnaissance into the interior. We know everything there is to know about Shantung.'

'But that is invasion,' Philip protested.

'Well, of course. But it will be properly done. Attacks upon Japanese merchants are already being organised. We shall go in merely to protect our nationals from abuse. Such a manoeuvre has a hundred historical precedents.'

Philip stared at him. He respected Yamamoto more than any other man in the navy, saving only his uncle. Yet at this moment he was talking like a member of that very Kempai he affected to despise. 'I thought our duty was to restrain the army from mad adventures,' he said.

'From mad adventures, yes. However, this is not such an adventure. It will have a seriously restraining effect upon Chiang Kai-shek's plans, and limit his northward advance.'

'In order to declare war upon us.'

'I do not think he can do that, until he has reunited the country beneath his government,' Yamamoto pointed out. 'And he can never reunite the country while we occupy the Shantung Peninsula. It is a very simple idea, like all the best ideas. Of course, we will offer to evacuate the moment Shantung is restored to order and the lives of Japanese businessmen are protected. But equally, of course, we shall see to it that this happy state does not come about until the army is ready to move into Manchuria.'

'My God,' Philip said. 'And when America intervenes?'

Yamamoto shook his head. 'America will not intervene, at this time, at any rate. Our political experts are sure of this. Certainly not under the present administration, and everyone is quite sure, with the American economy booming the way it it, that Coolidge will be succeeded by another Republican president, probably Hoover. However, their Far Eastern experts will begin to watch our future activities very closely, which is why the sooner we have a battle fleet superior to their own, the better. Should an administration come to power in the future with more global and less isolationist points of view than the present one, then we may have a problem.'

Philip scratched his head. These people spoke as if everything was a game of cards. Will North trump East's ace? No, because he should save his trump to force an entry later on. What happens if he does play his trump? Well, we may lose a trick or two, but we should win the hand. After all, these are only pieces of pasteboard. They don't bleed.

'What of Soviet Russia?' he asked, desperately. 'Do you suppose they will stand idly by if the army invade Manchuria, right up to their borders?'

Yamamoto smiled. 'The army have contingency plans for any move the bear may make. I understand there are even some hotheads who would begin by declaring war on Russia, just to clear the air, as it were. But common sense will prevail. Russia, like the United States, is at this moment a nonentity. It is virtually in the throes of another civil war, between the followers of Trotsky and the followers of this man Stalin. Do not look so glum, Philip. War with anyone – except, perhaps, China – is a most remote contingency at this time. Certainly over Manchuria. But as it is probably inevitable, one day, we must always be ahead of them, in ships and design. That is your duty, Shimadzu San. It is probably the most important duty in the entire navy. Far more important than ferrying a few thousand men to Shantung. I envy you, Philip, for being where you are now, at such an exciting time in the history of Japan.'

But he frowned as he gazed at his protégé; the pencil Philip had been holding had snapped in his hand.

Japan! How often in the past, Anne Freeman wondered, had that word exploded in her brain and seemed to open a whole new book of experience in front of her. But this would surely be the final chapter.

Or would it? She had, after all, nearly not returned. For set against that part of her which cried out for the sights and smells and experiences she remembered so well was another part, almost as large, which recalled only fear and horror, and which had, over the past seven years, become firmly rooted in the peaceful prosperity of the United States.

Save that now there was no peaceful prosperity, even in the United States.

They had been a bitter seven years, in many ways. It had taken her almost a year to be able to settle down to any work, after her return, a year in which her aunt Hilary had had to remain in America to look after her; both her aunt and her uncle William had obviously been afraid she might even commit suicide. Remarkably, she had never contemplated this. She was not that steeped in Japanese culture. In fact, at that time her sole idea had been to get as far away from Japan as possible, in mind as well as body. Work had helped. It had been hard, and time-consuming; but also mind-consuming. Female medical students were not that thick on the ground, and it had been a struggle to maintain her position as a human being, and a future doctor, while so many around her wanted to see only the woman, who would necessarily faint at the sight of blood, who would necessarily blush at the dissection of genital organs, before whom it would be bad manners to swear or tell risqué jokes. She believed she had destroyed those masculine misconceptions, at least as regards herself. Even if she knew she would never be a great surgeon, she had never actually wanted to be a surgeon at all. She stuck by her original love, children.

Proving herself had, she supposed, been only an aspect of growing up. She had gone to medical school as a girl; now she was very much a woman. She was tall, blonde, attractive – only a determined modesty kept her from

240

admitting, whenever she looked in a mirror, that she could actually be called beautiful – and self-composed. She had dabbled in love – without loving, but consciously as part of the experiences she considered necessary to make up the woman she wanted to be. She knew that the fact that her background contained utter tragedy actually made her more desirable to many men who had the father instinct, just as the fact that she had once had polio made her seem a totally weak and helpless female. That she had, apparently, so completely shrugged off that dreadful memory, and that she was, actually, as fit and as healthy as any of them, had seemed to upset her escorts nearly as much as her refusal to become involved, even after a night in bed.

In fact, the nights in bed – there had only been half a dozen of them – had been totally disappointing. She had determined to approach sexual matters with the freedom and absence of inhibitions she was sure she would find in a Japanese . . . and had discovered that the average American male apparently had more hang-ups and inhibitions than even her mother. They had accused her of frigidity, and she, utterly turned off by their coy and self-conscious approach to the business of touching her body or exposing theirs to her touch, had been content for them to think that. She still possessed a dream, even if it was now indistinct, and no one she had met since returning from Japan had measured up to it.

Yet the word 'frigid' was a damning one, and had occasioned more than one sleepless night. Perhaps she *was* frigid. Perhaps all those boys had needed was patient understanding, and that was something she was apparently incapable of giving another adult.

Because of the guilt, still lingering? She did not think so, any more. She had grown out of the guilt. Where a hundred and fifty thousand people had died in a few minutes it was impossible to feel guilty for any three of them. The earthquake had to have been an act of God and

241

nothing more. But perhaps it was a more tantalising, and more disturbing complex even than guilt. She found it difficult to understand, and had to resort to mental parables. The one which came closest was about being on the point of stepping into a shower-bath, having actually pulled the curtain and turned on the water, and taken the first step so that the jet had brushed across face and body and legs, lightly, cold, stimulating . . . and then being called away, suddenly and urgently. There had been no time to dress, no time even to dry. She had been jerked out of the bathroom, with the cold water and the memory of that first liquid caress slowly coagulating on her flesh, and in her mind. The water had dried, and left her cold all over. But it was the coldness of nipple-hardening titillation. Compared with that, America had been a warm tub.

She did not know, even now, as the ship allowed its tugs to push it against the dock, whether she truly wanted to re-enter that shower again. Everyone had taken it for granted that she did. It had been her oft-expressed dream, as a girl, and now that she was qualified and her uncle had secured her a position in the rebuilt Anglo-American hospital, once again dominating the cliffs to her left.

The Freemans had been delighted that she was returning to their land. Their only fear was that she might be concerned by Japan's sudden isolation in the world and the criticism constantly levelled at the island people, nowhere more so than in the United States. The occupation of the Shantung Peninsula had gone almost unnoticed, but the sudden flare-up in Manchuria, only two years afterwards, had concerned everyone. This was out of keeping with the accepted norms of twentieth-century politics.

That criticism had angered her, even while she had known it was justified. It had done more than anything else to drive her back across the Pacific, to see for herself.

That, and the crash. This, she knew, was unpatriotic of her; she was an American. Buh she felt bitter about the crash. Not for personal reasons, although even her once-considerable holdings and income, carefully invested by her uncle from her lion's share of her father's estate, had been more than halved by the slump. The bitterness was because she felt the whole disastrous situation was a result of American greed and American carelessness of their neighbours in their mad determination to become a nation of millionaires. And they already had so much. What right had they to criticise the Japanese, so many of whom had so very little.

Even when the Japanese were actually killing people? The worst any American was doing was killing himself. But the anger was there. And the attraction of Japan was now reaching out to her like the scent of cherry blossoms in the spring. So she smiled, and waved, and tried to forget that the last time she had seen these docks they had been tumbled ruin.

Just as she tried to pretend, as she peered at the crowd, and made out William and Hilary, and Shikibu and Maureen, all waving back, that she was not disappointed because she could not make out the tall figure of Philip Shimadzu standing with them.

'My dear, Philip is in England, would you believe it?' Hilary said. 'Attending some naval conference.'

'I read of it,' Anne said. 'I didn't know he'd gone.' She looked at her uncle, who had kept her informed, over the years, of most of Philip's movements.

'Well, he'll soon be back,' William said. He looked grave, however much he was trying to dissemble it beneath a show of excited affection.

'You'll have to tell me what's really happening in Manchuria,' she said, squeezing into the back of the car with Shikibu and Maureen. 'There are so many rumours.'

'Oh, those Chinese,' Shikibu declared. 'They murdered a Japanese officer. Would you believe that such a thing could happen?'

Again Anne looked at her uncle, who caught her eye in the rear-view mirror. 'That's what we have been told, certainly.'

'There is so much . . . ' she checked.

'Condemnation of our attitude in the States?' William asked.

'Well, I guess it's as much speculation as to what is going to happen next.'

'The guilty must be punished,' Shikibu said.

'There is certainly talk of a punitive expedition,' William agreed.

'While everyone knows that it is part of Japanese strategy to expand into Manchuria,' Anne said. 'If you use the murder of Major Nakamura as an excuse, Japan will stand condemned before the world.'

'As if that matters,' Shikibu snorted. 'What would Washington do if one of your officers was murdered in cold blood?'

'Well . . . demand reparations, I guess.'

'Reparations,' Shikibu said, scornfully.

'We will do what needs to be done,' William said. 'And hope that no harm comes of it. Now tell me, my dearest girl, did you come out here to quarrel with us, or to be one of us?'

She flushed, and then smiled. 'I am sorry, Uncle Bill. I just hate to see the Japanese people dismissed as international thugs, when I know they are not.'

'And yet,' William said sadly, 'all nations contain a goodly element of thugs. We must be patient, and hope that in the long run good sense prevails.'

'The Chinese murdered a Japanese officer,' Shikibu said again. 'Whatever happens is their fault. My Peter is in Korea. He knows what truly took place. The Chinese are guilty.'

*

244

But by the time they had reached her house, Shikibu was all smiles again. 'We thought you would like to stop here first,' she said. 'To see Iyeyasu. He is living with me while his father is away. You will not recognise him,' she added proudly.

Anne dropped to her knees before the little boy. He was six years old, going on seven, in fact, and looked more Japanese than she had expected. But he was also already tall for his age, and he possessed his father's blue eyes. 'Do you know me?' she asked, in Japanese; she had kept up her studies of the language side by side with medical school, and now considered herself quite fluent.

'You are Auntie Anne,' he replied, in English, and she gave a shout of delight and held him close.

'We are going to be such friends,' she told him.

'You are going to be his doctor,' Shikibu said.

Anne raised her head to gaze at the older woman.

'Do you not wish to be?' Shikibu asked Anne.

'Does Philip . . . ?'

'He will wish it too,' Shikibu said.

That promise made a whole day suddenly seem brighter. But then Anne looked at the woman standing in the inner doorway. The woman looked back at her, and then bowed.

'You will excuse me, honourable mistress,' she said to Shikibu. 'But it is time for Master Iyeyasu's milk.'

'Off you go,' Shikibu said, patting her grandson on the rump, and glancing at Anne as the door closed. 'His nurse. Her name is Idzuma.' She stood up. 'Oh, she is also Philip's mistress.' She shrugged. 'A man needs a woman, and I do not think he will ever wish to take another wife. She is good for him. And I think, in her way, she is even fond of him.' She smiled. 'You Americans do not indulge your desires and your needs so openly.'

'I wish we did,' Anne said, because it was necessary to say something. The brightness had vanished.

And yet, had she really supposed he would be standing

245

on the dock, or waiting at his home, panting to hold her in his arms? After seven years? If she had all but forgotten him, would not he entirely have forgotten her? And she *had* all but forgotten him, until today. It was just that the sight of Japan had brought memory flooding back with such startling clarity.

And Japan had not changed, certainly so far as she could see. Hilary, with whom she would be staying until she settled in, might in fact be a very American lady in her domestic habits, but she was utterly tolerant in a way Elizabeth had never been, and she was utterly devoted to the Japanese attitude to life. Shikibu was as softly feminine, Maureen as boisterously cheerful, as ever. The country was as she remembered it before the earthquake. Most of all, so were the seductive ambience of the bath and the delicious comfort of the kimono.

Even the hospital was as she remembered it before the earthquake. She went there for the first time with sweat trickling down her back, remembering only the shaking light-fittings, the splitting floors . . . and found only solidity beneath her feet. More, Dr Azuma was there himself to welcome her, as a colleague rather than a patient, and show her the pediatric ward, for which she was to have complete responsibility. He did not seem concerned about her age. 'You know us, and we know you, Freeman San,' he said. 'That is all that is necessary.'

To imagine that a people like this could have just committed an act of wanton aggression, and even now be extending that aggression . . . not for the first time, she recalled Philip's letter of 1924, the almost agonised self-appraisal it had contained, and disguised but obvious mental anguish at the requirements of his duty . . . had he even then realised what was coming? But in the navy he was presumably aloof from such maniacal goings-on. The army seemed to be a law unto itself, at least for the time being; it surely could not represent the true spirit of this most gentle of lands.

As for Philip . . . She could not believe that he had found happiness with a woman like Idzuma. But he had found contentment, and a freedom from memory; because *she* had not yet found those things, that was no reason to disrupt the even tenor of his life. She must find her own placebos, from now on.

Which she was sure she could do, in her daily duties. She adored children, and her only complaint with her new job was that there were insufficient Japanese amongst her patients; as its name indicated, the Anglo-American hospital catered mostly to the non-Japanese elements of Tokyo and Yokohama society.

The majority were victims of childish accidents – cuts and bruises which might need anti-tetanus injections; or childish illnesses – persistent coughs which might well be allergies or caused by inflamed tonsils (she carried out no operations herself but passed such cases on to Dr Azuma), with occasional cases of whooping cough or measles. Mostly the children were afraid, because it was in the nature of children to be afraid of a hospital and a lady in a white coat, but where the English and the American and the French complained loudly and cried copiously, her Japanese patients were indeed patient, sitting there with their black eyes moving from side to side as she prepared their medicines or their shots, only occasionally reaching out to touch the hand of an anxious, but equally patient, mother. To Anne's great relief, there were no polio cases during the first months, and her most serious crisis was a badly broken arm, which had to be reset, and an acute appendicitis – but there all she had to do was make the diagnosis, and Yoshiye Azuma took over.

Azuma offered her quarters within the hospital itself, where there was a staff wing. Much as she enjoyed life with her aunt and uncle, she realised that he was right, as to be called out at night for an emergency meant a long drive down to Yokohama. Hilary pretended to be sorry to see her go, and William talked at length about the impropriety of young girls living alone, but after she had pointed out that she would not be alone, as the wing was always filled with nurses and sisters – who outnumbered the doctors by about ten to one – they agreed that it was a sensible thing to do. And as William had given her an automobile of her own, a Model T, she was able to visit the family whenever she could spare the time to do so.

In fact, she was relieved to be by herself, and had had an ulterior motive for accepting Azuma's invitation. If she was going to live a life of her own, and perhaps even find some happiness of her own, she could only do that as what she was, an American. William, and even Hilary, were so steeped in Japanese traditions, and Japanese ideas of modesty and propriety – which meant that young girls and women behaved as they had apparently done in Boston in 1800 – that they could only prove the most utter wet blankets should she ever actually find a man for herself. Not, she soon realised, that this was going to be easy.

Partly because of the crash the Anglo-American hospital was very poorly staffed, and in addition to her pediatric duties she was required to handle a large out-patients department – she soon found herself working some sixteen hours a day, which left absolutely no time to meet anyone outside the hospital. There were two other young doctors working with her, and they also had apartments in the staff wing. One was an American and the other Japanese, and neither of them was married, while both of them were very interested in their lovely young colleague.

She enjoyed their company on their rare moments off duty together, flirted with them, and even on occasion shared the bath-house with them, to their obvious delight – but only when at least one of the nurses was also present. But she permitted nothing more. They simply did not attract her, quite apart from the fact that she was

248

exhausted a great deal of the time. The trouble was, she told herself, that she was just not ready for any lasting relationship – she was, after all, only twenty-four years of age.

And then knew that she was lying to herself, and that in truth she was only waiting for Philip to come home. Because she had not forgotten him after all. Because to acquire a beau and then meet Philip, and see a want in his eyes as he looked at her, would be unbearable. As if he would have a want in his eyes, when he had Idzuma to go home to, waiting, subservient and eager, for his embrace. Was that not what he truly wanted?

Of course. But she dreamed that it would not be, that he had sufficient American blood to want more from a woman; just as she had sufficient Japanese upbringing to want more from a man. And in any event, waiting meant she was free from having to make decisions. She could enjoy her work, and her life, and her freedom, after so many years of restraint and inhibition. She could even be happy, she realised. For the first time since 1923.

With a free weekend in front of her – her first holiday for six months – Anne drove up to Tokyo early in September 1930. It was amazing how, in six months, she had entirely settled in to her new life, her real life. In Japan the rest of the world seemed unutterably remote – she could well understand how these people had contentedly shut themselves away from the rest of humanity for two hundred and fifty years.

Now, what was happening in Manchuria seemed to have no effect on everyday life, or even on everyday people. There was increasing unemployment because of the international slump in trade, but this was less evident here than in other countries; the young man who had sought his fortune in the cities and now found himself out of work, instead of joining a dole line and hanging about a street corner, merely returned home to his family, as the

Japanese had always done in times of trouble. His return undoubtedly meant greater hardship for the family, as the same amount of rice would now have to feed an extra mouth, but this was a family matter, and Japanese families invariably kept their crises to themselves.

Equally, there was, of course, a great number of families with sons or even husbands serving in the army, but this was also a Japanese tradition, and here again no one allowed any fears that their loved ones might be killed to show – especially when they were fighting the Chinese. Even Shikibu hid whatever fears she might have for the safety of Peter, stationed with his regiment in Seoul, beneath a mask of total confidence. Certainly no Japanese seemed to consider fighting the Chinese, or biting off huge chunks of Chinese territory, as remotely unreasonable or aggressive or immoral, much less criminal. The Japanese had fought the Chinese since the dawn of history, and their leaders were not hidebound by Christian principles. As for what the rest of the world might say about it, the average Japanese, as he stood on his beaches and watched the mighty battleships of the Imperial Navy steaming slowly by, could not care less.

Democracy had been thrust at the Japanese only two generations before, within the living memory of many of the older, and therefore most influential, members of each family. It had not yet taken root. Every prime minister, and most of each cabinet, was a count or a prince or a noble of some sort, even if hereditary nobility had been officially abolished, and the Japanese people were content that it should be so. They wanted to be led, not to be faced with a choice of several leaders, several policies, on the American model. This acquiescence in the omnipotence of authority even extended to William, and more remarkably, through him to Hilary.

As a young man – Anne knew because her father had told her – William, at least partly because of his American father and education, had been doubtful of his country's expansionist policies. But as a loyal officer he had fought beneath the banner of the Rising Sun, and Japan had always won. He might be doubtful again, now . . . but he did not doubt that Japan would win again, and that the world would once again accept the victory. Besides, he would say, this is not even a war: we still have diplomatic relations with China. This is an incident. Apparently both nations preferred it that way.

She wished she could be sure what she truly felt about it. But she preferred not to think about it at all, to be like any Japanese, and pretend the outside world did not exist. But she also wondered what Philip thought about it, whether he was still the man of the agonised letter, or whether he too had decided to follow the flag and the lessons of history, blindly and without comment. It occurred to her that might be what she was truly waiting to find out.

She stopped by Shikibu's house, as she always did when visiting Tokyo, for a romp with Iyeyasu and a cup of tea with Shikibu herself, and discovered neither of them there.

'The mistress has gone to Master Philip's house,' explained Shikibu's housekeeper.

'Master Philip's house.' Anne frowned, even as her heart went pit-a-pat. He must be on his way home.

'Oh, indeed, Mistress Anne. She has been there all week. Since Master Philip returned.'

Anne stared at her. 'Returned? You mean he's back?'

'He returned on Monday, Mistress Anne.' The woman looked mystified that she should not have been aware of this fact.

But Anne was not mystified. Clearly he had instructed his mother not to mention his return to her, and however good a friend Shiki was to her, she was Philip's mother first.

She felt a sense of total deflation.

'You must go to Master Philip's house,' the woman

recommended. 'He will be most happy to see you, Mistress Anne. And Master Iyeyasu is there too.'

With Idzuma, of course.

'Yes,' Anne said, and got back into the car. But she drove to Hilary's house instead.

'Oh, I suppose Shiki forgot to tell you,' Hilary said. 'She has been so excited. And of course she hasn't seen you for a fortnight.'

'Surely she knew he was coming home more than a fortnight ago,' Anne pointed out.

'Oh, well, as I say, she probably forgot. Don't worry about it, for goodness sake, Anne. They're all coming here for dinner tonight. We'll have the whole family together again.'

And I must smile and pretend it is unimportant, Anne thought. When she felt exactly as if she had been slapped in the face with a wet towel.

'Ah,' she said. 'Oh, that is a pity. I have to be back in Yokohama tonight. This is just a rush visit.'

'Oh, Anne! I thought you told me on the phone you had the whole weekend off?'

'Well, I did . . . but one of the boys has come down sick, and I have to pinch hit for him tonight. I'm so terribly sorry, Aunt Hilary. Do make my most humble apologies.'

'I'm sorry too, my dear. I know Philip was so looking forward to meeting you again, after all these years.'

'Well,' Anne said, 'I'm sure we can hardly avoid bumping into each other, some time, now he's back.'

She drove back down to Yokohama with tears dribbling down her face. Was she cutting off her nose to spite her face? No. That was a delusion. If he'd really wanted to see her he'd have written to her, or at least told his mother to let her know about his imminent return. Was he still piqued because she had never answered his letter? Oh, how she wished she had. But that was so long ago. And totally irrelevant. He just didn't want her coming

252

between him and Idzuma. And she knew the real reason she was fleeing was simply that she could not bring herself to face him, knowing that he had probably just left that woman's arms. She had supposed she had washed him right out of her hair – and she had been wrong.

Well, she would just have to try harder. That evening she allowed Johnnie Corcoran, the American intern, to put his hand inside her blouse for the first time. But almost the moment he touched her, she pushed him away and sent him off, as puzzled and angry as she was herself.

'There is a telephone call for you, Dr Freeman,' said the ward sister. 'You may take it in my office.'

Anne patted the arm of the little boy who had just had his tonsils removed, and went into the office. 'Yes? Anne Freeman speaking?' Her voice was brusque; she was always irritated at being interrupted on her rounds.

There was a moment's silence, then the voice at the end of the line said, 'This is Philip. Philip Shimadzu.'

She gazed at herself in the mirror behind the sister's desk. Three weeks, and not a word. Three weeks in which she had stubbornly kept herself out of Yokohama, refusing to visit any of her relatives in Tokyo, waiting for such a call. But . . . *three weeks*.

'Oh, hello, Philip,' she said. 'I heard you were back.'

'Yes,' he said. 'Anne . . . can you come out to see me?'

She frowned at herself. The utter cheek. 'Come to see you?' she asked. 'Where?'

'I am at my house. I will wait for you here.'

'At your house? No, I don't think that would be a very good idea, Philip. Besides, I am very busy. I cannot just leave the hospital like that.'

'This is very important,' he said. And indeed his voice did sound upset. 'Iyeyasu is ill. He complained of a head-ache yesterday, and it got worse today, and now he is vomiting and running a temperature.'

Anne's frown deepened. But her pique was already

dissipating in professional interest and family concern. 'How high a temperature?'

'A hundred and two.'

'Is there any discoloration of the skin? Any spots?'

'No spots. But he's very flushed. I suppose it's the fever causing that, though.'

'Is the flush only on his face?'

'No, that's the odd thing. It's right down his throat and on his chest as well. I really would like you to see him, Anne, if you can possibly come out here.'

'I'm on my way,' Anne snapped. 'Now listen to me very carefully. Put him to bed, if you haven't already done so. And stay there, with him. Don't let anyone leave your house, and don't let anyone in, except me. I'll be there in half an hour.' She put down the receiver, then lifted it again. 'Connect me with Dr Azuma please,' she told the switchboard, and drummed her fingers on the desk as she waited, trying to calm her own nerves. 'Hello? Yoshiye? Anne. Can one of the boys possibly come down here to hold the fort for me?'

'Of course,' he said. 'But what is the problem?'

'I have to go up to Tokyo,' she explained. 'I think there may be a case of scarlet fever up there. Iyeyasu Shimadzu.'

He whistled through his teeth. 'You will have to inform the authorities and impose quarantine, you know, if it is scarlet fever.'

'I know,' she said. 'I'll notify the authorities as soon as I've made an examination. Yoshiye . . . if it shows any sign of being toxic, I'll have to bring him back here.'

'Of course. I'll have a bed made ready in the isolation ward.'

'Thanks. I'll be in touch.' She replaced the receiver, hurried back to her own office to change her white coat for a herringbone tweed, and then ran for her car.

A man she had never seen before opened the door, bowing low. 'Come in, please, Miss Freeman.'

She glared at him; she had a built-in dislike for people who called her 'miss' rather than 'doctor'. But he probably didn't know any better; he wore the uniform of a Japanese sailor. Then what on earth was he doing here. 'How long have you been in this house?' she demanded.

He looked surprised. 'I am always here,' he protested. 'I am Hagi. I am Captain Shimadzu's servant.'

'Ah,' she said. 'Well, you are not to go out. Do you understand me?'

'Oh, yes, Miss Freeman. The honourable captain has already told me this.'

Anne handed him her coat, took off her shoes, and hurried into the bedroom with her bag. Iyeyasu lay on the mattress, uncovered but wearing pyjamas; he appeared to be asleep. Philip sat beside him on one side, and the woman Idzuma on the other; Anne's nostrils dilated – she had forgotten Idzuma. But she could almost have been the boy's mother, from her attitude. Both she and Philip got up as Anne came in.

'Anne,' Philip said. 'My God, it's good to see you.'

It was difficult to decide whether he meant it personally or in a professional sense. She ignored him and dropped to her knees on the mattress. The little boy's eyes flopped open. 'Auntie Anne,' he said, his voice little more than a whisper.

Gently Anne held his chin and moved his head to and fro; his throat was quite pink. As was his chest. 'Open wide,' she invited, and peered into his mouth. Already the telltale scales were forming on his tongue. She looked at Idzuma. 'Have you no blankets?'

'He is so hot . . . '

'That is the fever. But the slightest chill could induce nephritis or permanent rheumatism. He must be kept covered up at all times.'

'Fetch the blankets,' Philip said.

Idzuma hurried from the room.

Anne stood up. 'I should like to wash my hands.'

'In here.' He waited in the bathroom doorway. 'Is it serious?'

'With fortune, no. But it could be. He has scarlet fever.'

'Scarlet fever? What is that? Where did he get it?'

She shrugged. 'It can come from anything. If some other child had it, and Iyeyasu even touched his clothing . . . It is highly contagious.'

'But what is it?'

'No one knows for sure. Obviously it affects the blood and the nerves, but the actual bacillus has not yet been isolated. There is work going on all the time, but all we know at this moment is that it is a bacillus. It is also very contagious, as I say. I'm afraid I am going to have to put this house under quarantine, although hopefully Iyeyasu will not have to go to hospital. When last did he go to school?'

Philip looked at Idzuma, who was returning with a pile of blankets.

'Two days ago,' the woman said.

'And he was all right then?'

'Well, he had a slight cold. Nothing serious. It was yesterday he complained of the headache, so I kept him home.'

Anne nodded. 'But he was at school during the incubation. That means he could have infected half the school. I must use your telephone. You weren't here, Philip?'

'No. I've been very busy at the Admiralty, compiling my report. I slept down there. I only came here today because Idzuma called me.'

'I was so worried,' Idzuma said.

'Of course,' Anne agreed. There was no reason to doubt the woman's sincerity, or her fondness for the boy, however much she might dislike her as a woman; Iyeyasu was not only her meal-ticket, but also undoubtedly her key to Philip's affections.

Anne got through to the local health officer and

reported the situation. 'He agrees that Iyeyasu may stay here,' she said as she hung up. 'He will take immediate tests of all the children in the class at school. It may be necessary to quarantine all of them.'

'Will he be all right?' Philip asked.

'With fortune, yes. You must take his temperature every couple of hours, and if it goes up at all, call me again immediately. Scarlet fever is only really dangerous when it enters the toxic stage, and his temperature will tell us if there is any chance of that. For the rest, he must be kept warm, and once the temperature starts to drop, you must give him a warm bath every day. You'll find that his whole body will become scaly, in a day or so, but these scales will just drop off or wash away when he begins to get well. Give him as much liquid as he'll take, milk and water. When the temperature comes down he can be fed light meals. Milk puddings, fruit, that sort of thing. But no meat or eggs.'

'Why not?'

'Because they cause increased functioning of the kidneys. I will wish a urine sample every day. One of the possible side-effects is kidney damage, and we must look out for any signs of this.' She smiled. 'In most cases the recovery is complete and without any after-effects whatsoever.' She went to the door. 'Oh, by the way, Philip, I'm afraid I must quarantine you as well. Scarlet fever very seldom affects adults, but they can carry the bacillus and give it to others.'

'Me? But what about my report?'

'Can't you write it here?'

'Well, yes. But all my papers are in my office.'

'Well, can't you telephone and have them sent over? No, telephone them and ask them to have the papers put in a briefcase, and I'll bring them over myself when next I come. That way no one else will be exposed.'

'Hm,' he said. 'They are top secret . . .'

'So have the briefcase locked.'

'I'll see what can be done. But what about you? Aren't you in danger of contracting the disease?'

'Goes with the job,' she said. 'But I'm more alert to the symptoms, you see, than someone who isn't in medicine, so I would hope to nip it in the bud. I'll bring the papers tomorrow morning.'

'Ah . . . I'd like to get working again this afternoon, if possible.'

Anne found herself nodding before she had properly thought about it. 'Then fix it up, and I'll bring them in after lunch. Will that be soon enough?'

'That'll be fine.' He went with her to the door, helped her into her coat. 'It *is* good to see you again, Anne. I wish the circumstances could be different. But . . . my God, how long is it?'

She looked into his eyes. 'Seven years, just about.'

'I suppose you never got my letter?'

'I did,' she confessed. 'I apologise for not replying. I guess I had a lot on my mind at the time.'

'I wish you had replied,' he said. 'Oh, I wish you had.'

They stared at each other.

'Yes,' she said. 'I wish I had too.' They inclined towards each other, but then her gaze drifted over his shoulder to Idzuma, standing in the doorway, watching them. She pulled back. 'I'll see you get your papers,' she said.

Had that been a hedge, she wondered, as she drove away? Because of the woman. Only because of the woman.

She had waited seven years to see him, and to see, too, the wanting look in his eyes. And it was there. He could not even wait until tomorrow. He wanted her, and at this moment he wanted her more than anything else in the world.

But he had Idzuma. So was she once again going to let selfish pride stop her doing what *she* wanted? She just didn't know. She did know that he was even more hand-

258

some than she remembered. And that his personality had become more wistfully attractive through being touched by tragedy. But could they ever fall in love? Dared they? It was not a question of consanguinity. They were no closer than half cousins; the blood of one man, Ralph Freeman, flowed through their veins, but that was three generations ago. It was a question of things remembered, things experienced, things felt. Of senseless attitudes. She had so deeply resented his refusal to see her after Haruko's death. That had been senseless, when he had been overcome by grief. Then she had not answered his letter. And he had so resented that, he had never written to her again, and had taken his time about wishing to see her again. But was that not perhaps because he felt as strongly for her as she for him? She didn't know. And she didn't know if she dared risk finding out. Just as she didn't know if her pride would let her go back to him, knowing that he wanted to make love to her – but knowing also that Idzuma was in the house, a thin partition away. Because Idzuma *would* be in the house; *she* had expressly forbidden her to leave.

But if she didn't go back now, if she didn't swallow her pride, if she didn't find out, once and for all, if they could love each other . . . there was really very little she could ever do with her life. So she telephoned Yoshiye Azuma and told him she would be late returning that afternoon. Even then she hadn't quite made up her mind. But she knew she had when she drove to the Admiralty.

'Dr Freeman?' The lieutenant gave a stiff bow. 'Captain Shimadzu says this briefcase is to be delivered to you.'

'Yes. I'm afraid he cannot leave his house for a few days. Probably a week. He explained the circumstances?'

'Yes,' the lieutenant said. 'Please give him my regards. You will take the case directly to him, please, not letting it from your sight? You understand these are highly classified papers. It is irregular for any civilian to have them at

259

all. But Captain Shimadzu assures me they will be safe in your care.'

'I'm not about to give them away,' she said. 'Or break the lock. Captain Shimadzu and I are . . . cousins,' she said, not wishing to be reminded of that in the slightest degree. 'And very old friends. He'll get the papers.'

The lieutenant bowed again, as she drove away. She had lunched very lightly, but her stomach still seemed entirely choked with butterflies. Because she was going back to him, as he wished. And she knew she was never going to return from this meeting. Not as the same woman.

'Anne!' Philip himself opened the door. He had changed his uniform for a kimono, and looked more relaxed than this morning. And so pleased to see her.

'One briefcase containing secret documents,' she said, holding it out. 'And I didn't see a single Chinese spy following me.'

'I'm glad of that,' he said, taking the case in one hand, and her arm in the other to draw her close. 'And I'm so glad you came back.'

'Are you?' she asked.

'So glad,' he said again.

The briefcase fell to the floor, and she was in his arms. For this she had waited nine years, she knew. Just as for all of that time, whatever the distractions and the traumas, she now knew she had never doubted it would happen.

Nor had he, she thought. She could feel him against her, as he almost swept her from her feet; but he did not need to, because she so nearly matched him for height, knee to knee, thigh to thigh, shoulder to shoulder, mouth to mouth . . . and groin to groin.

Presumably there were other people in the house. Idzuma and the manservant Hagi. And the woman mattered. Only she did not really matter at all, at this moment.

Philip released her and looked into her eyes. 'I'm giving you scarlet fever.'

'You're giving me more than that,' she said, and released him. She went into the bedroom, knelt beside Iyeyasu. 'How are you feeling this afternoon?'

'Aunt Anne!' he said, as if her presence made everything right. 'Aunt Anne!'

'I just have to take your temperature,' she said. 'Roll over.'

He obeyed, and she greased the thermometer and inserted it into his rectum. But he was only a hundred and one.

'Well?' Philip asked, standing above her.

'I think he's come down a shade. He's going to be all right.' She got up, went into the bathroom to wash her hands and her instrument.

'Thank you for bringing the briefcase,' Philip said.

She faced him. 'Your aide-de-camp was very reluctant to let those papers go. I suspect I may have become a name on a file.'

'On my file, certainly,' he said, and took her in his arms again.

'Are you sure my being here won't disrupt your domestic arrangements?' She couldn't resist that.

'Not if you'll stay. Will you stay?'

She gazed at him. 'I could stay, for perhaps an hour. I would like to do that. I would like that more than anything else in the world, Philip.' There was more she should say, she knew. They had reached a stage of arrangements, because what was not arranged now would never be arranged at all. But she didn't care.

She walked in front of him into the main bedroom, and then turned towards him again. There was no sign of life in the entire house. The professional ethics which now

261

ruled her life threatened to rebel. 'You haven't let your servants go out?'

He shook his head. 'I've told them to take the afternoon off, to rest. Idzuma was up all night.'

She looked at him.

'Caring for the boy,' he said, smiling.

'But she has played an important part in your life,' she remarked, and hated herself for it. Now was simply not the time.

'Has no one ever played an important part in yours?'

'No one but you,' she said. 'Although several have tried.'

She turned away from him, but he came against her, and his arms went round her waist, sliding up to her blouse. His fingers touched her breasts, moved again, and as she did not protest, returned. Her nipples had never been harder. Nine years, waiting for that touch.

'I have wanted you,' he said. 'From the first moment I ever saw you.'

'Snap,' she replied.

'But . . . ' he sighed. 'I loved Haruko.'

'I think I did too,' she said.

'Anne . . . '

She turned, in his arms, so that his fingers stroked across her armpits before coming to rest on her shoulder blades. 'I would replace her, Philip, if I could. But you will have to teach me.'

He wore nothing beneath his kimono. She was a mishmash of Western clothes, blouse and skirt, suspender belt and silk stockings . . . she wasn't even sure whether she actually got them off. Then she was kneeling against him. Because this was Japan, and this was her Japanese lover. She could touch him as she chose, knowing he only wanted her to touch him again. And he could touch her . . . Her breasts swelled and her belly swelled and her buttocks swelled and her vagina swelled . . . And, most of all, her mind and her heart swelled, to accommodate him, to want him and to satisfy him, to understand that here was loving where all other sensations were as nothing.

And most of all to satisfy herself, as she sat on his lap and he came in and in and in, and she knew the first orgasm of her life, and knew too that she had found the only man in the world, for her.

CHAPTER 10

The Dreamers

'Sex in the middle of the afternoon,' Anne said. 'I never knew it could be so good.'

'It is the only time,' Philip said.

They gazed at each other, and smiled, and leaned forward to kiss each other. He held her shoulders to look at her. Then he touched her, stroked the contours of her breasts, the quickly reawakening nipples, caressed the sweep of her thighs, sifted the silk of her pubes, even sought the perfection of her calves and toes, aware always of the clear grey eyes, the classical features, the magnificent golden hair, magnificent even when worn short. Here was beauty he had always suspected existed, but had never known for sure, before today. Here were so many things. And here, too, was disaster. But why should that necessarily be so?

She could see the shadow slide across his eyes. 'You don't . . . ' she hesitated, and lay down again. 'You don't have to do anything, you know, Phil. I'm a big girl now.'

He lay beside her, on his elbow, looking down at her. 'Don't you think I want to do everything? Or anything, just to make sure you never leave this bed?'

'I'd like that. But there's a but. Isn't there?'

He sighed, and rolled on his back.

'Haruko?' she asked.

'No. Not any more. There is . . . I don't know how to put it. It sounds so ridiculously pompous.'

'Try me.'

'My country.'

She frowned. 'You mean that you feel you should have only a Japanese girl?'

'No. I wasn't meaning that at all. I meant . . . I've never told anyone this, Anne.'

'Okay,' she said.

He returned to his elbow, gazing at her. 'What do you think of what is happening in China?'

'Not a lot. Sounds rather nineteenth-century type politics to me. But then, a lot of Japan is still nineteenth-century, and I find that attractive. Anyway, your mother is sure it is all the Chinese's fault, and your uncle thinks it will all blow over.'

'They could both be right, in the short term. There is no question that Nakamura was murdered by a Chinese mob . . .'

'And I seem to remember,' she interrupted, 'that when a Japanese mob murdered a British missionary back in 1865, the Royal Navy turned up and blew Shimonoseki flat.'

'Oh, yes,' he agreed. 'My – our – grandfather was there, trying to defend the place. But that was 1865. This is 1930. And no one could doubt that the British were inflicting reprisals. A bit drastic, perhaps, but reprisals.'

'You trying to tell me something?'

'I'm afraid so. These things didn't just happen, I mean Shanghai, Shantung, Nakamura's death.'

'My God,' she said. 'Should you be telling me all this?'

'I have to tell someone,' he said. 'I tried to tell you before, once.'

'I know,' she said.

'And I didn't even touch on it. There are secret plans . . . Sometimes I think the people who are running Japan are absolutely mad. At least, I don't know that *they're* mad, but they feel so obliged to listen to what the army tells them to do. And now even the navy . . . I've spent the last few months in England.'

'I know.'

'So everyone over there is really feeling the pinch.'

'They are in the States, too.'

'I imagine we will as well, some time soon. But that means nothing to our admirals. Everyone's broke, say the British and the Americans. So let's extend the naval holiday for another ten years, and this time let's even limit the possible total tonnage of cruisers as well. In other words, let's take the opportunity really to reduce armaments.'

'Sounds like a good idea to me.'

'It's not a good idea to my superiors. I've spent the last three years in the Office of Naval Design. My people plan our future developments in naval ships, and do the best we can with what we have as well. If you knew some of the things I have been asked to do . . . and some of the tragic consequences.'

Anne waited. She knew he wasn't going to stop talking. She realised he had wanted to talk like this, to someone, for at least seven years. And had not done so. But now he was talking to her. That had to make her the most important person in his life. Even if it distressed her to see him so unhappy.

'There was a line of destroyers,' he said. 'We were stuck with the tonnage, but they wanted heavier armament. I did what I could. And last spring one of them capsized in a typhoon. Do you know, I was congratulated by their lordships, because even upside down the ship floated and could be towed back to port. A magnificent achievement, they said. More than a hundred men dead, but a magnificent achievement. At least I got them to agree to reduce the overweight on deck. Then I was asked to design a fifty-thousand-ton aircraft-carrier.'

'Fifty thousand tons?'

'That's right. She'd be as big as a passenger liner. And way beyond treaty regulations. But they said, do it.'

'Did you?'

'Sure. But I tacked on an itemised cost account which

made them shiver, so the idea was dropped. But it'll come back as soon as the money can be found.'

'Won't this new agreement stop it?'

'No. Because while they are recommending to parliament that the new agreement be ratified, they are already making plans to withdraw from it.'

'Can they do that?'

'Who's going to stop them?'

'But won't it mean the condemnation of all the other nations?'

'Don't you think that is going to be the eventual outcome of the China business? Anne, the army means to have Manchuria, no matter how many incidents it has to manufacture.'

'Um.' She sat up, clasped her arms around her knees. 'It's all pretty grim. And I know how bitter you must feel about the men on that destroyer. But you were obeying orders. Nothing that has happened, or can happen, need affect us, Phil.'

'I tell myself that. And then I wonder, what if the orders were to fire on a United States ship?'

'No one would be silly enough to give you an order like that.'

'I wish I could believe that.' He sighed. 'What would you like to do?'

'Anything you wish me to.'

He knelt beside her, stroked her hair and her shoulders and her back, felt the velvet of her flesh rippling beneath his fingers. 'I would like you to become my wife.'

'Would you, Phil? Really and truly?'

'Really and truly.'

She gazed at him.

'But you aren't sure it's a good idea,' he remarked, and then smiled. 'Anyway, let's take a bath and think about it.'

'I'd like that.' She got up, and he wrapped her in one of his own kimonos. She had to hold the skirt from the floor, tall as she was. He slid open the door for her, and she stepped through, and faced Idzuma. 'I guess,' she said in English, 'that I really want us both to be sure.'

'Philip!' Shikibu cried, and hurried forward to embrace him. 'My dear boy. Are you all right? Is Iyeyasu all right? Oh, you should have let me come. I am far too old to catch scarlet fever. I don't even know what it is.'

'No one does. And I wasn't going to take that risk.' Philip held her close for a moment, then looked past her at a beaming William Freeman. 'Honourable Uncle! I'm glad you're here. I wished to talk with you both.'

William clasped his hand. 'The boy is really going to be all right?'

Philip nodded. 'He really is. It was just a mild attack. The quarantine has been lifted, from my house, at any rate. That's why I'm here. Anne has been marvellous.'

'Of course.' Shikibu led him inside and gestured him to a cushion, clapping her hands for her housekeeper to bring tea. 'She is a marvellous girl.'

'And I must congratulate you on your report,' William said. 'I'm not sure it will please everyone, but it is very well put together, and I doubt anyone can fault your facts.'

'Thank you, honourable Admiral,' Philip said, and drew a long breath. 'Now, honourable Mother, honourable Uncle, I have something I wish to discuss with you.'

'You wish to marry again,' Shikibu said. 'Oh, I am so glad.'

'Oh!' Philip was taken by surprise. 'How did you know?'

'Well, what else would you wish to discuss with me? I know nothing of naval matters.'

'Ah. Well, I do wish to marry again.'

'I think that is splendid,' William said. 'It is what you need, and now that you are forty . . . By forty a man needs a wife in every way. A happy domestic life is the key

268

to a contented old age. You have chosen the girl?'

'Yes.'

'Oh, William,' Shikibu cried. 'Philip has undoubtedly already spoken with her. This is 1930, not 1900, you know.'

'Nevertheless, there are forms which need to be observed, as you well know, Shiki,' William said severely. 'Have you spoken with this young lady, honourable Nephew?'

'Yes,' Philip said.

'About marriage? That is really unseemly. I do not know what this modern age is coming to. However, now that you have approached me, we shall from here on conduct the affair in the correct fashion. I will go and speak with this girl's parents, and make a formal proposal. I take it she is of good family?'

'The best,' Philip said.

'Good. Good. And the father?'

'Her father is dead,' Philip told him. 'It will be necessary for her guardian to give his consent.'

'Very well. Who is this fellow?'

'You,' Philip said, and hurried on as his uncle stared at him in consternation. 'You will have to give your consent on my behalf as well.'

'You . . . ' William appeared at a loss for words, and turned to his sister.

'You are not speaking of Anne?' Shikibu demanded.

'Yes, honourable Mother.'

'You mean this whole thing is some kind of joke. Really, Philip . . . '

'I am not joking, honourable Mother. I wish to marry Anne Freeman.'

'But, that is quite impossible.'

'Why, honourable Mother? We love each other. We have loved each other for a very long time, as I think you know. Now we have decided that we would like to be married.'

269

'You never cease to amaze me, Philip,' William said. 'Well, I am afraid I am going to have to refuse you permission for such an absurdity.'

'An absurdity?' Philip cried. 'Is it an absurdity to love?'

'It is an absurdity to love your own cousin, in that way,' Shikibu asserted.

'You mean it is an absurdity to describe Anne and me as cousins,' Philip said angrily. 'The relationship is so slight as to be almost non-existent.'

'Nonetheless, marriage between Anne and yourself is quite impossible,' William Freeman repeated.

'I would like you to explain that to me, honourable Uncle.'

'Well . . . ' He looked at Shikibu again, and then back at his nephew. 'You belong to different races, different backgrounds . . . '

'With respect, honourable Uncle,' Philip said, 'but that is another absurdity. Our backgrounds are very similar. And our ancestors have already bridged the racial gap.'

'You cannot deny that she is an American citizen,' William said quietly. 'And that you are a Japanese naval officer.'

The two men gazed at each other.

'You know,' Philip said. 'About the Strike South Plan.'

'Of course,' William said. 'I doubt I know as much about it as you, as you were one of its originators . . . '

'I have always been against it,' Philip said. 'It was you who told me never to oppose it openly.'

'Well, as to that . . . '

Shikibu looked from one to the other. 'What are you speaking of?'

'Uncle William is just reminding me,' Philip said, 'that it is the avowed intention of Japan to go to war with the United States.'

'Is that true?' Shikibu demanded of her brother.

'No,' William said, gazing at Philip. 'It is not true. But it is true that Japan understands that the proper fulfil-

270

ment of her legitimate needs as a nation is very likely to bring about such a conflict, and has thus been endeavouring to prepare for such an unhappy eventuality.'

'And you condone such thinking,' Philip accused.

'I do not consider it my duty, as a serving Japanese officer, to condone or not to condone any of my country's actions,' William said. 'Any more than it is your duty. We are required to carry out our country's will, that is all.'

'And you honestly believe it would be our country's will?' Philip demanded. 'In *any* circumstances? To go to war with the greatest industrial power in the world? Can you believe our people would wish that, if they were told the truth? Is it not, in fact, the will of a few ambitious generals which is driving us to this suicidal course?'

'Such talk is very close to treason,' William observed, mildly.

'And how can it be suicidal?' Shikibu asked. 'Do you really suppose America can defeat Japan?'

'Oh, Mother!'

'Your mother has raised a very valid point,' William said. 'We are not speaking of a war to the death, such as might take place between two adjacent nations, such as did take place between France and Germany. We are speaking of limited war, fought at a distance of six thousand miles, of our being able to demonstrate to Washington that to attempt to drive us from positions we have already occupied and are prepared to defend with all our strength will not be worth their while. So to make things right we pay China, or whoever is involved, an indemnity, perhaps. No one supposed Japan could ever conquer Russia in 1905, least of all the army or the navy. But we knew we could beat them, here in East Asia. And we did, and thereby obtained our objectives.'

'Uncle William,' Philip said, 'if you or anyone else honestly believes that the Americans will fight a limited war, and accept a negotiated defeat, simply because bringing their fleet across the Pacific may prove too costly

271

and too difficult, then you are living in a dream world. Anyway, how can you, of all people, even consider such a thing, however "limited" it may be? You told me it could never happen. That Japan was governed by sane men, that—'

'When I said that,' William Freeman pointed out, 'I was under the impression that the rest of the world was also governed by sane men. Not lunatics who can bring down their entire financial system by reckless speculation. What do you expect us to do? Starve, because we have not the funds to pay for the importation of rice? No one will buy our exports – there is no money any more. Tell me what we do?'

'To seek a solution by conquest is none the less wrong,' Philip said. 'It has to be.'

'The survival of the nation has to be *right*,' William insisted.

Philip sighed. 'I can see there is nothing to be gained by continuing this discussion. I will leave.' He got up, and bowed. 'Honourable Mother. Honourable Uncle.' He was so angry he was afraid he might be going to be rude.

'There will be no marriage between Anne and yourself,' William said a third time. 'If there should ever be a war, however brief and limited, between our two countries, it would mean the end of your career to have an American wife, and it would bring utter misery to her. I cannot permit it.'

'And do you not have a woman already?' Shikibu demanded. 'Is not Idzuma everything a man could wish? And a good mother to the boy? Why, I am sure that he looks on her *as* a mother now. He can hardly remember Haruko.'

Philip gazed at her in amazement. Only a few minutes before she had been saying how good for him, and for Iyeyasu, a marriage would be. 'I have already dismissed Idzuma,' he said.

'You have done what? How could you, Philip? She has

272

been at your side for seven years! How could you? And who is going to care for Iyeyasu?'

'Anne will be caring for Iyeyasu from now on, honourable Mother.' Philip bowed again, and left the room.

'Which does not alter the fact that we have been forbidden to marry,' Philip said gloomily, as they sat together eating sushi in a small Tokyo restaurant; Hagi was at home performing the unfamiliar duties of baby-sitter.

'That is ridiculous, Phil,' she protested. 'You are forty years of age. And I am twenty-four . . .'

'Uncle William is our guardian, and thus must be regarded as our father, for as long as he lives.'

'Oh, really, Phil,' she said. 'Of all the absurdities . . . Oh, I'm sorry. I don't mean to get angry. But surely you can see . . . Why, in the States such a notion would be laughed to scorn.'

'This isn't the States, Anne. This is Japan.'

She gazed at him for several seconds. 'And in Japan, age and seniority govern everything. Do you know, once I thought that was a great system? The best system in the world.'

'I still think it is better than any other.'

'You reckon? Is that why you are all blindly following your senior statesmen into a war you cannot win and no one will every forgive you for starting?'

'I am sorry, Anne. To marry you would be an open act of defiance against my mother and my uncle, against my ancestors. And yours. I would stand condemned before all society.'

'So I'm supposed to crawl away and hide beneath a bush. Well, I did that once before. But like I said, I'm a big girl now. I'm going to move in with you, married or not.'

'You cannot.'

'You mean, you don't want me?'

'Oh, Anne, for God's sake. Of course I want you. But Uncle William . . .'

'Can hoot and snoot as much as he wants, as far as I'm concerned. Oh, of course I'm enormously grateful to him, and to Aunt Hilary, for taking care of me after Daddy and Mother died. For sorting out the finances. For sending me to college. And I know how much you feel you owe him for being a father to you all of your life, for getting you into the navy . . . But nothing that he has done for you, and nothing that he has done for me either, means that he owns us. And to attempt to rule us for the rest of his life is emotional blackmail. I know what I want to do with my life, and the only opposition I am ever going to put up with is from you.'

He held her hand. 'My dearest girl, that is the most wonderful thing you, or anyone, has ever said to me.'

'So ask me again to come and live with you.'

He stared at her, and she stared back. Of course she didn't understand what she was asking, he knew. She was asking him to go against everything he had been taught since he was a boy, against all his beliefs, against every tenet of his society, against his mother, and against the man he respected more than any other in the world. She was asking him to divorce himself entirely from his family, and turn only to her. But she was offering to do the same. And she was also telling him that if he did not take her now, he would lose her forever. He could not contemplate that. And she was right in denouncing the system as one in which the Japanese people would blindly follow their seniors right into a war against the whole of the rest of the world. Such a system couldn't be perfect. Or even desirable. Besides, he had been unhappy for too long. Again as she had reminded him, he was forty, past the median of his life, with only decline in front of him, and here was the most marvellous girl he had ever seen, hardly more than half his age, offering him her all. To refuse that would surely be the greatest of all the absurdities.

Providing she really knew what she was doing.

'I want you to come and live with me,' he said.

'Whew! Do you know, for a moment I thought you weren't going to say it?'

'But my darling . . . what about the hospital?'

'Well, I'll quit if you want me to. But I'd hate to do that. They really need me.'

'Of course I don't want you to quit. I was just wondering how it would work out with them.'

'Oh, I guess there's the odd night I might have to spend there. But only if an emergency crops up.'

'I meant, won't there be a problem with Azuma? We can hardly set up house together without it becoming known.'

She smiled. 'You leave Yoshiye Azuma to me.'

'And Aunt Hilary? Uncle William?'

The smile died. But her expression was no less determined. 'You leave them to me, too.'

Yoshiye Azuma played with the pencils on his desk, not looking at Anne. 'Of course such a step on your part will not affect your responsibilities here, Anne, or the trust we have in you. Yet I cannot help but advise against it.' At last he raised his head. 'You know, if you love Philip, and I am sure you do, would it not be possible to have an affair with him and leave it at that?'

'That's what I am having,' she pointed out. 'As he cannot marry me.'

'Yes. What I meant was, an affair in which you see each other whenever possible, and you spend a night with him, whenever possible . . . but you don't actually move in with him.'

'But I intend to move in with him,' she said. 'To do anything else would be an absolute sham. Besides, it's what I want to do.'

'Yes,' he said again. 'You will of course find few Japanese women to understand that point of view. I mean, few Japanese ladies.'

'I don't expect them to. But I am not Japanese, you see.'

'Yes,' he said a third time, more sceptically than ever.

'However, Yoshiye, if you have the slightest fear that my personal behaviour in my private life will affect the hospital in any way, I will resign here and now.'

'You? Resign from the hospital? I thought you loved it here?'

'I do. I love the children. But I love Philip more.'

He gazed at her, and she kept her face in its most determined mould. She had no doubt that she would win, if she just refused to weaken.

'I can see that,' Azuma said at last. 'And I am sure that your private life will not affect your position here in the slightest. I certainly shall defend you to the board, should the question arise. But *I* must be concerned with your private life. Your family will never forgive you. Because they *are* Japanese. You will find yourself rather isolated. Except for Philip, of course.'

'I do not wish anything more, Yoshiye.'

'Yes,' he said for the last time. 'He is a very fortunate fellow, is Philip Shimadzu. Let us hope he knows that.'

'Please to go in,' said the maid.

Anne took a very long breath, then stepped through the doorway into the lounge of Shikibu Shimadzu's house. And stopped. All four of them were there, seated on their cushions, staring at her, rather like a panel of judges, she thought. And were they not judges? My God, she remembered, only a hundred years ago, here in Japan these four people would have had the power to lock me up for the rest of my life, for attempting to defy them.

But this was not a hundred years ago, and these people, much as she loved them and hated to hurt them, had no power at all over her. Besides, they were in the wrong, for holding on to such archaic ideas of right and wrong, and of family authority. She simply had to remember that. Just as she had to remember that Hilary at least, was as

American as she was, and as broad-minded. Surely. And equally, she needed to remember how much she had shared with Shikibu, how close they had always been.

So she smiled, and bowed. 'Reporting as instructed,' she said.

'Anne,' William said. 'Come here and sit down.'

She obeyed.

'I really must apologise for my son,' Shikibu said. 'For suggesting such an arrangement. Sometimes I think he is quite out of touch with reality.'

'Please do not apologise for Philip, Aunt Shikibu,' Anne protested, making a mental note of how the family apparently intended to play this game, and deciding to take up the challenge from the start. 'It was I who suggested the current arrangement.'

'The current arrangement?' William inquired, frowning.

'I moved my things from Yokohama to Tokyo this morning,' Anne explained. 'Dr Azuma has very kindly given me a week's leave to get settled in.'

There was a thunderstruck silence.

'You have done this, without reference to me?' William asked at last.

'I am referring to you now, Uncle William,' Anne said.

'You are a wicked, wicked child,' Shikibu declared.

Anne stared at her in surprise, quite taken aback by the suddenness, and the vehemence, of the attack. 'For loving your son?'

'It is not right.'

'Love is always right, Aunt Shikibu. If it is real, and genuine, and deep-seated. I do not think anyone, knowing Philip and me, knowing anything of us, can doubt that our love is real, and deep, and genuine.'

'And the fact that he is your cousin?' Shikibu demanded.

'That is not a fact of sufficient importance to concern us, Aunt Shikibu. We are not within the proscribed

277

bounds of consanguinity.'

'What of the fact that I, your guardian, and all of your aunts, all of your family, indeed, strongly disapprove of this liaison?' William demanded.

'That alone concerns us,' Anne agreed. 'Thus I am here to ask you to give us your blessing. To agree to our marriage. Because we do love each other, and we do intend to live together, for the rest of our lives.'

'And by making this declaration you think you can come here and bully us, your elders, into agreeing to this infamous thing?' Shikibu snapped.

Once again Anne knew a sense of shock. She had experienced Shikibu's vehemence before, understood her almost rabid patriotism, her equally rabid hatred of the Chinese who had killed her husband . . . But she had never been anything less than a charming, sensual, delicate companion to her, until this moment.

'I had hoped you would understand,' she said quietly.

'As it *is* done,' Maureen began.

'Oh, yes,' Shikibu remarked. 'I might have known *you* would side with them. Had you been a man you would have liked to be Anne's father.'

'If I were a man,' Maureen answered, 'I would slap your face for that.'

'For heaven's sake,' William Freeman said. 'Can we not conduct this conversation as Japanese, and not Americans? Quarrelling will get us nowhere.'

'I believe that Aunt Maureen, through having spent so much of her time travelling round the world . . . ' Anne said.

'In the company of your mother,' Shikibu growled.

Anne ignored the interruption. 'Has achieved a more balanced point of view than those who have no experience of life outside of Japan,' she went on. 'I am grateful for your support, Aunt Maureen. Aunt Hilary, I appeal to you . . . '

Hilary hesitated, then looked at her husband. 'I am

Japanese now,' she said. 'I must agree with my husband's point of view. But even if we lived in America, Anne, I could not approve of what you are doing.'

Anne gazed at her for a moment, then got up and bowed. 'Then there is nothing more to be said.'

'But you will persist in this mad course?' William asked.

'I intend to spend as much of my life as I can with the man I love,' she said. 'You have but to give us permission to marry. If you will not do that, then I will, as you say, persist in this mad course.'

'Then we do not wish to look upon your face again,' William said. 'Until you have come to your senses.'

Anne drove slowly towards Philip's house. She supposed the realisation that she had just been banished by her family had not yet sunk into her brain – or it was too nineteenth century for her brain to accept. She was actually more angry than anything else, far more angry than before she had entered Shikibu's house, prepared to be angry. How people could be so *wrong*, and yet believe utterly they were right. How they could not see that it was their archaic intransigence that was causing all the trouble, that would be responsible for all the scandal, when it became public knowledge – if it was not already. She waited at a traffic light, fingers drumming impatiently on the wheel, and an open touring-car pulled up beside her. She ignored it, but turned her head sharply as someone said, in English, 'Anne? Anne Freeman, by George!'

She stared at the man, who wore the uniform of a British naval officer.

'I bet you don't remember me,' he said. 'John Graham. I last saw you . . . well . . . '

'The day of the earthquake,' she said. 'Oh, I remember you, Mr Graham. Oh, how great to see you again. I had no idea you were still in Tokyo.'

'Just about my life's work, I'm afraid,' Graham said, without regret. 'But you . . . What are you doing here?'

She had the oddest feeling that he already knew, that the question was a gambit. Or part of a gambit. 'I'm working down at the Anglo-American hospital in Yokohama,' she explained. 'I'm a doctor now.'

'Good lord,' he commented. 'Well, my best congratulations. Next time I'm ill I'll come down and see you.'

'Oh, please do,' she said. 'But does Philip know you're in Tokyo? He hasn't mentioned you to me.'

'Ah, well . . . we sort of drifted apart, don't you know.'

She frowned. 'You didn't quarrel?'

'Good lord, no. I still regard him as one of my favourite people. But he was transferred to Shanghai . . . '

'He'd love to see you,' she said. 'I know he would. He . . . ' She was interrupted by the blaring of a horn from behind her; the light had changed to green several seconds before. 'Pull in on the other side,' she shouted, and did so herself.

Graham parked his MG behind her, and got out.

She stayed behind her wheel, smiling up at him. 'He would love to see you, I'm sure,' she said. 'He . . . we . . . well, friends are a little thin on the ground, at the moment. Well, maybe you've heard sufficient rumours to make you want to give us a miss as well.'

'Rumours?' he asked. 'What rumours?'

This time she knew he was lying – but now he was being the perfect English gentleman. She thought she could do with some of that. 'Follow me home,' she suggested. 'I know he'd like to see you.'

Now she drove more quickly. Of course it was possible for Philip and herself to make a perfectly happy and normal life together, even without the support of their family. Tokyo was full of people like John Graham. Although John Graham was obviously the best. She parked the car and ran into the house.

'Philip!' she cried. 'Philip.' She knew he'd be home from the Admiralty by now, anxious to learn how her meeting with the family had gone. 'Oh, Phil, I have John Graham with me . . . ' She checked at the expression on his face. 'Phil? Is something wrong?'

He kissed her perfunctorily, then looked past her at Graham. 'Hello, John. I'm not supposed to see you, you know. Not in my present assignment.' He shook hands. 'But I don't suppose it matters, now.'

Graham looked questioningly at Anne, who clung to Philip's arm. 'Phil, for heaven's sake tell me what's happened.'

'How did your meeting go?' he asked.

'Oh . . . ' she shrugged. 'They said no.'

'So?'

'So I told them, nuts. We're going to do it anyway. Now, Phil, please . . . '

He sighed. 'I've been given a command,' he said. 'The battleship *Mutsu*.'

'The *Mutsu*?' she cried. 'But that's marvellous. Isn't she the biggest ship in the fleet?'

'Other than the carriers,' Graham said. 'Oh, best congratulations, Phil, old boy.'

Philip looked from one to the other. 'You don't understand,' he said. 'I am to assume command tomorrow morning, and the ship leaves on an extended goodwill cruise at the end of the week. Round the world. It is estimated we shall be away from Japan for approximately two years.'

'Two *years*?' Anne whispered.

'The order transferring me was signed yesterday morning,' Philip went on. 'Before you ever saw Uncle William.'

'Hm,' Graham said. 'It looks as if they mean business.' Thus proving that he did indeed know all about it; probably, Anne thought, everyone in Tokyo knew all about it. She was so angry that for a moment she could not speak.

'I have also been informed by my mother that I must return Iyeyasu to her for the time I shall be away,' Philip said.

'And you intend to do that?'

He sighed again. 'It is normal procedure. She is the boy's nearest living female relative.'

'I have just been ordered from their presence, forever,' Anne said.

'I think I had better leave,' Graham said, and did so.

'I cannot refuse a direct command,' Philip said.

'Of course you cannot, my darling. And such a command. Your next appointment can hardly be less than admiral. But I suppose you do not feel you can oppose your mother, either.'

'If I could make you understand . . . '

'I do understand,' she said. 'Just as I understand that this is a deliberate plan to separate us. Okay, they've won a round. But Phil, they can only win the battle if we let them. All I want to be sure of is that you will come back to me here, no matter what happens, no matter how long this voyage of yours lasts. Tell me you'll do that, and I'll wait. I'll move back to Yokohama, and I'll sit tight, and wait. Because surely, if we do that, and still get back together when you come home, the family will just *have* to say okay. So just say it, my darling. That you're going to come back to me.'

He kissed her. 'I'm going to come back to you, my dearest girl. Oh, I am going to come back to you.'

PART THREE

The Traitor

CHAPTER 11

The Plot

'Honourable Major.' Ikita Kitabake got up and came round his desk, bowing low before the small man in civilian dress.

'Honourable Captain.' Mori also bowed.

'I had heard you were returning to Tokyo,' Kitabake said. 'Will you not be seated?' He offered Mori a cigarette.

'Thank you.' Mori sat down and crossed his knees, accepted a light. 'Yes. It is felt that I may be a target for assassination in Shanghai, should I remain there much longer. And in fact, honourable Captain, ten years is long enough in one posting. Even a posting like Shanghai.'

'Ten years,' Kitabake murmured. 'That is indeed a long time. And now . . . ?'

'I shall remain in Tokyo for the foreseeable future,' Mori told him, and smiled. 'You will be making your reports to me, Kitabake San. As in the old days.'

'How nice!' Kitabake did not look altogether pleased.

'And there is much for us to do. You are aware that what has happened in China is irrevocable?'

'You mean the battle outside Mukden, and our occupation of Manchuria?'

'It was not a battle, Kitibake San,' Mori said, severely. 'It was an incident. Nothing more than that. It is very important to keep this fact always in mind. But I am talking about the occupation of Manchuria, yes. It is obvious that we had no choice, what with the murder of

287

Nakamura last year, and Chinese troops firing upon us . . . ' He paused to gaze at Kitabake.

'Oh, indeed,' Kitabake agreed, keeping his face straight.

'However, as you are no doubt aware,' Mori went on, 'the League of Nations has taken it upon itself to investigate the circumstances, and has sent a commission, headed by some English milord, to learn the truth of the matter.'

'I have heard that.'

'Are you also aware that there is virtually no chance the findings of this commission can be favourable to us?'

'Well, if it is allowed to interview *everybody*,' Kitabake said cautiously.

'There is no chance,' Mori repeated. 'I would therefore like you to give me your estimation of what will happen, when this report, unfavourable to Japan, is ultimately published.'

'Well . . . ' Kitabake looked even more cautious. 'Presuming the report is handed to the League of Nations, and presuming that it brands us the aggressor, presuming even the worst . . . ' He glanced at his superior. 'That it suggests it was actually our troops who fired on the Chinese, and not vice versa . . . '

'All of those assumptions should be made, honourable Captain.'

'Yes. Well, no doubt the League of Nations will order our forces to withdraw from Manchuria and pay China an indemnity.'

'And should we refuse to do that?'

'Ah. Well, they may impose sanctions. This could be a grave matter, honourable Major.'

'Can you conceive of us withdrawing from Manchuria? Can you estimate the loss of face that would entail?'

'Undoubtedly,' Kitabake said. 'On the other hand . . . '

'It is considered unlikely that the commission will complete its investigations and release its report for at least another year,' Mori said. 'So to all intents and purposes there will be no crisis before 1933. Are we expected to stand still for another year, waiting? Plans are already advanced for the creation of a puppet Chinese government in Manchuria. We are already in negotiation with the former Manchu emperor, Pu-I, and he is responding favourably to our proposals. Can you imagine being forced to abandon all of that?'

'Well,' Kitabake said, 'having set up this state, what is it to be called, Manchukuo?'

Mori smiled. 'You are better informed than I had supposed, Kitabake San.'

'Well,' Kitabake went on. 'Would it not be possible to say that we have now liberated Manchukuo from Chinese tyranny, and will now withdraw our forces?'

'Never,' Mori declared. 'We intend to keep Manchuria. Of course, we shall stay because Pu-I begs us to, but I doubt that will fool many people. No, no, Kitabake San. Should our recent movements be condemned by the League of Nations, I can tell you in confidence that the army means to force our government to leave that body.'

Kitabake frowned. 'But that . . . '

'Will mean what? In real terms. The Western Powers are all bankrupt. They have bankrupted themselves by this absurd financial system they have used for so long, and which has now collapsed beneath them like a house of cards. They are in no position to take any positive action against us, other than raise their tariff barriers, and they are doing that anyway, as a consequence of the Depression. What is more, our financial advisers say the situation is unlikely to change for some considerable time. We shall never have a better opportunity to assert ourselves, here in East Asia.'

Kitabake shook his head. 'If you mean now is the moment to launch the Strike South Plan, I do not believe it can be done. Our navy is simply not ready, and our oil reserves are too low. If oil sanctions were to be imposed on us . . . '

'These are matters I mean to discuss with you in a moment, honourable Captain. However, they are not truly relevant. What was the purpose of the Strike South concept? It was to free us from the risk of American or British interference while we obtained our requirements from China. But that risk no longer exists, as I have just demonstrated. So the plan can be shelved for the time being. No, no, my friend, I will tell you where our most serious opposition will arise: right here in Japan.'

Kitabake's frown deepened. 'I do not understand.'

'We are aware that there are many people, many people in high positions as well as amongst the nation at large, who do not approve of what the army is doing. The poor short-sighted fools believe it is possible to prosper in this world without fighting for the right to do so. We have no doubt at all that these white-livered weaklings will react most strongly to a condemnation of Japan by the League of Nations.'

'If they are the majority,' Kitabake murmured. 'Then . . .'

'Bah! What nonsense. It is we, the samurai, who decide what the nation does. Not a majority composed of honin. I have been returned to Tokyo to draw up a list of all prominent people who might oppose our will over the next few years. They will have to be dealt with, one way or another.'

Kitabake gazed at him. Assassination of one's opponents was a very old means of conducting politics in Japan, and he was not the least concerned by the moral implications of what Mori had just told him. But he was staggered by the immensity of the task proposed.

'So I will rely upon you to supply me with the names of all potential opponents in the navy.'

'I think you will find that the navy, and its officers, will carry out whatever duties are required of it by the government of the day, Mori San, as it has always done.'

'Will I find that, Kitabake San? Who is the most senior of our admirals?'

'William Freeman.'

'A man with American blood in his veins. The man who negotiated the infamous Washington Agreement.'

'That is not quite correct, Mori San. Admiral Freeman was part of the negotiating team.'

'By far the most influential part,' Mori pointed out.

'Possibly. Possibly he has always taken the view that Japan is but one member of an international brotherhood of nations . . .'

'Aha!' Mori cried, pointing.

'But he is on the verge of retirement,' Kitabake added.

'On the verge. He has not yet retired. And he is not due to do so for three years. Three years is too long. And even after he is retired, he will carry too much weight. Then there is that nephew of his.'

'Yes,' Kitabake said thoughtfully. 'It is odd that you should mention Captain Shimadzu.'

'He let you down with a bump,' Mori reminded him. 'You recommended him for the Shanghai posting.'

'On the recommendation of his uncle,' Kitabake pointed out. 'But I agree with you; he did let me down with a bump.'

'And now I am told that he commands our finest battleship.'

'That is true, yes. He is presently on a round-the-world goodwill cruise.' He smiled. 'To undo some of the damage done to our reputation by the army.'

'Bah!' Mori said. 'Goodwill cruise. What nonsense.'

'Nevertheless, it was undertaken on the instructions of Viscount Saito personally. And of course a man like Shimadzu is ideally suited for such a task, with his international background. However, he was really appointed to command *Mutsu* to extricate him from the design office.'

'Explain?'

'The pattern is very indistinct. He is, of course, an internationalist, like his uncle. That is not surprising, as his uncle is also his guardian. He is also perhaps a romantic, as he proved in Shanghai . . . '

'He should have been cashiered for that,' Mori growled.

'He has powerful friends. Anyway, it was felt that the design office would be a good place for him, because, make no mistake, Mori San, he is a brilliant man. He has an imagination, which so many of our officers lack. Well, he was in fact a great success at the design office; he managed to steer that very narrow path between giving us the best in weapons and equipment, and especially anti-aircraft defences, and yet not openly contravening the Washington Agreement. Oh, there was that unhappy incident of the destroyer capsizing, but it was a typhoon, and it was in any event proved not to be Shimadzu's fault, as he had indeed advised against adding additional guns on deck because of the top-heaviness that would be induced.'

'I understand he also refused to commission a design for a larger aircraft-carrier than any now in existence,' Mori commented.

Kitabake raised his eyebrows. 'You are also well informed, Mori San,' he said. 'But that is not altogether correct. Shimadzu did commission the design, but he also commissioned a very careful costing of the project, and when he first submitted it to their lordships they knew at once that it was not a practical proposition, given the existing naval budget. He has obtained a reputation for the highest integrity. Even the Shanghai affair helped that.'

'So?' Mori did not look pleased.

'That is what makes an incident which has been reported to me so odd. Nearly two years ago, just before his appointment to *Mutsu*, he removed, or in fact, which was worse, he caused to be removed, some top-secret documents from the design office to his home. It is of course possible that he saw nothing irregular in doing this, as the documents were his own compilation, drawn up by himself during the London Naval Conference, and containing his own notes on proposed future limitations in tonnage and armaments, and how we could circumnavigate such limitations. There was also ample reason for his act in causal terms; his son had contracted scarlet fever, he had himself been placed under house quarantine, and he was in the middle of preparing his report. Therefore, like the conscientious officer he is, he sought to continue his work even while unable to attend his office. But nonetheless, it was an irregularity.'

'Go on.' Mori's face was beginning to relax.

'Even more irregular was the means he employed to obtain the documents. As he could not go himself, he sent a messenger. And the messenger was not even his personal servant, but a woman. And not even a Japanese woman, but an American.'

Mori sat up, now definitely looking happy. 'Her name?'

'It is in the file. Anne Freeman.'

'Freeman? But does that not mean . . . ?'

Kitabake nodded. 'Indeed. She is some kind of relative of Shimadzu's.'

'And she was here in Japan?'

'She is still here in Japan. She is a doctor, down at the Anglo-American hospital in Yokohama. But, and here is the sinister aspect of the situation, she is also Shimadzu's mistress.'

Mori's brows drew together.

'It is something of a family scandal. In fact, Admiral Freeman himself wished to do something about it, separate them, as it were, at the very moment that I was recommending Shimadzu's transfer from the design office. I did not then know of the irregularity concerning

293

the conference documents, but I had been informed that this Freeman woman had spent several nights at Shimadzu's house, and obviously any officer with a foreign mistress cannot be allowed to have access to secret documents.'

'That is true,' Mori said. 'So he was sent away to a plum job at sea. But you say the woman is still here?'

Kitabake smiled. 'No doubt waiting for him to come back. Which will be in another couple of months.'

'Yes,' Mori said. 'That is interesting. But not, unfortunately decisive. If the woman had left, or was known to have contacts with some foreign agent . . . How I would like to find something really important to hang on Philip Shimadzu.'

'I have not finished yet,' Kitabake said.

Mori raised his head. He played cards, and could tell when his opponent possessed a hitherto unsuspected trump.

'Have you ever heard of a man called John Graham?' Kitabake asked.

'The British Naval attaché?'

'That is quite correct. I have had him under surveillance for some time.'

Mori shrugged. 'So he is a spy. All naval attachés are spies. But very obvious ones.'

'Granted. But he is also a spy who has remained in one place for a very long time. Ten years.'

'I was in Shanghai for ten years,' Mori reminded him.

'Exactly. And you were engaged in subversion as well as observation. It is not a usual British custom to leave their men in one place for so long.'

'You mean you think Graham may be engaged in subversion? Here in Tokyo?'

'Yes, I do believe that. And yet, up to now I have never uncovered anything which might be held against him. He projects a hail-fellow-well-met image, comes across as rather a fool, in fact, and has a wide circle of friends here in Tokyo, and in Yokohama. He is very popular. None of those things can be considered as subversive activities. However, there is one thing about him which has always interested me: he is, or was, at one time, Philip Shimadzu's best friend.'

Mori's thoughtful frown was back.

'You did not know that, did you?' Kitabake demanded, triumphantly. 'But it is true. Graham was Shimadzu's groomsman, at his marriage to Haruko Tokagawa.'

Mori stroked his chin.

'Afterwards, of course, they saw less of each other,' Kitabake went on, 'although Graham from time to time visited Shimadzu on his first command, the cruiser *Yahagi*; he was certainly with him, for instance, on the day of the earthquake. After that Shimadzu was sent to Shanghai, as you know, and when he returned, he did not resume his friendship with Graham. In fact he hardly saw him. Well, of course he could not possibly be a close friend of a foreign naval attaché while serving in the design office.'

'Then I do not understand what you are trying to tell me,' Mori said. 'Shimadzu appears to have acted quite correctly regarding Graham while in the design office, and he left that office only a week before taking command of *Mutsu*, since when he has been at sea for well over a year. Or did he see Graham between removing the papers from his office and going to sea?'

'That I cannot say for certain.'

Mori gave a snort of impatient disappointment.

'But,' Kitabake went on, 'Graham has certainly come back into Shimadzu's life, Mori San, even if indirectly. Graham has been seeing a great deal of this Miss Anne Freeman.'

Mori snapped his fingers. 'Who is Shimadzu's mistress, and who is the woman sent by Shimadzu to take the confidential papers from the design office.'

Kitabake leaned back with a smile. 'I have to admit that the information was fortuitous. I had not yet learned of the incident with the papers when one of my people was approached by Miss Idzuma Kurosowa, who had apparently been in the employ of Shimadzu, and had been dismissed. One suspects she was more than just a servant, and hell hath no fury like a woman scorned, eh? She gave me the information that the woman Freeman had been seeing Graham. In fact, Kurosowa, who had apparently been watching Shimadzu's house, claims that Freeman actually took Graham there, a few days before Shimadzu assumed command of *Mutsu*.'

'Over a year ago,' Mori said. 'And you have done nothing? Well, I shall arrest this Freeman woman immediately. To have a woman belonging to Shimadzu at Kempai Headquarters . . . Is she handsome?'

'Extremely so,' Kitabake said. 'And I am beginning to believe what they say of you, Mori San, that you are nothing more than a thug. However, may I suggest most strongly that you control your impatience, for a little while longer? Because there are many aspects of this situation which need very careful consideration. Anne Freeman is an American citizen. The Americans may not be prepared to react to what is happening in China, but I suspect there would be a considerable reaction to the arrest and, ah, interrogation of one of their nationals by the Kempai. We would have to have irrefutable proof of her implication in spying. Then supposing she did confess to having passed secret papers to Graham, what could you do about him? Only demand his deportation as an undesirable alien; he is protected by his diplomatic immunity from arrest. And most important of all, I doubt you would uncover anything of value, even from Anne Freeman. Is not the real prize Philip Shimadzu?'

'To nail him I would give five years of my life,' Mori said.

'Well, why do we not just wait, and watch, and listen,

and see. Whatever information Anne Freeman gave John Graham, it is long gone. She has been able to give him nothing since, because her source, Philip Shimadzu, has been at sea all of that time. But Philip Shimadzu is on his way home, undoubtedly again to take up with his beautiful mistress, and equally with his old friend, who is also her old friend. Why do we not just be patient, Mori San. We may turn up more than we even dream of, in the course of time.'

The *Mutsu* was a dream come true, amongst warships. Seven hundred and thirty-eight feet long, more than a hundred feet wide, and thirty feet in draught, displacing more than forty-two thousand tons, powered by ten boilers which delivered eighty-two thousand horsepower to her four-shaft geared turbines, armed with eight sixteen-inch guns in four double turrets, plus a myriad of lesser weapons, and carrying three aircraft, manned by one thousand, three hundred and sixty-eight men, she was, with her sister ship *Nagato*, still the largest battleship afloat; the British giants, *Nelson* and *Rodney*, because of the British determination to keep as close to the Washington Agreement tonnage limitations of thirty-five thousand tons as possible, outstripped the Japanese ships only in possessing one more sixteen-inch gun – they were neither as long nor as heavy. As she rode to her mooring amongst the lesser ships of the Imperial Japanese Navy in Tokyo Bay, she looked what she was, a triumph of naval design and engineering. It was in fact impossible not to look at her and feel a thrill throughout the body, not to have tears come to the eyes.

But there were more reasons for Anne Freeman to have tears than just the beauty and majesty of the ship, or the fact that she was now home after more than two years. In the crowd that had watched her moor, and now waited patiently for husbands and brothers and sons, and lovers, to come ashore, there were also Shikibu and Iyeyasu.

How the boy had grown. The boy she would have made her own, Anne thought. He was all but ten years old now, far too tall for a Japanese, although his lank black hair and yellow-brown complexion merely made him seen an incipient giant himself, rather than an alien. And in fact, he was not an alien. He possessed only an eighth American blood. She herself had been going to turn him into an alien, Anne knew, however inadvertently. So perhaps it had all turned out for the best after all.

But how she longed to run forward and take him into her arms, and smile at Shikibu. A temptation to be resisted. In nearly two years she had seen nothing of her aunts or her uncle. There had been no scandal, because of Philip's banishment, but she had still transgressed, and she was the one who had to return on her knees and beg forgiveness. She would never do that. At least, not until she knew whether she had anything to beg forgiveness for.

But she did, and she would. Because she had all of Philip's letters, mailed from every port where the *Mutsu* had brought up, and where, no doubt, admiring crowds had filed on board, to cast respectful glances at her handsome captain. Those letters had shown no diminution of his love.

At last the waiting was over, and the liberty boats were coming ashore, headed by the captain's pinnace. The crowd clapped its admiration as he came up the steps from the floating dock and saluted, and then bowed to his mother, before taking both her and his son into his arms. His greeting was warm, loving . . . and perfunctory. His eyes searched the crowd even as he held Shikibu close, and when he saw Anne, he nodded his head for her to come forward. When she hesitated, he nodded again.

Anne took a deep breath, and stepped from the throng. 'Phil,' she said. 'Oh, Phil!'

'Auntie Anne!' Iyeyasu cried, in a mixture of pleasure and surprise. She wondered what they had told him, that she had gone back to America, perhaps?'

'Iyeyasu,' she said in reply, but was already in Philip's arms. The crowd once again applauded, but its attention was now distracted by the arrival of all the other men who had been for so long absent from their families.

Anne found herself released, and looking at Shikibu. 'Aunt Shiki,' she said, and bowed.

Shikibu hesitated, and then suddenly reached forward and took her into her arms. 'My dear girl,' she said. 'My dear, dear girl. There is a car waiting.'

'For us all,' Philip said.

Shikibu hesitated once more, and then sighed. 'For us all,' she agreed.

Shikibu sat in the back with Iyeyasu and Anne, leaving Philip to share the front with the driver. 'I will speak with your uncle, of course,' she said. 'But I do not know . . . he has much on his mind.'

'Haven't we all,' Philip said. But at this moment he had only love on his mind, and delight at being home again.

'When can I go on board, honourable Father?' Iyeyasu asked. 'When can I?'

'Why . . . tomorrow,' Philip promised. 'I will show you everything.' He turned his head to smile at the women. 'I will show all of you everything.'

'No one knows what is going to happen,' Shikibu said gloomily. 'There are rumours that we are going to leave the League of Nations . . . I do not know what to say. There is considerable feeling in the country. And then, the assassination of Prime Minister Inukai, only a year after Prime Minister Hamaguchi was shot . . . '

'I heard about it,' Philip said. 'It is a serious situation.'

'Who'd be a prime minister,' Anne said, trying to lighten the conversation.

'Viscount Saito is now in charge,' Shikibu said.

Philip nodded. 'He is a good man. And strong.'

'Of course. He too resists the more extreme demands

of the army. But will he not also be assassinated?' Shikibu asked.

Philip turned his head again to smile at her. 'You paint too sombre a picture, Mother. It is an unfortunate fact that political assassination is as common in Japan as gangland assassination is in Chicago. But we will eventually bring these murdering thugs to book. And curb the army too. As for leaving the league, well, there have been international crises before, and we are still here. I am still here. Now. Home. And you and Anne are going to be friends again. Are you not?'

Another brief hesitation. 'If this is what you truly wish, my son, who am I to stand in your way? But I cannot answer for your uncle. He is an embittered old man. And not only as regards you. He is embittered about Japan, too.'

'I feel sorry for him, you know,' Philip confided to Graham, as they sat in the bar of the Officers' Club after their bi-weekly game of tennis. 'He is reaching the end of his active life, and he sees everything that he has sought to create for Japan being squandered by these military hotheads.'

Graham nodded. 'It is a potentially explosive situation. And I am amazed that you can still describe them merely as hotheads.'

'I would say that the worst thing any of us can do would be to adopt hysterical attitudes,' Philip said. 'Or over-react in any way. Oh, I am not attempting to belittle the murder of two prime ministers in two years. In many countries that would indicate a state of anarchy. But do you see any evidence of that in Japan? Assassination has been used as a legitimate political weapon here for too long.'

'I thought you were intent on entering the twentieth century,' Graham remarked.

'I sometimes wonder if we are ready for it,' Philip

observed. And smiled. 'Or if the twentieth century is ready for us. Of course it makes the blood boil to know that no one has ever been convicted of either of those crimes . . . The actual assassins merely committed suicide on arrest. But this again is time-honoured custom. Although you would think that the famous Kempai would have a lead by now on who is financing these crimes.'

'I imagine they do,' Graham ventured.

'Perhaps. In which case the situation could be more serious than I thought. But I have the utmost faith in Viscount Saito. You know, Hamaguchi and Inukai were both civilians, professional politicians. Saito is an army man himself, who fortunately opposes the extremists. Is this not a good sign?'

'Until they bump him off too,' Graham said.

'They will have to think long and hard about that. He has considerable support in the army. And he is a very strong, hard man. He knows what is best for Japan, and he will do it.'

'Like taking you out of the League of Nations?'

'Oh, that. Is not everyone making too much of that? The League of Nations is a great idea, but it hasn't worked, has it? I should like you to tell me why there is so much fuss about our announcing we are leaving the league, when countries like the United States or Soviet Russia have never even bothered to join.'

'Russia is about to become a member,' Graham told him.

'Well, perhaps they feel the need. We do not. I cannot see that refusing to belong to such an international organisation has to brand us as pariahs.'

'Um,' Graham said. 'Your circumstances are a little different to the Americans, surely. They refused to come in from the start, for fear of having to become involved in another European war. You are leaving because of criticism by just about every other nation in the world.'

301

'Because of Manchuria. Well, maybe we can rejoin when that furore dies down.'

'But you will not give it up?'

'How can we, now? We have established an independent state there.'

'Independent?'

Philip smiled. 'As long as Japanese bayonets are holding it up. That is why we cannot quit now. There would be a massacre of all those who have supported us.' His smile widened. 'The British have the same problem in Ireland, have they not? And don't tell me you conquered Ireland a very long time ago. You still conquered it.'

'Oh, hell, who am I to argue against history,' Graham acknowledged. 'But can you promise me that Manchuria . . . I beg your pardon, Manchukuo . . . will be the last of your conquests? What about that fighting down in Shanghai last year? That was a pitched battle between Chinese and Japanese forces.'

Philip nodded. 'It has been brewing for a long time. It makes you wonder . . . When I was down there, the military was really in the hands of a most detestable man named Mori. I expected a pitched battle to take place almost any day. But it never did. Now I believe Mori has been recalled to Japan. And what happens? Fighting breaks out. Maybe he was better at his job than I thought.'

'Maybe. It was still an ugly incident. And now, is it true you people are withdrawing from the naval agreements?'

'We have given notice of such intention, yes. To take effect in 1936.'

'But you have already started building vessels outside the treaty limits.'

Philip gazed at him. 'I do not know. I am no longer in charge of the design office. And if I were, old friend, I could not possibly give you such classified information.'

'Oh, forgive me,' Graham said. 'Would you accept that

I am really worried for you? I mean, for Japan. I suppose I've lived here so long now I almost consider myself a Japanese. I like everything about this country. And whether you care for it or not, Phil, Japan needs the rest of the world, and belongs in it. This planet is just too small, nowadays, for any nation to opt out completely. I would hate to think your leaders are dreaming of attempting another two and a half centuries of isolation.'

Philip slapped him on the shoulder. 'No chance of that. And shall I tell you something? There is going to be a change.'

Graham frowned. 'What sort of change?'

'I don't know. But you can feel it in the air. The army has really gone too far, because most Japanese feel as you do, or as I, for that matter. We are not a politically minded people. I mean the people, not the generals and the professional politicians. So we have ambled along now for too long, thirty, nearly forty years, with the ambitious generals telling us what to do next. When we were small and irrelevant to the West, the English and the Americans and the French patted us on the shoulder and said, good show, knocking over the wicked Manchus and the wicked tsars. So the people cheered. Now that we have grown into a first-class power, the West isn't so happy. Instead of the wicked Manchu it is poor Chiang Kai-shek, only trying to reunite his country. So we have been criticised and isolated for opposing him. These things have filtered through to the people. A regiment of soldiers was booed the other day, down in Kyushu. The people know where our troubles originate. Once Viscount Saito is sure he has the support of the people, it will be possible for him to take a firm line with the army. I would say there is very little risk of further expansionism.'

'And the navy?'

'The navy has always done what the government of the

303

day asked it to do, John. Not vice versa.'

'Then it was the government's idea to abrogate the naval treaties?'

'That I cannot say. And you should not ask me. Now, let us get dressed and hurry home. Anne is waiting dinner.'

They stood up. 'I envy you,' Graham said. 'Your happiness. Your confidence.'

'Perhaps the two things go together,' Philip said. 'Do you know, I sometimes envy myself, and wonder how it came about.' He grinned. 'But I don't ask myself that question, either.'

If only it were true. Acting to Graham, however distasteful, was simple enough; he had simply to remind himself of all the propaganda which was continually pumped at him and at every other naval officer. At the entire country. And the country undoubtedly swallowed it whole. But then, so did most naval officers. Because not sufficient of them knew of the files lying in dusty drawers, the plans for the Strike South concept? He wondered what John Graham would say, if he ever discovered the existence of those plans.

Or had they been thrown away by now? Certainly the army had gone ahead with its plans without turning to the navy at all. It was almost as if the Japanese armed services belonged to two different countries.

But how did one explain away, in 1933, the murder of two prime ministers in consecutive years? Even the average Roman emperor had managed to last more than twelve months. All without trial, or without released investigation. Anarchists. Paid by the army? Or far more sinisterly, as Graham had hinted, by the Kempai itself? What happened to a country when its secret police, and a secret police as vicious and ruthless as he knew the Kempai to be, actually took control? Did the Emperor know? Of course not. No one would have dared tell him.

304

But did the generals know? Or did they suppose they could still ultimately control this cancerous growth in their midst?

A growth for which he worked. There could be no doubt of that. If Japan was ever forced to go to war, because of her aggression on the mainland or to the south, he would be on the bridge of the *Mutsu* as she steamed into action, her sixteen-inch guns blazing away.

Did Anne realise that? It was not a possibility he dared discuss with her, for fear of upsetting the delicate balance of their relationship. Because, incredibly, they *were* happy. He had not, in fact, known or dared hope it was possible to be so happy.

Only the opposition of William in any way cast a shadow across their domesticity. Even Hilary allowed herself to be invited to Shikibu's house when she knew Anne and Philip were going to be there. But William would not relent. It was pure pride, of course; the fact that Anne had moved in with her handsome cousin had not caused half the scandal they had feared it might – she was recognised as a foreigner, and foreigners behaved in foreign ways. But William could only see that they had defied him, and he was the guardian of them both. He would not relent. Nor, Philip knew, would he accept any overtures towards a reconciliation as long as they continued to live together.

But how could they contemplate anything else? Because they were three, a family. And Iyeyasu worshipped the ground Anne walked upon. Shikibu had been quite correct when she claimed that the boy did not remember anything of Haruko; she had been incorrect when she claimed that he must therefore look on Idzuma as a mother – perhaps subconsciously, he had always been aware that Idzuma was a servant. Anne he only ever remembered as a friend, and the woman who had nursed him through his illness, and as a woman he in any event adored because she represented the huge wide world

305

outside of Japan, a world in which he was intensely interested. It was in fresh, keen young brains like Iyeyasu's, indeed, untainted by that overwhelming dependence on the past which so handicapped Japanese thought, that the best future for the country lay, Philip knew.

While Anne herself was perfection, and not merely towards the boy; she was perfection towards all children. But she also loved. Even though, as he knew, she was not as happy as himself. She wished to be married, and have children of her own. Until that happened, she was determined to use all available contraceptive devices to prevent a pregnancy. It was not a point they ever quarrelled about, much as he too would have liked other children, and much as he wanted to make her the happiest woman in the world. And much as he knew that her American mind must reflect on the absurdity of the situation, where they were both total adults. But she had lived in Japan long enough to know that for someone in Philip's position to marry in the face of his, and her, guardian's determined opposition would cause a family crisis all over again, would even rock Tokyo society, and would certainly have the most adverse effect on Philip's career. And Anne was still young enough to be patient, even as she approached her thirtieth birthday, and to pray that William would relent. Hilary was working on him, they knew, and she had some hopes that his attitude might change when he retired, which was due to happen in only a year's time.

Philip dared not attempt to envisage what Anne's attitude might be if their uncle still opposed their marriage then, but for the moment it was possible to be happy. They loved. Even though he was away for long periods, taking *Mutsu* to sea, for manoeuvres under Isoroku Yamamoto's command. Often, indeed, the fleet commander actually flew his flag in *Mutsu* – and how good it was to be working with Yamamoto again at what they both knew, and loved, best: commanding ships at sea. But that only made their reunions the more entrancing, their family holidays the more enjoyable. During the next two years, when he was home, they would take long weekends and go up into the Hakone Mountains, to swim and climb, and when longer vacations were available, they would go right down south to Kyushu, the home of Philip's ancestors, taking the water route by the Inland Sea, wandering over Japan's most spreading countryside, climbing the immense slopes of Mount Aso to stare down at the bubbling lava beneath them, and wonder at the immensity of the crater, which stretched some twenty-three miles and contained a dozen prosperous villages.

Often John Graham accompanied them. He was almost like a brother, the brother that Peter had never been. Being an introspective man, Philip even occasionally wondered if he should be jealous. Apparently, during his round-the-world cruise on *Mutsu*, Anne had seen a lot of Graham. He had taken her to dinners and nightclubs, played tennis with her, gone swimming with her . . . but all without, according to Anne, ever crossing the bounds of the perfect English gentleman. This had puzzled her. 'Do you think he's well . . . odd?' she asked. 'You know, it's called the English disease.'

Philip had offered no opinion. Homosexuality was equally a Japanese vice, or pastime; but it was not considered a vice in Japan. And if Graham was a homosexual he was certainly discreet about it. And if he was, did it matter? He was masculine and athletic, and the most pleasant and charming man Philip had ever known. 'You mean you're upset because he's never made a pass at you,' he joked.

'Grateful,' she countered. 'I wouldn't have known what to do.'

'Because you fancy him?'

'Because he's your best friend, silly.'

Which he supposed was absolutely true. Even if they might one day have to fire guns at each other? He could not believe that. That was insanity, and an impossibility, too. Whatever the army thought.

It was possible to be happy, not only because of their love, and their love for their separate occupations – for she adored her hospital as much as he adored his ship, and they both recognised that mutual adoration – but also because Japan itself was a suddenly and strangely happy place during those three years before 1936. The very worst had happened, and yet nothing had happened, and thus it was possible to feel that the worst was past. The country had been roundly condemned by the entire world as an aggressor nation – but it had not been forced to disgorge a single one of its conquests, and indeed it was those conquests, and the continued pressure they were able to put on China to accept Japanese goods at a low tariff rate, that kept the nation economically viable.

And if both the army and the navy were continuing to expand and arm – Philip could not help but thrill to some of the leaked information emanating from the design office concerning giant battleships and even that fifty-thousand-ton aircraft-carrier Yamamoto had once dreamed of – the army had, as he had prophesied to Graham, lost much of its clout since the China incident. The people of Japan had held their breaths at the audacity of it . . . and allowed themselves a great sigh of relief as it had worked. They did not wish to repeat so harrowing an experience. And undoubtedly most of them all knew enough to relate the assassinations of the two consecutive liberal prime ministers to army machinations, and wanted no more part of that, either.

Viscount Saito and his largely civilian government were now firmly in control. The general election they had called for February 1936 would undoubtedly increase that control, according to the political experts, as their majority would grow, and thus enable them to increase their attempts to mend Japan's fences with the West. Of course, they could never go so far as to offer to abandon Manchuria, or Formosa, or Korea; no Japanese, even a liberal, would forgive them for that. But by illustrating how prosperous and well run those countries were beneath Japanese rule, and how apparently happy and contented their people, as compared with the rest of China – where civil war had now become endemic in a vast three-sided contest between Chiang Kai-shek and his Nationalists on the one hand, half a dozen warlords on the other, and the Communists, who had developed into a formidable fighting force, on the third – the Japanese leaders felt they were making a very good case for their conquests to be recognised. Misery, starvation and death were the lots of the average Chinese. This could not be said of Manchuria or Korea.

And if *he* knew that both countries were really under the heel of the Kempai, and woe betide anyone who attempted to oppose or even criticise Japanese rule, well, he had to reflect that that was the way of the world. And be grateful that at least he, now nearly the senior captain in the fleet, with flag rank surely only a year or two away, need no longer have any dealings whatsoever with that organisation.

After so many years of trauma and uncertainty, he had at last arrived at a plateau of happiness, with only greater happinesses to come. Or so it appeared on the day that his brother came to see him.

Philip was in his day cabin on board *Mutsu*, reading over the log just before going ashore for a weekend with his family, when Hagi appeared in the doorway, bowing, to announce General Peter Shimadzu. Philip leapt to his feet. 'Peter! Good heavens. Peter!'

They gazed at each other. In the twelve years that had elapsed since Haruko's death they had seen very little of each other, only for the odd meal at Shikibu's house when they had both happened to be in Tokyo at the same time. Peter had certainly prospered. Although only two years the elder, he was, at forty-seven, a full general, and in command of the Seoul garrison. But it was remarkable how little he had changed over the years, the same little moustache, the same abrupt manner, even in his bow. And he had never married. Philip wondered if behind that coldly military bearing his brother also had a loving mistress, and also loved.

'Philip!' Peter came into the cabin, and they embraced. 'It is good to see you.'

'And you. I had no idea you were in Tokyo. Is it long leave? We could go shooting together.'

'I have returned to Tokyo for good,' Peter said.

'Transferred?'

'Yes.' Peter sat down, looked at the door in a pointed fashion. Philip closed it. 'I applied for the transfer, actually. One gets tired of existing in a colonial town, when there is so much to be done.'

'Oh, quite.' Philip sat down himself. 'Sake? Tea?'

'Perhaps later. This is a magnificent vessel you command.'

'Yes,' Philip agreed. 'There is none like her.'

'Although she is rather old, is she not?'

'Well, yes, I suppose she is. We try to keep her arms and equipment updated of course, but twenty years is old. As a matter of fact, she is due to be replaced by one of the new battleships now under consideration, but heaven knows when that will actually happen. To be honest, they are so hush-hush not even I know anything about them.'

'So you will command one of these new ships?'

Philip bowed. 'I would hope to, honourable Brother.'

'Surely you should hope *not* to,' Peter pointed out. 'Are you not ready for flag rank?'

'I am ready, certainly,' Philip agreed. 'But it is a matter of dead men's shoes, you know.'

'Oh, indeed,' Peter said. 'Thanks to the policies of our

masters. The absurdities of our masters.'

Philip suppressed a sigh. He hoped he was not going to receive a political lecture.

'And how is Anne?' Peter asked.

Philip raised his eyebrows in surprise. 'She is well.'

'I would like to come and visit her, and you, of course,' Peter said.

'You are welcome. She would love to see you. Why not come ashore with me now, and have dinner with us tonight? We – well, as you may have heard, our arrangement is not regarded with universal approval. In fact, I had no idea *you* approved . . . '

'I hardly wish to be classed with Uncle William,' Peter pointed out, 'in my views of the world. I am sure you both know best how you wish to conduct your personal affairs.'

'Well, if I may say so, honourable Brother, that is the best news I have heard in years. I really think this calls for some sake.'

'When we have talked,' Peter said.

Philip, reaching for the bell to summon Hagi, lowered his hand. He frowned. His brother certainly seemed to have something on his mind.

'I would ask your opinion of the state of the nation,' Peter said.

Philip raised his eyebrows. 'I would say it is as satisfactory as can be expected, given the circumstances. Viscount Saito seems to have got on top of the political instability, and as long as we have China as a market we shall not starve, even if we may not actually prosper at this moment. But as the rest of the world pulls out of the Depression, and as we are, shall I say, forgiven for our misdeeds and thus faced with lower tariff walls, why, I see nothing but prosperity ahead of us.'

Peter gazed at him. 'You are incredibly naive, honourable Brother. But then, you always were.'

Philip waited to be enlightened as to his naivety, with a

sinking heart. He was, after all, in for a political lecture.

'Do you really suppose that the rest of the world, as you put it, by which I understand you to mean the Western bloc of powers, will ever treat with Japan as an equal, unless we force them to do so? Have they ever done so?'

'Well . . .'

'Consider,' Peter said. 'They have accepted our expansion, simply because we told them we would brook no interference from them. They have taken what revenge they could by raising their tariffs against our goods, but that is the revenge of a child. Yet what do we see now? A government which is getting ready to kowtow to London and Washington, to make amends. To crawl on its belly, not realising that our enemies will merely step on its head. But that head will be Japan.'

Philip sighed. He had had too much of this sort of thing, from people like Mori, and even Yamamoto, his immediate commander.

'It is a fact that, throughout life, throughout history,' Peter went on, warming to his theme, 'the only prosperous and successful, and, I may say, happy nations, have been those who have been strong, and have demonstrated their strength to themselves. Indeed, nations at war. Victorious war.'

'Oh, come now . . .'

'Why do you not listen? Was not the fifth century BC the greatest in the history of Greek art and literature and sculpture, a time when they made their greatest contribution to the thought and progress of mankind? And it was a century of unending warfare, against Persia and even against each other.'

'Yes, but . . .'

'And when did Shakespeare and Marlowe and Spenser and Milton flourish? When Great Britain was fighting for its life against Spain, or during the Great Rebellion.'

'Well, I suppose there is some argument in that direction,' Philip agreed, unable to think of an adequate counter at such short notice.

'We in the army have long been aware of these facts,' Peter said. 'We have always conceived it to be our duty to remind the nation of these facts as well, to raise it to a full understanding of its duty, not only to itself, but to posterity. And what do we now see all around us? A people sunk into slothful anxiety only for peace and a preservation of the status quo, encouraged in that direction by this white-livered government now in power.'

Philip frowned. He had heard that derisory adjective somewhere before. 'The government represents the people,' he pointed out. 'That is their prime duty in life.'

'Bah! When have the people mattered? When have the people truly known what they wanted? It is us, the samurai, the leaders, who matter.'

Once again, familiar words.

'This is intolerable,' Peter declared. 'Every officer in the army knows that it is intolerable.'

Philip sat up. 'I think you should reflect very carefully before you continue, honourable Brother,' he said.

'Or you will have me arrested for treason?'

'Of course not. But you may say something you may regret.'

'I do not mean to. How can I? You are my brother. May not brother speak freely to brother?'

'Yes,' Philip said. 'But . . .'

'But I will ask you to swear to me that you will never repeat a word of what I am about to tell you.'

Philip stared at him.

'Swear, by every ancestor of ours who ever wore a sword, and most of all by the bones of Ralph Freeman,' Peter said.

Philip opened his mouth to protest, and then closed it again. Yet he had to know what Peter, and presumably his army friends, had in mind. Nor could he possibly hope to alter the course of events, whatever they might

313

be, without knowing. 'I will swear,' he said. 'On one condition, that you are not speaking of revolution. If you are, I *will* have you arrested, brother or not.'

Peter considered him for several seconds. 'No,' he said at last. 'We do not intend revolution. Because, as you say, we would not succeed. There are too many people supporting the government of Viscount Saito. It is our purpose merely to awaken the people's hearts to the glories of the past, the glories that should be their future, the shame that is their present.'

'We?' Philip asked.

'There is a group. Large enough, but every man carefully selected and utterly dedicated.'

'Of which you are a member?'

'Yes.'

'And just what does this group intend to do?'

'On a given day, we intend to seize the various government offices, including the parliament house and the cabinet office.'

'And you do not describe that as revolution?'

'It is not. It would be a revolution if we were meaning to take control of the country afterwards. But we do not. It would be a revolution if we intended any bloodshed. But we do not. We have taken an oath to this effect. We merely mean to protest, in the most public possible manner, against the sloth and lethargy and downright dishonour which is pervading our current government.'

'I think you are quite mad,' Philip said. 'Have you given any thought to the consequences of this action?'

'Indeed we have. What do *you* suppose will happen after we have seized these buildings, and the fact becomes generally known?'

'His Majesty will instruct the military commander of Tokyo to call out his troops and surround you. Or is the military commander of Tokyo also in the plot?'

'He is not in the plot. And it is not a plot. It is a planned protest.'

314

'Then . . . ' Philip scratched his head. 'I do not understand. You will have to surrender.'

'Exactly. And?'

'My God! You will be charged with at least mutiny. Probably treason. Either way you will be condemned to death. Do you realise that?' He frowned. 'Or do you mean to use your trials as some sort of political springboard?'

'There will be no trials,' Peter declared. 'We intend to anticipate our sentences.'

'You . . . '

'In public,' Peter said. 'Before all of Tokyo.'

'You *are* mad!'

'We are samurai.'

Philip realised that his brother was in deadly earnest. There was no society in the world which would accept such a course of action – save the Japanese. There was no society in the world which would react to such a course of action except in terms of revulsion and horror – save the Japanese. But Peter . . . 'You intend to participate in this?'

'I have been elected leader.'

'You are a Christian. How can you contemplate committing suicide?'

'I am also a samurai, and the descendent of a long line of samurai. This is the more important.'

'You have a mother.'

'So have all of my fellows.'

'And you think I shall not attempt to stop this craziness?'

'Of course you will not attempt to stop me, honourable Brother. To do so would be to break every law of bushido. You would disgrace yourself, and you would disgrace the name you bear and every member of your family. You would ruin your son's career before it has even begun. Can you contemplate that?'

Once again he was in earnest, and he was right. It was

315

necessary to be sure that every man, woman and child in Japan would condemn what he was proposing to do. But it was also necessary to understand that they would accept the atonement he was proposing – and even more was it necessary to understand that they would abhor the man, and especially the brother, who would attempt to dissuade him from what he considered an honourable course.

Philip sighed. 'Then why have you come to me at all and told me all this?'

'Because there is something I wish you to do for me.'

Philip waited.

'The Admiralty is, of course, one of the buildings we intend to take over,' Peter said. 'In fact, it is a part of the exercise I intend to command myself. Now, I understand that Uncle William has been relieved of active command and placed on the staff.'

'That is so. Until he retires next summer.'

'Our action will necessarily take place before next summer. It is, of course, largely dependent on the outcome of the elections. If, as we hope, the electorate show a swing to the right and turn out Saito and his crew, then there will be no necessity for action at all. However, if, as we fear, the people are sucked in by these liberal promises of peaceful prosperity, it will be necessary to act promptly. Now, on receipt of a message from me, you must act yourself, immediately. The message will contain but a number, nothing more. The number will be the day on which our action will take place, in that month. On receipt of such a message I wish you to keep Uncle William away from the Admiralty, on that day.'

Philip stared at him.

'Call me a coward, if you wish,' Peter said. 'But I would prefer not to have to face him. Besides, although it is our intention to avoid bloodshed wherever we can, mistakes do happen. Everyone will be in a state of high excitement. And it is not forgotten by many that Uncle William was a prime instigator of our acceptance of the Washington Naval Agreement, which is at least partly responsible for our present weakness. He is also an utterly fearless, outspoken man, and a total upholder of the government, however misguided its policies. You are aware of these things?'

'Yes,' Philip said.

'So you will see my anxiety. I neither wish to face the old man, nor to risk any harm whatsoever befalling him. He must not attend the Admiralty on the day in question.'

'I appreciate your concern,' Philip said sarcastically. 'But I think you should understand, as I thought you did, that Uncle William and I are no longer on speaking terms.'

'I am relying upon you to engineer a reconciliation. Do so by the end of the year. And then do as I ask.'

'You mean, sit back and watch you perform seppuku?'

'It is an honourable way to die,' Peter said. 'I have your word?'

'That I will not betray your plans?'

'And that you will keep Uncle William away from his office on the selected day.'

Philip tried to think. He was, in fact, being asked to accept, and not to betray, a *coup d'état*. And yet he knew that if Peter was telling the truth, and he could not doubt the word of his own brother, the conspiracy did intend only a formal group suicide to remind the nation of the laws, and the obligations, of bushido. It was an absurd concept, viewed with any Western ideas of either logic or ethics, but it was entirely Japanese. Thus, he was being asked to acquiesce in his own brother's suicide, because it would be an even greater crime against bushido to attempt to dissuade him. So, was *he* now accepting bushido as a way of life? He refused to believe that – but it no longer mattered, because *Peter* had accepted it.

'Will you swear to me that you and your people contemplate no assassination, and no subversion of the

317

legally elected government of this country?'

'I have already done so,' Peter protested.

'I wish you to do so again.'

'Then I do. I swear by the bones of Ralph Freeman. Will that satisfy you?'

Philip sighed. 'It seems it must. I think you are wrong. Utterly wrong. I think you will bring great misery to our mother. And I also think you will bring great misery to Japan.'

'But you will do as I ask?'

'It is that, or hand you over to the Kempai.'

'And you will never do that, my honourable brother,' Peter said. He smiled and got up, and put his arm round Philip's shoulders. 'Now come, did you not invite me to dinner, with your beautiful mistress?'

CHAPTER 12

The Tragedy

Anne stood with Philip in the doorway of their house to watch the lights of Peter Shimadzu's car disappear into the night. 'That really was a treat,' she said, 'to see him again after all these years. I'd forgotten how entertaining he could be. I'm so glad he came to see us.'

'Yes.' Philip closed the door.

'And I think you should be too,' she said severely. 'You really were quite rude this evening, Phil, sitting there glowering. Okay, so you and Peter have had your differences. And maybe he's taken a long time to give us the thumbs-up sign, but he has done so. I'm in the business of letting all bygones be bygones, just as quickly as possible.'

Philip looked at her for a moment, and then went into their bedroom; Iyeyasu had retired some time earlier; now that he was twelve years old he was studying like mad to get into the Naval Academy – not that there was much risk of that not happening, with his background.

Anne followed him, frowning. 'Phil, is there something wrong?'

Philip undressed, washed himself at the basin, then sat on the mattress. 'I have been so happy, these past three years. Too happy. Perhaps a man is not intended to be too happy.'

She knelt beside him. 'I wish you'd tell me what's eating you.'

'I cannot.'

'Oh? You've always told me everything before. Do you think I'm going to rush outside and shout it to the neighbourhood?'

He looked at her.

'And maybe I could help,' she said. 'I hate to see you looking like this. Why, you haven't had that look on your face since . . . since the day of the earthquake. I'd swear to that.'

'You didn't see me all the time, after the earthquake,' he reminded her, and lay down, his hands beneath his head.

Anne undressed in turn, washed and sat beside him. 'Please, Phil. I've never betrayed your confidence. Don't tell me you're being sent on another world cruise?'

'I wish to God I was,' he said.

'Then what *is* it?'

He stared at her. Of course he could tell her. She was the most trustworthy person he knew. And he simply had to discuss his dilemma with someone. What dilemma? He had spelled it out to Peter himself: do as his brother wanted, or betray him to the Kempai. There was no other course. Expose Peter to Mori? Even Peter, a general officer, would be subjected to Mori if a single word of the conspiracy leaked out. But just to sit here . . . And Peter was, after all, an essentially noble character. His sole concern was to save his uncle from possible assassination, or even injury, by some fanatic . . .

But could Anne, so American in her outlook, understand the laws of bushido?

'Phil?'

He drew a long breath. 'I have just agreed to assist my brother in committing suicide,' he said.

'You have done *what*?'

'He and some other army officers feel that the nation is degenerating, because it will no longer back their aims, and they mean to commit seppuku in public as a protest, and hopefully thus re-awaken the people to the respon-

320

sibilities of being Japanese. It is, unfortunately, an old bushido custom.'

'But, my God! You must stop him. And he was here tonight, so gay and charming . . . Holy Cow! When did you first find out about it?'

'This afternoon.'

'Je*sus*! Phil, you have to talk him out of it.'

'I cannot do that, Anne.'

They stared at each other. But she knew he was right; beneath all the charm and the culture and the civilisation and the china-doll prettiness of Japan, there always lurked that grim, implacable rule of the warrior. 'What about your mother?' she asked.

'She will have to understand. She will understand. She is Japanese.'

'God, how you people drive me up the wall. You can just lie there and talk about your brother dying, as if he had some incurable disease . . .'

'He has,' Philip said. 'It is called the code of the warrior.'

Once again they looked at each other, and once again she knew she really had nothing to argue with. 'And what part do you play?' she asked in a low voice. 'Do you strike off his head when he has disembowelled himself?'

'He has not asked me to do that, thank God,' Philip said. Because she knew he would do that, he would have to do that, should Peter request it of him. Or be himself dishonoured.

'Do you know when it's going to happen?'

'No,' Philip said again. 'Although I am to be informed, just before the day. No, they intend to make their protest as publicly as they can, and thus they mean to invade the parliament building as well as the service ministries. Peter is afraid that there just could be some resistance, although he swears they certainly do not intend to fight anyone if they can avoid it, and thus he wants me to keep Uncle William away from the Admiralty on that day. I suppose he really does love the old fellow, despite their differences.'

'Shades of Gunpowder Plot,' Anne muttered. 'And just how are you supposed to keep Uncle William away when he won't even speak with you?'

'Yeah,' he said. 'That's my problem. Seems I have some time to work it out. Peter indicated nothing would be happening before the election next year.'

'You mean, if there's a swing to the right, they might abandon this stupid scheme?'

'I think so. We'd better pray for that to happen.'

'Only it's not going to.' Anne lay down beside him. 'As you say, maybe we're just not meant to be happy. My God! I really thought such things only happened in history books. Phil, will you swear to me that no matter what happens, *you* will never commit seppuku?'

He looked down at her. 'How can I swear something like that, my dearest girl?'

'Then you do believe in bushido, just like Peter.'

'I don't know,' he said. 'Would you believe this is the first time I have ever come face to face with it? I just don't know.'

Japan, Anne thought. She looked through the open door of her office at the row of men and women sitting on the benches outside; today, she was on out-patient duty. They would come in, one at a time, with minor complaints and ailments, but some of them in real pain, and some of them truly ill and unaware of it, and they would do whatever she told them to, and listen to her gravely, and watch and wait, with patient resignation and the most utter politeness. And, she supposed, if by any chance she told one of them that he was suffering from an incurable disease and would be dead in a week, the man would merely bow and say, 'So sorry to have troubled you, honourable lady doctor.'

Would he then go home and commit seppuku? No,

because his honour was not involved. It would, indeed, be dishonourable, because it would be cowardly of him *to* kill himself, instead of patiently awaiting the inevitable end. Besides, those people out there were mostly of peasant stock, honin. It was the samurai who clung to the tenets of bushido. Bushido! How romantic it had always seemed in the pages of a book. The Code of the Warrior. Thoughts of King Arthur and his Knights of the Round Table, or the Crusaders swearing to smite the infidel or die in the attempt. She had never before wondered what the wives of the Crusaders had thought about the business; the romances she had read always suggested they had been universally happy to see the backs of their lords in order to have a bang with their pageboys. Because their lords would be doing their dying in faraway lands, and not before their eyes.

The thought of Philip ever doing something like that . . . Yet she knew that he had already come close to it, because of the Shanghai affair. He had not told her everything of that, or anything of that, really, only that he had clashed with the local secret police commander over the treatment of a Chinese woman . . . She had not even thought to ask if the woman had been pretty. Had he been condemned for that, he would have been required either to live a life of disgrace, with his family also disgraced . . . or cut open his belly.

She shuddered, so lost in her own thoughts she hardly saw the man in front of her. She automatically pronounced the swollen wrist to be a sprain, made a note on his card and handed it to the nurse.

She did not know Peter as well. Indeed, she hardly knew Peter at all. But she knew Shikibu, and William, and Maureen. She just did not see how she and Philip could go on living their normal lives for the next few months, knowing what was going to happen . . . And yet she also knew that she had to, because she had chosen this position for herself, of being Philip's mistress – and therefore she had to be bound by his concepts of honour, not hers. For her to attempt to interfere, and betray Philip's trust, would be worse than unforgivable – it would earn her his hatred instead of his love.

The next man had obligingly dropped his pants and the nurse was standing by with the needle for the anti-tetanus shot. Anne made the injection. 'You must return for another in six weeks' time,' she told him. 'Do you understand?'

'Oh, yes, honourable lady doctor,' he said, dressing himself.

'And for goodness sake be careful the next time you wish to open a tin can,' she told him. 'You could have lost that finger.' She sat down, made a note on his card, handed it to the nurse, looked up as the door opened again, and saw John Graham.

'John,' she cried. 'How good to see you. Or is it good, here?' She remembered that he had said he would come down to her whenever he was ill; she had supposed he was joking.

'It's rather a delicate complaint,' he said. 'Do you think I could see you privately?'

'I'm afraid not,' she said. 'Hospital rules, and that sort of thing. But my nurse speaks no English, if that's any help.'

'Ah.' He glanced at the girl, who smiled back; up to now they had been using Japanese. 'Yes, well . . . if you're sure.'

'Of course I'm sure.' She pointed to the chair. 'Sit down. And tell me what's on your mind.' She smiled in turn, as he very carefully lowered himself to the seat. 'Don't tell me you've extracted something unpleasant from a geisha house.'

'Would that take long to diagnose?' he asked in English.

'One glance.'

'Then I haven't. What would take longest to diagnose?'

She frowned at him. 'Is this some kind of a joke, Johnny? I have a room full of patients out there.'

'And I have to talk with you on a vitally important matter. Please Anne. It is vitally important to you, too.'

She gazed at him for several moments, aware of a succession of very odd sensations. Even if she had been joking when she discussed the subject with Philip, she *had* always found it odd, and even rather insulting, that Graham had never made the slightest pass at her, even during the long two years that Phil had been away, when he had squired her quite regularly. He had not been her only squire. She had accepted dates from several Japanese men, and also from Johnnie Corcoran, and none of them had been the least bit backwards in making advances – especially Johnnie Corcoran. Nor had her protests that she belonged to another been very effective – as she wore neither a wedding nor engagement ring – and she had had to be quite aggressive on occasions. But from Graham, nothing. Yet this morning he was looking quite intense.

'Don't you think it is something we should discuss at some other time?' she asked.

'No. It has to be somewhere I have every reason for visiting you.'

'Johnny,' she said, as gently as she could. 'I happen to be in love with Phil. For God's sake, you of all people must know that I'm his mistress. So really . . . '

'That's why I'm here, Anne. It is desperately important. What I have to tell you can affect all of your lives.'

She frowned, then turned to the nurse. 'I shall need a complete new card for this patient,' she said in Japanese. 'He has not been here before.'

'Of course, honourable doctor. But would you not like me to fill in the particulars?'

This was normal practice, and while that was being done Anne could see perhaps another three patients before coming back to Graham.

She shook her head. 'No. I think I will take down the

particulars myself.' She took the card. 'I cannot allow you very long, John,' she said, reverting to English. 'So shoot, every time I ask a question. Now, let's see. Full name?'

'John Harrison Graham. Have you seen anything of Peter Shimadzu since his return to Tokyo?'

Anne's head jerked up before she could stop herself. But she kept writing. 'Date and place of birth? Of course we have.'

'Fourth September 1897, Paisley, Scotland. Has anything he has said or done seemed strange to you?'

Now her heart was pounding and her stomach seemed to be rolling. 'Why do you ask that? Name of father?'

'George Harrison Graham. Anne, I believe something very serious is going on.'

'Name of mother? Please explain that.'

'Margaret Graham. Née Abercrombie. I have information that there is to be a *coup d'état* aimed at eliminating the present liberal ministry.'

'Occupation? I cannot believe that.' God, she thought, what do I do?

'Naval officer, attached to the Tokyo Embassy of Great Britain. Well, I think my information is correct. And Anne, according to my source, the *coup* is to be led by Peter Shimadzu.'

'Previous illnesses? Where did you get such absurd information?'

'Whooping cough, measles, mumps, all as a child. Nothing since twelve. Information is my business.'

'Operations? Are you saying you are some kind of a spy?'

'Appendix removed in 1919. Well, of course I am, I'm a naval attaché. But I am also vitally concerned with what happens here in Japan. That's my job.'

Once again she gazed at him. 'I shall devise a complaint for you,' she said, 'which will take some diagnosing. Don't worry, I will do all the writing down. It'll be stomach pains, which could be anything from hernia to constipation. Tell me what you have to say. And please hurry.'

She wrote slowly and carefully.

'I . . . What I am telling you is in the utmost confidence, Anne. Please understand that. My principal job is in maintaining relations with a group of Japanese who are, well . . . best described as Westward looking in their ideals and sympathies.'

'This is an organised group?'

'To a certain extent.'

'Organised by you?'

'In so far as it is organised at all, yes.'

'I see. You mean you are admitting that you have formed and are operating a spy ring, here in Japan.'

'I would put it differently. It is a group of people, as I say, who have done their best, and are still doing their best, to keep Japan's leaders from committing an irrevocable act. I once hoped that Philip would become a member of the group.'

'And he refused?'

'Circumstances prevented me from ever approaching him on the matter. Just as I was about to, the earthquake happened and he was left utterly distraught. Then he was sent to Shanghai. I had to write him off.'

'You are an utter thug,' she remarked dispassionately. 'Do you mean to say that is the only reason you cultivated his friendship?'

'In the first instance, yes, I cultivated him as a source of information and a possible recruit. Then I genuinely grew to like him.'

'I don't believe you. And you have the most unmitigated gall in coming here and telling me all of this. Do you have any idea what would happen to you if I were to take this story to the police?'

'I would be deported.'

She glared at him.

'And Japan would take another step towards confront-

327

ing the whole world. Listen to me, Anne. We, my people and I, have almost thought we were winning, these last few years. We *are* winning. Japan is adopting a more conciliatory attitude to world opinion than at any time in the last three centuries. And the army knows it, too. That's why it is planning this *coup*. Anne, they have got to be stopped. And if Peter is the leader, then Philip is the man to do it, hopefully with the least harm to anyone. All he has to do is talk to him, tell him he knows all about it, and Peter will have to forget it.'

Anne had written all she could. 'I had better examine you,' she decided. 'Please go behind that screen, undress and lie down on the bed. The nurse will assist you.'

She watched him go, drumming her fingers on her desk. The panic had past, but in its place there was a deadly fear. She had to think, clearly and concisely. Where had he got his information? Obviously from one of Peter's group. Presumably she should be thanking God the traitor had gone to Graham and not the Kempai. But had the man given Graham correct information? If he had, that meant that Peter had lied to his brother about the intentions of the conspirators. She could not believe that. Graham had just confessed to being more than a spy; he was actually an *agent provocateur*, even if he claimed his intentions were merely to keep Japan at peace. It was obvious that he would interpret any information of that nature as leading to a *coup d'état* – because he was British: for all the years he had lived in Japan, he could not accept that sane men might choose to commit suicide in public in order to shame their countrymen. She could hardly blame him for that; she found it difficult to accept herself.

'The patient is ready, honourable doctor,' the nurse said.

But what was she going to do about it? What *could* she do about it that would not betray both Peter and Philip . . . save shoot Graham down in flames. And suddenly she wanted to do that. Life was difficult enough without this Scottish twit putting his oar in, where he was neither wanted nor needed. And where he was so mistaken.

She went behind the screen. Graham lay on his back with his hands clasped beneath his head; he was a bigger man than she had supposed, and far more heavily muscled than she had imagined. She began to test the stomach walls. 'What do you want me to do?' she asked in English 'Supposing I can bring myself to believe a word of what you've been saying.'

'I wish you to tell Philip everything I have told you, and ask him to dissuade Peter from such a crazy course.'

'And where am I supposed to have got my information?'

'Oh, tell him it came from me, if you wish. In fact, I would be more than happy if he were, after all, to join our group. It has to be very secret, of course; I know the Kempai are interested, but they've never been able to raise a shred of evidence against me or any of my associates. But including Philip would really present no problem because we see so much of each other already.'

'You wish me to persuade Philip to become a traitor to his country?'

'I would argue that,' Graham protested. 'I would claim I am asking him to become a super-patriot. If the military seize power, God alone knows what is going to happen.'

Anne inserted her finger into the sac of his right testicle and pushed upwards, as hard as she could. 'Cough.'

'Ahahaha,' he went. 'My God, I feel as if I really do have a hernia.'

'I pressed a little hard,' she said. 'Because it is what you deserve. I thought you were our friend, John Graham. Now I see that you are nobody's friend. You're just doing a job of work. So I suggest you get dressed and get out of here, and don't bother to come near either Philip or me ever again. Or I'll tell him *just* what you are, and he will probably have you deported. As for your *coup d'état*, forget it. There is no possibility of Peter leading such a thing.'

She returned behind her desk, and a moment later the door closed; he had not said another word.

'Honourable English gentleman is not truly sick?' asked the nurse.

'No,' Anne said. 'Honourable English gentleman is not sick at all – only in the head.' She looked up. The girl was obviously puzzled. Anne forced a smile. 'I think he fancies me,' she explained. 'But I don't fancy him.'

She seethed. The thought of Philip, with his so delicately balanced sense of honour and responsibility and loyalty, being approached by some British agent . . . The unutterable cheek of the man, pretending to be their best friend for so many years, and all the time sizing Phil up as a potential member of his 'group'. She wondered, indeed, if she should not tell Philip about it. But as Graham had said, what would that achieve? He would merely be deported, and his people, left leaderless, would surely fall into the hands of the Kempai. She knew nothing of *that* organisation, but Philip obviously had a total distaste for it. And if Graham was telling the truth, they were actually people who had only the future of Japan at heart. It was, in fact, possible to suppose that Philip, with his fears of the effects militarism might have on the future, might be prepared to sympathise. She could not risk that. Because then his guilt problems, his uncertainty as to whether his was the right course, as to whether or not he was betraying his country and his ancestors and the laws of bushido, might well escalate into an unbearable mental strain. All of her life she had discounted seppuku as a fairy-tale; now the thought of it haunted her every nightmare. Because it was that very confusion of what was right and what was wrong that was now driving Peter to suicide.

That she had expelled Graham from their lives was sufficiently upsetting to Philip, even if he did not know what had happened. 'Now that is very strange,' he remarked, putting down the telephone. 'John has cancelled our tennis game, and he has also declined Christmas lunch with us. For the first time in four years. He was distinctly cold, too.'

'Are we going to have Christmas lunch?' she asked.

He sighed. 'What else can we do?'

Save behave as normally as possible. So Shikibu and Maureen came to lunch with them and Iyeyasu; Hilary and William, as ever, declined. Philip had made no headway in approaching his uncle; William Freeman simply refused to see him. It had been impossible, of course, to explain to Hilary why it was so important that he should speak to his uncle, and to his importunings for a reconciliation, she continued to recommend patience.

'To tell you the truth, Philip,' she said, 'he is growing increasingly testy at the thought of having to retire at all. After next summer, when it has actually happened, things will be different.'

'Next summer,' he said to Anne.

'There is a way you can see him immediately,' she said. 'Renounce me. Or at least say you're going to.'

'Oh, yes?'

'That is the only block between you.'

'Yes,' he agreed.

'But you won't do it?'

'I will if I have to. When Peter's message arrives. The fact is, my dearest girl, playing that sort of deceitful game doesn't appeal to me in the least, and anyway, what am I to say to him? I cannot possibly risk telling him to stay away from the office until I know the very day. That's how it'll have to be.'

Peter also declined to attend Christmas lunch, pleading pressure of work at the War Office. That was actually a relief; Anne just could not see them all toasting the hoped-for successes of 1936 with him there. But it was a sufficiently sombre occasion, for her, in which the forced gaiety of Philip and herself only made the entire day more of a travesty. That night they lay in each other's arms, both unable to sleep.

'No word yet?' she asked, stupidly. Because of course he would have told her the moment he knew.

'Not a thing,' he said. 'You know, I cannot help but hope that the whole thing has fizzled out. It could have happened. These things do.'

'Oh, pray God that it has,' she said. 'Oh, pray God!'

And as January passed, a cold January, with snow falling even in the streets of Tokyo, somehow she felt that it had. By then, of course, the entire country was caught up in vigorous and at times violent electioneering, as the parties of the right, and those of the left, the Liberals, or Minseito, presented their differing points of view – although even the Minseito was actually about as far to the right as the most dedicated American conservative. They never saw Peter at all throughout the month, although he had often dropped by to have a cup of tea with them before the turn of the year. So it was possible to believe that he was having problems with his fellow conspirators. Surely they were realising the enormity of what they had intended . . . but always the shadow of the elections hung over them, and she at least was left actually hoping for a decisive swing back to the right, no matter what it might mean for the future of Japan. By the evening of 20 February, however, it became clear that the Minseito had gained an overwhelming victory at the polls.

It seemed all Japan celebrated. Anne went out with Philip, and found herself being booed because she was with a naval officer. They returned home, and gazed at each other.

'This will put them off,' she said. 'It has to. They cannot go against so clearly expressed a will of the people. Surely.'

332

'I hope to God you're right,' he agreed, and tried to telephone Peter. But his brother was nowhere to be reached, and in fact no calls were being received at the War Office at all. Philip left a message asking his brother to call back, but he never did.

It was necessary for him to spend the next four days on board *Mutsu*, where an anti-aircraft gun turret was in the process of being changed, and he did not return home until the evening of 25 February. In his absence, Anne had been instructed to open all his mail, and to contact him should there be any news. But there had been nothing of interest at all. They spent a quiet evening, as they usually did on the days he came home, retired early, and slept heavily. Next morning they shared a long, languorous and sexy bath; as it was a day off for him she had arranged one for herself as well. It was ten o'clock when they emerged from the bath-house, wrapped in kimonos, debating what they should do with the day, to find the mail neatly piled up for them by Hagi. Philip sifted through the envelopes, and suddenly checked, his face frozen.

'From Peter?' she asked.

'It is his handwriting.' He slit the envelope. Inside there was a single sheet of paper. It slipped out, drifted to the floor between them; they could both read what was written on it, perfectly clearly: simply a number – 26.

'Oh, my *God*!' Anne gasped. 'That's today!'

For a moment Philip was unable to think, as a thousand and one reflections galloped through his brain. Peter had promised him more notice than this. And for it to happen now, when Viscount Saito had just received the most conclusive vote of confidence in Japanese political history, was desperation. But the more dangerous for that. And he had been caught quite literally with his pants down.

'Get out my uniform,' he snapped, and ran for the

333

telephone to call his uncle's house. 'Hello? Hello? Aunt Hilary? Is Uncle William there?'

'No,' Hilary said. 'Of course he isn't, Philip. He has already gone to his office. Is there something wrong?'

'Something . . . Listen, Aunt Hilary, can you possibly call him and ask him to return home? Immediately? *Tell* him to.'

'Philip? Are you drunk?'

'I'm in deadly earnest, Aunt Hilary. Please do as I say. Listen, tell him Mother has had a heart attack, or something like that. Tell him he must hurry. But get him out of there.'

'Philip . . . '

'Please,' he shouted. 'His life may be in danger. Please do as I ask.' He hung up. 'Listen,' he told Anne. 'Get dressed and get over to Aunt Hilary as quickly as you can, and make sure she calls him.'

'What are you going to do?'

He dragged on his trousers, buttoned his jacket. 'I'm going down to the Admiralty. It's still early, I should be in time. With luck she'll have got him out of there before I even reach him. If not, I'll just have to drag him out, and face the consequences after.'

'But Phil . . . ' She hesitated, biting her lip. The temptation was there to say Don't go, don't get involved; why should you? And with Uncle William dead . . . supposing he was dead . . . But that was an utterly inhuman thought. He might have turned away from them, but the dedicated old man was only acting according to his lights. 'Be in time,' she said. 'Oh, please be in time.'

Philip ran out of the house, leapt into his car and gunned it out of the garage and into the drive. He refused to let himself think any longer of anything save reaching his uncle. Peter had promised him more warning than this; how that thought kept banging at his mind. But Peter also was probably supposing that his brother had already effected a reconciliation with his uncle, and that getting him from the office would simply be a matter of a telephone call.

He swung on to the first main road, went through a red light and immediately heard the howl of a siren behind him. Well, that was to the good. The more policemen he accumulated on his way to the Admiralty the better, just in case. In case of what? He simply didn't know what to expect to find. He glanced at his watch, while keeping his left hand pressed to the wheel; it was twenty minutes to eleven. With luck he wouldn't find anything – save an angry uncle.

The car slid round corners, scattering pedestrians with its blaring horn, and once cannoned off a lamp post to leave a deep gash in the rear mudguard. But now Philip could see the Admiralty building. He braked in the drive, and showed his pass to the marine guardsman. 'Have there been any visitors to the Admiralty yet this morning?' he asked.

'Why, yes, honourable Captain,' the guardsman replied. 'A group of army officers, led by General Shimadzu himself, arrived only ten minutes ago for a conference.'

'Oh, Christ!' Philip said, his fingers curling round the wheel. They were inside the building. Doing what? According to Peter, they would already be preparing themselves for seppuku. To go crashing in now might bring about the one thing he wanted to avoid. But just to sit here . . .

A motorcycle drew up beside him. 'With respect, honourable Captain,' said the policeman. 'But you have just violated every traffic regulation in Tokyo.'

'Not enough,' Philip snapped. He would have to go into the building, come what may. But he had to be prepared for any eventuality. 'Have you got a weapon, constable?'

'Of course, honourable Captain,' the policeman said, frowning as he reached for his book of tickets.

335

'Good. I will need you to come with me. You . . . ' He turned to the guardsman. 'What weapons do you have?'

'Weapons, honourable Captain?' The man looked astonished. Philip knew that even his rifle would be unloaded. But he could see past him into the guardhouse, where the sergeant was sitting at his desk, and hanging from a hook on the wall behind him was a holster and belt. 'Sergeant,' he shouted.

'Honourable Captain!' The sergeant got up and saluted.

'Are there bullets in that gun?'

'Why, yes, honourable Captain. It is fully loaded.'

'Give it to me.'

'Sir?'

'That is an order, Sergeant.'

The sergeant hesitated, glanced at the private, then took down the belt and handed the pistol to Philip.

'I have written out these tickets, honourable Captain,' the policeman was saying. 'If you will kindly . . . '

'Yes, give them to me.' Philip crammed them into his pocket, unclipped the holster, took out a nine-shot Luger automatic pistol and checked the magazine. 'Now, Sergeant, I want you to turn out the entire guard, and make sure they are adequately armed and that their weapons are loaded. Then I wish you to enter the Admiralty and arrest every officer wearing an army uniform. Understood?'

'Yes, honourable Captain,' the sergeant said, although he still looked totally mystified.

'Then get to it. You . . . ' He turned to the policeman. 'Constable, come with me.'

'Me, honourable Captain? I cannot enter the Admiralty compound.'

'I am giving you an order, Constable,' Philip told him.

The policeman looked as if he would have protested, when suddenly there came a flurry of shots from the building itself.

'God Almighty!' Philip shouted, and gunned his engine. Behind him he heard the wail of the siren. Maybe that would distract them from whatever they were doing.

He braked at the front entrance, ran up the stairs and bumped into the marine doorman. 'Honourable Captain,' the man panted. 'Shots . . . '

Philip pushed him aside, ran into the corridor beyond the swinging glass doors and looked left and right. On this floor there were only clerks, but all the doors to the various filing rooms were opening, and people were looking out, asking anxious questions. There was another burst of fire from upstairs. Philip took the steps three at a time. Arriving on the first landing, he was faced by a man wearing the uniform of an army lieutenant. And carrying a revolver.

'Stop there,' the man said. 'And return downstairs. No one is allowed past this point.'

'Drop your weapon and raise your hands,' Philip snapped. 'I am placing you under arrest.'

The man raised his revolver instead, and Philip shot him. Blood spurted from the khaki tunic, and a look of utter surprise crossed the young man's face as he slumped to the floor, while Philip stared at him for a moment – he had never shot anyone before in his life, but the reaction had been instantaneous.

Now there was pandemonium from all around him. Someone actually stepped out of an office and shot at him, but missed, because he was already on the next flight of stairs; he was interested only in William Freeman's office. The next flight had a right-angle bend, and he checked there, listening to the bark of the policeman's gun from behind him, and to more wailing of sirens in the distance. The next landing appeared deserted, but as he ran up to it another army officer appeared. This time Philip did not even challenge him. He fired immediately, three times, and the man came tumbling down. Philip jumped over him, gained the corridor, sent a shot wing-ing in the direction of a door which opened towards him, and then himself pulled open the door to William Freeman's office. He leapt in, and gazed in horror at his uncle, lying on his side on the floor, still half in his swivel chair; from his shoulders a trail of blood drifted towards the wall. In front of the desk a male secretary lay in a crumpled heap, also bleeding.

'Oh, Christ,' Philip said. 'Oh, Christ!'

He felt something hard jab into his back. 'Drop your weapon.'

Philip hesitated, then obeyed. The gun barrel jerked against him, and he moved away. He turned, to see a man he did not know; but that he was responsible for the two murders in this room could not be doubted.

'Captain Shimadzu,' the man said contemptuously, and raised his revolver, but hesitated as the door burst open. Peter ran into the room.

'I was told you were here,' he snapped at his brother. 'Why on earth . . . ' He looked past Philip at the body of William Freeman. 'You shot him?' he gasped, turning to the captain. 'You shot my uncle? In the name of God . . . '

'In the name of the army,' the captain said.

'But . . . ' Peter looked at his uncle again, his face betraying utter horror. Then he looked at Philip. 'You were to keep him away.'

'And you swore to me there would be no killing,' Philip said.

'I . . . there was not to be. I have tried to stop it.' Peter turned to the officer. 'You have dishonoured me. You have dishonoured us all.'

'And you are a fool, *honourable* General,' the officer sneered. 'Did you not know that it was our purpose to rid Japan of this whole liberal blight that lies across it like winter snow? You were always a fool. Now I will complete the job.'

The gun exploded before Philip knew what was happening. He was aware of a tremendous jolt in the chest

338

and of turning right round, before finding himself on his hands and knees beside his uncle. Amazingly, he heard no sound for several moments. He tasted blood, and seemed to be on some kind of a roller-coaster, from which he now fell, hitting the floor with a crash. The fall seemed to restore his hearing. Dimly he made out other shots, and a heavy thud as of a body hitting the floor. Then Peter was kneeling beside him. 'Philip,' he was saying. 'Oh, Philip . . . oh, God. Listen, I will get help.'

Philip could only gasp for breath, and stare in horror as the figure of his uncle moved.

'Uncle?' Peter whispered. 'Uncle? You are alive?'

'You are dishonoured,' William said, blood dribbling from his lips as he spoke. 'In the name of all your illus-trious ancestors, I curse you from here to eternity, Peter Shimadzu. You are *dishonoured*, and with you, the army.' Then his head drooped as he died.

'I swear,' Peter said. 'I swear . . . I am indeed a fool.'

The office door swung open, and Philip heard the gasp as the new arrival took in the charnel-house that the office had become. But he had even more important things on his mind. 'The building is surrounded, honour-able General,' the man said. 'And we have accomplished our purpose. We must go to the balcony and commit seppuku. Will you not lead us?'

Peter gazed at him, then looked down at his brother, 'Help will soon be here,' he promised. 'I will fetch it for you myself.' Slowly and carefully he lowered Philip's head to the floor, and stood up.

'We must hurry,' the man said.

'I am not coming with you,' Peter said. 'I am going downstairs, to surrender, and fetch a doctor.'

'Surrender?' The man's tone was incredulous. 'But you will be dishonoured, honourable General. You will be stripped of your rank. You will be cashiered. You will be condemned to death. And you will die in shame.'

'Yes,' Peter Shimadzu said. 'As you have forced me to

339

live in shame, honourable Colonel. Can I die differently?'
He walked through the door.

CHAPTER 13

The Conflict

Pain. Nothing but pain. Pain whenever he breathed, pain whenever he moved. And pain whenever he thought.

And weakness. Of the mind as much as of the body. Nothing was distinct any more. He had no idea where he was, only with difficulty making out faces through a thick haze. Anne, weeping. His mother, weeping. Maureen, weeping. Hilary, surprisingly not weeping, but her face a mask of tragedy. Isoroku Yamamoto, his grim face glowing with admiration. Various admirals. Even Hagi, utterly griefstricken. But not his uncle. Never William. Never again.

He wondered if his uncle had had any idea, just before he died, that the nephew from whom he had been estranged for so long had been trying to save his life. He had to belive that. He could not face the thought that his uncle had condemned him equally with Peter – or even that he had died still angry with him for having sought love in his own way.

But that was something he would never know.

Gradually his surroundings began to swing into focus, and the pain subsided. Only the weakness remained. But now he could see, as well. 'Anne,' he said.

'Oh, my darling,' she replied. 'Oh, my darling.'

Another doctor came in, and they conferred, and then nurses unbandaged his chest. He tried to look down, but they were careful not to let him.

'You were very fortunate,' the doctor said. 'The bullet

only nicked a lung, and then exited to the right, through the shoulder.' He smiled. 'The shoulder is the most serious now.'

Philip wished he hadn't said that, because now he was aware where most of the pain was coming from. 'Will I lose the arm?' he asked. He was right-handed.

'No, no. But it will take time. A very long time. As will the lung. You must be patient. I repeat, you were very fortunate. It seems that your brother shot Colonel Tarawa at the very moment that the colonel shot you, and this threw the colonel's aim off.'

'My brother,' Philip said. 'Tell me of my brother.'

The doctor's face clouded. 'It is not my place, honourable Captain,' he said, 'to speak of your brother.' He left the room.

'Tell me what happened,' Philip begged Anne when they were left alone.

'You must rest,' she said. 'Excitement is the worst possible thing for you.'

'And do you not think I will be excited, and stay excited, until I know what happened?'

She sighed. 'It was just terrible,' she told him. 'There were several groups, and they took over nearly all of the government buildings. But Phil . . . they had planned wholesale assassinations from the start. Then even killed Viscount Saito.'

'The Prime Minister?' He could not believe his ears. Saito had seemed so massively permanent; he had been prime minister, on and off, since just after the Great War.

'And several members of his cabinet,' Anne went on. 'Mr Takahashi, the Finance Minister . . . Oh, the list is endless.'

'Then what has happened to the government?'

'The worst,' she said miserably. 'The country has been placed under martial law, and what is virtually a military dictatorship has taken office. Hirota is the new Prime

Minister. He has also taken charge of the Foreign Office.'

Koki Hirota had always been a tool of the generals. 'And what of the conspirators?' Philip asked.

'Most of them committed seppuku on the spot,' Anne said. 'On the balconies of the various buildings, in front of all the crowds, exhorting the people to remember them and be ready to do the same, for the honour of Japan. Phil, it's just awful. They are being spoken of as heroes. Martyrs.'

'That was what they intended.'

'Yes,' she said. 'Oh, Philip. What are we to do?'

'What of Peter?'

She sighed. 'He refused seppuku, as you know. They tried twice. Well, I mean, when he didn't do it on the day, and allowed himself to be arrested by the police, he was given his swords and locked in a cell by himself. But when they returned the next morning . . . he still had not done it. So . . . oh, Philip, they handed him over to the Kempai for interrogation.'

'The Kempai? My God! What happened to him?'

'I do not know. Save that he is to be placed on trial, together with the other survivors; some of them were too badly wounded to commit seppuku.'

'Mother?'

'She is distraught. You can imagine. There was a time when we thought you were going to die as well.'

'You must bring her to see me. And Iyeyasu. And Anne, I would like to see Peter.'

She frowned. 'I don't know that can be done. And I don't know you should. I mean . . . '

'He saved my life.'

'After lying to you in the first place.'

'I would like to see him,' Philip insisted.

Yamamoto came again. 'Well, Philip San,' he said. 'What does it feel like to be a hero?'

'Am I a hero, honourable Admiral? What did I accom-

343

plish? Am I not as guilty as anyone?'

Yamamoto frowned. 'Listen to me carefully. Your aunt came to me with some story about how you attempted to get your uncle to leave the office, minutes before the mutiny. I told her that she must be mistaken, and not to mention that to a soul.' He held up his finger as Philip would have spoken. 'I think I understand. Peter was your brother. You could not betray him. But you could not let your uncle die, and you determined, however late, that the mutiny could not be allowed to proceed. I have no doubt that you had no idea of the scale upon which this insurrection was planned. So you nearly got yourself killed trying to protect your uncle. That is all that need be said about the matter. That you happened to be arriving at the Admiralty on the morning of 26 February, and heard shots coming from the building, and leapt into quite remarkable action, is at once a coincidence and an event greatly redounding to your credit. Remember this.'

'I thought Uncle was already dead,' Philip said. 'He was, just about. We will never make that story stick, honourable Admiral. I am surprised I have not also been arrested.'

Yamamoto smiled. 'There was some talk of that, to be sure. You have some virulent enemies in the Kempai, you know. And Kitabake is amongst them. But I would brook no argument from that lot. You have come through the whole affair with exemplary honour, in the eyes of the nation. You are a hero, while your brother is a disgrace. These things are well understood. Now it is your duty to get well again as quickly as possible. We have need of you. I have need of you.'

'I would like to see my brother, honourable Admiral,' Philip said.

Yamamoto's smile changed into a frown. 'Dr Freeman has told me of this. Why, Philip? He betrayed you.'

'He also saved my life. And he is my brother. I would

like to see him.'

'Then you will have to get well even quicker. He will never be allowed to come here. But if you can leave the hospital before he is executed . . . '

'Which will be when, honourable Admiral?'

'Oh, not for some time. He has not even been tried yet, much less convicted. There is time. I will see what I can arrange.' He stood up. 'But remember, his is the disgrace, for all eternity. He broke the laws of bushido, in every way. He is disgraced.'

'Honourable Father!' Iyeyasu stood by the bedside, his face grave. He wore the uniform of a naval cadet.

'Congratulations,' Philip said, and squeezed his hand. 'I did not know.'

'He passed his examinations with flying colours,' Shikibu said.

'I am very proud,' Philip said.

'I too am very proud, honourable Father,' Iyeyasu said. 'Of you.'

'And you, honourable Mother?' Philip asked.

Shikibu sighed. 'I, too, have to be proud. It is good to have something to be proud of. My house is painted white.'

Poor Mother, he thought. Her mother was killed when her entire clan was destroyed by Imperial troops, and she was only a child; her husband was murdered by the Chinese; now her brother had also been murdered as her half-brother had perished in an earthquake. And now, too, her eldest son was to die a traitor's death. Could any woman have been so unfortunate?

'Peter saved my life,' he reminded her.

'Do not speak to me of him,' Shikibu said. 'I do not wish to hear his name again, as long as I live. He was my son, and I loved him. He is my son no longer. Do not speak to me of him, Philip. You are the only son I now possess.'

*

345

Hilary came to say goodbye. 'I have been told by Admiral Yamamoto,' she said, 'that I am not to inquire into the events of that dreadful day, Philip. But I do know that you tried to save your uncle's life, even at the cost of your own, and I am therefore forever in your debt.'

'But you are leaving Japan.'

'Yes.'

'After . . . How long is it since you first lived here?'

She smiled, sadly. 'I first came to Japan when I was ten years old,' she said. 'That was nearly sixty years ago. But I only settled here permanently in 1905.'

'And that is more than thirty years ago,' Philip said.

'Japan was always one man, for me, Philip. Not a people. Now he is dead . . . ' She hesitated.

'And the people are now hateful to you?'

'I do not know about these things, Philip. I do not wish to know. I find it distressing, yes, that they should be calling my husband's murderers martyrs. But no doubt William would have explained it to me. He always showed me where to go, and I willingly followed him. I am not leaving Japan because I disapprove of it. I am leaving because I cannot bear to be reminded of William, wherever I turn, wherever I look. Will you ever come to visit me?'

'As soon as I can,' he promised. 'But first, I must get out of this bed.'

It was May before he was allowed to leave the hospital, and then only under Anne's care, to make sure he continued a slow and steady course of convalescence. By then much of the furore over the attempted *coup* had died down, but the new regime was still firmly in control of the country, and obviously intended to remain that way; the trials of the captured officers were just beginning.

Philip wished to give evidence, but his doctors ruled against it. Anne agreed with them. 'You were shot through the chest,' she reminded him. 'You still cannot breathe properly, and the slightest exertion leaves you exhausted. Do you have any idea how lucky you are to be *alive*? Half an hour in court could start the haemorrhaging again.'

So he made a deposition, which he was promised would be read to the judges. 'It can, of course, have no effect on the verdict,' Yamamoto told him on one of his weekly visits. 'Your brother has confessed to treason. But I have arranged for you to be able to see him.'

He went to the prison on 30 June. Anne accompanied him to drive the car, as he was still very weak and his right arm was still useless. But she waited in the antechamber while he was taken into a private room, where Peter was brought to him.

Peter bowed as he came through the door, flanked by guards. 'Honourable Brother. It deeply grieves me to see you so weak. I would not have had it so. But I am told you will recover.'

'Yes,' Philip said, studying him. Had he really been in the hands of the Kempai? Of Mori? Had his testicles been squeezed by a pair of pliers? He stood straight enough, but there was a certain stiffness to his movements. 'Why did you lie to me?' he asked.

'I have never lied to you,' Peter said.

'You told me I would receive forewarning of your *coup*,' Philip said. 'Your message arrived at my house half an hour before you entered the Admiralty.'

Peter nodded. 'I have been told this. I gave the message to my secretary to mail. He betrayed me.'

'You also told me there was no bloodshed intended.'

'I would not have had it so.' Peter sat down.

'How can a brother lie to a brother?' Philip asked again.

Peter raised his head. 'I did not lie to you, Philip,' he repeated. 'What I told you was what I understood was going to happen. What I had organised. What I commanded. It was to be a protest, nothing more.' He

347

shrugged. 'In many ways, it was a protest, nothing more. None of my men attempted to seize power. I did not lie about that.'

'Yet they committed wholesale murder.'

'Of men who were not fit to live,' Peter said.

'Uncle William?'

'I would have saved his life, had I known what was intended,' Peter said.

'But you think he also deserved to die?'

'He has consistently opposed every plan for increasing the greatness of Japan, and supported every plan to perpetuate our inferiority to the Western Powers.'

'You *are* a fool,' Philip said. 'Whatever his feelings, he of all the men in Japan would have marched forward to do his duty, regardless of what was involved. Even if it involved war with all the world. You will never replace him.'

Peter sighed. 'It is not my province.' He stood up. 'You have paid me much honour in coming to see me, honourable Brother. To everyone else in Japan I am a traitor and a coward. There can be no man in all the history of our nation as dishonoured as I. Even my mother spurns me.'

'I know that you saved my life,' Philip said, also rising.

'That was read out in court,' Peter said. 'And I am grateful for your act of gratitude.'

'When are you to die?'

'Next week.'

'You are told so far in advance?'

'Perhaps they think it is an additional punishment. But it is good to know so far in advance, do you not think? I am not a coward, you know, Philip, no matter what they say of me.'

'I never supposed you were.' Philip went round the table.

'It is not permitted to touch the prisoner,' the guard said.

'Then arrest me,' Philip told him, and embraced his

348

brother. 'Would you like me to be present?'

'Ah, no, thank you,' Peter said.

Philip sighed. His thoughts drifted back to the day following the Battle of Tsushima, when he and his brother, both teenage cadets, had stood with their mother to watch William Freeman's battered ship returning to the port of Shimonoseki. Glorious days. 'To know the future,' he said. 'Oh, to know the future.'

Peter smiled. 'I think we are fortunate not to have to bear that cross as well, Philip. Tell me one thing: do *you* think I lied to you?'

Philip shook his head.

'Then there is nothing more to be said.'

'Yes, there is,' Philip said. 'Do *you* believe in your course, the course of the army? Do you believe it is the right course for Japan?'

'Naturally,' Peter said.

'And do you know that you may have achieved your objectives? That there is now a military government in Japan?'

'Yes,' Peter said.

'Then can you understand that I am against their principles? That I believe they will lead to the destruction of our country?'

'I understand that you are against our principles, Philip,' Peter said. 'I do not happen to share your point of view. Only time will tell which of us is right. And I . . . ' He smiled again. 'I will not be there to share in either the triumph or the defeat. But I would like to know that *you* understand that I have only ever had the glory of Japan, and of our name, at heart.'

'I understand that,' Philip said.

'Then I will say, God bless you, and keep you, in the times to come.' Another quick smile. 'They will be tumultuous. I only regret that I shall not be able to stand at your side when the bullets begin to fly.' He bowed, and turned, and left the room.

*

'And they call him a coward,' Philip said. He sat in his lounge and stared at the wall. 'It is at times like these that you discover who are truly your friends.'

'You do not lack for them,' Anne said. 'Admiral Yamamoto has been magnificent.'

'Because he wants me back under his command. He is well aware that it is very necessary for the navy to present a unified front against the ambitions of the army, now that the army has taken control. And he knows he can rely on me. Were I ever to let him down, he would throw me to the dogs without a second thought. I am speaking of *friends*. Where is Graham? We were close. Closer than I have ever been to any man, even Peter. And he has not even sent a letter of condolence. Not even a get-well card.'

'Yes,' Anne said. 'Perhaps he had his reasons.'

He frowned at her. 'Would you explain that?'

'I . . .' She flushed. 'You would be very angry. Now is not the time.'

'Now is always the time, my dearest girl. There is no time like now.'

'I . . .' She bit her lip, sighed, and told him of her interview.

He said nothing until she was quite finished. 'I don't know if he really knew what was going to happen,' she said. 'Or if he was just guessing. But I feel so terribly guilty. If only I had told you, there and then . . .'

'I would not have believed you, as you did not believe him.'

'Yes,' she said. 'But Philip . . . what happens now?'

'He is attempting to subvert the will of the Japanese people.'

'Is he?' she asked. 'Is it not the army which has already subverted the will of the Japanese people?'

'Oh, God, I do not know. To see him would be to become a traitor, knowing what I now know. And it would make you a traitor. I should pick up that telephone

350

and call Kitabake, right now. That is the only correct thing to do.'

'And if, through arresting Graham, they gain the names of his associates, you would be destroying God alone knows how many men, and probably women, who share only your ideal of Japan.'

He sighed. 'Sometimes I wish Peter had not interfered, that day at the Admiralty, and let his accomplice shoot a little straighter.'

'Philip! Don't talk that way. But you know as well as I that Hirota and the generals are going to lead this country straight into war. If you can, you *must* do something about that. Everyone always felt that the navy would restrain the army from any really crazy adventures. The navy, as represented by men like Uncle William. But Uncle William isn't there any more.'

'I must speak with Yamamoto.'

'To what end?' She frowned. 'You mean to tell him about Graham?'

'Good heavens, no. Not at this moment, anyway. But Yamamoto is a good man. He knows what should be and what should not be, and more important, he knows pretty well what is going to happen in the immediate future. I will speak with him.'

Anne's turn to sigh. 'But you won't speak with John Graham.'

'You are asking me to break my vows of loyalty to the Emperor, Anne. To become a traitor. How could I do that, and not commit seppuku?'

'How can you be a traitor, when you are trying to *save* your country from annihilation?'

'We do not *know* what the army, what Hirota, intends. We do not *know*. And until we do know, until we also know that the navy will not be prepared, or perhaps not be able, to stop them, to oppose them would be treachery. I have taken an oath to follow the Emperor's orders to the limits of my life. I cannot now break that oath, simply

351

because of a supposition. I do not know if I can ever break that oath, no matter what happens. I will speak with Yamamoto. When I have done that, I will decide whether or not to tell John to seek an immediate transfer from Japan. I do not believe he can remain here, in any event.'

'Then I will have betrayed him,' she said.

'He asked you to tell me, didn't he?' Philip smiled, and kissed her on the cheek. 'I will speak with Yamamoto.'

'Come in, honourable Captain, come in.' Isoroku Yamamoto rose from behind his desk, beaming. He gave a suitably short bow in response to Philip's deep one, and then hurried round the table to embrace his friend. 'It is good to see you in uniform again, although I had not expected it so soon. You cannot be ready for duty again, already?'

'I believe I am. My doctors say I am not. They are talking of months, yet. Months.'

Yamamoto gestured him to a chair. 'Can you use your arm?'

'Not yet. But it is no longer part of a naval officer's duty to lead boarding parties, sword in hand.'

'And your lung?'

Philip shrugged. 'My chest aches, and sometimes I have difficulty breathing. But . . . '

'You are also far too pale and thin. The doctors have spoken with me also, or rather, I have spoken with them. They recommend at least six months more of convalescence. Then you will be totally fit again. And that is the Philip Shimadzu I wish.'

'Six months?'

'It is not so long a time. Do you know what I recommend for you? That you take that beautiful mistress of yours for a long holiday. Go down to Kyushu, and soak up the sun, and eat lots of rice, and drink lots of sake, and return to me, next year, with some weight on those shoulders.'

'It is very kind of you to suggest that, honourable Admiral, but . . . '

'There is something else I strongly recommend, Philip.'

'Sir?'

'That you marry the girl.'

'Marry her?'

'Is that not what you wish to do? I know your situation. Your uncle often discussed it with me. I did not agree with his point of view, but it was not my place to interfere with the judgement of the head of a family on a strictly family matter. But are you not the head of the family now?'

'Good heavens,' Philip remarked. That thought had not occurred to him before. And of course it was not true; it would not be true, at least in his estimation, until after Peter was dead, however easily the rest of Japan might write off his elder brother.

But Peter was very soon to be dead.

'It is truly said,' Yamamoto continued, 'that out of evil cometh good. Not always perhaps a commensurate amount of good, to be sure. But we are thumbing our noses at the gods, and at the fates they control, if we do not attempt to extract *some* good out of every misfortune that overtakes us. I recommend that you do so. There is no need – indeed, I doubt that it would be appropriate at this time – for you to have a great wedding. Both you and Doctor Freeman are Christians, are you not? You can therefore hold a small private ceremony to satisfy the dictates of your religion, and it can still be registered as a legal marriage.' He leaned back with a smile. 'And if you were to be kind enough to ask me, I would be honoured to give the bride away.'

'Why, honourable Admiral . . . I am quite overwhelmed. I do not know what to say, except thank you, both for your advice, which I shall assuredly follow, and for your kind offer, which I most assuredly accept.'

'Then that is settled. And then, take that six months'

honeymoon down in Kyushu. I have important things in mind for you when you return.'

'It is the future that I wish to discuss, certainly, honourable Admiral,' Philip said. 'That is, if I shall have a future.'

'Why should you not?'

'Is not my family disgraced?'

'Your family is honoured, Captain Shimadzu, because you belong to it. Only your brother is disgraced. You should always remember that. I wish to hear no more talk of disgrace. You have a great future in front of you, one that I have mapped out with much care. You understand that you now possess sufficient seniority to receive flag rank?'

'Yes, honourable Admiral.'

'And I would be the first to congratulate you. However, with your permission, Philip, I would like to defer that honour for the next couple of years.'

'The decision is yours, honourable Admiral,' Philip said. But he was aware of a feeling of sickness spreading away from his stomach. Yamamoto was being very kind, as kind, indeed, as he knew how . . . but even he could not gainsay the fact that his senior captain's brother was a condemned traitor.

Yamamoto smiled at his expression. 'Have faith in me, Philip San. Now, firstly, I am going to confirm Captain Tiridata in command of the *Mutsu*. He has been acting for you since your injury, and has proved himself a capable officer.'

Philip bowed his head.

'When you return to duty, you will assume command of the cruiser *Tone*,' Yamamoto continued.

Philip's head came up. 'A cruiser?'

'She is still on the slip. In fact, I doubt she will be ready for launching for another year. But that will give you ample time to become familiar with her. What, do you regard this as a demotion?'

'Well, with great respect, honourable Admiral . . .'

'The *Tone* is one of the ships of the future, Philip. She will displace fifteen thousand tons, deep loaded, and that is larger than any battleship your illustrious uncle ever served on. True, her armament is only eight-inch, and you are used to something twice that calibre, but this ship is a totally revolutionary design. She will cruise at thirty-five knots, Philip. Think of that, in a ship of that size. She will have the very latest in anti-aircraft batteries. And she will carry six aircraft. She is virtually a battle-cruiser, but is yet immensely well armoured. But even more important than that, Philip, she is a floating laboratory. She will include every advance in the science of navigation, the science of gun-laying, and the science of detecting an enemy, that we have made since 1919.'

Philip nodded. 'I have read of her in the *Naval Review*. Was she not one of the first ships laid down after the decision to abandon the Naval Treaties was taken?'

'She was actually laid down before then,' Yamamoto said. 'As a light cruiser, of course, as that was all we were then allowed. Our decision to abandon the treaties allowed us to develop her into the magnificent ship she now is. I wish you to have command of her, for a limited period.'

'Of course, honourable Admiral. I can only hope that during this limited period, I will be able to convince you of my readiness, and suitability, for a more important command.'

Yamamoto laughed. 'You are deeply hurt. Well, you should be. But I have asked you to have faith in me. I have told you that I wish you to retain captain's rank for a few years more, and that I wish you to command this finest ship in the Japanese Navy, for a limited period. Why, do you suppose? It is because even the *Tone* will be the finest ship in the Japanese Navy for only a limited period. Then we will have another ship which I wish you to command, because she will be the greatest warship ever to put to sea, and I think you are the finest seagoing captain there is in this fleet. Would you not say that would be the perfect marriage?'

'The greatest ship ever to put to sea?' Philip asked, unsure what he was being told.

'Not a word of what I am about to say, no idea of what I am about to show you, must ever leave this room, Philip.'

'Of course, honourable Admiral,' Philip replied, without thinking.

Yamamoto got up, went to the filing cabinet in the corner, and from one of the drawers took a roll of stiff paper, which he proceeded to spread on his desk, holding the edges down with various inkwells and paperweights. Then he looked up. 'What do you think of her?'

Philip stood beside him, and looked at quite the most beautiful sketch of a warship he had ever seen, with magnificent flared bows, a fighting top as high as an apartment building, and three obviously massive gun-turrets. There were no scales shown, so it was impossible to estimate her actual size – but he was certainly looking at a very large battleship indeed.

'This is only an artist's impression, of course,' Yamamoto explained. 'The plans are still on the drawing board, being worked over, and she is still being costed – I have not yet had even the design presented to parliament. But they know what I have in mind, and they will undoubtedly be prepared to fund it. Or rather, them. I think we need two of these.'

'She is certainly a lovely looking ship,' Philip ventured.

'And she will be the greatest fighting ship in the world,' Yamamoto sat down again. 'Seventy thousand tons.'

'Seventy . . . ' Philip also sat down again, without intending to. 'But that is double the treaty limitation.'

'We no longer adhere to the treaty, Philip. Nor are we going to be bound by any restrictions whatsoever. Let the British and the Americans rack their brains about how to fit sixteen-inch guns and adequate armour into thirty-five thousand tons designed weight. Let the Americans worry about whether or not they can afford to widen and deepen the Panama Canal. We are going to *do*, and when it is done, we shall possess a fleet which no one will dare oppose. Do you see those guns? They will be eighteen-inch calibre. Eighteen-inch! Do you realise that each gun will hurl a shell of more than three thousand pounds in weight? A broadside of twenty-seven thousand pounds? More than two tons?'

Philip scratched his head. The idea of any opposing vessel being hit by two tons of flying high explosive, or, indeed, near missed by such a colossal discharge, was mind-boggling.

'She will have twelve modern boilers, Philip, developing one hundred and fifty thousand shaft horsepower. That will give twenty-seven knots. These ships will not only be half as big again as *Nelson* and *Rodney*, and far more powerful, they will be four knots faster. And yet they will be the best-protected ships in the world as well; those turrets will have twenty-five inches of steel around them; the conning tower will have nineteen inches; the hull will have sixteen and the deck, the deck, Philip, will carry nine inches of steel. Aerial bombs will merely bounce off that. They are a dream. They have been my dream, ever since I was in the design office myself, when such things could only be dreamed of. But now I am going to make my dreams come true. And you are going to command one of these ships.'

'Once again, honourable Admiral, I do not know what to say,' Philip confessed.

Yamamoto smiled. 'Then do not say anything. Follow my instructions, beginning with Doctor Freeman. Just let me know the day. Now, there was a matter you wished to discuss with me, I believe?'

For a moment Philip couldn't think what it was. The design of the new super battleship still lay on the desk, and in his imagination he was already standing on the bridge of such a ship . . . She would be virtually unsinkable. Unfightable. Such a ship . . . He realised that Yamamoto was still gazing at him inquiringly, and sat up straight. 'I . . . I have not yet had the opportunity to discuss with you, honourable Admiral, recent political events. To discover how you feel they will affect the role of the navy.'

'Ah. You have been lying there on your hospital bed, brooding on the events of last February. Those were shocking, reprehensible . . . And yet, as I have said, out of evil can come a great deal of good.'

'You mean you privately approve of what was done?'

'I mean that the nation certainly needed to be reminded of who and what we are,' Yamamoto said evenly. 'I do not hold with assassination. It has always seemed to me to be the ultimate in cowardice, to surprise a man with the intent of taking his life. But those officers at least had the courage then to take their own lives. Most of them.'

'And are now considered martyrs,' Philip said bitterly.

'Every nation needs a few martyrs now and then,' Yamamoto reminded him.

'And so now the army is in command,' Philip said. 'Utterly and completely. Do you not regard this as a grave step, honourable Admiral?'

'That remains to be seen. They are proceeding with suitable caution at the moment. And at least, with the army in command, we are going to be allowed to create the kind of navy Japan needs. This kind of navy.' He tapped the drawing. 'That can be no bad thing.'

'With whom are we going to fight, honourable Admiral, when we have these ships? The entire rest of the world?'

Yamamoto sighed. 'You are too eager to adopt an apocalyptical view of the situation, Philip. I cannot help but believe it is this Christianity you espouse. Having the greatest fleet in the world does not mean we wish to destroy every other fleet; it means every other fleet in the world will have to think twice about fighting *us*. That is the important factor. As for being isolated against the rest of the world, that is changing, most rapidly. This, too, is confidential, but if it will reassure you, we are about to sign a treaty of friendship and alliance with Germany.'

Philip frowned. 'Germany? That is of value to us?'

'Ah. You have not kept up with recent political events, Philip San. You still think of Germany as a defeated nation. Well, perhaps she is. But under her new government, under the leadership of this Adolf Hitler, she is determined to regain her former Great Power status, and she is doing it. She is now re-arming at a great pace, and she is building a new navy, as well. No one is objecting. The British have even given this new navy their blessing. And they are seeking to borrow our expertise, in battleships and aircraft-carriers.' He smiled. 'We shall not, of course, let them into *this* secret.' Once again he tapped the drawing.

'But you see, Philip, it is as I have always felt, that we have but needed to be patient, for the circumstances of which we have always dreamed to fall into our lap. There are cracks appearing in that monument to hypocrisy, the apparent unity of the Western Powers. Italy has become engaged in a wild African adventure, and is herself now an outcast amongst nations. Spain is on the verge of civil war. And Germany foresees that the real enemy of the future is Soviet Communism. Well, so do we. That is the official reason for our pact. However, in the short term we still consider China to be our prime enemy, and therefore our prime target. The importance of our new relationship with Germany is that we are no longer isolated, and that no one at this moment is in a position to point a censorious finger at us, except the Americans, of course, and they have been doing that for years – without much effect.

'Believe me, Philip, I am as much against mad adventures as I ever was. But I wish to see Japan as strong and respected as she should be. I will do everything in my power to accomplish that, and I expect my officers to share my points of view. I know that you do. Now, I uggest that you go down to Yokohama, as soon as you feel able to, and inspect the *Tone*, and appreciate her, and then . . . marry Doctor Freeman, and look forward to a glittering career in the new Japanese Navy.'

'Honourable Admiral.' Philip stood up, bowed and then saluted. 'The wedding will have to wait until after my brother's execution.'

Yamamoto inclined his head. 'I understand that, honourable Captain.'

The family sat together on the morning of 7 July 1936. What was left of it. Maureen Freeman and Shikibu Shimadzu, Anne Freeman and Philip Shimadzu, and Iyeyasu Shimadzu. The boy was now, of course, old enough to be told what had happened, and was happening today. He scarcely knew his uncle, but he could still regard the thought of him with disgust. Because however Western their upbringing, the family was yet Japanese. Peter's failure to commit seppuku had disgraced them all.

They assembled at dawn, and maintained a silent vigil, until the clock struck eight. Then Philip got up. 'It is done,' he said.

A single tear rolled down Shikibu's cheek.

'The body will be released within an hour,' Philip said. 'I have arranged a hearse. Will you attend the cremation, honourable Mother?'

Shikibu shook her head.

'I will come with you,' Anne said.

'And I,' Maureen said.

'And I,' Iyeyasu said.

'No,' Philip said. 'You will stay with your grandmother. And Aunt Maureen, I would beg you to allow me to go by myself. With Anne.'

Maureen bowed. He was the head of the family.

'I know it's a terrible thing to say,' Anne said, as she drove towards the prison – his right arm was still useless. 'But I suddenly feel I can breathe again. It's as if I've been holding my breath all of these months.'

'I know,' Philip said.

She glanced at him. 'You never told me how your interview with Yamamoto went.'

'Very well. He told me a great number of very interesting facts. Held out the most magnificent views of the future; he seems quite confident that the new government will be as circumspect as the old. And he appointed me to a new command, as soon as I am again fit to serve.'

'Oh, Philip, how splendid. A new battleship?'

'There isn't one, yet. Although there will be. For the time being I am to be captain of our newest cruiser, the *Tone*.'

'A cruiser?'

'Yamamoto swears it is not demotion. He says it is a necessary step to prepare me for command of one of the new battleships, when they are built. Technology has advanced so much in the past few years, you see, that even ships like *Mutsu* and *Nagato* are just about out of date. I believe him. He is an honest man.'

'And he regards the situation as satisfactory,' she observed, staring ahead of the car.

'Yes,' Philip agreed. 'Nevertheless, I think it would not be a bad idea for me to speak with John Graham.'

She turned her head. 'Oh, Phil. Thank God! You mean Yamamoto *did* say something?'

'Whatever he said to me was in the strictest confidence, my dearest girl. And I gave him my word to that. But there are some questions I would like to ask Graham. I will not betray him. I give *you* my word on that. I merely wish to ask him some questions.'

'That is simply splendid,' she said. 'When can I invite him to dinner?'

'I think it can wait until we return from our honey-moon.'

'From our . . . ' Once again her head turned sharply.

Philip gazed at her. He thought that perhaps, at thirty years of age, she had reached her full beauty. She had allowed her golden hair to grow, as she was now living in Japan, where every woman's hair was long; but instead of dressing it in a huge coiled bun as did most Japanese, she let it flow down her back, secured on the nape of her neck by a bow and kept in place on her scalp by a headband. Her features were as crisply beautiful as he had ever remembered, only now they were more sensitive and therefore more attractive than when she had been a girl. Her body was splendid, tall and strong and athletic, and utterly feminine. She would be a prize, even if he did not love her, and know her, and know that she was the only woman in the world for him. And at last he could make her his very own.

'Will you marry me, Anne?' he asked.

'Marry you? Oh, Phil. But . . . '

'You can thank Isoroku Yamamoto for reminding me that there is no one to stop us, now. I am the head of the family, as of eight o'clock this morning.'

'Gee whiz,' she commented, lapsing into pure Ameri-canism. 'I just never thought it would ever happen. Oh, Phil . . . Do you mind awfully if I cry a little?'

'Congratulations,' John Graham said. 'Oh, very best con-gratulations.' He bowed to Anne. 'Mrs Shimadzu. But when did it happen? I knew nothing of it.'

'Well, in all the circumstances, we thought it should be strictly a family affair,' Anne explained. 'We were mar-ried three months ago. Then we took a long honeymoon. Philip is still on sick leave, you see.'

'Yes. I do wish to say, Philip, how much I admire your actions on . . . ' He checked, but Philip did not reply. 'Still,' Graham went on, deciding to change the subject.

'If I had known earlier, I could at least have brought you a present.'

'As Anne said, it was a very small, private ceremony,' Philip said. 'But we thank you for the thought, at any rate. Will you not be seated?'

Cautiously Graham lowered himself to his cushion. The doors to the lounge were closed, so that the maid-servant could hear nothing that was said, but Anne had brought in the kettle to prepare sake.

'So now he can beat me whenever he chooses,' she said, desperately endeavouring to make at least one of the two men smile.

Neither did so.

She gave them each a cup of sake, and sipped her own. 'I did as you asked, John,' she said. And sighed. 'But not until after the event.'

Graham also sipped, and waited.

'I doubt anything Anne could have told me would have altered those events,' Philip said. 'As I understood them. It seems you knew more than I did.'

'Still not enough,' Graham said. 'I learned there was to be some kind of an attempted *coup*. I certainly did not know it involved the murder of most of the Cabinet, or I would have warned one of my people, who was actually a member of that Cabinet. And who is now dead.'

Philip frowned at him. 'One of your agents was a member of the Japanese cabinet?' he asked incredulously.

'I wish you could understand,' Graham said. 'I have no agents. I am a member of a group of people who are seeking to keep the peace of the world. Nothing more than that.'

Philip gazed at him. 'You understand that my first reaction to what Anne told me was to hand you over to the police?'

'That's reasonable,' Graham agreed. He was very watchful. Perhaps, Anne thought, he expected Kempai agents to be waiting behind the wall.

363

'Anne persuaded me that perhaps you have the good of Japan at heart, and I chose to wait. But now I wish you to explain certain things to me. You came here for the express purpose of setting up an anti-militarist regime?'

Graham shook his head. 'Good Lord, no. I came here as a naval attaché. But as things began to hot up in China, and as I spoke with various people, I realised that there was a considerable difference of opinion in Japan as to whether your country should follow a path of aggression in East Asia, or not. I communicated these impressions to my superiors, of course, and was told in return to cultivate those who could be called peace-lovers, and discover just how deep were the divisions between them and the warmongers, and what advantage we, I mean Britain, could obtain from it.'

'Was that when you cultivated me?'

'No. I cultivated you because I was told to. You were, and are, a Japanese naval officer who spoke English fluently, and who has an American background. It was thought you might be a useful source of information, especially as you were on the staff.' At last he smiled. 'You never revealed any information of any value. But I liked you as a man. I was honoured to be your friend.'

'But you still thought I could be useful to your group,' Philip said, recalling various conversations on board *Yahagi*, and one in particular, many years before, when Graham had raised the point as to whether there could ever come a moment when a serving officer would have to reject the course his country was taking.

Graham shrugged. 'I hoped so, certainly. But then the earthquake, and your transfer . . . '

'The earthquake appeared to have ruined my nerves, and my posting to Shanghai meant I would be too close to the Kempai.'

'Something like that. Regretfully.'

They gazed at each other. 'I appreciate your honesty,' Philip said at last. 'Even if I regret the discovery that our friendship was so false.'

'It was real enough to me,' Graham said, not lowering his eyes. 'And it would be real enough again.'

'But only if I join your treasonable group.'

'Unfortunately, that appears to be the only way you will again consider friendship with me. But I would ask you to consider, what can be treasonable for a group of intelligent men to get together occasionally and criticise a course of action being undertaken by their government?'

'The fact that they are doing so with the agent of another government,' Philip pointed out, and Graham flushed. But instead of seeking to capitalise on the point he had just gained, Philip changed the subject. 'What do you know of this new German Government?'

Graham frowned. 'Nazi Germany? It is a collection of the most unmitigated thugs who have ever ruled any country, much less a potential power like Germany. We thought, and we still think, that Lenin and his crew were bad, but Hitler and *his* crew are a darned sight worse.'

'Why?'

'Because they have come to power on a wave of racial hatred, principally anti-Semitism, and because they are unashamedly creating a military dictatorship. In fact, they have already done so. They make no bones about wishing to overturn the Versailles Treaty and restore Germany to her position under the Kaisers, as the predominant power in Europe.'

'I see,' Philip said thoughtfully. 'And what will Great Britain and France do about it?'

'They do not appear to be doing anything, at the moment.'

'But if Germany is breaking treaties . . .'

'There is a large body of public opinion in Britain that considers that the terms of Versailles were too harsh. Maybe they were. But the fact is that the present British Government is not disposed to challenge any of Mr Hitler's transgressions. And France appears to be in the throes of some kind of civil war.'

'So you do not think there is going to be a general European War?'

'I am sure there will have to be, when we come to our senses. No one who has read *Mein Kampf* – that's a sort of autobiography Hitler wrote a few years ago, in which he sets out his aims – can possibly have any doubt about that. But, as I say, it won't happen until the British come to their senses, unfortunately. May I ask why you are interested? I don't see Germany ever being in a position to trouble Japan.'

'Still, they seem to be the people we may have to watch out for eventually,' Philip said. 'Tell me of your group.'

'I cannot do that.'

'Unless I join you?'

'Not even then. Should you join us, in the course of time you will meet more of my associates. We occasionally get together for discussions.'

'But never to plan subversion?'

'I have told you, that has never been considered. Because it has never been necessary. During the last three years Viscount Saito's Government has moved steadily in the direction we have always thought best. Our people, who are prominent in their individual fields, whether it is business, or sport, or politics, or even religion, have of course played their part in discussions, formal and informal, with the members of that government, and we like to feel that we have helped shape its policies. As I have told you, one of our members was actually a member of the cabinet as well. He was, unfortunately, gunned down in the February *coup*.'

'And now?'

'Well, I will admit that what has happened has been a catastrophe, for us no less than for Japan.'

'Do you think the army know of your existence?'

'I am sure they do not. Or the Kempai would have

interfered before now.'

'Are you sure the Kempai knows nothing about you?'

'Quite sure. For the reason I have already stated.'

'Yet you have sworn me to no oath of secrecy.'

'I trust you, Philip,' Graham said, simply. 'And I know that you believe in the same things as I do. I also believe that as a member of our group you would become its natural leader, should circumstances ever make it necessary for us to have a leader.'

Once again they gazed at each other.

'You must have some plans for what happens next,' Philip said.

'We have none,' Graham replied. 'As I have said, the assassination of Saito and, even more, of men like Takahashi and our representative has been a catastrophe. I believe it will prove a catastrophe for all Japan, in the long run. But up to now nothing has happened to prove me right. I am not, repeat not, in the business of seeking insurrection here in Japan, Philip. My brief is influence, not revolution. I deplore what is happening inside Japan at this moment, but as long as it remains a domestic matter I can and will do nothing about it. Your new leaders are pressing ahead with armaments, of course, and so is everyone else right now. They have taken no overt steps towards resuming any expansionist programmes as regards China. So I, we, must hope that they will act with the same common sense and true appreciation of the situation as their predecessors.'

Yamamoto's sentiments, Philip thought. But Yamamoto also looked forward to the alliance with Germany – and perhaps Spain and Italy as well – whom Graham obviously felt were hell-bent on war. 'If I joined your organisation, you would require information from me?'

'Only what you might wish to volunteer,' Graham promised. 'I would not compromise your honour.'

'And if I tell you that I can give you no information at

all, although I may from time to time be privy to certain developments which might affect your estimation of the situation?'

Graham shrugged. 'That is up to you. If you joined us, I would have to believe that you are prepared to work in the same direction as my colleagues and myself.'

'Yes,' Philip said. 'Well, it is something I shall have to think about, very carefully. But I also think we have talked enough treason for one night. Anne has a splendid shabu-shabu prepared for us. Why do we not eat?'

'You are torturing the poor man,' Anne observed.

He had thought her asleep. Now he rolled over to take her in his arms. 'I had supposed I was torturing myself.'

'Well . . . that as well.' She sighed. 'But to keep him waiting for a reply, week after week after week . . . Can you not believe that he has only the future at heart?'

'I do believe that, my dearest girl. But whose future? He confesses that he was sent here to do a job of work, by his superiors. Now, he may be utterly naive. That does not alter the fact that Great Britain has enormous interests here in the Far East, interests which financially and even, perhaps, physically, she is finding it more and more difficult to protect adequately. Obviously it is to her advantage to have a friendly government in power in Japan.'

'Is that so very wicked?'

'Perhaps not. Except that Great Britain, seeking her own advantage, not ours, was the one to abrogate the treaty she already had with us, back in 1922. Had she not done so, there would be no problem; we would, as part of our obligations under that treaty, be obliged to protect all British colonies from anyone. Certainly we would never have regarded them as potential spoil ourselves.'

He turned his head to look at her; that had been a slip of the tongue. But she had not apparently noticed, was concentrating on the main theme of the argument.

368

'But if they had done that, they might have antagonised the United States.'

'Have they achieved so much by opting for friendship with the United States?'

'They must hope so.'

'Yes. Well, on the evidence, it would seem they are mistaken.'

'So you will not join Johnny's group.'

'I said, I must think about it. I must be absolutely sure.'

Think, about becoming a traitor. Because that was what was involved. It was quite possible – even if it might be morally unacceptable – for a lawyer or a doctor or an author or an artist, one of that dreadfully amorphous group lumped together under the title of intellectuals, to criticise the Government. Even to go so far as to join a discussion group with a representative of a foreign power, in order to influence the actions of one's own country's leaders, was not possible for a serving officer, who had sworn an oath to obey whatever commands were given him by his superiors, confident always that such commands emanated from the Emperor.

But what happened when such a serving officer doubted the commands had indeed emanated from the Emperor? The present Mikado, as Crown Prince, had attended his first wedding. He was a man of quiet charm – and not a great deal else. But he was also a god.

This question had bedevilled Japanese history, since time immemorial, as he well knew. A god was omnipotent. But the Japanese ruling class had, centuries ago, recognised that their emperors, while certainly gods, and direct descendants of the Sun Goddess, Amaterasu, were none the less fallible beings. More fallible than most.

The Fujiwara Clan had begun the process back in the ninth Christian century, banishing the Emperor to monastical seclusion and taking the reins of power themselves. Thus had begun an almost inevitable process of delegation of power. When the Fujiwara had grown weak, as they had to with the passage of time and incestuous marriage, they had been replaced by a new family, the Minamoto, amongst whom indeed he numbered his own distant ancestors. The Minamoto had ousted the Fujiwara in fact, but not in name. The Fujiwara, the Regents for the Emperors, had joined the Emperors in seclusion, and the Minamoto had had to find a new name for themselves. Thus Yoritomo Minamoto, greatest of the clan, had called himself Sei-i-tai-Shogun, or Barbarian Subduing General. In that name, the Minamoto had ruled the country until they in turn had been overthrown by the Ashikaga. The Ashikaga had claimed the title of Shoguns, but they had been overthrown by Oda Nobunaga, whose great general, Hideyoshi Toyotomi, had eventually come to power. Unable to claim the title of Shogun, because he was of humble birth, Hideyoshi had called himself Kwampaka, Regent for the Shoguns. The Tokugawa, replacing the dead Hideyoshi and his family after the bloodiest of civil wars, had been both of noble heritage and ruthless determination. They had killed every relative of Hideyoshi they could find, and announced themselves as the new Shoguns; Iyeyasu's great forebear had been the first to take the title. His descendants had then ruled Japan for two and a half centuries. But always in the name of the living Emperor.

Then in 1867 a remarkable thing had happened. An emperor had died while his eldest son had still been a boy, his energies not yet chanelled by his advisers into nothing better than contemplation and the judging of poetry competitions. And that boy, aided by some remarkable people – amongst them Philip's own grandfather, Ralph Freeman – had dared to attempt to regain the imperial power from the Shogunate . . . and had succeeded.

But Mutsuhito had been a remarkable man. Neither his son, Yoshihito, nor his grandson, Hirohito, the present Emperor, had revealed quite such qualities of leadership and decision. Thus the country had slipped back into inferior hands. Those hands had first of all belonged to capable, and utterly loyal, generals and admirals, who had sought only to establish the independence of Japan, to prevent it from becoming a field for Western exploitation, as had happened to China. Now those men were dead. He supposed his Uncle William had been the last of the breed, he and Viscount Saito. And now the country was again in the hands of a shogun, only this shogun was nameless, a many-headed hydra, a committee of generals rather than a single military dictator. And under that leadership, Japan was bound . . . where?

But as history showed, shoguns had been overthrown before – in the name of the Emperor they pretended to obey. Was that the ultimate recourse? Was he designated to lead such a desperate venture? He could hardly be less; John Graham had hinted as much. But he, Philip Shimadzu? A man who had always sought nothing more than the paths of peace wherever possible, in order to enjoy the prosperity that comes with peace? He found that an incredible concept. The leader of any revolt against this new shogunate should be a man like Osoroku Yamamoto, bold and determined, confident and capable . . . and already an admiral. But Yamamoto wanted only to use the generals and their ambitions to achieve the fleet of which he had always dreamed, and then, one day, to lead that fleet into battle; Philip did not think his mentor really cared who his enemy might be. Could such a man ever act for the country as a whole? Such a shallow man, he realised with surprise; and he had always regarded Yamamoto as the epitome of nobility.

'What will you do?' Anne asked next morning at breakfast, as she had asked every morning at breakfast for the past fortnight.

'What I decide to do,' he replied, and touched her hand; it was the first time he had ever snapped at her.

She bowed her head, as a Japanese wife should, and he

strode to the door, where Hagi was waiting with his shoes and cap and belt and weapons. And there was a young lieutenant waiting too, just arrived, panting and breathless.

'Honourable Captain,' he gasped. 'Oh, honourable Captain. Admiral Yamamoto has himself sent me to summon you to the Admiralty. Honourable Captain, we are at war.'

CHAPTER 14

The War

'War!' Iyeyasu screamed, jumping up and down. 'War! Oh, isn't that splendid, Father? Isn't that splendid?'

'War?' Anne asked in bewildered horror. 'But war with whom?'

'With China,' Philip told her.

'China? But . . . my God!'

'My reactions entirely. It seems that Chiang Kai-shek has patched up his differences with the Communists, and with the warlords, and they have determined to present a united front against us. Thus they have declared war.'

She gazed at him; he had been unable to keep the excitement out of his voice. 'And that makes you happy?'

'Well, they have declared war on us, my dearest girl. Not us on them.'

'Ours was the provocation.'

'Some years ago. Manchuria has virtually been accepted as ours, now. This is an entirely new development.'

'One of which you do approve,' she said angrily.

'Of which we must all approve,' he pointed out. 'Our nation is at war. Fighting for its life . . . '

'Oh, balderdash,' she shouted. 'We, fighting for our lives, against China? All they want is their own country back.'

'You do not understand,' he told her. 'Without Manchuria we are nothing. And if we were to lose, do not suppose it will stop at Manchuria. They would claim

Korea and Formosa as well. We would be reduced to our heartland, and be disgraced and dishonoured before the eyes of the world. We would collapse into nothing.'

'Dishonoured,' she said angrily. 'Is that all you can think about, your precious honour?'

'Is there a finer goal for a man,' he asked quietly, 'than to live all his life in perfect honour? Can there be?'

She flushed. 'Oh, Phil . . . ' She put her arms round him and hugged him. 'You were against the annexation of Manchuria.'

'Yes, I was. But I knew it was a necessary step. Perhaps, then, I would have settled for a smaller Japan, a second-rate Power. Because I feared a huge conflagration. That did not happen, and our country has benefitted. Oh, my darling, perhaps in my heart I still do not approve of it. But I do know that for us to be driven out, for us to be defeated in war by China, would be disastrous. Believe me.'

She sighed. She did not know how to argue against that. Because it could be true. Japan had never lost a war, since the restoration of the Mikado. And it had been the Japanese realisation of their helplessness in the face of the strength of the Western Powers which had inspired that revolution. It was impossible even to imagine what sort of revolution might be inspired were Japan to be defeated by China.

'It's just that . . . I guess, it seems every time we seem on the verge of achieving something, something happens. Phil, what about John Graham?'

'You will have to see him on my behalf. Tell him that in the present circumstances I can no longer even consider joining his group. But tell him more, that he must disband this group immediately. Meeting to criticise the Government and its policies in time of peace is perhaps just possible; to do so in time of war is treason. Tell him I make this demand of him.'

374

'While you march off. Phil, suppose America comes in on the Chinese side.'

'They won't. China has decided to fight us. For vengeance on the past, not for any new aggression on our part. If America did not go to their aid when we invaded Manchuria, why should they go to their aid now?'

'Because they'll see that it's all a set-up,' she cried, once again becoming angry. 'Can't *you* see that? Can't you see that this is what the generals have been trying to engineer for ten years? Ever since they occupied Shantung, they have been willing the Chinese to go to war with them, so that they would have an excuse to gobble up more territory. And the Chinese haven't obliged, until now. They've had more sense. And they probably trusted Saito. But Saito is dead. Killed by the generals. So now the army has got everything it wanted. But it's still the same army we have always known was a catastrophe for Japan. Don't you think it should be opposed more than ever, now?'

'How can I think that?' he demanded. 'How dare I? China has declared war upon us. And we have responded, in the name of the Emperor. I have sworn to carry out his commands to the best of my ability, the very last drop of blood in my veins. How can I oppose him now?'

It was no longer a time for thought, but for action. What a relief that was. He had supposed, from time to time during the past year, that he might be going mad. Through trying to think. Through trying to resolve the hundred and one conflicting emotions and ideas and understandings which had tugged at both his brain and his heart. Militarism appalled him; yet he was a serving officer. Because he had never been offered the choice of any other profession; carrying weapons, and using them, was his heritage. And the thought of battle undoubtedly thrilled him, despite all. His uncle William had first earned his spurs in battle against the Chinese. Might not all of history be about to repeat itself?

All of history? He would hope for a better fate than William's. But that was a long time in the future.

And at least part of his anti-militarism had always been fear of being drawn into a conflict with the United States. Not from physical fear of defeat – although he knew that was inevitable – but because of that other heritage, handed down by his grandfather, and now additionally, because of Anne. He had felt the risk was greater than ever when he heard of the pact with Germany; he did not think Japan should ever consider becoming involved in Western affairs, even if only by proxy.

Graham's opinion of the new German regime disturbed him. It had sounded too much like a copy of the worst of Japanese militarism. Thus he had even been tempted to join the discussion group, to oppose the government as far as he could, and hope to bring about a change – even a change by armed *coup*, if need be. But he had held back because of his oath, because of his ambitions . . . and because of his family. The conflict over which direction the country should take had bedevilled his mother's entire life. It had cost her her husband, her brother and her eldest son. To suppose that she could sit back and watch her other son entering into the same conflict with equanimity was impossible. And there was Iyeyasu as well, also about to commence his career; how could he follow such a career, how could he ever honour and love a father who had set himself against the proper development of such a career?

Against them there was only Anne. Of course she was right, in cold terms. China had been goaded into this war, and it was a war of liberation, for the Chinese. But Anne, much as he loved her, just did not understand the truth of the matter. China and Japan had hated each other since before the dawn of history. They would always hate each other, and they would always be rivals for the leadership of East Asia. The Chinese were his natural enemies; they had murdered his father. They deserved to be smashed.

Even a woman like Wu Chi, for whom he had nearly ruined his career? Yes, he now knew. Even she. Because she, had she lived, would be as anxious as anyone to destroy Japan.

Anne did not understand these things. America had no such natural, historical enemy. So the war would make her very unhappy. He regretted that. But could he, in honour, afford to weigh her opinions at a time like this?

Admiral Isoroku Yamamoto smiled at his senior captains, assembled in the wardroom of the battleship *Nagato* and gazing at him in rapt attention; their eager tension filled the air.

'I understand that this is what you, all of us, have waited for all of our lives,' he told them. 'We are fighting seamen, who have only ever wished to be given the right to fight. Some of us, indeed, may have from time to time doubted that right would ever be ours again. But how may a man endure an entire lifetime, and never see action? That is against the very laws of Nature.

'Alas, my friends, I can promise you little glory in this enterprise. Yet this is not to say your duties will be anything less than arduous, and at times even repugnant; they must still be carried out with ruthless determination. China, mighty China, more than five hundred millions of people, united and determined, has thrown down the gauntlet to little Japan. Make no mistake: this is a war of revenge. They would wipe out the catastrophe of the Manchu, the memory of our past successes. And do not make the mistake, either, of assuming they will easily be defeated; their very numbers make the task difficult. Yet defeated they must be, and crushed. They have chosen to throw down the gauntlet to us; we must seize this heaven-sent opportunity to settle with China once and for all.

'Our leaders are aware that it would be quite impossible for us to seek to conquer so vast a country. Nor do we have any ambitions to try. Out aims are, first, to defeat the Chinese armed services wherever they can be encountered, and utterly destroy them. Secondly, to seize, and keep, control of all the great seaports, and indeed the entire Pacific coastline; by doing this, we control all the great rivers, and indeed, we control China; nothing can leave or enter the country without our permission. Once that is accomplished, all else falls into place. The third objective we have is to install in the rest of China a government which will support our aims, and not pursue ambitions of its own. But that is a political matter, and does not concern us. Our responsibility is the second aim, the sealing up of the Pacific seaboard.

'To do this, we must, first of all, defeat the Chinese fleet. Well, there hardly is a Chinese fleet, worth mentioning. But every Chinese vessel must be destroyed, wherever it can be found. This includes civilian vessels. There must be no hesitation in this. And such destruction must be accompanied by the most total ruthlessness. Our principal aim is to break the Chinese will to resist, make them rue the day their leaders chose war, and therefore make them repudiate those leaders. Thus no Japanese ship will ever pick up Chinese survivors. I wish this clearly understood. Every Chinese man, woman and child, every Chinese dog, is of this moment our enemy and must be destroyed. Those who put to sea must perish, that those who remain behind will be afraid to put to sea.'

He paused, to look from face to face. 'At the same time, I must impress upon you that no shots must be fired at foreign vessels, whatever the provocation. I am thinking here principally of those flying the Union Jack or the Stars and Stripes. It is not our intention to offer the Western Powers the slightest reason for intervention to save China from its just desserts. Remember this.

'Our second objective is the support of the army in

securing the seaports and the river mouths. The rivers we will simply blockade. Support to the army will be given by bombardment as and when required. The battle fleet, led by *Mutsu* and *Nagato*, will sail immediately.

'Our first destination will be Shanghai, to seal off the Yangtze Kiang. Now here again, my friends, my captains, I must impress upon you that you must carry out your duties with the utmost determination, and in close co-operation with the army commanders on shore. You will blast Shanghai, regardless of whether fire is returned or not, regardless of whether you may be inflicting civilian casualties or not, until the army commander requests you to cease fire as the city has surrendered or is about to fall to assault. Is this understood? I repeat, civilian casualties are a necessary concomitant of war, and the Chinese Government should have taken the possibility of such casualties into account before going to war with us. Of course, it goes without saying that no gun will be aimed at the International Concession. Thank you, gentlemen. That will be all. The honour of Japan is in your keeping. Your safe keeping.'

The officers bowed, and filed from the wardroom. Philip remained.

'Well, Shimadzu San,' Yamamoto said. 'The hour of reckoning has arrived.'

'You have no doubts?'

'Which doubts were you thinking of?'

'That we can do the job?' Philip temporised.

'That is the army's business,' Yamamoto said. 'I know we can do our job, Philip, simply because, as I said just now, there is no real opposition. But I see no reason why the army should not also accomplish its set purposes.'

'Well, then, no doubts that the Western Powers may intervene?'

'None at all. At least, overtly. I have no doubt they will criticise us, and perhaps even condemn us for waging war with all our might, as if they would not do the same in similar circumstances. That sort of criticism we can treat with contempt. They will also undoubtedly sell arms and munitions to Chiang Kai-shek, but they are also selling such items to us. Making money is all they really care about.'

'Well, then, honourable Admiral, have you no doubts concerning the morality of what we do?'

Yamamoto regarded him for several seconds, as if considering the point; but Philip knew he was only considering his reply. 'No, Philip,' he said. 'Because a man can have no morals when the existence of his people is the stake. China is, and has always been, and will always be, our enemy. You know this as well as I. During the next few months we are going to be given the opportunity to eliminate her as a threat to our future prosperity, perhaps for a century. The crime would be not to take that opportunity. More, possession of the entire Pacific seaboard of Asia will enable us to develop that industrial strength which is so essential, and so elusive. The Japanese people can only benefit from this war. Now you tell me, do *you* have doubts?'

Philip shrugged. 'I always have doubts. But none that will interfere with my duty, honourable Admiral. I wish a command.'

'You have one. *Tone.*'

'*Tone* will not be ready for action for another year. I am ready for action now.' He extended his right arm, clenched and unclenched his fist to prove that he had regained full control. 'You have just indicated that this war could be over in months.'

Yamamoto smiled. 'Perhaps I was being optimistic.'

'So I must kick my heels ashore for a year, while my fellow officers are engaged in fighting a war. Is it that you do not trust my willingness to fight, honourable Admiral?'

Yamamoto's head came up. 'If I did not trust you, Philip,' he said, 'you would not be on board this ship. I have told you, there is no honour to be found in this war. There will be no fleet actions. Indeed, there will be no ship-to-ship actions. It will simply be a matter of the destruction of enemy lives and property. From a naval point of view, we are using a sledgehammer to crush a nut. I would rather you prepared yourself for whatever may still lie ahead. Of course . . . ' He smiled. 'If China should still be fighting in a year's time, then we may well have need of both *Tone* and yourself, to finish the job.'

'Thank God for that,' Anne said. 'Oh, thank God!'

Philip refilled his sake cup.

'But you are sorry,' she accused. 'You want to go and bombard Shanghai. You actually want to.'

'My country is at war,' he said. 'I wish to have a command, to be at sea. That is my profession. Is it criminal to wish to exercise it?'

She bit her lip.

'Would you like to return to America?' he asked.

She stared at him. 'Return to America? Whatever for?'

'Simply because you are obviously unhappy here in Japan.'

'Unhappy here? I am your wife. I can only be happy where you are.'

He held her hand. 'If you are my wife, my dearest Anne, then you must *be* my wife. You must support me with all your heart, all your soul. You must believe that what I choose to do is right, above all things.'

She would not lower her eyes. 'You once said to me, how can you expect me to swear something like that?'

He threw her arm away from him. 'Then go.'

'But I will swear it, for you,' she said.

His head turned slowly.

'Because I love you,' she said. 'I am not being disloyal in thanking God that your duties are keeping you at home for a while longer. That is because I love you. And I will support you as you wish. I will come and cheer when the

Tone puts to sea, Philip. And I will trust that your own humanity, your own sense of honour, and your love for me, will always guide you in the path you should follow.'

He put his arm round her shoulders. Could any man ask as much of any woman? Because she trusted in his integrity. A trust he could never betray. Just as his oath of allegiance was a trust he could never betray. And at this moment that had to come first, surely. Above everything else. Making Anne understand that would have to follow.

But there were other vital matters to be settled, as well. 'Have you seen Graham?'

'Yes.'

He frowned. 'How did you do it?'

'I have told you. I am now his doctor. He comes to me regularly, with unidentifiable pains in his stomach. I listen to him, and make notes, and examine him, and find nothing wrong. So he goes away, and thus comes back again, the following month, with more pains.'

'Do you not suppose someone may find that suspicious?'

'Why should they? I have many patients who come to see me every month.'

'But the things you discuss . . .'

'No one can tell what we actually discuss, because we speak English. My staff nurse, who is the only one in attendance, does not speak English.'

'So you have told him what I have to say?'

'Yes.'

'And?'

'He is saddened by your decision, just as he is deeply saddened by the course of events.'

'But he will do as I ask?'

'No.'

Philip frowned.

'He will not seek a transfer,' Anne said. 'Nor will he promise to break off discussions with those who still

382

agree with his point of view.'

'Is he so confident that I will never hand him over to the Kempai? Japan is at war.'

'He, too, trusts your good sense, my darling,' she said. 'And your honesty. And your honour. And he still believes you may one day have need of him, and his friends.'

Philip got up and went to the bedroom door. 'And to think he was once my closest friend.'

Anne followed him. 'I think he is still your closest friend, Phil. Your closest male friend, at any rate.'

'Now that we are at war,' Mori said, 'we may take off the gloves, so to speak. We have been given very wide powers of search and arrest. It is time to dispose of all the subversives in our midst, Kitabake San. I would have you prepare a list of all those serving in the navy or in any ancillary departments who are at all open to suspicion.' He carefully smoothed his sleeve insignia; war had also permitted a proper evaluation of his services, with consequent promotion.

'I have already prepared a list, honourable General,' Kitabake said, and handed him the sheet of typewritten paper.

Mori ran his eye down the names, a frown slowly gathering between his eyes. 'I do not see the name of Shimadzu.'

'That is true.'

'Or of Dr Freeman.'

'Agreed. She is not, of course, connected with the navy in any way.'

'She is Shimadzu's wife.'

'Agreed.'

'And what of Graham?'

'I have no reason to put his name there either, General Mori.'

Mori raised his head to stare at him. 'No reason? You

383

have now been investigating these people and their nefarious activities for four years, and you have found no reason to arrest any of them? I repeat, we do not have to be so careful with regards to proof now.'

'There is absolutely no proof against the Shimadzus or Commander Graham, honourable General,' Kitabake insisted, 'of anything. In the beginning, I thought there was something brewing. During 1933, and 1934, and 1935, Shimadzu saw a great deal of Graham, but always in the most open and above-board manner. Since the assassination of his uncle, he has seen him only once, when Graham went to dinner at Shimadzu's house.'

'Aha!'

'It was immediately after Shimadzu and Dr Freeman returned from their honeymoon,' Kitabake pointed out, somewhat wearily. 'Graham was undoubtedly offering congratulations. There was no development of that meeting.'

'Then what of Mrs Shimadzu? This so-called Dr Freeman?'

'As you say, she is now Mrs Shimadzu. She has seen Graham somewhat more often than her husband, to be sure. But in a professional capacity. She is his doctor.'

Mori frowned. 'His doctor?'

'Indeed. She is actually a doctor, you know.'

'And you do not find this suspicious, Kitabake San?'

'No. She is an American, and Graham is British. It is perfectly reasonable for him to go to the Anglo-American hospital whenever he feels unwell.'

'To see a woman?'

'I have checked with our agents in America,' Kitabake said, even more wearily. 'It is not uncommon for American males to have female doctors. Presumably the same applies in England. It seems to me to be perfectly reasonable for Graham to wish Mrs Shimadzu as his doctor. They are already old friends.'

'Nonetheless,' Mori insisted, 'it is suspicious. It is the

384

perfect set-up, is it not? I wish you to keep Dr Freeman under the closest surveillance, honourable Captain.'

It was Kitabake's turn to frown. 'You are aware that Captain Shimadzu has powerful friends? He is connected with the Tokugawa family, through his first marriage, and he is a close friend of Admiral Yamamoto. He is also a national hero, since his remarkable efforts to oppose the *coup d'état* of February last year.'

'Yes,' Mori said grimly. 'He did not succeed.'

'But he tried, and all but died for it. It is impossible to conceive that such a man could be connected with any anti-Japanese subversion.'

Mori stood up. 'He was attempting to save the life of his uncle. I find all of that very suspicious, Kitabake San. Here we have the captain of one of our battleships, who happens to be on shore leave, deciding to visit the Admiralty on the morning of 26 February. I would like you to discover for me how often he "decided" to do that. Everyone says what a remarkable coincidence that he arrived just as the first shots were fired. I do not believe in coincidences, Kitabake San. What no one seems to have considered, but what I have ascertained, is that on the morning in question Captain Shimadzu also picked up a ticket for reckless driving. Does a man drive with reckless speed when he is merely going to visit his uncle? And that is another point: is it not true that Philip Shimadzu and his uncle were estranged, had been estranged for several years? This is fairly well known about Tokyo. Yet on the morning of 26 February, the very morning of the attempted *coup*, Philip Shimadzu decides to visit his uncle, breaking several traffic laws in doing so. I would like you to consider these things, Kitabake San.'

Kitabake stroked his chin; his suggestion of weariness had vanished. 'That is certainly an interesting thesis, honourable General. Are you suggesting that Shimadzu had prior knowldge of the *coup*?'

'It was led by his brother,' Mori reminded him.

'And did you not ask his brother about it? You had him in your custody for weeks on end.'

'Yes,' Mori said thoughtfully. 'He would tell us nothing. Do you know, I have heard him scream so loud my ears were ringing. I have watched the veins in his neck seem about to burst through his skin. Yet he would do nothing but deny that anyone was implicated save himself. I cannot understand a man of such courage, such determination, refusing seppuku when those fools in the police gave him the opportunity.'

'Yes,' Kitabake said drily. 'But are you supposing that Philip Shimadzu was trying to take part in the *coup*, or prevent it happening?'

'That is something I wish one day to have the pleasure of asking Shimadzu personally,' Mori said. 'I doubt he has either the courage or the resolution of his brother. But whatever his intentions, he is a man who knows more than he either pretends or admits, and that is always suspicious.'

Kitabake nodded. 'I will take note of what you say, honourable General. However, may I ask you one question, in the greatest confidence, as we are on this subject.'

'Of course.'

'Was the Kempai aware of the existence of this plot? Because I was not.'

Mori's features slightly relaxed. 'The Kempai is aware of all things, Kitabake San. But we do not tell everyone everything we know.'

'But you permitted the plot to proceed.'

'Do you not think that was a wise decision, as we have obtained all of our objectives? Do you think Chiang Kai-shek would have been so mad as to declare war on Japan while Viscount Saito, a man with whom he hoped to be able to deal, was in power? We have forced his hand. And this is what we set out to achieve.'

'I should have been told,' Kitabake insisted. 'Why, I could have been at the Admiralty myself, that day.'

'But you were not, were you, Kitabake San? And even had you been, no harm would have come to you. I wish Dr Freeman watched at all times, and I wish you to gain every possible access to her daily life. I also wish to be kept in the closest possible touch with your investigations in that direction. Is that understood, honourable Captain.'

Kitabake also rose, and bowed. 'It is understood, honourable General.'

With a screaming of sirens, and to the accompaniment of gun salutes from the other vessels in Tokyo Bay, the heavy cruiser *Tone* slipped from her mooring and proceeded out towards the open sea, just a wisp of smoke rising from her funnel.

'Oh, isn't she magnificent, honourable Stepmother?' Iyeyasu cried, squeezing Anne's arm.

'Yes,' Anne agreed. Because she was, a magnificent ship. And for her, the saddest of sights. She had never believed that this could happen. The war with China had now lasted a year; in another few weeks it would be Christmas 1938. She just had not believed the fighting would last for a full year. Or that no end would be in sight at this stage, either.

In the beginning, the Chinese had merely been slaughtered. Peking had fallen within a few weeks of the commencement of hostilities, then Shanghai, then the Japanese Army had pushed up the Yangtze Kiang Valley itself and taken even Nanking, the old capital of China. The country had thrilled to the unending succession of victories, even if her blood, at any rate, had run cold as she had looked at the published photographs of the destruction wreaked by indiscriminate bombing attacks, or by indiscriminate shelling from the Japanese Navy, and as she had read of the wholesale destruction of life and property. Yet this wholesale and utterly ruthless assault had at least promised a quick and easy victory –

and certainly a victory before Philip would ever be able to take his ship to sea.

But that had not happened. The Chinese, beaten again and again, had continued the fight with unflinching and unyielding courage. And not without successes of their own. Last year, at Tai-er chuang, a Japanese army had been surrounded by guerillas, and had only fought its way out with heavy casualties. And this very past summer, when the decision had been taken to launch an all-out advance upon Hankow, the city Chiang Kai-shek had made his capital following the fall of Nanking, the Chinese had broken the dikes restraining the Yellow River, flooding millions of acres of arable land, changing, indeed, the very course of the river, killing many Chinese and destroying the livelihoods of many more – but also drowning many thousands of Japanese soldiers, with their tanks and equipment.

It was war to the absolute edge of the knife. And yet it could still only have one end. For the advance on Hankow had been resumed, this time farther south, up the Yangtze instead of the Yellow River, and farther south still, Canton had recently fallen. No matter how hard the Chinese fought, the Japanese were slowly and relentlessly strangling them to death, and certainly achieving their objectives, as outlined to her by Philip, to control the entire Pacific seaboard; that task was nearly complete.

And now Philip himself was about to take part in the slaughter. In some ways she was almost glad of this. He had been very difficult to live with, this past year; he had chafed as he devoured every newspaper and every radio broadcast, and he had read of the exploits of his comrades with glowing eyes. The good-humoured, liberal-minded, anti-militarist had become the aggressive patriot. And he was, of course, in no danger; the last Chinese warship had long been swept from the sea. Now at last he could command his ship and fire his guns and feel that he was playing his part . . . But would he come back a relieved or a changed man?

She had devoted all of her life to Philip, as she had devoted all of her life to his people. A people she now hardly knew, and that was the most difficult thing of all to accept. Like Philip, the Japanese had changed. They might have wanted peace, in the main – but only because they had been afraid of the imponderables of war. Now they had had war, for more than a year – and they had known only victory. There were many houses in Tokyo and Yokohama flying the white flags of grief, and she saw many patients who had lost sons and husbands and brothers in China. But no mother or sister or wife doubted that those men had died for the honour of their country, or mourned them as anything less than dead heroes. And the dead were confined to fighting men. No bomb had ever fallen on a single Japanese village, much less city. Thus the people were inspired. They were beginning to wonder if they had not indeed been faint-hearted at having for so long rejected the concept of war. Books and pamphlets and newspaper articles were flooding Tokyo, recalling the history of the centuries-old struggle with China, of the many indignities the Japanese had had to suffer in the days of the Ming, and the Yuan, and even the early Manchu. But also of the defeat of the Mongol fleet in the thirteenth century, and the great victories gained over China in 1894. For a people so steeped in the past, that past was as important as the present. Now, they were told, they would end the Chinese menace forever, and become the greatest force in Asia. What people, however dedicated to beauty and art and the contemplation of the finer things in life, could possibly not be drawn to such a concept – because to be the greatest force in Asia *was* one of the finer things in life, if it could be accomplished without personal disaster.

These were the feelings she must applaud, whenever she was in public. But she must also applaud them in

389

private, because both Iyeyasu and Philip subscribed to them. She had lost the only two men she loved to the hideous god of war. She could only pray that they would come back to her, one day. One day soon, before the blood-lust had taken over their minds irrevocably.

She returned Iyeyasu to his college, from which he had been given the morning off to bid farewell to his father, went back home, and then, restlessly, drove down to Yokohama. She had the entire day off, but what was she going to do with it? Mope around the house? Go to visit Shikibu, and be exposed to even more rampant patriotism? She would rather work.

She parked her car and went into her office. Nurse Harya bowed in surprise. 'I did not expect you, honourable doctor.'

'I'm a glutton for punishment,' Anne pointed out. 'Any calls?'

'Why, yes, honourable doctor.' Nurse Harya opened the desk diary. 'The Englishman, Commander Graham, has been trying to reach you. He left a number for you to call. He says it is most urgent that he speak with you.'

Anne hesitated, gazing at the figures. She had told Graham she could not see him again, because Philip had commanded her to. She did not resent the command; she accepted it as a concomitant of being married, not only to a Japanese man, but to a Japanese officer, in time of war. If she did not believe in the war, and was sure that in his heart Philip did not do so, either, yet she could understand his determination to do nothing which could conceivably interfere with his country's plunge for victory.

Yet she trusted Graham. And needed to see him, she knew, if only to remind herself that there was a world outside Japan, watching and waiting as she was.

Would she be betraying Philip? How could she, by just listening to what the man had to say?

She might even be helping him, in the long run. Anne picked up the telephone.

390

CHAPTER 15

The Plan

As usual, Anne made the notes herself, while Nurse Harya retreated to the back of the office and waited patiently. Whatever her thoughts — which presumably ranged over the apparent likelihood that her superior, although now a seemingly happy married woman, was also indulging in an affair with the British naval attaché — she kept them to herself.

'I hope this is as important as you made it sound on the phone,' Anne remarked, in English. 'You know Philip's feelings about us seeing each other.'

'Has he gone to sea?' Graham asked.

She nodded.

'For trials?'

'No. He means to go straight on patrol, and work the ship up while he's doing that.'

He sighed. 'He's really caught up in it, then. Who is he going to fight? Or is he merely on his way to blast some coastal village which hasn't been obliterated yet?'

'He conceives that he is doing his duty,' Anne replied, somewhat coldly. She couldn't allow Philip to be criticised like that when he was only obeying orders. 'As you will presumably do your duty, whatever may be involved, when Great Britain goes to war with Germany.'

'There isn't going to be a war with Germany,' he told her.

She raised her eyebrows. 'Hitler's dropped his plans for Czechoslovakia?'

Graham's shoulders drooped. 'No. We seem to have dropped our opposition to such plans.'

She frowned at him. 'Does the Japanese Government know that yet?'

'I imagine they do by now.'

'Well,' she said. 'I imagine it will be a relief to them. I think they still fear a British intervention, out here.'

'Well, that has become somewhat more likely, I suppose.'

'Oh, come now. You're afraid to take on somewhere like Germany, which Britain and France could surely smash to bits in a week, and you're still going to take on Japan?'

'I wouldn't write the old bulldog off yet,' he said. 'The fellow sometimes gets the most quixotic notions. And all Europe, all the world, it seems, is staggering under what happened at Nanking.'

'Why is that so staggering? What about the Germans bombing Guernica, in Spain?'

'I'm not talking about the bombing, although God knows that was bad enough. But the Germans didn't then go in and butcher men, women and children at the point of the bayonet. They didn't rape and loot and destroy everyone and everything they could lay their hands on.'

'And you think the Japanese Army did that in Nanking?'

'I know they did. You people just don't realise how censored is all the news you get here.'

She stared at him. 'You expect me to believe that?'

'It happens to be true. Tell me something; have you ever heard the name *Panay*?'

'Should I have?'

'Perhaps not. I keep forgetting that you keep trying to be one hundred per cent Japanese, and not American. The *USS Panay* is, or rather was, an American gunboat on the Yangtze Kiang. She was attacked by Japanese bombers and destroyed. Over a year ago.'

'I don't believe you. Philip would have known.'

'Didn't he?'

She bit her lip. Philip and she had come to a mutual agreement not to discuss the war. And he had certainly been increasingly pensive over the past year; she had thought it was frustration at not being able to get to sea. But suppose . . . 'If that were true,' she said, 'then what has happened about it?'

'Japan and the United States nearly came to blows, if that's what's worrying you. But the Japs have climbed down, and are to pay an indemnity. So the danger has blown over for the time being.'

'How do you know all of this?'

'We receive secret transcripts from London. Anne, listen to me. Everything that has happened in the past is academic. But there is no doubt in my mind that we, the whole damned world, is moving towards some kind of a climactic showdown, and it's only a couple of years away. If that long. When it happens, Japan, this Japan you claim as your own, is going to be fighting alongside Nazi Germany, because they are allies, and very probably Italy and Spain as well, as the Fascists seem to be firmly in control in those countries. But the odds are that the United States will be fighting alongside Great Britain and France.'

'Never,' she said. 'No American president would ever dare involve us in a European war again.'

'Maybe. But this isn't going to be a European war. It's going to be global, if Japan is in it too, and China. Anne, it is going to happen.'

She chewed her lip. 'Why are you telling me all of this? What am I supposed to do about it?'

'Well, I would certainly recommend you go back to America.'

'Me? Desert my husband? Desert my son? Iyeyasu is my son, you know. I regard him as that, anyway.'

'All right. I didn't really expect you to abandon Philip.

But that makes it all the more important for us to do whatever we can to head off the showdown. The moment Philip returns from this patrol, I want us to get together.'

'I don't know, John. I really don't. I don't think he'll do it, while there's a war on.'

'A war with China. Don't you think he'll talk to me if there's a question of war with America?'

'You don't know there is going to be such a war,' she objected. 'You're supposing. And maybe hoping, because you reckon Britain and America together will be unbeatable. John, it *isn't* going to happen. And Philip knows it isn't going to happen. He knows things he has never discussed with me. But he does know them, because he's so close to Yamamoto. And everything he knows makes him quite sure there won't be a war with America.'

'Does he know the Japanese Navy is laying down, or maybe has already laid down, at least one battleship bigger than any ever built before, by any nation? What's the aim behind that? To fight a non-existent Chinese fleet?'

Her frown was back. 'You know this?'

'I know enough to suspect it.'

'You mean you don't know anything at all. You're back to supposing.'

'London has information on it. So definite that a directive was sent out only a week ago to the Ambassador, asking him to put a direct question to Hirota; he's Foreign Minister as well, you know. Well, the Ambassador took me along. And we asked Hirota if it was true that his country was laying down battleships with a designed displacement of forty-five thousand tons. As you no doubt know, designed weight does not include fuel and ammunition and water, and is usually exceeded, deep loaded, by between five and ten thousand tons in big ships. So we are really talking about a possible fifty-five thousand ton battleship, which, again as I am sure you know, is bigger than anything else in the world today.

Even the pair the Germans are building, *Bismarck* and *Tirpitz*, aren't going to exceed forty-five thousand tons, deep load.'

'I know that,' she said. 'What did Mr Hirota say?'

'He looked us in the eye and said, smiling as he did so, "Gentlemen, I can give you a categorical denial that Japan is building, or is considering building, any forty-five thousand ton battleship. It is not our principle to build ships of that class." '

'Well, then you can't possibly suppose Hirota would lie to you? He may be a Fascist, but he is also a Japanese gentleman.'

'Oh, agreed. But the denial was so flat, and as he put it, categorical, I'm left wondering just what he did mean. I put it to the Ambassador when we got back to the embassy, that perhaps he should have pressed the point. Because supposing, just supposing, the navy's design office is contemplating something even *bigger* than fifty-five thousand tons deep load?'

'Bigger? But that's absurd. You're talking of something as big as the *Queen Mary*.'

'So? She floats. And crosses the Atlantic at over thirty knots.'

'The idea is incredible.'

'Philip has never mentioned anything of this to you?'

'Well . . . ' She frowned. 'He did say, when he was given *Tone*, which was really something of a demotion, you know, for a captain of his seniority, that it was merely to give him practice at handling modern vessels, so that he could command one of the new battleships when they were ready. But he said nothing about size.' She gazed at him. 'He never talks shop at home, and I never ask him. It's the only way. So many of the things he knows are top secret.'

'Like these battleships. Anne . . . ' Graham leaned forward. 'If the Japanese are building such a warship, it is because they intend to use it. Or them. And if they do build such ships, and use them, they will be unstoppable. On any ocean in the world.'

'So what am I supposed to do about it?'

'Find out if it's true.'

'And tell you?'

'If you wish. I would find out for your own peace of mind, if I were you.'

Because the one would follow the other, she thought. 'Now you are actually asking me to become a spy.'

'I think the time is coming when you are going to have to choose sides, Anne.'

'I am married to a Japanese naval officer.'

'Who you *know* will not fight against America. So anything you can do to stop such a war coming about has to be done. Right?'

'And telling you Japanese naval plans will stop a war?'

'Yes. Listen to me. If we can tell the Americans for sure that the Japanese are building some kind of super battleship fleet, which can only be aimed against them, and the Americans say right, Mr Hirota, we know what you are up to, and we are going to build something even bigger, the Japanese will have to think again. Isn't that logical?'

'Oh, God, I don't know. It just sounds like some super arms race to me. Oh . . . look, you simply have to go. You've been here half an hour.'

'My God, have I?' He got up. 'May I come again?'

'Well, all right. But not too soon. You're making my nurse suspicious.'

He frowned. 'Suspicious of what?'

Anne smiled. 'She thinks we're having an affair, stupid. Now for God's sake, get out of here.'

The door closed behind him.

'Honourable doctor did not need to examine honourable English gentleman, this time,' Nurse Harya remarked.

God, Anne thought. I should have done that. 'No,' she said. 'I did not think it necessary.'

*

'That is the woman,' Kitabake said. 'Wearing the nurse's uniform.'

He sat in the back seat of his automobile, which was parked at the side of the road; General Mori sat beside him, watching the passengers get off the bus. It was still the depths of winter, and the days were short; the street lights were already gleaming through the light drizzle, and it was not possible to see the woman's face clearly. As for why *they* were here at all, acting like a couple of field agents when they were the two most senior Kempai officials in Tokyo – that was because Mori was taking a personal interest in the affair. Kitabake did not think it was purely because his superior meant to avenge himself on Philip Shimadzu for the Shanghai business; he also meant to get his hands on Anne Shimadzu. He *was* a thug, and totally bestial. But he was virtually running the interior affairs of Japan at this moment, and simply had to be humoured.

'Pick her up,' Mori commanded.

Kitabake shrugged. 'Signal,' he told his driver.

The driver blew the horn, three times quickly, then one long blast. The V-sign.

The woman ignored the sound, as did everyone else; horns were blaring all around her. She walked away from the bus briskly, and turned down the next side-street. Her apartment was just down that street.

'Where will they take her?' Mori asked.

'Where you wish, honourable General,' Kitabake said.

'Let them take her to your office,' Mori said.

Kitabake frowned. 'My office is not soundproofed, honourable General.'

Mori smiled. 'I do not mean to make her scream, Kitabake San. I wish to talk to her.'

Kitabake tapped his driver on the shoulder, and the automobile moved forward, turning down the side-street behind the nurse. But the street was suddenly empty, save for a black van parked at the side of the road. Kitabake's

397

automobile pulled up beside the van, and he rolled down his window. 'Report.'

'The subject is in the back, honourable Captain,' the driver of the van said.

'Very good,' Kitabake said. 'Take her to my office. We will await you there.'

The automobile gathered speed behind its whirring windshield wipers, and drove to the Admiralty, parking in the shadows round the back of the building. The entire mansion was nearly in darkness; only the duty cipher clerks and radio operators spent the night there, along with one senior officer, to cope with any emergency that might arise. Kitabake led Mori through a side door and down a corridor, then into a large room, almost empty of furniture save for a desk and two straight chairs; the floors were bare. But the walls were covered with maps and lists.

'I fink it disturbing to informants,' he explained to Mori, 'to enter such stark surroundings. They find themselves wondering if the people they will encounter here are similarly stark.'

'A sound principle,' Mori agreed. 'You will leave this woman entirely to me, honourable Captain.'

'Of course, honourable General,' Kitabake said, with some relief. He was essentially a gatherer of information; he had never allowed himself to be employed on the executive side of the Kempai before. Indeed, despite his boast to Mori, he knew he would not know how to begin to interrogate a suspect. Or to bully someone into being cooperative. All of his informants had come here at least partially because they wanted to.

They listened to feet outside, and what might have been a cat mewing. Then the door opened and four men entered. They wore civilian clothes and between them they carried a sack, which wriggled and from which the mewing sound was coming. They dropped the sack on

398

the floor, and immediately water trickled away from it; at some stage on its journey to the Admiralty it had been doused in a puddle; but Kitabake was suddenly overwhelmingly aware of the smell of dampness pervading the entire room.

The men released the neck of the sack, and two of them thrust their hands inside and seized a leg each; by this means they dragged the woman out on to the floor. She still wore her white nurse's uniform beneath her blue cloak, but all the almost sterile neatness had disappeared into crushing dampness; one white shoe had come off, her white stockings were twisted, two buttons had burst from her bodice as she had fought in the sack – and with each gasping breath her white brassière surged most disconcertingly into the gap. Her starched white cap had also disappeared, allowing her black hair to drift untidily; some of it lay across her face.

There was a strip of sticking-plaster across her mouth, which was preventing her from making any sound above the mew. But now Mori nodded, and one of the men tore the plaster away. The woman gasped again, and rolled on to her front, then rose to her knees, staring at the man in front of her and slowly taking in the office.

'Do you know who I am?' Mori asked.

The woman's head moved slowly left and then right.

'Well, from this moment I am your employer,' Mori told her.

Once again she shook her head, slowly, uncertainly. 'I work at the hospital,' she said, her voice low. 'I work for Dr Azuma.'

'You work for me,' Mori said, and walked towards her. She watched him coming, her eyes dilating. Mori reached her, stooped slightly, closed the fingers of his right hand on her throat and lifted her to her feet. She gasped, and almost choked. Mori released her, and her knees buckled, but she caught herself in time and remained standing. The sound of her panting filled the room, and two of the men moved forward to stand at her shoulders.

'What is your name?' Mori asked.

'Akiko Harya, honourable sir.'

'And as you say, you are a nurse at the Anglo-American hospital. A senior nurse?'

'Yes, honourable sir.'

'You are married?'

'Yes, honourable sir.'

'Where is your husband?'

'He is with the army, honourable sir. In China.'

'A loyal and patriotic family,' Mori observed. 'You have children?'

'I . . . I have a baby girl.' Her nostrils dilated; she knew these people were not her friends – the mention of her child made her more apprehensive than she had hitherto been, for herself.

'Ah,' Mori said. 'And where is she now?'

'She is with her grandmother, honourable sir. I am to collect her, now.'

'I am sure you will, Nurse Harya. You say she is a baby. How old is that?'

'She is four years old, honourable sir.'

'That is not a baby. That is a child. A child who can no doubt feel.'

Akiko Harya gasped.

'Now, Nurse Harya, you work for the American woman doctor, Anne Shimadzu, is that correct?'

'I am her assistant, honourable sir.'

'I understand that she has been receiving visits from an Englishman, a man called Graham. Is that right?'

Akiko Harya stared at him.

'Is that right?' Mori asked again.

Akiko licked her lips. 'It . . . it is forbidden to reveal the names of patients, honourable sir.' Mori gazed at her, then his hand went out again, to grasp her throat, and this time he squeezed. Akiko gasped and choked, and tried to kick him. But as she raised her right foot, one of the men standing behind her promptly kicked her on the left leg just behind the knee, throwing her off her feet so that she was entirely supported by Mori's fingers. But Mori then let her go. The men caught her before she could hit the floor, but still laid her out on the wood.

Akiko lay still for a moment, and then attempted to move. One of the men stepped on her right wrist, which was still extended above her head. He did not put all his weight on to his leg, but merely sufficient to prevent her moving, and to make sure that she understood he *would* put all his weight on the slender bones if she tried. She subsided, her bodice rising and falling.

Mori stood above her, and with the toe of his shoe lifted her skirt, flicking it back over her stomach to uncover her thighs, her white drawers. Akiko clamped her legs together with all the ingrained modesty and thus outrage of a Japanese woman. 'Tell me of this Englishman,' Mori said.

Once again Akiko licked her lips. 'He is Dr Freeman's patient,' she said.

'And what is his illness?'

'I do not know.'

Mori thrust the toe of his shoe between her legs, forcing them to part. For a moment the muscles attempted to resist him, then instead Akiko raised her knees, and then, realising how she was exposing herself, she let her legs fall to the floor again, while she panted. Mori, his shoe still between her thighs, inserted the toe in her crotch, very gently.

Akiko writhed, and the man pressed a little more heavily on her wrist. She gasped. 'I do not know,' she cried.

'You are Dr Freeman's assistant. You must know.'

'She interviews him herself,' Akiko gasped. 'She records stomach pains. But she has been able to make no diagnosis.'

'Ah,' Mori said. 'She can make no diagnosis. How often does he come to see her?'

'About . . . about once a month.'

'Ah,' Mori said again. 'And she has sent him for X-rays, or a second opinion?'

'No,' Akiko said. 'He is not ill. Dr Freeman knows this.'

'How interesting,' Mori remarked. 'Then why does this Graham go to see her?'

'He is in love with her,' Akiko said.

'Oh, really?'

'That is what she says,' Akiko said.

'I see. So he visits her to tell her of his love. How does he do this? What does he say to her?'

'I do not know.'

Mori prodded her vagina with his toe.

'I do not know,' she shouted. 'I do not know.' Her voice broke into a sob.

'You are always there, are you not?'

'Yes. But they speak in English. And all she records on his card is stomach pains.'

'You do not understand English?'

'No, honourable sir. Please . . .'

Mori nodded, and stepped away. The man moved his foot from Akiko's wrist, and also stepped away. Slowly, cautiously, as if she could not believe her good fortune, Akiko Harya sat up. Her hands instinctively went down to clasp her groin, as if to reassure herself that she had suffered no permanent damage, then she pulled down her skirt, looked at the men, and rose to her knees, then got to her feet. She trembled.

'Now, Akiko,' Mori said kindly. 'This is what I wish you to do. I am going to have you enrolled in an English-speaking evening class immediately, and I wish you to

402

attend this class every night, beginning tomorrow. You will learn the language just as quickly as you can; to this end you will attend this class every night. Understanding the spoken word is all you have to achieve, but I wish you to be able to do this within a month at the outside. Do you understand me?'

'Yes, honourable sir.'

'You will tell no one that you are doing this, Akiko. Least of all Dr Freeman. Then, once you can understand English, I wish you to listen very carefully to everything that is said in Dr Freeman's office, in English, whether between her and this English lover of hers, or between her and anyone else. Then I wish you to visit an address I will give you, once in every week, and repeat every word of every conversation that you can remember to one of my people. Is this understood?'

Akiko stared at him.

'If you do not do this, Akiko,' Mori said gently, 'or if what you have to tell us is not sufficiently interesting, I am going to hurt you very badly. I am also going to hurt your little daughter very badly. I want you to understand these things.'

Akiko inhaled, slowly.

'And of course,' Mori went on, 'should you repeat to any living soul, and especially Dr Freeman, one word of what has happened here tonight, or what I have asked you to do for me, then words will not be able to describe what pain I will cause you. Do you understand that?'

Akiko nodded.

'Because this Dr Freeman is an enemy of Japan,' Mori told her. 'She and this Englishman are not in love. They are spies, and they are devoting all their energies to harming Japan. To seeing that Japanese soldiers get killed. Your husband, Akiko. They wish to see your husband dead. Remember this. She is your enemy. So you must help us to catch her out. And this Englishman. Where is Nurse Harya's shoe?' he demanded.

One of the men reached into the sack and took out the shoe, together with her cap.

'Good,' Mori said. 'Now, Akiko, dress yourself properly, and one of my men will drive you to collect your daughter, and then take you home. I look forward to hearing from you.'

'The wind is rising, honourable Captain,' said Commander Fushiro.

'I will come up.' Philip replaced the telephone, put on his cap, left his day cabin, and went up to the bridge. It was blowing about forty knots, he estimated; the seas were big, and were starting to topple over in foaming white and blue crests, and the swell was already high enough to half-lose the cruiser in each trough; yet with the sun peeping through the clouds it was a scene of remarkable wild beauty. And *Tone* rode as buoyantly as a duck, sliding down, skimming up, cutting the waves, her engines never losing their even beat. While the bridge hummed with the subdued sounds of the various navigating and radio equipment, always reassuring. Everything about this ship was reassuring; she was the most beautiful thing he had ever handled, even more beautiful, however much he hated to admit it, than *Mutsu*. He had no doubt that he could drive *Tone* through a typhoon, if he had to. But he did not think this was going to be anything more than a severe storm; the distinctive cyclonic pattern of the typhoon was missing. However, the motion was growing increasingly severe, and they were merely on patrol, some seventy miles off the Chinese coast.

'Reduce speed, Mr Fushiro,' he said. 'Twelve knots will be sufficient until the wind drops.'

'Aye-aye, honourable Captain.' Fushiro gave the necessary order to the engine-room, and the movement became perceptibly easier.

Philip sat in his chair, mounted so that he could see

down through the bridge windows over the bows, and gazed at the seas. He was happy. He was always happy at sea, regardless of what the weather might be doing, and it occurred to him that over the past year or so he had *only* been happy at sea. The world was becoming an increasingly grim place; no one could doubt that Europe was moving increasingly in the direction of war, as Germany continued to expand, regardless of promises given to the Western democracies, and as Great Britain and France became increasingly aware that Hitler was not to be trusted. Yamamoto kept assuring him that even if there was a European conflagration, Japan would not be involved; the pact with Germany did not allow for mutual support in the field or at sea, only morally. Yet once war began, it was always impossible to say where it would end.

The situation was affecting his home life, and that was far more serious. Anne was very tense nowadays. And she had started asking questions, which she had never done before. She had asked about the *Panay*, an incident about which all naval officers had been sworn to secrecy. Then how had she learned about it in the first place? He had an uneasy feeling that she was still seeing Graham, but had not wished to press the point for fear of causing a quarrel.

But then she had started asking about his next command. She seemed to have some idea that it was going to be a very large ship, even if she really had no conception of how large. Graham again? Setting her to ask him questions? He had allowed himself to become angry at that, and she had apologised; their incipient quarrel had dissipated as they had held each other close.

He should, of course, become really angry with her. If she was being briefed by a representative of a foreign, and basically hostile, power – his own wife – he should beat her and then send her away, back to the States. He loved her too much to do either of those things; there was the trouble. And even worse, he felt too much, deep in his belly, that her obvious apprehensions were well founded, despite Yamamoto's repeated assurances. If only it *were* possible to discuss things openly with her. Or if only it were possible to see an end to this constant, and constantly increasing, tension.

'With respect, honourable Captain.' The duty midshipman stood to attention at his shoulder, a sheet of paper in his hand. 'There is a radio message.'

Philip frowned at the words:

IMPERIAL JAPANESE SHIP *TONE* FROM HIS MAJESTY'S SHIP *VENTURA* STOP ASSISTANCE REQUIRED STOP POSITION THIRTY ONE DEGREES TWO MINUTES NORTH LATITUDE ONE HUNDRED AND TWENTY FOUR DEGREES TWELVE MINUTES EAST LONGITUDE STOP CIVILIAN VESSEL IN DANGER OF SINKING STOP MARSTON.

Philip read the message again; it was most unusual for such a communication to be signed with the name of the captain of the sending vessel, unless the contents were of a personal nature. He had never heard of this man Marston. He looked at Fushiro, handed him the paper, and then inspected the chart, where the *Tone*'s position was plotted every hour. 'He is not ten miles away,' he remarked. 'How the devil did the Britisher know we are in his vicinity?'

'He will have been listening to our radio traffic, honourable Captain.' Since the Chinese fleet had entirely disappeared, the Japanese had ceased to bother with radio silence when on patrol.

'Hm,' Philip said. 'What is *Ventura*?'

Fushiro had already opened the reference book. 'She is a destroyer, honourable Captain. Fifteen hundred tons. Based on Hong Kong. She will be on patrol, as are we.'

'Does she not know this is a war zone?' Philip grumbled. 'However, if there really is a civilian vessel in difficulties . . . ' And actually, he thought, he would not much care to be on a fifteen-hundred-ton destroyer in weather like this. 'Make the necessary course alteration, Mr Fushiro, and increase speed to twenty-four knots.' Which was as fast as he wanted to go in such big seas. He turned to the midshipman. 'Make to *Ventura*.'

The boy poised his pencil above his pad.

' "Message received and understood," ' Philip said. ' "Will be at your position in thirty minutes." ' He hesitated; the Englishman had made the first advance. 'Sign it "Shimadzu",' he said.

The boy saluted, and hurried to the radio room.

Fushiro stood beside his captain. 'You do not suppose it could be some kind of a trap, honourable Captain?'

'Set by a British destroyer?'

'Well . . . who can tell? It is unusually phrased.'

'Quite. He is making a personal appeal for my help because he fears we may not be inclined to leave our patrol, even for a few hours. There can be no trap. Great Britain and Japan are at peace. And anyway, a little destroyer, taking on *Tone*? We would sink her in seconds.'

'I was considering a torpedo strike, honourable Captain.'

Philip glanced at him. The idea was impossible. And yet, with the whole world in such a state of knife-edge tension . . . If the Germans should have invaded Poland or Rumania, countries to which the British had given unqualified promises of support . . . This destroyer might know something he did not. And in the eyes of the world Japan was certainly Germany's ally. 'Double your look-outs,' he said, and reached for his own binoculars.

Now the *Tone* was crashing through the waves as her speed increased, but now, too, she was running down-wind, and the motion was easier, save when she overtook a wave in front of her and buried her slender bows in the back of the swell, sending hundreds of tons of green water cascading along the decks, and white spray splattering even over the windows of the fighting bridge some forty feet above the waterline. It would, he reflected, be quite impossible for anyone to launch a torpedo in these conditions with any hope of hitting its target; he did not know he would be capable of hitting anything even with his radio-controlled guns, as the ship rose and fell some twenty feet in every few seconds.

'There,' said Commander Fushiro.

Philip levelled his glasses and made out the tiny shape of the destroyer, only two hundred feet long, bravely trying to keep herself between the worst of the seas and the very large junk, several times her size, which was wallowing in the troughs, having been dismasted in the storm. Some of the waves were breaking right over the British ship, but the white ensign still fluttered bravely in the breeze.

'Message from *Ventura*, honourable Captain,' said the midshipman.

Philip read:

THANK GOD FOR YOUR PRESENCE STOP SHIP SUN LILY DISMASTED AND MAKING WATER STOP UNABLE GET ALONGSIDE TO REMOVE PASSENGERS STOP CAN YOU PUT DOWN OIL MARSTON.

An oil slick would stop the waves from breaking, as long as it held together, which could be for perhaps half an hour – long enough to remove most of the passengers. Philip levelled the binoculars again, looking beyond the warship at the merchantman. She flew no flag, all her rigging had gone overboard. But she was crowded with people waving and shouting in a fine state of panic.

'This will be a difficult manoeuvre, Commander,' Philip said. 'That destroyer cannot possibly remove all of those people. We will have to go alongside ourselves. Take up a position upwind of the junk and prepare to

408

discharge oil; we will drift down with it.'

'With respect, honourable Captain,' Fushiro said. 'That is a Chinese vessel.'

Philip lowered his glasses and gazed at his second in command.

'Our orders, honourable Captain, are to destroy every Chinese vessel that we encounter, and all who sail in such ships,' Fushiro said.

Philip looked at the junk and the destroyer again. But Fushiro was right; the junk was most certainly Chinese. And they were allowed no room for discretion in their orders. Not to destroy the junk, and all on board, would be dereliction of duty. But the thought . . .

Fushiro smiled. 'It will not actually be necessary to waste a shell, however, honourable Captain. The enemy is most certainly sinking.'

Indeed, the junk was visibly getting lower in the water, and the panic on her decks was just as visibly increasing.

Still Philip hesitated. What he was being asked to do was mass murder. But it was what Yamamoto had instructed all his captains to do. And without Yamamoto, he was nothing. Nor was Yamamoto an easy man to please; Philip knew he was a favourite of the admiral's, but he also remembered what he had once told Anne, that should he let the admiral down, he would be thrown aside forever. It was entirely due to Yamamoto that he was now standing on this bridge, with so much more to follow; any ordinary naval officer whose brother had been executed for treason, would have had no career left at all, even if he had not been cashiered.

'We must send the Britisher away, honourable Captain,' Fushiro said.

Philip nodded. 'Make to *Ventura*,' he told the waiting midshipman. ' "Are you escorting *Sun Lily*?" ' Oh, how he hoped and prayed the answer could be yes. If somehow the junk could be under the protection of the Royal Navy . . . 'Reduce speed, Mr Fushiro,' he commanded.

'We are close enough.'

The midshipman was back. Philip scanned the paper:

NEGATIVE STOP WE SIGHTED AND AN-
SWERED DISTRESS ROCKET STOP MAY I SUG-
GEST SPEED IS IMPERATIVE STOP SUN LILY IS
SINKING MARSTON.

'Make to *Ventura*,' Philip said. ' "You have done your
duty stop I congratulate you stop you may now leave *Sun
Lily* in our care." Sign it "Shimadzu".'

Speed had been reduced to ten knots, and the heavy
cruiser was riding the waves easily, although heeling to
each massive gust of wind. The junk was only a mile
distant, as was the destroyer, although she had now
drifted astern, as the Japanese ship was between the
stricken merchantman and the worst of the weather.

The midshipman was back.

WISH TO REMAIN AND ASSIST MARSTON.

'Make to *Ventura*. "Assistance not required,
Shimadzu".'

Fushiro was inspecting the junk through his binoculars. 'This could take time, honourable Captain,' he
remarked. 'They are pumping with all their strength.
They even have small children pumping.'

Philip also stared at the Chinese vessel. They were so
close that with his glasses he could make out even the
expressions on some of the faces, could see the crew
passing up towing hawsers as the Japanese ship
approached, anticipating that they might be taken in tow.

The midshipman presented a new message.

REGRET DECISION BUT WILL WITHDRAW
GOOD LUCK MARSTON.

Fushiro swung his glasses and watched the destroyer
begin to turn into the wind and the sea, to head south.

410

'I suggest we sink the enemy now, honourable Captain,' he said. 'It would be quickest and best. A single shot into her waterline should suffice.'

Yet again Philip gazed at the junk. The expressions of the people on deck were changing from hope and relief to amazement and despair as the cruiser continued slowly around the sinking vessel's stern, leaving her exposed to the seas, having made no effort to close her or put down oil. The captain was on deck, using a megaphone, shouting into the wind, but his words had no hope of carrying across the storm. Waves were now breaking right over the junk's decks; even as Philip watched, a gaggle of people were swept away, screaming and holding on to each other.

'Message from *Ventura*, honourable Captain,' said the midshipman.

Philip took the paper.

IN THE NAME OF HUMANITY MAKE HASTE MARSTON.

Philip crumpled the paper into a ball. 'There is no reply,' he said.

'She is returning,' Fushiro remarked.

Philip watched the destroyer turn again and come back towards them. 'Make to *Ventura*,' he told the midshipman. ' "You must leave stop this is an order stop you are in a war zone stop Shimadzu".'

'I was wrong,' Fushiro said. 'About the need for a shell. The pumps seem to have jammed.'

The *Sun Lily* was now almost submerged, a hulk swept by every huge wave; more and more people were being washed away. Some, despairing, were actually jumping into the seething waters to drown the more quickly. Others knelt and prayed, staring at the Japanese warship.

'*Ventura* is putting down boarding-nets, honourable Captain,' Fushiro said.

Philip nodded. He felt sick.

'That is a contravention of your orders, honourable Captain,' Fushiro said.

'My orders are to destroy all Chinese ships, Commander,' Philip said. 'As you have said, the weather is doing that for us. I cannot be concerned with the crew.' How calm and resolute was his voice. My God, he thought, if only I could be concerned with the crew.

'We should drive him away,' Fushiro growled. 'A shot across his bows. He is flagrantly disobeying Japanese orders.'

'Then we'd very probably have another *Panay* incident,' Philip reminded him. 'And I do not think the admiral would thank us for that. Anyway, the ship is gone.'

For indeed, the *Sun Lily* had slipped beneath the waves, leaving only human and animal flotsam desperately trying to keep afloat as the destroyer nosed her way amidst them, eager British sailors manning the boarding-ladders and the nets to take on as many as they could.

'Alter course due north, and resume cruising speed, Mr Fushiro,' Philip said.

Fushiro gazed at him. 'You mean to leave the destroyer to pick up survivors? That is a contravention of our orders, honourable Captain.'

'The Chinese vessel is sunk, Mr Fushiro,' Philip said. 'We have our patrol to continue.'

As he turned away from the bridge windows to go below, the midshipman came out of the radio room. The boy's face was flushed. Philip took the paper.

MAY GOD HAVE MERCY ON YOUR SOUL STOP IF YOU HAVE A SOUL STOP MARSTON.

*

'Tell me,' Anne begged.

'I have told you,' Philip said, stretching out on his mattress, feeling the entire room still going up and down,

412

as it always did when he returned from a long voyage. But should he really be here, lying on a comfortable bed, with his loving and lovely wife beside him? Would she want him here, if she knew what he had become?

'I know what you told Iyeyasu at dinner,' Anne said, sitting beside him. 'You made it all sound so very easy. So very glorious.'

'Is that not what war is?' he asked. 'Easy, when you have overwhelming superiority, and always glorious?'

She hesitated, then lay down beside him. 'There are letters,' she said.

'I saw them. I'll look at them tomorrow.'

'There is one from the academy. A report. Iyeyasu is doing very well. In two years' time he will be commissioned. And have to go to sea. To war. Do you not think it would be a kindness to tell him what it is really like?'

'No,' Philip said. 'And in any event, the war will be over, in two years' time.'

'You think so? You've heard the news from Europe?'

'Of course. Germany has invaded Poland, and Great Britain and France have declared war. There does not seem to be much actual fighting, except in Poland.'

'Isn't it going to involve us?'

'No. We are remaining at peace with all the world. Save China. At Germany's specific request, I believe. They do not want a world war, at this time. They are sure the British and the French will make peace, once they realise that Poland cannot be saved.'

'And if they don't?'

'They will.'

She sighed. 'John Graham doesn't think so.'

'Are you still seeing Graham?'

'Yes.'

'In the name of God, why?'

'I happen to be his doctor, Phil.'

'So whenever he feels like a chat he comes in to see you. What does your staff nurse think about it?'

'I have no idea. She doesn't speak English, so she really doesn't know. Although . . . ' She smiled. 'I think she thinks we are having an affair.'

'And are you?' He sat up.

'For God's sake, Phil.'

'Then why do you keep on seeing him? He is an enemy to our country.'

'Do you really believe that, Phil?'

'Oh, God . . . ' He lay down again. 'Why do you not get pregnant?'

She looked down the bed. 'Chance would be a fine thing.'

'Oh . . . I am exhausted. And yes, war is not all glory and derring-do. It is the most filthy, ghastly mess. I need a day or two to recover. But Anne, my dearest girl . . . ' He rolled towards her and took her hands. 'Why do you still take precautions? We've been married three years. You always said . . . '

'I don't take precautions, Phil. Not any more. Maybe . . . maybe we left it too late.'

'Too late?' He rose on his elbow to look at her.

'Well, I am going on thirty-four.'

'And still the most beautiful woman I have ever known. But Anne, have I really done that to you?'

'Of course you haven't. You know, I don't think either of us has really wanted children, these past three years. It's no kind of world to bring them into, is it?'

'Has it ever been any different sort of world?' He took her in his arms. 'Oh, Anne, my Anne, it is a terrible world. I have watched women and children drown . . . and been unable to help them. I have become a mass murderer. I have . . . '

She kissed him. He was telling her the truth, at last. 'As you said, when has it ever changed, my darling?'

He held her so close she lost her breath. 'I am so unhappy, Anne. So very unhappy.'

'Not now,' she whispered, feeling him move against

her. 'Not this moment. *We* can be happy, Phil. You and I. No matter what.'

Isoroku Yamamoto stood on the gantry, looking down on the dry dock and the monstrous hull which sat there, waiting to be launched. 'What do you think of her?'

The hot July sun glinted from the freshly painted steel, flickered from the protective hats of the myriad construction workers down there; flickered too from the guns and bayonets of the guards who constantly patrolled, not only the gantry but the dockyard floor itself. No ship could ever have been constructed with more secrecy.

Philip Shimadzu said, 'She is incredible.'

'A great ship, for a great captain.' Yamamoto smiled. 'Oh, I intend to sail on her too, whenever I can. What, could you imagine a finer flagship?'

'What is to be her name?' Philip asked.

'*Yamato*.'

'*Yamato*,' Philip repeated. 'And she is to have a sister?'

'The keel is already laid. *Mushashi*. But you are to have *Yamato*.'

'Am I, honourable Admiral?'

'Indeed, it is all arranged. In fact, if you wish it, I will second you from *Tone* immediately, so that you can be here to supervise every aspect of her completion. She is to be launched next month. And once that is done, I want her in commission just as rapidly as it can be done. Certainly by the end of next year.'

'We are at war,' Philip reminded him. 'Should I not serve?'

'You will be performing a far greater service by having *Yamato* ready for sea by December 1941 than you ever could by sailing up and down the China Sea,' Yamamoto told him. 'Anyway, you have had four tours of patrol duty, and what is there to do out there?' He gazed into Philip's eyes. 'Save sink unarmed junks. Or rather, watch them sink.'

'Yes,' Philip said.

'You are aware that Commander Fushiro filed a report on your actions, regarding the junk *Sun Lily* and the British destroyer *Ventura*, last September?' Yamamoto asked.

'No. But I was surprised that he did not appear to do so.'

'I suppressed it,' Yamamoto said. 'I think your actions were entirely correct.'

'Thank you, honourable Admiral.'

'You and I, Philip, are fighting seamen. We must always find commerce destroying repugnant. It is the tragedy of our lives that we have never had to steam into battle, as commanders. However, that day will surely come. I *will* relieve you of command of the *Tone*, immediately, and allow you to devote all of your energies to *Yamato*. Because that is the most vital task in the navy today. Our moment is approaching too rapidly to risk any delays.'

'Honourable Admiral?' Philip was mystified.

'Well, consider recent events, Philip.' Yamamoto led him down the ladders from the gantry to the waiting automobile, got into the back seat and gestured Philip to sit beside him. 'France has surrendered to Germany. This is an important event. It means not only that Great Britain now fights alone, but that all the various French overseas possessions have now been neutralised. This is a sufficient change of situation here in East Asia. Would you not agree?'

'Well, yes, honourable Admiral,' Philip said, not at all sure to what he was agreeing.

'Do you remember a conversation we had in the planning room at the Admiralty, not long after your return from Washington? My God, eighteen years ago, Philip. Eighteen years! How time flies.'

'I remember, honourable Admiral.' Philip found his heart pounding.

'We discussed certain eventualities.'

'Yes,' Philip said.

'And certain possibilities, and certain hazards as well, for the fleet. You were the one who raised most of the hazards, remember?'

'Indeed, honourable Admiral.'

'Can you remember what they were?'

'Yes,' Philip said. 'That any movement of the fleet to the south would expose it to risk of attack by shore-based bombers from Malaya and French Indo-China.'

'But French Indo-China is now to be regarded as at worst a neutral,' Yamamoto pointed out. 'In fact, I can tell you that we have already opened negotiations with Vichy for the use of bases there. Continue. What next?'

'That any violent expansion to the south would inevitably bring us into conflict with the Royal Navy,' Philip went on, feeling exactly as he had done when watching the Chinese women and children drown.

'But the Royal Navy is fully committed to the North Atlantic and the Mediterranean. Are you not aware that both *Bismarck* and *Tirpitz* are virtually complete? The Royal Navy will soon have its hands full. The third hazard?'

'That any movement of our main forces to the south would expose us to invasion by Russia in the north,' Philip said desperately.

'True. But I can tell you in confidence that before too long the forces of Soviet Russia are going to be neutralised as well. But there was a fourth hazard, was there not?'

'The most important one, honourable Admiral: intervention by the United States. There is a battle fleet of at least six battleships and three aircraft-carriers in Hawaii.'

'Indeed. I agree with you that that is our most important consideration. However, I can also tell you, again in confidence, that there are moves afoot to . . . how shall I put it? Persuade the United States to cease interesting herself in events here in the Far East, at least for long enough to enable us to achieve our aims, and create an unbreachable defence perimeter. I can say no more than that at this time, but obviously it is a necessary part of our strategy to possess the strongest fleet in the world. Which is why we need *Yamato* to lead us into action. And that has to be by the end of next year.'

'She will be but one ship, honourable Admiral,' Philip said.

Yamamoto smiled. 'One ship can be decisive, when she is the only one of her class, Philip. I will promise you this: you will have the opportunity of commanding *Yamato* in action, and soon. It is the intention of the Government, the moment all the factors we have discussed become favourable to us, as they are going to within the next eighteen months, to launch the Strike South Plan.' He pinched Philip's arm. 'With suitable modifications, of course.'

CHAPTER 16

The Decision

John Graham sat before Anne Shimadzu's desk. 'You've heard the news?'

'That Hitler has invaded Russia? Yes.'

'And is smashing the hell out of it?'

'Yes. The war does seem to be spreading.'

'What do you suppose Japan is going to do about it?'

'She's not going to go to war with Russia on Germany's behalf, John. I can promise you that.'

'Because Philip has told you so?'

'Well . . . yes.'

'What else has he told you?'

'Nothing. There is nothing else to tell. He has not even been to sea for several months, as you know. He is waiting for *Yamato* to complete.'

'And when will that be?'

'I don't know. He hasn't told me. And even if he had, I could hardly tell you, John.'

'Has he told you anything about the ship itself?'

'No. And the same thing applies.'

'Not even how big she's going to be?'

'John, please!'

Graham leaned across her desk. 'Listen to me, Anne. It's been two years now, and I've just pumped information into you, hoping it would reach Philip and make him think. Now it has to come the other way.'

'Has to?' She gazed at him; was he threatening her?

'Why do you think the Japanese have refused to aid

419

Germany against Russia? Don't you think they owe Russia a thing or two? Zhukov gave them a bloody nose on the Manchurian border two years ago. Don't you think they want to avenge that?'

'I don't know,' she said. 'They probably aren't going to war because Hitler doesn't need them.'

'Oh, he needs them all right. Stalin has several whole armies posted in Siberia, just in case the Japs try something. Once he reckons they aren't going to, those troops will be released to defend Moscow, and Hitler knows that. He has actually appealed for Japanese help, and been turned down. You tell me why.'

Anne glanced at Nurse Harya, waiting patiently in her chair in the corner. 'You simply must not be so vehement. You're supposed to be telling me about a tummy ache, not the end of the world.'

He sighed. 'It could be the end of the world. The reason, my dear girl, is that Japan intends to seek its own place in the sun, right here in East Asia. I am informed that plans are being laid for a massive drive to the south, which would overrun Malaya, and the Dutch East Indies, and perhaps even the Philippines.'

'Oh, come now.'

'They'll never have a better opportunity. French Indo-China is theirs, virtually. I happen to know that they're pouring men and planes into Saigon. The British are fighting for their lives in North Africa, and have still to keep most of their troops in England to repel an invasion. There simply is nothing to spare to defend the Far East, save a couple of Australian divisions. There are no ships and virtually no aircraft. The Japanese know these things. And they know they will never have a better opportunity than now, to seize an empire which will make them self-sufficient in raw materials, and virtually unbeatable. Why do you think the army has replaced Konoye by Tojo? Now you actually have a general as prime minister. That can only mean one thing – war.'

'And don't they also know that the US would never sit by and allow them to overrun South-East Asia?'

'I reckon they do. But let me tell you something else. I happen to know that the US has virtually given Japan an ultimatum this year: pull out of China or face an economic war, with a total embargo on US goods entering or leaving Japan. Now, this government isn't going to pull out of China, is it? But at the same time, an economic embargo on that scale would ruin Japan. So what's left? I would say they are committed to the conquest of those raw materials they need, even if it means physical war with America. And I would further say that is why they are hurrying ahead with their plans to complete *Yamato* and *Mushashi* just as quickly as possible, to give themselves the edge in capital ships. Don't forget they also have this massive new fifty-thousand-ton aircraft-carrier just about ready. Anne, there are rumours that *Yamato* is going to be *seventy* thousand tons on completion. Do you remember that I warned you, two years ago, that there was going to be a ship that size?'

She nodded unhappily.

'And Philip is going to command her. Has he any idea against whom?'

'I told you, we have a pact, Phil and I, that I don't ask questions and he doesn't answer any. It's the only way.'

'Well, now you simply have to ask questions, Anne. You have to find out when *Yamato* is going to be ready for action, and you have to find out where Philip is being sent first.'

'So you can pass the information on to the Americans?'

He returned her stare. 'Yes.'

'You are asking me to become a traitor to my country.'

'Your adopted country. Aren't you an American citizen as well?'

'It would destroy Phil, John. You know that. It would destroy my marriage, my life, to give you information like that.'

'Then make Philip do it. It is his life, too. I can't believe he wants to go to war against America.'

'Did you want to go to war against Germany? But you went, because your government decided to do so.'

'Anne . . .' He reached across the desk and took her hands. 'I am begging you for help. If Japan makes a move now, and catches us all hopping, well . . . the consequences could be too terrible to imagine. Just imagine those hellhounds from Nanking being let loose in Manila or Hong Kong or Singapore? Or even, you know, San Francisco. It could happen. Anne, they have to be stopped, or checked. Or if necessary, defeated. Philip has to be made to understand that. For God's sake, it is a matter of life and death. Everyone's life and death.'

She chewed her lip. 'We are going on holiday down to Kyushu next week,' she said. 'Just the two of us; Iyeyasu will stay at college.'

'Then talk to him. Please talk to him, Anne.'

She sighed, and nodded.

'This is splendid, Nurse Harya,' General Mori said. He scanned the sheet of paper again. 'You even have a good memory. Splendid. Be sure that I shall remember your cooperation, always. Now, had you not better go back to your duty?'

The nurse, as she always did, positively ran from the room.

'A very useful young woman,' Mori reflected aloud.

'Certainly she has supplied us with sufficient evidence to have Commander Graham declared *persona non grata*,' Kitabake agreed. 'I shall take these steps immediately.'

'No, no,' Mori said.

Kitabake raised his eyebrows.

'I agree,' Mori said, 'that we have here more than sufficient evidence to have Graham deported. But what would that achieve? We know nothing of this so-called

422

"group" of his. And of course we cannot at this time actually interrogate him. Deporting him would be a grave mistake, in my opinion. Even more important, we have nothing against the Shimadzus. Mrs Shimadzu has steadfastly refused to divulge any information to him. It is possible that she may now be going to try to obtain some from her husband, but we cannot be sure that she will succeed. We must have proof that she has. We must never forget that he is a close friend of Yamamoto's, and Yamamoto is now fleet commander. What is more, he cannot be replaced, as he is the only man our masters have confidence in to defeat the American fleet. That means they will humour him in everything. When we arrest Shimadzu, we must have incontrovertible proof of his treason. Proof which even Yamamoto will have to accept. So I suggest we let Captain and Mrs Shimadzu go on their holiday to Kyushu. We know Mrs Shimadzu will be working on her husband. When they come back, now, well, then we may have everything we want, eh, Kitabake San?'

But Kitabake knew what Mori really wanted.

They walked over the sands, on the beach south of Nagasaki. Nagasaki was nearly the southernmost seaport in the whole country, at times almost sub-tropical; certainly on a warm September afternoon. The sea was blue and there was hardly a cloud to obscure the blue of the sky; there was hardly any wind, either, and not a ripple on the water. Yet there was no peace. Not only did Nagasaki hum, like an enormous factory situated just beyond the headland of Nomo Zaki – as indeed it was an enormous factory, a prime ship building port as well as an industrial hub – but overhead Mitsubishi Zero dive-bombers flew constantly to and fro, climbing high into the sky, and then zooming down as if about to crash into the headland, before booming away into the bay beyond, making descents close to the surface of the sea, then once again climbing into the distance.

'Who'd choose a holiday within fifty miles of a naval base,' Philip said. And smiled. 'As if it is possible to have a holiday, in Japan, more than fifty miles from some kind of a base.'

He was very relaxed. More relaxed than she had known him for some time. 'Happy?' she asked, squeezing his hand.

'With you, yes. I don't think a man can, or should, be happy, in wartime.'

A cue, perhaps. 'Phil . . . ' She held his arm tighter yet. 'What's going to happen?'

'God knows.'

'I'm serious. You must have some idea. Last year you said the war with China would be over in two years. But it just seems to get more and more involved. Next year Iyeyasu will be commissioned.'

'He won't be in any danger, at least from the Chinese,' Philip said, some of the good humour leaving his voice.

'But? Because there is a but, isn't there?'

'Oh, God, I suppose so. I still don't think Iyeyasu is ever going to be involved in a shooting war. Not next year, anyway.'

'But there is going to be one, this year? With someone else than China?'

He sighed, and sat down on the sand, arms clasped about his knees. 'I think so.'

She sat beside him. 'You think so?'

'Well . . . maybe I know so. Maybe I've known for a long time.'

'Since you left *Tone*,' she suggested.

He glanced at her. 'Who's observant, then?'

'Of my husband? Shouldn't I be? Tell me what's going to happen, Phil.'

'I don't know what's going to happen, my dearest girl. I wish I did. But I have my suspicions. God, I have my suspicions.'

'Tell me, Phil. Please tell me.'

Another quick glance. 'You do realise this is absolutely top secret?'

She bit her lip. 'Yes.'

'Um.' He lay down, moving his hands to clasp them behind his head, and watched yet another aircraft dipping out of the sky towards the high, bold headland that separated them from the city and the port; the planes were very definitely training by sighting on the headland, and then appearing to drop their bombs at specified distances beyond. Only, of course, they weren't actually dropping any bombs. Yet for some reason he found the spectacle disturbing, although for the life of him he could not think why.

'Phil?' She lay down beside him.

'Well, you know of course that all armies, and all navies, spend their time deciding who are the people they are most likely to have to fight, one day, and preparing plans for war against those people.'

'Yes.'

'So obviously all of our plans have always been laid for a war with China, a war just like this one, in fact, except that the Chinese are holding on somewhat longer than our planners had anticipated. That doesn't alter the fact that they are beaten. However, when the plans were first drawn up, and I am talking of something like twenty years ago, it was assumed that the British and the French, having so many financial interests in China and so many colonies in the Far East – as well, of course, as the Dutch, and perhaps even the Americans – might object to our defeating China and might wish to come in on the Chinese side. Or at least deny us imports of oil and rubber and other war materials; the sort of thing they threatened to do to Italy during the Ethiopian crisis. Now, obviously, such economic sanctions would face us with an impossible situation, mainly because we are so short of raw materials of our own.'

'Yes,' she said, aware of a peculiar breathlessness.

'Therefore the idea grew that at the same time as the army invaded China, it would be necessary for the navy to strike south, and secure the tin and rubber of Malaya, the oil of the Dutch East Indies, and the additional rice supplies of French Indo-China and the Philippines.'

'My God!' she said.

'It was felt that while that might incur hostilities with Great Britain and France and the Netherlands, and possibly even the United States, if it was done quickly enough and ruthlessly enough, we could establish a perimeter which would be very difficult for any of those nations to assault, operating so far from their home bases. And within that perimeter we would be totally independent of the rest of the world for all our necessary commodities. In these circumstances, it was envisaged that the injured colonial powers would almost certainly accept a negotiated peace, leaving us in possession of our gains, and them with perhaps indemnities or something.'

'Je*sus*!' Anne commented.

'Yes. But it really was planned. I know. I was one of the planners.'

'You?'

'I was on the planning staff then. One of Yamamoto's blue-eyed boys. It was just before my marriage to Haruko.'

'And you went along with that?'

'No. I didn't like the idea at all. Especially the idea of war with the US. I discussed it with Uncle William, who I think was just as appalled as I. But being Uncle William, he counselled patience and diplomacy. He pointed out that the plan was obviously impractical, as it depended upon too many imponderables being in our favour, and said that all *I* had to do was keep telling this to my superiors. Which I did. I produced every possible figure I could dream up to prove that it wouldn't work. And my figures were largely accepted. Which, remarkably, made me more of Yamamoto's blue-eyed boy than ever; I suspect he came to the conclusion that I was totally honest. I thought the whole project had been shelved, and in fact, the army went into China four years ago with nothing more than a protest from anyone, because everyone else had problems of their own, by then. But the Government has apparently never forgotten the Strike South Plan, and now they've taken it out and are dusting it off. Because you see, incredibly, all the reasons I gave for it not working have been resolved. Well, nearly all.'

'I don't understand,' she said.

'Well, I told them that our fleet, proceeding south to assault Malaya and the Dutch East Indies, would be utterly vulnerable to air attack from French Indo-China. But French Indo-China is now virtually an ally. Then I told them that we would find ourselves taking on the entire British fleet within a few months. But the British fleet has to stay at home, right now, to fight the German fleet. Even if they've sunk *Bismarck*, in the couple of days she was out she damaged *Prince of Wales*, sank *Hood* and caused the most awful panic. And there's still *Tirpitz* and *Gneisenau* and *Scharnhorst* waiting for the chance to get out, maybe all three together. Then I said that if we sent the fleet and our main army south, the Russians would probably invade from the north.'

'But now they're being overrun by the Germans,' Anne said. 'Oh, Christ. But what about the Americans?'

'Oh, yes,' he said. 'That was my trump card. But there are moves afoot to neutralise the Americans, at least for the immediate future. I imagine there is some sort of *quid pro quo* going on, but it also has something to do with *Yamato*, and thus presumably relative fleet strengths. Once she's commissioned, and she will be this December, we'll have the greatest battle fleet in history. *Yamato* is unsinkable. And she can destroy any conventional battleship with a single broadside.'

'And you'll be in command,' Anne remarked.

427

'Yes.' He sat up.

'And you're happy about that? You're going to stand on her bridge and sail into action against the Americans, blowing them to bits. You. Ralph Freeman's people. My father's people. *My* people.'

'I told you, that's not going to happen,' Philip snapped angrily. 'They're going to stay neutral.'

'Oh, yeah? Who told you that?'

'Yamamoto himself, as a matter of fact.'

'And you believe him'

'Absolutely. He would no more tell a lie than . . . than Uncle William. He refused to go into details, but he said – this was last summer, you know – that both the Soviet Union and the United States would have to be neutralised before we could move, and that this was going to be done . . . ' He checked, and watched another dive-bomber wheeling out of the sky. 'God damn!'

'Yes,' she said. 'The word is neutralised, not stay neutral. Neutralised, like being invaded by the Germans. Yamamoto *knew* the Germans were going to invade Russia, *last year.*'

'But it's not possible for anyone to invade the States. It simply isn't possible. It . . . the whole concept is too crazy for words.'

'Tell me why?'

'Because even with *Yamato*, we don't have that much superiority.'

'Yes, but if it's her fleet that's to be neutralised, the same way that Russia has been neutralised, by a German attack, perhaps . . . '

He shook his head. 'That's the least possible of all. The main US fleet is concentrated in Hawaii, and there is no way any German fleet can get to Hawaii. Anyway, why should they? No . . . ' He watched yet another plane. Because something was ticking away at the back of his brain. 'You ever been to Hawaii?' he asked. 'Honolulu, specifically.'

428

'Well, yes, the ship I came out to Japan on stopped there. But that was eleven years ago. I don't remember much about it.'

'I was there on *Mutsu*, as part of the round-the-world cruise,' he said. 'I've swum below Diamond Head.'

'Diamond Head?'

He pointed at the headland, above which the Zero was swooping. 'I've just realised that headland is an exact replica of Diamond Head.'

Anne stared at it, and the wheeling and swooping aircraft. 'And those planes are using it as some kind of marker. Oh, my God, Phil. What are you going to do?'

'Come in, Philip, come in,' Yamamoto said. But he frowned as he glanced at his diary. 'You were not due to return from vacation for another two weeks.' He wagged his finger. 'That was your last vacation for some time, you know. Once *Yamato* is commissioned . . .'

'I felt restless, honourable Admiral. Permission to sit?'

'Oh, of course. Forgive me.' Yamamoto leaned back in his chair. 'You look as if you have something on your mind. No problem with *Yamato*, I trust?'

'All is very well with *Yamato*, honourable Admiral. I have been given a firm date for commissioning: 8 December.'

'Hm.' Yamamoto looked at his diary again. 'That is good. It does mean . . . well, that does not matter. That you will be in full commission on 8 December is very important.'

'Is it, honourable Admiral?'

Yamamoto gazed at him. 'You had better speak your mind, Philip.'

Philip drew a long breath. 'Is it the intention of Japan to go to war with the United States, honourable Admiral?'

Yamamoto's expression did not change. 'What leads you to that conclusion, honourable Captain?'

'I have just returned from Kyushu, honourable Admiral. My wife and I stayed at an hotel outside Nagasaki. And walking on the beach beneath Nomo Zaki headland, I watched several squadrons of navy bombers making dummy runs.'

Yamamoto's eyes narrowed. 'Continue.'

'They were using Nomo Zaki as a marker, honourable Admiral. Picking it up from a great distance, and then using it as a range-finder, to drop their bombs at a set distance beyond.'

'Yes?'

'Well, honourable Admiral, I have visited Oahu. The cliff outside Nagasaki bears a remarkable resemblance to Diamond Head outside Honolulu – beyond which is the American naval base of Pearl Harbor.'

'Do you know, Philip, that is quite brilliant?' Yamamoto remarked. 'I have always had the highest respect for your intelligence and observation, but you still continue to surprise me.'

'Then I am right?'

'Of course. Fortunately, I do not think any other casual observer would have so acute a reaction. Still, I will warn the fliers to vary their techniques somewhat. But identification of somewhere like Diamond Head is, of course, very important from the point of view of pilots who are approaching from a considerable distance, and who have not had the advantage of being able to reconnoitre the target area.'

'May I say, with great respect, honourable Admiral, that any idea of us carrying out a bombing raid on Pearl Harbor is absolute suicide?'

Yamamoto raised his eyebrows. 'Explain.'

Philip knew better than to confront the Admiral with the historical implications of what was intended, much less with his own personal involvement; Yamamoto was interested only in facts.

'Because the conditions which would make a war with

430

America possible do not exist, honourable Admiral,' he said. 'Our best assumption was that America would become involved in a European war or at least an Atlantic one, and would maintain more than half her fleet in the Atlantic. That has not happened, honourable Admiral, and there are at least six American battleships, and three aircraft-carriers in Pearl Harbor. It is also an intensely well-defended base. Once war is declared between our two countries Pearl Harbor will be *expecting* us to attack. We would come under assault by shore-based planes long before our ships could get close enough to launch any air strikes.'

Yamamoto nodded. 'All that is very true,' he agreed. 'But suppose, just suppose, that the Americans did not know we were going to attack them . . . until we attacked them?'

'But you mean, without a declaration of war?' Philip was aghast.

'Well, the first shot would be a declaration of war, would it not? Anyway, the formal declaration would be made at about that same moment.'

'But, honourable Admiral, the morality of such an action . . .'

'There is no room for morality in war, honourable Captain, as I have reminded you often enough, except in respect of one's own country. How do you suppose we defeated the Russian colossus in 1905? Simply because, two days before the declaration of war, our torpedo boats attacked the Russian fleet in its base at Port Arthur, and so damaged it the Russians could not put to sea for two months. By that time our transports, which could have been destroyed by those Russian battleships, had put our armies ashore, not only in Korea to win the fight for Manchuria, but on the Liao-tung Peninsula itself, to invest Port Arthur. Your uncle was in the navy then. So was I,' he added, reminiscently.

'But that was nearly thirty-seven years ago, honourable Admiral. Surely . . . '

'Surely what, Philip? Surely circumstances have altered? Circumstances never alter, except in degree. Port Arthur is now a day's sail from Shimonoseki. Yet it was vital to our victory in that war. Manila, Hong Kong, Singapore, Djakarta, are hardly further from our shores in terms of time now than Port Arthur was then. And they are vital to our victory in this war.'

Yamamoto leaned forward. 'Listen to me. I have no desire to fight the Americans, but it has been made obvious to us over the past year that they are preparing to fight us. They have warned us that if we do not cease hostilities in China they will put an embargo upon all strategic goods entering Japan. They would like to strangle us to death. Well, we cannot sit back and allow them to do that. Therefore the decision has been taken to strike south. But in view of the American attitude, we can no longer doubt that they will probably intervene the moment we move. It is not our place to hope that might not happen; it is our duty to make our decisions based upon our estimates of what is most likely to happen, and to act accordingly. Therefore, if we accept that war with the United States is inevitable, we must be sure we win that war, or at least put ourselves into a position where we cannot lose it.

'We are negotiating with Washington now, for a change of attitude. But if there is no change of attitude, within a given time, then we intend to attack their Pacific fleet, without warning, and destroy it. I am not a fool. I am well aware that they will build another fleet. But before they can do that, we will have our oil and our tin and our rubber, and our perimeter. If they want to knock their heads against that, that is their privilege.'

'Honourable Admiral . . . '

Yamamoto got up and came round his desk, to rest his hand on Philip's shoulder. 'Philip, I know and respect your high ideals of honour. Would that we could always order our national affairs in such a manner. But the national affairs must come first. You and I devised a scenario, many years ago. We required a certain set of circumstances to be favourable, and then we knew we could secure the future of Japan. But to expect all of those conditions, or even most of them, ever to be favourable at the same moment, was asking too much of fate. We have received more than our share of good fortune as it is. Every condition we set has been achieved, save one. And that one can also be achieved, sufficiently for our purpose, if we can eliminate the United States fleet for a period of even six months. Japan will never have such an opportunity as this again. Were we to turn our backs upon it now, then history would never forgive us.

'I repeat, we are negotiating with Washington. Let us hope and pray that our negotiations are successful. But whether they are or not, we must strike south. I promise you will be one of the first to know when the decision is taken. And Philip,' he added, gazing into the tortured eyes of his protégé. 'You will not have to take part in the attack on Pearl Harbor. You will not be able to, because the decision will be taken before *Yamato* is commissioned. I am glad about this. I know how difficult it would be for you to launch such an attack upon people whose blood flows in your veins, and to whom your wife belongs. I alone will bear the burden of any dishonour that may accrue to the navy as a result of that attack. I will bear it proudly, for the honour of my country. But I also know, Philip, that once the war commences, if it does, you will command *Yamato* to glory, the greatest ship the world has ever seen. For the glory and, more, the survival and the triumph of Japan.'

'Tell me,' Anne said.

'There is nothing,' Philip snapped. 'Nothing to tell. I was mistaken. We were mistaken. There are . . . there are talks going on now between Japan and the United States, talks designed to draw up a long-term alliance. I have told you this already. Do you not suppose that the Americans are as aware as anyone else of what is going on? Germany is going to win the European war, and Britain is going to be reduced to the level of . . . of Sweden. Her empire will be up for grabs, and will fall to the nation which acts first. The Americans intend to seize the West Indies – you know they already have bases in many of the islands – and exert a protectorate over Canada. They have agreed that we shall have a free hand to take what we wish here in East Asia. It is as simple as that.'

She stared at him with her mouth open. Because he had never lied to her before, and he was not very good at it.

'It is the truth,' he insisted. 'Therefore we shall have nothing to fear when we move south. Nothing.'

Anne closed her mouth, then opened it again to lick her lips. 'But you are still going to war with Great Britain,' she said. 'What am I to tell John Graham?'

'Nothing. You are not to see him again. Do you understand? I do not wish you to see him again, ever. He is an *agent provocateur*, and he represents a country which is going down to defeat and seeks to involve others in its ruin. You are not to see him again.'

She bowed her head, and they ate in silence. And did not speak after they retired, either. Which was as unique as his lie. She knew he had lied.

He heard her sob, once. But then, he wished to sob himself. With despair. For had he not always known this moment would come? He had known it since the first day he had sat in Yamamoto's office, after returning from the Washington conference in the spring of 1922. Nineteen years, during which it had lain at the back of his mind like some hideous disease, while he prayed that it would go away and never affect him.

But now he had to accept the fact that it had become active, and fatal.

What could he do? The imponderables, the enormities,

434

the risks, the catastrophes, seemed to crowd round his head like a dozen bottles of sake. There *were* talks going on with the United States. Yamamoto clearly did not expect them to succeed – but Philip believed the admiral when he claimed to be praying for that success. Therefore he must do the same. And nothing else? Because suppose they did succeed – and he had already taken action? The one overwhelming consideration was not the utter infamy of launching such an attack on any country, much less one that he considered his second home, but rather the utter certainty that the Americans, thus attacked, would fight, and fight, and fight, until Japan was stamped into the earth. Yamamoto did not know that. He did not know the Americans. Neither did General Tojo.

But what could *he* do? Save play the traitor. And would the Americans believe him, that the Japanese could plan such a thing? He could, of course, remind them of Port Arthur, but they would no doubt say, as he had done, that was thirty-seven years ago. Things were different now. Were they? As Yamamoto had said, he had been a serving officer then, and so had William.

And for him to play the traitor, complete the wreckage of the Freeman family, bring the last remnants of Ralph Freeman's fame, already tarnished by the dishonour of his eldest grandson, crashing into the dust. And the danger of it. Iyeyasu, Anne . . . He could not even play the traitor and then commit seppuku, he knew. Not with them alive and living in Japan. Because the Kempai, Mori, would take them just the same. Anne, stretched on a garage table before Mori and his wire . . . He felt quite sick.

And what of himself? His ambitions, his dreams? There was an insidious but terrifying thought. He often dreamed of *Yamato*. She was virtually ready to take her place in the fleet; he had already taken her on two trial voyages, and only one or two relatively minor details remained to be seen to. He had never handled such a magnificent vessel, had never known such pride as he felt standing on her bridge. In only another few weeks she would be sailing in all her glory, the greatest ship ever to put to sea. To fight the Americans, under his command. Even the Americans would have to bow to the superiority of so great a fighting machine. For a while. They would build bigger and better ships, eventually. No doubt about that. But he would have commanded her . . . to the end?

Suddenly he thought he saw a solution. Perhaps it was possible to let the Americans know what was planned, and still not betray himself, still retain his rank and prestige, his domestic happiness . . . and his place as captain of the *Yamato*. Then, if there had to be war between Japan and America, he would fight in that war, to the best of his ability. But he would know it was a war undertaken with honour, in which victor and vanquished could take just, and joint, pride.

He could do that, by means of Graham. Graham could see the news reached the Americans. Graham . . . Philip lay in the darkness, chewing his lips. It was what Graham had always dreamed he would do: play the traitor and turn to him.

Was he going to do it? He did not know. He simply did not know. Certainly he could not contemplate it until he knew for sure, that war was inevitable, until the last card had been played. And there were certain arrangements to be made. He would be placing his life in Graham's hands. He did not fear that. But he could not risk the lives of Anne and Iyeyasu as well. They must not be involved, under any circumstances. And time was short. Yamamoto had said the decision would be taken before *Yamato* was commissioned.

Did that mean he had already made up his mind to betray his country? No, to save it from utter destruction. He had to remember that. He had to enable the

Americans to say, We know all about your plans, and we will stop you if you try. That was his duty, to untold unborn legions of Japanese children.

He had to remember that.

'I would like you to take Iyeyasu for a holiday in America,' he told Anne at breakfast.

She raised her eyebrows. 'Now? In the middle of term?'

'We can say there is illness in the family there.'

'What family? Aunt Hilary?'

'Oh, we can say anything we wish. We can just take him away and get you both on a ship. I will answer any objections that may be made.'

She stared at him. 'Oh, Phil . . . ' Her eyes shone. 'You mean you're . . . ' She decided not to say it. 'Of course you're right. But if you're staying here, so am I.'

'Now, Anne . . . '

'No!' she said vehemently. 'You are my husband. I am staying at your side. No matter what happens.'

'I do not know if anything is going to happen, yet. I am hoping it will not. But I have to make sure that Iyeyasu and you are in safety, no matter *what* happens.'

'Are you planning suicide?' she asked.

'No.' He flushed. 'I believe it can be done without anyone tracing the source of the information.'

'By using John?'

'Perhaps. But Anne, once it is done, and I would only do it to avoid a treacherous attack, not to avoid war, I am committed to remaining here, and fighting for Japan. Against America.'

She considered the entirely new situation for several seconds. Then she nodded. 'I understand, Philip. And I respect you for that decision. I will remain here with you.' She forced a smile. 'Doctors are always popular in war-time.'

He sighed. 'You are missing the point. I *believe* it can be done. I believe I will be acting for the honour of my

437

country, not the dishonour of myself. But, Anne, if I did decide to act, and something were to go wrong . . . '

'I understand that, too,' she said. 'But what can go wrong? You have but to tell John the truth of what is happening, what is planned. He will never betray you, so no one will ever know from where the information came. It could have come from any of the group. And as you say, if you do that, you will have done your duty to mankind, Phil. And to Japan. And no one will ever know.'

'If that is truly the case, then there is no necessity to send Iyeyasu away. In fact, to send him away might be to betray us.'

'Yes,' she said.

Philip brooded as he drank his tea. As usual, she was offering nothing but common sense. 'All right. But suspicion will certainly fall upon every naval attaché in the country. And there is one possible source of information for Graham which must be closed immediately. You must not see Graham again, as I said last night. I am very serious.'

'Um,' she said.

'Have you seen him since returning from vacation?'

She shook her head. 'But he is coming to see me in two days' time.'

'Cancel the appointment. Do you understand?'

She hesitated. 'But . . . '

'I will contact him, when I am sure there is no alternative. But you must not be involved, under any circumstances.'

'Is it not more important to risk my involvement than yours? I'm an American citizen. Even if they could trace the information back to me, they couldn't harm me, only deport me.'

'Do you think so? If they have already made up their mind to go to war with the United States? You do not know these people as I do, my dearest girl. You simply must not see Graham again. Please promise me that.'

She sighed, and nodded.

'Now this is very interesting,' Mori remarked, studying Nurse Harya's report.

'So I thought, honourable General,' Kitabake said. 'It seems to indicate that Shimadzu has made up his mind not to be a traitor after all. That is, if he ever did consider it, and we have not been mistaken all of these years.'

Mori frowned. 'How do you arrive at that conclusion, honourable Captain?'

'Well . . . ' Kitabake tapped his copy of the transcript. 'Mrs Shimadzu telephones Graham, who has an appointment with her as his doctor, and tells him that she is cancelling the appointment, and that he must not come to see her, ever again. She would not have done so without being instructed by her husband, who clearly feels, now that matters are approaching a crisis, that any contact with a British naval attaché must be correct.'

'You think so? And what about this remark, "Philip may just be in touch one of these days"?'

'Well, would she not have to say something like that, honourable General? They have been friends for years.'

'I think you labour under a severe handicap in the execution of your duties, honourable Captain: you are far too anxious not to discover treachery in your precious navy,' Mori remarked. 'I think things are reaching a critical stage. You know as well as I that the orders to set the Pearl Harbor operation in motion will be given within a few days. It is obvious to me that Shimadzu is merely waiting to be sure the operation is going to commence before warning the Americans. We know it is going to take a matter of at least a week to get the fleet to their position, in the greatest secrecy. If the Americans have the slightest idea what is going on, the whole venture could turn out to be the most colossal catastrophe. Have you discussed this with Yamamoto?'

439

'Only in the most general terms, honourable General. We have, of course, discussed the security aspects of the situation, the utter secrecy which is required. No one, but no one, save Yamamoto himself, and of course General Tojo, knows such things as the actual date of sailing, or the actual course to be taken. There is no risk of that being betrayed.'

'Yet the various captains of the ships comprising the fleet will have to be informed at least of the sailing-date, at some stage,' Mori pointed out.

'Agreed. I put this point to the admiral, asking him if he had total confidence in all his captains, and he gave me one of his famous stares. And then said the captains are all already on stand-by to put to sea, although they do not as yet know the reason, and the date will be confirmed the day before sailing. The point is that Shimadzu will not even be sailing with the fleet, simply because *Yamato* will not be in full commission. So it is very possible that Shimadzu will not be included in those captains given a sailing-date and rendezvous until after the event, as it were.'

'*Yamato* will be in service early in December,' Mori said. 'According to my information. That means she will certainly be ordered to join the battle fleet at the earliest moment. What, possess the finest battleship in the world and not use her, at such a time? No, no, Ikita San, I do not like the way things are shaping up, entirely due to Yamamoto's over-confidence. I had hoped to have incontrovertible proof by now of Shimadzu's treachery . . . But I have also been warned that, at this juncture, I must cause no ill will between the army and the navy, that is why I have not even risked putting a tail on Shimadzu. But now we must act. We will have to force his hand.'

'How, honourable General?'

'We will arrest Dr Freeman.' He held up a finger as Kitabake would have protested. 'Very quietly, and secretly. Shimadzu is not to know. She will just disappear.'

'Do you not think Shimadzu will work out what has happened to her?'

'Of course he will. That is what we require him to do. But he will have no proof, and he will not be able to do anything about it. This will upset him. It will drive him mad with anxiety. I have told you, I do not think he possesses the resolution of his brother. I think that such a manoeuvre will bring Captain Shimadzu into the open, one way or another. And, of course . . . ' He smiled. 'Who can tell what information we may be able to glean by interrogating Dr Freeman? I am looking forward to that.'

Kitabake stared at him. And that is all you truly wish to do, he thought. He wondered if Mori was going to risk serious inter-service discord, and at such a time, merely for the sake of getting his filthy hands on the American woman, of possessing something that belonged to Philip Shimadzu. Possessing! The word, as applied to Mori, and as it would be applied by Mori, all but made him shiver.

Mori continued to smile; he was not a mind-reader. 'So you will organise the abduction of Dr Freeman, Kitabake San. As I say, in complete secrecy. Thus you will use my people, not yours. Mine are more experienced at this sort of thing, anyway. Also, you will use the woman Harya as your decoy. But do not let her go, afterwards. Once we take Dr Freeman, the nurse is redundant and may even prove a problem. You will take the women immediately to Kempai Headquarters. I will be waiting for you. Telephone me the moment your plans are complete, and tell me when to expect her. You understand everything you have to do, honourable Captain?'

'Yes, honourable General,' Kitabake muttered. 'I understand everything I have to do.'

*

441

Philip sat and drank jasmine tea with his mother. Anne had telephoned to say she would be late, because of an emergency patient who had just been brought in to the hospital. Tonight, of all nights.

But wasn't he actually pleased that she should have such a perfect alibi? If his meeting with Graham was ever discovered, she could not possibly be involved. Or even accused of knowing about it. Because she did not know of it. The sealed letter had been delivered to him only that afternoon. He had known what it contained before he even slit it open, with trembling hands. Then he had telephoned Graham.

So now he waited, with his mother. The mother he was about to betray, as he was about to betray all of Japan. No, he told himself fiercely; he simply had to remember that was not true. He was about to save Japan from herself, and from disaster. But Shikibu would never understand that. If she ever knew what he had done, that would be the end.

'You are pensive,' Shikibu observed. 'It is this war. It just drags on and on. Because the Chinese have no sense. This is something our leaders do not recognise. China has been in a state of war for so long that it matters nothing to them whether they are fighting each other or Japanese soldiers. What would really surprise the Chinese would be for them to wake up one morning and find themselves with no one to fight at all.'

'So what do you suggest we do?' Philip asked.

'I think we have done enough. We should consolidate our gains, not keep pressing on into that endless country.' She smiled, and squeezed his hand. 'I am just a silly old woman who understands nothing of these matters. I only know that we have now been at war for four years. It did not take us that long to beat the Chinese in 1894. That hardly took us four months. And it did not take us four years to beat the Russians in 1904, either. But I suppose General Tojo knows best.'

'Let us hope he does, honourable Mother. Now, I must leave you.'

'Oh? I had hoped you would stay for supper, if Anne is going to be late.'

'I must get back,' he said. 'I have work to do.' He kissed her cheek. 'It will all come right in the end, Mother. It must.'

He drove north through the brilliantly lit streets of Tokyo, slowly, hands tight on the wheel. It would all come right, he thought, because he would make it so. He crossed the canal, and turned towards the open country beyond Matsudo. Now he watched the milometer, and at the selected distance beyond the village saw the light gleaming from the automobile pulled in beneath the trees. He parked beside it. 'Real cloak and dagger,' he remarked.

Graham smiled. 'But it's good to see you, Phil. You're sure you weren't followed?'

'I saw no one behind me. Not even Mori would dare put a tail on a Japanese naval officer, anyway.'

'That must be reassuring. He certainly keeps a tail on me. But don't worry, I gave him the slip. Now, what's on your mind.'

Philip held out the envelope. 'I think you should see this.'

Graham hesitated, then opened the envelope, took out the sheet of paper, flicked on a small pocket-torch, and played the narrow beam over the Japanese characters.

'The fleet will put to sea at midnight tomorrow,' he read. 'Departure will be in the utmost secrecy. There will be no salutes or farewells. The Northern fleet will proceed directly to its rendezvous (A). The southern fleet will proceed to its rendezvous (B), together with the transports. Final instructions will be issued at sea. Orders for Captain Shimadzu: the *Yamato* will proceed to sea on 8 December. She will proceed as if to take up a position at rendezvous (A), but before then will regain contact with the Northern Fleet, which will be steaming west at that time. Contact should be made by 12 December at the latest, but full radio silence will be maintained throughout; all communication will be by reconnaissance aircraft. Good luck and good hunting. Yamamoto.'

'You will have to tell me what this means, precisely,' Graham said.

'It means that the main division of the Japanese fleet, including our best aircraft-carriers, is about to sail for a rendezvous north of Hawaii, with the intention of delivering a surprise attack on the American fleet in Pearl Harbor,' Philip said.

'Good God!' Graham gasped.

'At the same time,' Philip went on, 'the second division of the Japanese fleet, escorting transports carrying soldiers, will commence to occupy Hong Kong, the Philippines, Malaya and the Dutch East Indies.'

'Holy Jesus Christ! All without a declaration of war?'

'I imagine the declaration of war will be made at the very moment the attacks are launched.'

'Which will be . . . The fleet sails midnight tomorrow. That's 26 November. They'll be in position by about 3 or 4 December.'

'That is correct,' Philip agreed. 'And if I am supposed to encounter them as they return, a week later, they will have launched the attack some time in the three or four days after achieving their position.'

'Not much time,' Graham commented.

'Time enough. You say you have secret codes to London. A message could be in Washington by the time the fleet sails.'

'Um. If they, or London, will believe such a message. But Phil, what are you going to do?'

'Sail with *Yamato*,' Philip said. 'And fight for Japan, if I

444

have to. But if Washington can put out in every broadcast, every newspaper, that they are aware of what the Japanese High Command is doing, I think it will be sufficient to make them abort the attack.'

'That's not to say it will avert war.'

'No,' Philip agreed. 'But at least it will be an honourable war, engaged in after a formal and correct declaration on each side.'

'Yes,' Graham said. 'Yes. But Phil, if this news is leaked it will also launch such a witch-hunt here as Japan has never known.'

'I understand that.'

'But you feel secure.'

'I will have done my duty.'

'Um.' Graham knew that was a totally Japanese point of view. 'This information is couched in the most general terms, of course. It says nothing of what the course the fleet will take is actually going to be, or where the rendezvous point A is situated, exactly. Do you know these things?'

'No. No one knows these things, except Yamamoto. We shall receive such orders at sea. But even if I did know them I would not tell you. I do not wish the Americans to launch a surprise attack on our fleet either, you know. My aim is to make both sides turn away, if that is possible.' He took the envelope back. 'However, in all the circumstances, I doubt that you and I should ever meet again.' He held out his hand, and Graham took it. 'And of course you must stay away from Anne, at all costs.'

'I understand that. But if Japan does mean to attack Hong Kong or Malaya, I won't be here too much longer; I'll be given my passport along with all other British Embassy personnel.' He sighed. 'I'll never be able to tell Washington who gave them this information, you know.'

'I should say, thank God for that,' Philip said, and drove into the night.

*

'Ten o'clock. My goodness, that was a long one,' Anne Freeman said as she washed her hands. 'I hope my husband didn't wait dinner.' She glanced at Nurse Harya. 'Did you manage to telephone your mother?'

'Yes, honourable doctor. But I would be grateful, because of the lateness of the hour, if you would permit me to ride with you in your automobile to Tokyo.'

Anne raised her eyebrows; Harya had never made such a request before, although they had worked late together often enough. Was there at last some thaw in the Japanese woman's reserve? A reserve which had seemed to grow over the past year or so. Dr Azuma had explained it to her: although she had been a member of the staff for eleven years now, and was indeed next in seniority to Azuma himself, there were several members of the nursing staff who still could not accept the idea of a female doctor – and Harya was obviously one of them.

Anne smiled. 'Of course, Nurse Harya. It would be a pleasure.'

It was drizzling, as usual in late November, and she drove slowly, even on the open highway. She had told Philip that she would not be home before eleven, and she should still make that comfortably. While Nurse Harya . . . She glanced at her companion, sitting silently beside her. 'Is there news of your husband?' she asked conversationally.

'Sometimes there is a letter,' Nurse Harya said. 'But when it comes, he is already somewhere else. So I never know.'

'Yes,' Anne said. 'That's tough. I never know where my husband is either, when he's at sea. But at least I know he's on his ship.'

They entered the suburbs of Tokyo.

'You'll have to direct me,' Anne said.

'Take the third on the left, honourable doctor,' Nurse Harya said. 'And then the second on the left again.'

Anne slowed as she approached the corner, turned into

446

the street as directed, and frowned; this looked a very poor neighbourhood. She had no idea that someone like Harya, always so neatly turned out, so clean in her personal habits, could live in a slum area like this. When she took the second left turning, the houses looked even more dilapidated – and remarkably, there was absolutely no one on the street at all; it was not that late.

'The fourth house,' Nurse Harya said, her voice soft. Anne pulled into the side of the road; there was no kerb.

'Well,' she said. 'I hope you find all is well.'

To her surprise, Nurse Harya made no attempt to get out of the car. Instead she turned to look at her, her face sad. 'You understand, honourable doctor,' she said. 'That I did not wish to do this thing. But I have no choice.'

'What on earth are you talking about?' Anne asked, and heard her door opening. She swung back to face it, and caught a glimpse of two men, who reached inside for her arms to jerk her out of the car. She found herself standing in the drizzle, and opened her mouth to scream. A bag was dropped over her head, plunging her into a stifling darkness. For a moment she was too surprised even to kick, and then she felt fingers tearing open the sleeve of her left arm.

'Is it permitted to return home now, honourable sir?' Akiko Harya asked.

Kitabake glanced at her. 'No,' he said. 'You are to accompany us.'

'But my mother-in-law . . . my child . . .'

'General Mori wishes to speak with you,' Kitabake said. 'Get into the van.'

The black van had pulled in behind the parked car; Kitabake now reached inside the car and switched off the lights and ignition, and closed the door. Akiko Harya watched him, watched Anne's inert body being lifted into the van, and turned to follow her. As she did so, one of the waiting men stepped up to her, taking a length of steel pipe from his overcoat pocket, and hit her a tremendous blow across the back of the head.

Akiko Harya dropped without a sound, blood already soaking through her cap.

'You . . . why did you do that?' Kitabake demanded, keeping his voice low with an effort. 'You had no orders.'

'I had orders from General Mori, honourable Captain,' the man said. 'This woman is now useless to us, and knows of us. She could become an embarrassment.' He knelt beside Akiko, felt her heart and then hit her again, with even more savage force. This time her head had nowhere to go, merely ground into the roadway; blood flowed from her nose and mouth.

The man nodded, and one of his companions dragged the dead woman back to Anne's automobile, opened the passenger seat, and draped Akiko half in and half out. Blood trailed away from her head on to the road.

'Whenever you are ready, honourable Captain,' the man who had struck the blow said.

Kitabake inhaled. He had never before watched such cold-blooded murder. But there was nothing he could do about it now. Was there anything he could do about it, at any time? He climbed back into the back of the van, where two more men waited, Anne's unconscious body lying between them. The doors were closed, and the van immediately moved away.

The light was on in the back of the van; curtains were drawn across the small windows. Kitabake knelt beside the woman, watched by Mori's aides, and pulled the bag from her head. Her face was flushed, and half covered in clouding yellow hair, but she breathed evenly. Kitabake moved the hair, and one of the men leaned forward with a strip of sticking-plaster. With great care Kitabake placed the plaster over her eyes. Another piece was provided, and this he affixed across Anne's mouth.

Kitabake remained kneeling, looking down at her. There was more woman here than he had ever seen in his

448

life before, at close quarters; no wonder Mori had for so long dreamed of getting his hands on her. But to do it . . . The wife of a naval officer . . . Yet *he* was already an accomplice in the crime. As he was an accomplice to murder. The thought left him curiously breathless. As he was an accomplice, there was absolutely nothing to stop him, just for instance, touching this woman now, while she lay unconscious. Only the presence of the two men. But the men were members of Mori's staff, and Mori would do whatever he wanted to this woman, with all his staff looking on, sure of their support and encouragement.

And did he not want to touch her? He had never let himself go with a woman in his life. He had never married, and his visits to geisha houses had invariably been disasters. He was, he supposed, afraid of women. Certainly he was afraid of surrendering to them, to the desire of them. But more than any of those things, he was afraid of surrendering to his own baser instincts. He was a Japanese officer. He enjoyed intelligence work, and he was good at it. But he was also a gentleman. When he thought of how Mori had treated Nurse Harya when she had been arrested . . . And when he imagined Mori standing above this woman, his toe in *her* crotch . . . But Mori meant to make Anne Freeman scream. A naval officer's wife.

He drew a long breath. What would it feel like, to . . . His hand touched Anne's neck; she wore skirt and blouse, and her coat was open. His hand slipped lower, and he could feel the flesh, rising and falling beneath his hand, and beneath the three layers of material — blouse, slip and brassière. He could unbutton this shirt and put his hand inside . . . Mori would certainly do that. And then he would feel the warmth, and the nipple. His fingers moved to the button, and then he raised his head. The two men stared at him.

Kitabake got up and sat down. 'The heartbeat is

strong,' he explained. 'It is very necessary to check these things, if she is going to be interrogated.'

The men looked away.

Philip Shimadzu stood in the doorway of his bedroom, and scratched his head. It had been the longest drive home he had ever known – although it had taken just forty minutes. Nor was there any use in looking over his shoulder now. What was done, was done. But all he wanted was to hold Anne in his arms, very tightly. And she was not here.

He looked at his watch; the time was eleven-fifteen. She had said she might be late for supper, but that she would be home by eleven.

He picked up the telephone, gave the number of the Anglo-American hospital, listened to the various clicks. 'Is Dr Freeman still there?' he asked the receptionist. 'This is her husband speaking.'

'Why, no, honourable Captain,' the girl said. 'Dr Freeman left the hospital just after ten this evening. Nurse Harya was with her.'

Philip frowned. It was still only a thirty-minute drive, no matter how heavy the traffic. Late at night it could be done in ten minutes. 'Thank you,' he said. He replaced the receiver and gazed at the wall. She must have had a flat tyre. Although surely she would have been able to reach a telephone and call him; the road from Yokohama was built up almost its entire length, nowadays. So . . . He returned to his car and drove down the highway. Cars passed, to and fro, but none was Anne's. He actually reached the hospital and looked into the car park, but of course her car was not there, either.

He began to know a creeping fear, which affected his stomach like ptomaine poisoning; obviously, he told himself, because his nerves were on edge. Anne had had Nurse Harya with her. What *could* have happened? He went into the hospital, obtained Nurse Harya's home number from the receptionist, called, and received no reply. It was now past midnight. He replaced the receiver. The receptionist, who was busy answering other calls, suddenly frowned back at him. 'It is the police, honourable Captain, seeking to know where you might be found. They have tried your home.'

Philip snatched at the phone.

'Honourable Captain?' asked the lieutenant. 'I'm afraid we have some rather disturbing news. If you will stay there, I will come for you.'

'What news?' Philip shouted. 'What news?'

'Your wife's car has been found abandoned on a Tokyo back street, honourable Captain,' the lieutenant said. 'Wait there, sir, I beg of you. I will come for you immediately.'

Anne awoke to a feeling of deathly cold and total disorientation. She was aware of discomfort, as if she had been bounced on the ground several times, but there was no actual pain, apart from the cold. But she could not see, and her mouth tasted foul . . . and she was cold. And wet.

She realised that someone had just emptied a bucket of water over her, and that she was lying on a stone floor. And that she was both gagged and blindfolded with sticking-plaster. That accounted for all her feelings, save . . . there was something else the matter. She felt air on parts of her body where there should not have been air, and when she moved her feet her bare toes scraped over the coarse surface. Both her shoes and stockings had been removed. She rolled on her back, and felt the coarseness on her buttocks. She was naked!

That realisation brought memory flooding back. Harya, looking at her most apologetically, two men, reaching for her, the thrust of the needle, then nothing. And now she was naked, on a stone floor. Naked! Alone? No, someone had just thrown water over her.

Then it happened again, a flood of ice-cold liquid

which swept through her system and even soaked the blindfold plaster, although without releasing it. She wanted to shout to whoever it was to stop, and could make no sound save a high-pitched moan from the back of her throat, and that she choked off immediately; that was surrender.

'She is awake,' a voice said. She had never heard it before. Then she heard fingers snap.

Hands seized her arms and dragged her to her feet. She knew she was trembling. But it was as much with outrage as with fear or cold. Because she wasn't afraid at all. How could she be afraid, even of kidnappers? She was the wife of Philip Shimadzu, the most senior captain in the Japanese Navy, soon to be an admiral. How could she be afraid?

Someone was standing immediately in front of her. She sensed this, and could smell him. 'Such beauty,' the man said, the same man who had just spoken. 'Such beauty.'

Fingers pulled her nipples. She had large nipples, and the cold had made them hard. But only Philip had ever been allowed to touch those nipples, for more than ten years. Her sense of outrage grew, and she knew the man must be standing very close. She tensed her muscles and brought up her right knee, with all her force and quite without warning, feeling it crash into cloth, with flesh beyond. There was a gasp and a moan from in front of her. She expected a blow back, but only felt the hands on her arms tightening.

'Are you all right, honourable General?' asked a new voice.

'Bitch,' the first voice moaned. This was obviously the 'general'. 'Bitch.'

The general, she thought. That suggested some kind of military organisation. That suggested . . . Her muscles sagged with fear as she realised into whose hands she had fallen.

'I will put her in a cell,' the other man suggested. 'Until

452

you are feeling better.' Strangely, this voice had an undercurrent of amused contempt in it.

'No,' the general said, his voice less agonised. 'She has struck a Japanese officer. She must be whipped. Take her to the bar.'

The hands holding Anne's arms forced her forward, and she went with them, her bare feet stumbling over the stone floor. She wanted to fight them, but she knew the futility of it, and her brain was clouded with the understanding that she was in the hands of the Kempai. She did not wish to give them an excuse to hurt her. As if they were not going to do that, anyway. They were going to whip her. Whip *her*! Anne Freeman Shimadzu. It was not possible. It just could not be happening.

But it was, and Harya was a part of it. That was almost the most difficult part of the whole catastrophe to accept. Harya, who had worked with her for so many years, who . . . She felt cold steel against her groin, and automatically doubled forward. When she tried to straighten, she was held in that position, and her arms carried forward, and down, and then pulled apart and strapped to other pieces of cold steel. The uprights. She realised that she had been bent over a bar. Her legs . . . But the hands now grasped her legs, pulling them apart also, and securing her ankles to the uprights. She tugged, tentatively, but knew immediately she was not going to free herself. She was trussed, wrists almost to ankles, buttocks uppermost, in the most humiliating position any woman could find herself. And she could not even scream.

Her hair had flopped forward and was covering her face; she could feel the blood pounding in her temples as it rushed into her head. The noise seemed to obliterate the sound of the voices, and she had to concentrate on breathing, for fear she would choke on her own hair. But why didn't she want to choke? Would that not save her a great deal of pain? Of agony?

But she intended to live, and be avenged, and . . . The

first stroke of the bamboo cane was like a knife, cutting into her flesh. Her head jerked, and she gasped right through the sticking-plaster. But she had barely caught her breath when the second stroke cut even more deeply than the first. She moaned, and writhed, and felt the steel bar pressing into her flesh, and tried to tense her muscles to resist the third blow . . . and felt nothing. Instead she heard a voice saying, 'Go on, get out. Get out.'

Another voice, the one which had earlier been amused, said, 'I must protest, honourable General. This is the wife of a naval officer.'

'Get out,' the general said again.

Anne listened to doors closing, and got her breathing under control, and felt the searing pain, and wondered what was going to happen next . . . And felt the general's hands where the cane had descended, moments before, massaging her tortured flesh, and then moving between her legs, seeking her hair, and more . . . and knew, that her ordeal had only just begun.

Philip stared at the body of Nurse Harya, lying on the table in the police morgue. Although the back of her skull was a shattered mess, the rest of her was remarkably undamaged, poignantly petite. A woman he had often seen, and spoken to, in life, whenever he had had occasion to visit the Anglo-American hospital. Her face had always been calm. It was calm now. She had not known she was about to die.

'It looks very much as if Mrs Shimadzu has been kidnapped,' the police inspector was saying. 'In a most brutal fashion, seeing as how the thugs were prepared to murder Nurse Harya. And it was a premeditated crime. Nurse Harya was neither assaulted before death, nor was anything of value taken from her person. It was Mrs Shimadzu the brigands wanted. I want to assure you, honourable Captain, that we are doing all in our power to find some trace of these people. We shall. But it may take time. I must ask you, honourable Captain, to return to your home and wait. If the kidnappers contact you, as they undoubtedly will, seeking a ransom, you must come to us immediately.'

Philip gazed at him for a few minutes, and left the morgue. He got into his automobile and drove home, not knowing what he was doing. He could not believe what had happened. Anne, kidnapped? It was just not possible. But then, was it possible to imagine Nurse Harya with her skull split open? But that led to thoughts of Anne in the hands of people who could commit such a crime.

He closed the door behind him and stood in the lounge without even removing his shoes, staring from wall to wall. There was so much to be thought about, so much to be considered. Kidnappers! It was not a common crime in Tokyo. Therefore . . . But his brain rejected other, more terrifying concepts, could consider only that she should have been here, waiting for him. They should have been sitting down to their goodnight cup of sake together, and then lying on their mattress together, and enjoying the mutual warmth and comfort, and from time to time the surging passion, of two people who loved, and were also in love.

Instead . . . what was he going to do? He looked at his watch. It was two o'clock in the morning. Certainly he was not going to sleep. But what else could he do? Tell his mother? That made no sense. It would distress Shikibu and it would not help the situation. The same went for contacting Iyeyasu. Because there was always the chance this whole business would be resolved within twelve hours or so. A simple ransom demand . . . He had lots of money. So did Anne, and they maintained joint owner-ship of everything. Let the kidnappers ask for what-ever they wished, so long as she could be safely returned . . . If only his eyes did not constantly see the body of Akiko Harya, her skull split open by two savage blows.

He spun round as he heard a knock on his front door. Could they possibly have come here? No, they would not dare do that. But if they had; his fingers curled into fists, and he looked at his swords, hanging on the wall. Then he realised it might be Anne herself, miraculously escaped. He ran across the floor, slid the door open, gazed at . . . Ikita Kitabake.

'May I come in, Captain Shimadzu?' Kitabake asked.

'Now?' Philip demanded.

'It is very important,' Kitabake said.

Philip stood aside. Whatever Kitabake wanted, it would at least help to pass the time until the arrival of the ransom demand.

Kitabake removed his shoes and went into the lounge. 'You are waiting for your wife to return home?'

'Yes,' Philip said, alarm bells starting to ring in his brain.

'She will not return,' Kitabake said. 'The Kempai have arrested her. She is in the hands of General Mori.'

Philip stared at him. 'Mori?' His brain just could not take in the extent of the catastrophe. And yet, had his subconscious known this, all along?

Kitabake sighed, and sat down without being invited. 'I am betraying my position,' he said. 'There is nothing left for me but seppuku. But possibly there is nothing left for you but seppuku either, Shimadzu San.'

Philip dropped to his knees beside him. 'Tell me,' he said, his voice low and hard.

Kitabake shrugged. 'Mori has long suspected your wife of passing classified information to the British naval attaché, John Graham, under cover of their so-called love affair. We have never been able to obtain any proof of this. We even inserted Nurse Harya into Dr Freeman's office, to report on Dr Freeman's conversations with Graham, and learned nothing more than that your wife steadfastly refused to tell him what he wanted to know.

But Mori was determined that she was guilty. Partly this was, I think, to avenge himself on you, Shimadzu San, for what happened in Shanghai. He often said he wanted to implicate you as well. But I do not believe that is the whole truth of the matter. He wanted Dr Freeman. He . . . ' He sighed. 'He is my superior. I obeyed my orders, as I am required to do. He may have been right. So tonight . . . '

'Tonight you murdered Nurse Harya, and abducted my wife,' Philip said.

'I did not know Harya was to be executed,' Kitabake said, with dignity. 'That was carried out by Mori's men. But I arrested your wife, yes, as ordered to do so, and took her to Kempai Headquarters. And there . . . ' Another sigh. 'There I discovered what I have always feared. That Mori merely intended to abuse her sexually, and thus avenge himself upon you and gratify his own urges at the same time.'

Philip drew a long, slow breath. Once he had held that man at the end of the barrel of a pistol. 'And you did nothing to prevent this?'

'I left, and came here, Shimadzu San. I feel I have been dishonoured. I feel you have been dishonoured. I feel the entire Japanese Navy has been dishonoured.'

'Yes,' Philip said. 'And so you mean to commit seppuku, feeling that will make everything all right. And you would have me do the same.'

Kitabake looked surprised at his tone. 'What else is left for us?'

'We can get my wife out of Kempai Headquarters,' Philip said. 'And avenge her rape.'

Kitabake frowned. 'But that is impossible.'

'Why?'

'Because . . . well . . . '

'Because Mori is our senior officer? Mori should have been hanged, years ago.'

'Because it is impossible,' Kitabake repeated. 'The

457

Kempai Prison? It is the most strongly guarded place in Japan.'

'But you can come and go as you please.'

'Of course . . . ' Kitabake realised what Philip was thinking of. 'But once I attempted to release Mrs Shimadzu, I would need an army to fight my way out of there.'

'An army,' Philip said thoughtfully.

'Well, at least half a dozen dedicated men. Men who would not be afraid to die.'

Philip pointed. 'And you have already determined to die, Kitabake San. Therefore you will at least die with honour. More honour than merely slitting your belly open. Swear that to me.'

Kitabake sat straight. 'How may an officer in the Japanese Navy do less than that, Shimadzu San? If it were possible to rescue your wife, even if we died in the process, I would willingly assist, not only to save her from further shame, but to save the navy from further shame. But as it is impossible . . . '

'Just sit there,' Philip recommended. 'And wait.' He picked up the telephone.

John Graham came through the door, then halted, staring at Kitabake. He gave a brief laugh. 'Changed your mind again, Philip? I'm afraid it won't do any good, now; I've already relayed your message to London.'

'Message?' Kitabake asked. 'What message?'

'Shut up,' Philip said. 'And you shut up too, John. Just sit down and listen to me.'

Graham frowned at him, but sat down. And listened.

'My God!' he said, when Philip had finished. 'I really hadn't thought that would happen.'

'It has happened,' Philip said. 'So as you say, I have changed my mind again, John. I want Anne out of there tonight.'

'Bit of a tall order,' Graham said.

'Is it?'

Graham frowned some more, as Philip's intentions slowly dawned on him. 'You have got to be mad. You'll never do it.'

'Kitabake will get us in. But we'll need assistance to get back out.'

'Oh, yes? We?'

'I need every man you can raise.'

'Now I know you are mad, Phil. I can't ask my people to do something like that. I can't just destroy my organisation, to . . . well . . . ' He flushed.

'Organisation?' Kitabake asked. 'What organisation?'

'You can't ask them to rescue my wife,' Philip said. 'Who is at this very moment being raped and tortured by Mori.'

'Well, my dear fellow . . . '

'I have just given you the most valuable information any British naval attaché has ever received in history,' Philip said, grinding the words out. 'Now I am asking for payment. And isn't your organisation about to be destroyed, anyway?'

'Not necessarily,' Graham said. 'It will continue to function even with me gone.'

'Then you refuse to help me? You wish me just to sit here while Mori abuses my wife until he's ready to execute her?'

'Well,' Graham scratched his head and looked at Kitabake, who was clearly totally nonplussed by what he was hearing. 'I don't really think you have considered this matter in its entirety, Phil. Let us suppose I do help you, and we get in, and even manage to rescue Anne, and aren't actually shot to pieces but manage to regain the streets of Tokyo, what happens next? We all commit seppuku? If that is the case, I don't see that we've achieved all that much.'

Philip gazed at him.

'There are other points as well,' Graham went on.

'What about the rest of the family? Your mother? Iyeyasu?'

Philip sighed, and his shoulders slumped. He actually had not thought of them at all. 'So it is seppuku, after all.'

'That depends on how badly you want Anne out of there.'

Philip raised his head sharply, his heart pounding.

'It might just be done,' Graham said. 'But not for at least twenty-four hours.'

'Twenty-four hours?' Philip shouted. 'You expect me to leave Anne in there for twenty-four hours?'

'Well, it's actually less than that. About eighteen hours.' Graham glanced at Kitabake. 'Is she likely to be executed in that time?'

Kitabake shook his head. 'I do not think Mori will tire of her in that time.'

'Tire of her?' Philip cried. 'My God . . .'

'So she will still be alive. And she's old enough and tough enough to survive a few beatings, surely. The operative word is alive,' Graham said.

'You . . . you can just say that,' Philip gasped. 'You don't know what the Kempai do to people. My God, the wire . . .'

'Mori will not use the wire,' Kitabake said. 'Until he is ready to destroy her. The use of the wire is irreversible.'

'You don't know when he will decide to destroy her,' Philip groaned. 'And until then . . .'

'We have simply got to keep our nerves, and trust in Mori's lust. I'm sorry, Phil, but there it is,' Graham said. 'I am terribly sorry this has happened, but now that it has, we simply have to look the facts squarely in the face, and decide our best course of action. Do you want my help, or not? If I help you, it will mean destroying my own organisation, virtually. That will be going against everything I was taught. And not even for one of my own people.'

'You wouldn't describe Anne as one of your own people?'

460

Graham flushed. 'Well, do you wish my help?'

'Of course. But why do we have to wait twenty-four hours?'

'Simply because, firstly, I have to make contact with some of my people; that will take time, and it is already nearly dawn. Secondly, whatever we do has to be done at night. Thirdly, there is a British ship sailing from Yokohama at midnight tonight – that is, in twenty hours' time. Don't you think we should endeavour to be on that ship? It's bound for Los Angeles.'

'My God,' Philip thought. 'I never thought of that.' He frowned. 'But won't they send after us?'

'I don't think they will,' Graham said, 'in view of everything else that's going to be happening tonight. Superior officers, and especially Yamamoto, are not going to be available, and all anyone will know is that you took your wife back from the hands of the Kempai, supposing you succeed. That will be a serious breach of discipline and security, but not necessarily treason. And an international incident right now, such as stopping a British ship on the high seas to arrest some of its passengers, might just mess up a whole lot of plans. And the fourth point is that twenty hours will give you time to get Iyeyasu out of the academy. You are entitled to do that. His stepmother has been kidnapped, for ransom. You are distraught. You can also get hold of your mother. You don't have to tell them anything. Just have them handy, and make a rendezvous with them for tomorrow night.'

Philip stared at his friend. 'You really are a born conspirator.'

Graham grinned. 'Let's say I was trained to it. But Phil, I think Captain Kitabake should also spend the day in your company. Just in case he has second thoughts.'

'I do not understand,' Kitabake said. 'You mean to escape Japan? You, Shimadzu? At a time like this?'

'Can I remain?'

'You will be pronounced a traitor,' Kitabake pointed

out. 'As soon as . . . ' He glanced at Graham, unsure how much, if anything, the Britisher really knew. 'You know what I mean.'

'If I am a traitor,' Philip said. 'Has not Mori made me so?'

Kitabake sighed. 'It is sad. And you . . . *Yamato* . . .the navy . . . '

'Dreams,' Philip said. 'A man should never dream. Kitabake San, you have declared your intention of committing seppuku. Will you not at least assist me to rescue my wife first, that you may die without a stain on your conscience? I will give you my sacred word that my wife has never done anything in her life to harm Japan.'

Kitabake stared at him.

The douche of cold water awoke Anne. Incredible that she should have slept, lying on a cold stone floor. But she had been exhausted, and afraid to move. She had never realised how mentally immobilising it was to be suddenly blinded, to know there were people all around her, watching her every movement, waiting to kick her or beat her . . . or rape her again. Certainly it had been more than once. When the 'general' had finished, he had called his men back, and commanded one of them to enter her. Apparently he had wanted to watch. The other men had laughed, and made obscene jokes. Only one voice had been conspicuously absent: that of the man who had protested against her treatment. One gentleman, one honourable man, amongst so many.

She had not fought any more, even when they had released her from the bar and allowed her to stand. Instead, her knees had given way and she had merely slumped to the floor. She still had not been fully able to believe what had happened to her, the pain and the shame and the humiliation. She had lain on the floor, helpless, and been dragged some feet away over the stone floor, and there left. If she had then moved her hands and feet cautiously, it had been experimental. She had raised her hands, to touch the plasters across her mouth and eyes, perhaps to pull them off, if only to be able to lick her lips – her throat was absolutely parched. But immediately she had been prodded in the ribs by a booted toe. She had then lain still.

And slept? For how long? She had no idea. Only the increasingly unbearable thirst, to which were now added the rumbles of her empty belly, made her realise it must have been for some time. And she was again cold. But was she ever going to be warm again?

Had she surrendered? She refused to admit that. She had closed her brain to what was happening, because in doing that lay her only defence. Her brain must stay closed until Philip came for her. She knew he would. She had to be certain he would. If she ceased to believe that, then she might as well cease to live.

But he had not yet come, and there was another hour of agony in front of her. Only an hour? Pray that it could only be an hour.

'Well, Dr Freeman,' the general said. 'Are you ready to speak with us?'

Anne turned her head towards the sound, and pushed herself to sit up. That was instinctive; she felt too vulnerable lying down. But she was too vulnerable, no matter what she did.

A hand touched her head, and another seized the end of the sticking-plaster and whipped it from her mouth. The pain was intense, but the relief was enormous. Would they now free her eyes?

Apparently not.

'Last night we played with you,' the general said. 'Today we are going to play with you again. But this time we wish you to talk to us. We wish you to tell us of your husband's treachery.'

Anne opened her mouth, but no words would come out. She licked her lips.

'She is thirsty,' the general said. 'Give her something to drink.'

A mug of water was held to her lips, and uptilted. A lot of it ran down her neck and on to her body. But sufficient got down her throat. It tasted like nectar.

'Well, Dr Freeman?' the general asked.

'Treachery?' Anne asked. 'I know nothing of any treachery.'

'Do you deny having a regular rendezvous with Commander Graham, and passing him information? Secret information, about the Imperial Japanese Navy? Tell us about that, Dr Freeman.'

Anne's brain flickered. How could they know about that? Harya! My God, Harya. But Harya did not know what she had said to Graham. Yet they knew what Philip meant to do. But how could they, when he had not done it yet, and the only person he had discussed it with was her? They were guessing. Because Philip had been right all along; her seeing Graham had become known to the Kempai. Therefore the fault was hers. And Philip was in danger.

'Come along, Dr Freeman,' the voice said.

'My husband is an officer in the Imperial Japanese Navy,' she said. 'A senior officer. He has committed no treachery. And when he learns what you have done to me . . .'

She felt his breath on her face. 'I am going to *hurt* you, Dr Freeman,' the voice said. 'Oh, I am going to *hurt* you.'

Anne sucked air into her lungs. Do your damndest, she thought. Oh, do your damndest, General Mori. Because suddenly she knew who he was, who he had to be.

Hands grasped her arms and dragged her to her feet, half pulled and half pushed her across the room again. Back to the bar? No, this time she brought up against the edge of a table, and now they were seizing her legs as well to lift her from the floor. She did not fight them; she lay inert in their hands, as they stretched her on her back. The

464

table was made of steel, and was thus a special table. Oh, yes, she realised, it was a special table; her legs and arms were being pulled apart, as far as they would extend, and secured by leather straps, which were obviously permanent fixtures. Was she to be raped again? She could hardly imagine she was in the least attractive at this moment, all her make-up gone, her hair plastered to her scalp, her body a lather of dried sweat.

Yet she tried to tense her muscles when she felt the fingers on her breasts again. Touching her nipples. Always her nipples. Mori was fascinated by those nipples . . . But he was not playing with them this morning. Instead the fingers were attaching something metallic to each teat, something which gripped and at the same time bit into her flesh. Something . . . There was a sudden bolt of pain, unlike anything she had ever felt before, seeming to cut through her chest almost like a liquid bullet. The scream which issued from her throat was entirely involuntary – a gush of agony, even as the arc her body made, straining against the leather straps which secured her wrists and ankles, was equally involuntary.

She hit the table as she came down, mouth sagging, breath rasping, whole body tingling and trembling.

'There now, you see, Dr Freeman,' Mori said. 'That hurt. And there are even more interesting, and more tender, places for us to attach these clips, you know. So why do you not tell us about your husband's treachery?'

O Philip, Anne thought. O Philip, please hurry. Please, please hurry. Or it will be too late.

'Oh, my dear boy,' Shikibu said. 'Oh, my dear boy.' She held Philip close. 'Why did you not come to me sooner?'

He had, in fact, delayed going to Shikibu until the last possible moment, until after he had brought Iyeyasu from the academy; the superintendent had raised no objections – he had indeed been anxious to help.

'I kept hoping something would turn up,' he explained.

'You poor darling,' Shikibu said, and then embraced Iyeyasu as well. 'You must be so worried.' Not for the first time she looked at Ikita Kitabake with a somewhat puzzled expression. 'What are we going to do?'

'I am expecting a call from the kidnappers,' Philip said. 'I am hoping to see them tonight, and get Anne back, if it is possible.'

'Are the police going to cooperate?'

'Oh, yes,' Philip said. 'They are standing by. Everyone is going to help. That is why Captain Kitabake is here. You have met Captain Kitabake?'

Kitabake gave a stiff bow. He had grown increasingly morose and silent throughout the day, but Philip felt sure it was the thought of his own approaching suicide; he did not think he would let them down, now. He dared not think that.

'You are so kind, honourable Captain,' Shikibu said. 'It is reassuring to know that my son's fellow officers are rallying round, at a time like this.'

Time, Philip thought. Time! His mother was clearly both surprised and gratified at his air of massive calm; she had no idea of the surging fears and emotions which were making him want to scream, and drink several bottles of sake, and sink into blissful oblivion.

And of all the tensions pulling him apart, time was the worst. His eyes kept dropping to his watch. It was five o'clock in the afternoon, and already almost dark. Graham had to move soon, or they might miss the ship. But it meant that Anne had now been in Mori's hands for nineteen hours. Nineteen hours of mistreatment and abuse . . . and perhaps of worse. Nineteen hours!

He dared not consider what was going to happen this evening. There were too many imponderables. He did not know what he would find when he broke into the Kempai Headquarters, or even if he would succeed in breaking in. Or out again. He did not know what Shikibu's and Iyeyasu's reactions were going to be when they learned the truth, that they were about to flee their country forever; he had not even been able to risk telling them to pack any clothes. And he did not even know what *his* reaction was going to be, when this was over. He was destroying his career, his dreams, his entire life . . . to save perhaps an already destroyed wife. There was no logic in that. But when was love, or honour, or manhood, logical?

The telephone rang. The four people all sat straight, and Philip picked up the receiver. It had to be Graham.

'Philip? Admiral Yamamoto.'

'Admiral? But . . . ' Yamamoto was with the fleet, waiting off Hokkaido in the north.

'I am about to embark, Philip,' Yamamoto said. 'But I had to call; my dear boy, I have just learned your dreadful situation. Philip, I am so very sorry.'

'Thank you, honourable Admiral.'

'Is there news?'

'I am hoping to hear shortly.'

'She will come back to you, Philip. Of this I am sure. Have faith in that.'

'I will, honourable Admiral.'

'But Philip, at this greatest moment in our country's history, nothing, I repeat nothing, can stand in the way of our duty. I know you understand this.'

'Yes, honourable Admiral.'

'Therefore, no matter what happens, Philip, you will bring *Yamato* to me, in a fortnight's time. That will be the sweetest sight I can see, *Yamato* steaming over the horizon, with you on her bridge. And Philip, by then we will have been launched on the greatest adventure in history. Victory or death, Philip. But it will be victory. Remember this, and come to me, with *Yamato*.'

The phone went dead. Philip looked at his mother.

'The admiral?' she asked. 'He is a great man.'

'Yes,' Philip said. Who is about to steam blindly to disaster, taking his country with him, no matter how many temporary triumphs he achieves along the way. And who expects me, in honour, to be at his side. But where did honour begin and end? He thought it was not a word he would ever wish to hear again.

Shikibu prepared a light supper, but they hardly ate anything. Iyeyasu was so bewildered by the whole situation it was almost tragic to look at him. His life had always been so serene and secure, his future so preordained. As *his* had always been, Philip thought. Now, the boy could only think that his dearly beloved stepmother had been kidnapped. He had no idea, yet, that his future was also about to be shattered beyond repair.

And it was nearly time. 'Now, honourable Mother, listen to me very carefully,' Philip said. 'When I receive a telephone call, shortly, I am going to go out with Captain Kitabake. We will use the captain's car. When we have done that, I wish you and Iyeyasu to take my car — Iyeyasu will drive you — and go down to Yokohama. Go to the Green Funnel docks, berth number six, park the car, and stay there. Anne and I will come to you.'

Shikibu frowned at him. 'I do not understand. Do you mean that Anne is in Yokohama? That you know where she is?'

'I . . . we believe so,' Philip said. 'I must ask you to do this thing for me, Mother. I will explain it all when we come to you. I promise you this.'

'Well . . . ' Shikibu looked at her grandson.

'We must do as honourable Father wishes,' Iyeyasu said. 'But I would prefer to accompany you, sir.'

'Your duty is to take your grandmother to Yokohama,' Philip said. 'This is vitally important. Go there, and wait. There is a Green Funnel ship in berth six. She is due to sail at midnight. Wait there until either I bring Anne to you, or the ship sails. If I have not come to you by then, return home, and wait for me here.'

He could do nothing more than that. And if that happened? They could commit seppuku as a family.

468

'I understand, honourable Father,' Iyeyasu said, even if he clearly did not. But he was resolved to obey his father in everything; he still wore the uniform of a naval cadet – for the last time.

The telephone rang again. Philip looked at his watch. It was eight o'clock. He picked up the receiver.

'Move,' Graham said.

'Where is General Mori?' Captain Kitabake asked.

The captain on the guard desk stood to attention. 'The general has gone to dinner, honourable Captain.'

His gaze flickered over Philip, whom he clearly recognised, and then over the other men. He was equally clearly totally surprised.

'And the woman prisoner,' Kitabake asked.

Once again the captain stared at Philip. 'I believe she awaits further interrogation, honourable Captain.'

Philip gave a faint sigh of relief.

Kitabake was nodding. 'I will go through to her immediately. You will observe that I have placed Commander Graham under arrest?'

The Kempai captain looked at Graham uncertainly. The Scot's wrists were handcuffed, and he was escorted by four men in the uniform of naval policemen. Only four men. Kitabake had been appalled, and Philip had himself been taken aback. But Graham would use only volunteers, and as he had said, if they could not do it with four men, then they would need four thousand.

'I do not understand,' the Kempai captain said.

'This is an outrage against international law,' Graham declared. 'There will be considerable repercussions.'

'I have acted on General Mori's personal command,' Kitabake said.

'I did not know of this,' said the guard captain.

'Nevertheless, the general gave his orders to me. You will admit us, Captain.'

'Yes, but . . . ' The captain turned his bewildered gaze

469

on Philip, who nodded, as grimly as he could.

'I know,' he said. 'My wife has proved a traitor to Japan. So I am told. A confrontation with this man will prove the matter one way or the other.'

The captain gave a faint sigh, no doubt thanking the gods that he was unmarried, and he would therefore never have to face such a terrible situation. 'I will telephone to the inner guard.'

'No,' Kitabake said. 'The woman must not be forewarned. It is essential that she be confronted with this English spy before she understands what has happened. You will merely admit us.'

The officer hesitated, and then nodded. 'Very well. Your people will remain here, however, Captain Kitabake. Only Kempai personnel are allowed into this building, as you well know. And . . . ' He glanced from Graham to Philip. 'Those with business here.'

Philip looked at Graham's men; their muscles were visibly tensing, and their hands were dropping towards their holsters.

But Kitabake appeared unconcerned. 'Of course,' he said. 'You will remain here,' he told the men. 'But try to stay awake.' He nodded. 'We are ready, Captain.'

The captain unlocked the door behind his desk. There were actually only three men on guard duty, in this outer office of what merely looked like a large office building in downtown Tokyo. They could have been overwhelmed, presumably; but Kitabake had assured them that he could get them to Anne without resorting to violence, which would necessarily give them away. If the four men they had left behind did not betray themselves by nerves. But Graham seemed unconcerned by the situation, although he was giving a very good impression of a deeply injured and frightened man. And once through the door and into an inner room, Philip was very glad they had followed Kitabake's advice; there was another complete guard in here, a dozen men, off duty, playing cards, talking or reading . . . But still twelve men with weapons close to hand, who leapt to attention as the officers entered.

The captain pointed. 'You,' he said to one of the men. 'You will take Captain Kitabake and Captain Shimadzu and their prisoner to the lower level.'

The man stood to attention, put on his cap and strapped on his automatic pistol.

'Down there,' the captain said.

Kitabake nodded. 'Do you not suppose I know the way, Captain?' he inquired.

Philip gave Graham an appropriate push, and the four of them went through a door at the end of the guard-room, and found themselves in a long corridor. Several offices opened off it, but at night they appeared to be locked and empty; yet Philip had a sudden understanding of how Peter might have felt, as he and his fellows had invaded the Admiralty.

At the end of the corridor there were staircases, one leading up and the other down. The soldier escorted them to this, and took them down, into a world of bare electric light bulbs, stone floors and the stench of disinfectant.

At the foot of the stairs there were four more soldiers playing cards; they also stood to attention at the sight of the officers.

'This will do, soldier,' Kitabake said. 'You may return to your post. 'You,' he said to one of the waiting men. 'Do you know who I am?'

'Of course, honourable Captain. You are honourable Captain Kitabake,' the man said.

'And you have the key to Level B?'

'Yes, honourable Captain. But General Mori instructed that the level was not to be opened until his return.'

'This is urgent,' Kitabake said. 'And is being done on General Mori's orders. Give me the key.'

The man hesitated. But not only was Kitabake a senior

471

officer in both the navy and the Kempai, and accompanied by another man wearing the uniform of a captain in the navy, as well as by a prisoner, but he was also known to be Mori's right-hand man. He gave Kitabake the key.

Kitabake led them along the corridor, and unlocked the door. Philip's heart was pounding so hard he thought he was going to be sick. The door swung inwards, and they stepped through – into darkness, but a world of odours. Kitabake closed the door and switched on the light, and Philip inhaled sharply. His gaze took in the benches, tables, bar, the instruments hanging on the walls . . . No Torquemada had ever possessed such an array of ghastly tools.

'There,' Graham said.

Philip ran forward. Anne lay on the floor, naked, and though there was no blood, no obvious cuts on her body, *bruised*. Her wrists were tied together behind her back, and there was a strip of plaster across her eyes. She was either asleep or unconscious, but certainly alive; her breasts moved as she breathed. He stood above her for a moment, afraid to touch her, It was as if every pore in her body was crying out, silently telling him the hundred and one things that had been done to her.

He knelt, lifted her shoulders, cradled her in his arms.

'No,' she whispered. 'Please, no.'

'It is Philip,' he said, and pulled the plaster from her eyes.

She winced, and blinked, and wept – but the tears were partly joy and partly the shock of seeing light again after so long. She shuddered, squeezed her eyes shut, and then opened them again. 'Philip,' she whispered, clinging to him. 'Oh Philip.'

'Would you mind releasing me,' Graham said to Kitabake. 'The sooner we're out of here, the better.'

Kitabake unlocked the handcuffs, while Philip looked around the huge, empty room. Anne shivered constantly, and was clearly suffering from prolonged shock; there was no sign of her clothes. But there were some blankets in a corner. 'We're going to take you home,' he promised. 'All the way home.' Gently he laid her on the floor, and went to the blankets.

'Now, do you think you can talk us back out again?' Graham was asking Kitabake.

'Of course. But I am not going to.'

'Eh?'

'I have done what my honour demanded. I intend to remain here, and when Mori comes, as come he must, I will demand my swords, and the right of seppuku,' Kitabake explained.

'And what happens to us?' Graham demanded.

Kitabake bowed. 'I would recommend that you follow the same procedure. However, if you must try to leave, what happens must lie in the hands of the gods.'

Graham looked at Philip, who was wrapping Anne in a blanket and lifting her from the floor. Philip returned the look, put his hand in his pocket and drew his revolver. 'You will accompany us, out of here, Kitabake San. This is my understanding of our bargain. When we leave, you may commit suicide, if you wish.'

Kitabake stared at him.

'My sentiments exactly,' Graham said, producing an automatic pistol. 'Let's go.'

'Philip,' Anne moaned. 'O Philip.'

'Just five minutes, my dearest girl,' Philip said, holding her close with his left arm. Five minutes, he thought, to freedom, or to eternity. 'But you are going to have to walk,' he said. 'Stay immediately behind me.'

'I can walk,' Anne said, releasing him and holding the blanket herself.

Graham had opened the door. 'Let's go,' he said again.

Kitabake hesitated, then went to the door and stopped once more. The voice of Mori drifted to them, quite plainly. 'Captain Kitabake is down here?'

*

473

Kitabake looked at them.

'Oh, Christ,' Graham said. 'That guard captain must have telephoned him.' He closed the door.

'We are lost,' Kitabake said. 'But if we all call for our swords . . .'

'Bugger that,' Graham said, and felt in his other jacket pocket. 'Catch.' He tossed Philip a Mills bomb, held another in his own hand. 'I kind of suspected the going might get rough. If we have to go, we're going to take the Kempai with us. Right?'

'Right,' Philip said, and looked at Anne. She said nothing, but there could be no doubting her resolution, or her determination to die rather than be recaptured.

'You in there,' Mori called. 'Open this door and surrender. You cannot escape. There are twelve armed men out here. I am talking to you, Kitabake. You have just committed suicide.'

'Twelve,' Graham said. 'That's most of the upstairs guard as well. They're making it easy.' He had already pulled the pin from his grenade. Now he counted to twelve. 'Dive,' he said. He pulled the door open and rolled the bomb along the floor into the corridor, at the same time flattening himself against the inner wall. The explosion was almost instantaneous, an immense shock wave which reverberated through the inner room and pinned both Philip and Anne against the wall, while their eardrums seemed to have been punctured.

Kitabake had been blown right off his feet. Now he sat up, reaching for his own pistol. 'Betrayed,' he cried. 'Betrayed.'

Graham levelled his arm, and shot him through the head.

'God almighty,' Philip said. 'I am *glad* you're on our side.'

'Training,' Graham explained, and stepped into the corridor. The men outside lay scattered about, four of them dead, the other eight bleeding and mutilated, groaning as they tried to collect their wits; the floor was slippery with blood.

'Look out!' Anne screamed, and Philip turned, to see Mori, at the very back, slowly trying to regain his feet; he had obviously avoided the worst of the blast by being at the rear of the crowd trying to break down the door.

Now he snarled. 'Shimadzu,' he said. 'You!'

Philip shot him through the heart, and fired twice more.

'Was that Mori?' Anne asked.

'Yes,' Philip said.

'Thank God,' she whispered.

'The stairs,' Graham said, drawing another Mills bomb from his pocket and running in front of them.

There was a great deal of noise from up there – men shouting, alarm bells jangling. Graham lifted the bomb to his mouth, pulled the pin with his teeth, and charged at the stairs, making the action of a fast bowler at cricket, leaping at the moment of delivery and releasing the bomb to send it flying through the air at almost roof level. It landed on the upper floor and exploded on impact, tearing a vast hole in the floor itself, destroying the stairhead. Several men fell through the gap, gasping and screaming. Graham continued on his way, vaulted upwards, and reached the next level. Philip was immediately behind him, grasping Anne round the thighs to lift her up, then pulling himself up by the shattered timbers.

'Use your bomb,' Graham snapped.

The corridor in front of them was packed with men staring at them in consternation, unable to bring themselves to fire on an officer. Philip had already drawn the pin from the bomb and counted to twelve. Now he hurled it into their midst. One of the men actually caught it, realised what it was, gave a shriek, and dropped it; it exploded between his legs, filling the hallway with smoke.

Graham was already running towards the door, leaping over dead and dying men, apparently out of bombs, but with his pistol in his hand. As he did so, the outer door opened, and one of his men looked in. 'We did not know what to do,' he admitted.

Graham looked at the three men lying dead behind the desk, and through the open door at the automobile waiting, engine running, one of his people behind the wheel. 'You did fine,' he said. 'Just fine.'

Shikibu held Anne close. 'Oh Anne,' she said. 'My dear girl. Oh Anne. But I do not understand.' She looked above Anne's head at Philip. 'You want us to board that ship? To flee Japan? Now, Philip, you know I cannot do that.'

'You *do* not understand,' Philip said. 'I cannot remain here. I have just destroyed Kempai Headquarters.'

'I know you have,' Shikibu said. 'Our lives have been a tragedy, Philip. My entire life has been a tragedy. And you . . . you were going to be the one to redeem it all. But you married an American, and she betrayed you.'

'No, Mother,' Philip cried. 'No. She did not. She is innocent. I am the one who has betrayed Japan. But I refute that, too. I have tried to save Japan, from the rule of people like Mori, and his superiors, like Tojo. Even from Yamamoto. They seek only to rule by the laws of bushido. And bushido has no place in this world today. Mother, you must believe that.'

'I believe nothing,' Shikibu said. 'Save that Japan, and the Japanese people, have a destiny. Circumstances have forced you to go against that destiny, my son. As circumstances slew my husband, and my brother, and my eldest son. I am stricken by the gods. But I shall not desert my country.'

'Mother,' Philip said desperately.

'You either bring her by force,' Graham said. 'Or you leave her. The ship is ready to sail.'

Philip hesitated, and Shikibu pulled herself free of his arms. 'I will walk,' she said. 'Back to Tokyo.'

'Have you ever had the feeling that you are damned,' Philip said.

'Aren't we all damned?' Anne asked.

He gazed at the blue water sparkling away from the ship's sides. They had been at sea eleven days. And as Graham had prophesied, no attempt had been made to halt them. There were more important matters in hand, and not enough senior officers to decide what should be done. Isoroku Yamamoto was at sea, maintaining radio silence as he pursued his grim mission. So they were safe, at last; tomorrow they would dock in Los Angeles.

But equally, tomorrow he should have been sailing on *Yamato*, the proudest man on earth.

'But you have acted the hero, Philip,' Anne said.

He turned his head. 'You think so?'

'I know so,' she said, and squeezed his fingers.

'You have never said . . . ' He hesitated.

'No,' she said. 'I have never said. And I will never say. What Mori did to me can never be explained. But I did not surrender to him, Philip. And I knew you would rescue me. I never doubted.'

He sighed. 'At what cost. Mother . . . '

'She must live her life as she sees it.'

'And Iyeyasu?'

She looked along the deck, where the boy sat, also staring at the waves. 'We have a problem there. But a problem we can solve, Phil, together. A problem we *must* solve, together. But you . . . you have done everything right.'

Graham came along the deck, followed by his faithful four. What did they think, Philip wondered. Because they too had had to abandon homes and families for the unknown.

'There's a radio message,' Graham said. His face was grave, and yet contented.

Philip raised his head.

'At dawn this morning,' Graham said, 'Japanese

bombers attacked Pearl Harbor.'

'Oh God!' Anne cried.

'It seems they achieved complete surprise, and a considerable victory,' Graham said. 'At least two battleships sunk, and an enormous amount of other damage. But the aircraft-carriers were not there, at least. And the damage is only relative. We are in this together now, Phil. Great Britain and America. There can only be one result.'

Philip could not doubt that, if there were even a few dozen other fighting men in Great Britain like John Graham.

Yet the sense of failure loomed above him. 'You mean they ignored our warning,' he said bitterly. 'It was all for naught.'

'I don't think so,' Graham said. 'Pearl Harbor was certainly alerted that a surprise attack was possible, and imminent. And besides, you tried. You know, they don't know who you are yet, Philip, but there's quite a reception waiting for you in Los Angeles. What does it feel like to be a real, dyed-in-the-wool hero?'

'You mean, a real, dyed-in-the-wool traitor,' Philip said.

'That's for mankind, and history, to judge,' Graham said. 'But you know what, old son? I reckon, taking everything into consideration, they're going to be on your side.'